SOMEBODY Like Me

STEFANIE K. STECK

Book Cover by Melody Jeffries

Chapter Header and Space Illustrations by Melody Jeffries

Ranch Map and Family Tree Illustrations by Erika Plum

Edited By Caitlin Lengerich and Allie Samberts

Proofread by Tessa Frank and Caitlin Lengerich

ISBN (Paperback) 979-8-9866169-4-0

1st edition 2024

This is for those who ever felt like they were a "problem,"
I can assure you that you never were a problem.

Author's Note

A year ago, I fell in love with the rodeo, and this novel formed the moment I saw my first tie-down event. I just knew it was going to be centered around a rodeo, and a cowboy falling in love. *Somebody Like Me* contains adult content. Though it is fade to black and no explicit details are on page, the intimacy is implied. It deals with topics that have taken research, such as a working cattle ranch where branding/vaccinating of calves takes place and, rodeo events and rules. Even with research, creative liberties were taken. Content warnings include family deaths, gaslighting, verbal abuse, panic attacks, anxiety, and depression. Having had many panic attacks myself, I hope I have handled these topics with care. Your mental health matters, so please protect yourself. Thank you for choosing to read *Somebody Like Me*, I hope you love reading it as much as I loved writing it.

Hartwell Hills
RANCH
Lake
Lottie's River
Lachlan's House
Cow Pastures
Main Barn & Events
Horse Pasture
To Gardens
Stables & Indoor Arena
Bunkhouse
Garage
Rhett's Cabin
Main House
To Town

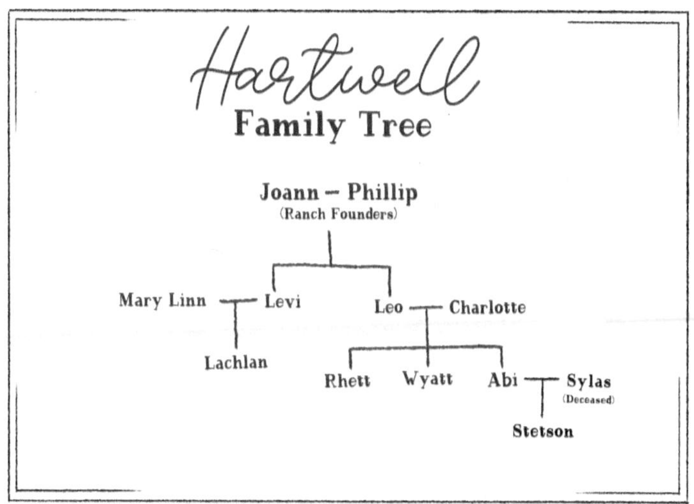

Hartwell
Family Tree
Joann — Phillip
(Ranch Founders)
Mary Linn — Levi
Lachlan
Leo — Charlotte
Rhett   Wyatt   Abi — Sylas
(Deceased)
Stetson

ONE

Kyla

"**H**EY GIRL, WHAT'CHA DRINKIN'?"

Oh great . . . here we go.

This was not why I was here.

Here was a dark, dingy bar, that smelled like wings and bad beer, in some no-name town in Idaho. There weren't any neon signs hanging on the wall, but there were bull skulls and cowboy hats hanging from the rafters. Pool tables lined the walls, and the crowds were pouring in. This was clearly a local bar that really didn't have anything for me. I was thankful they at least had Captain Morgan and Dr Pepper.

Even though I wasn't quite sure what I was doing in this exact bar, I knew for sure I wasn't here to have some man in a cowboy hat ask me "what'cha drinkin'."

The audible groan I let out would have filled the entire bar if the country music wasn't so damn loud. Not that I didn't like country music. On a normal day it would have calmed me, but I just wasn't in the mood for it. Give me some grunge hate music right now—not Shania.

"I'm going to stop you right there," I answered, my eyes focusing on the drink I already had, completely turning away from him.

"Oh, wait," he interrupted, "I'd just love to buy you a round." His arm fell on the bar top in front of me as he let a small chuckle out of his throat. It was deep, raspy, and it *definitely* caught my attention.

His voice still vibrating in my ears, I looked at his forearm on the bar top and followed it up to his shoulders to finally look at him.

And *damn* . . . I shouldn't have looked.

I saw him earlier, sitting on the opposite end of the bar as me with two other men. One wore a baseball hat, and the other sat in the corner with his arms folded over his chest. Out of all of them, Cowboy was hard not to notice. The man would be able to stop oncoming traffic. His tan cowboy hat sat perched on what I could only assume was a gorgeous, full head of light brown hair, his light beard only defining his perfect jawline. He had a slight smile on his lips and his blue eyes were standing out over the shadow of the hat. He was stunning.

I blinked and looked back at the drink in front of me, running my fingers along the condensation. I inhaled, letting my breath sit in my lungs for a few seconds, and then let it out through my lips.

"Listen," I began, trying to keep my voice steady, "I'm done with relationships, so if you could please. . ."

"Who said anything about a relationship? I just asked if I could buy you a drink." His voice was solid, sliding off his tongue like butter. Calm. Collected. Deep. Seductive. And that smile . . .

I squinted my eyes as my nose scrunched. "Yeah, I guess I did jump right to that didn't I?" I mumbled.

"What was that, Princess?"

Princess?

I shook my head. "Nothing."

He let out a raspy chuckle again as his chin dipped. Looking up at him again, I almost felt my stomach drop. God he was gorgeous. And his laugh . . . *oof* . . . if I wasn't sitting my knees would be liquid by now, just from his laugh alone.

I would be lying if I said my mind didn't wonder what his laugh, his *voice,* would sound like if he whispered against my ear. Heat began to rise and the butterflies settled in my stomach. Even though it had been only six months since I left my ex and all the manipulation that went with him, we hadn't slept together in over a year—and even then, it wasn't the best sex I'd ever had.

And to think I was almost stuck with him forever.

I was meant to be starting fresh here, figuring everything out. But now, there was Cowboy here, sending chills up my spine simply by talking. Making me think all sorts of things I shouldn't be thinking.

His hands on my waist, his fingers against my skin.

His lips on me . . .

Snap out of it, Kyla. Remember you don't need, or want this.

"Okay, humor me. What made you come over here then? Just saw a pretty girl sitting by herself and thought you'd come over and flirt?" I spun in my chair, facing the striking man in front of me, and leaned my elbow on the bar top.

He smiled again, the corners of his lips twitching as his teeth came into view, a dimple becoming visible on his right cheek. He really needed to stop smiling.

Reaching up, he took his hat off, confirming my suspicion that his hair was indeed beautiful. He rested his hat on the bar top before taking a seat on the stool next to me. Clearing his throat he said, "I saw a beautiful woman sitting alone and a lot of idiots more than willing to make fools of themselves." His eyes began to roam the bar. He did have a point. There were more men than women in the small space. "I decided to—"

"To what?" I interrupted him this time, taking him by surprise. "Make a fool of *yourself*?"

He let out a loud laugh as his chin dipped. "No, I came over here to hopefully buy you a drink. To talk."

"Before your *friends* could beat you to it?" I narrowed my eyes at him, not breaking his gaze while I lifted my glass to my lips, taking a sip.

"My friends?" he parroted, turning back to the table he came from. The two men weren't even paying attention to us. "Wyatt is . . . well . . ." He turned his back to me. "He's a couple of beers in. Lachlan will make sure he makes it home, but . . . I couldn't stop thinking about why you were sitting here alone ever since you came in." His eyebrows raised, the corner of his lips twitching.

Wyatt. Lachlan.

I narrowed my eyes. Glancing back at the table, I studied them for a moment, before my focus went back to the man in front of me. He was dressed like your typical, run of the mill, cowboy. A white t-shirt was tucked into his Wrangler jeans, topped with a shiny belt buckle, a blue, and button-down shirt opened showing the tee underneath, the sleeves rolled to his elbows, showing off his toned forearms, and brown boots tucked in his pants with mud on the toes. The only thing he didn't have was the southern drawl, but being in Idaho I didn't expect him to. His voice was still vibrating in my ears and—southern drawl or not—I wanted him to talk again.

But I wanted him to leave me alone.

I also really wanted him to stay.

Why did I want him to stay?

I hated the way the anxiety ate at every decision that came my way. Inhaling, I dug deep in my gut for courage I knew existed there. I'd leave it up to my favorite game if he stayed or not. That way it wasn't my decision.

"Alright, Cowboy," I sighed, lifting my drink, downing the rest of the alcohol inside.

"Cowboy?" he emphasized, the grin only growing.

"How about we play a game." I stared him down.

"A game?"

I nodded, eyeing him up and down once more. "I'm decent at reading people. I bet if I can guess five things about you, you get out of my hair. If I can't, you can buy me that drink."

"Five things? You don't know me."

I flipped my hair over my shoulder. "You're easy to read."

He raised his sandy eyebrows. "Excuse me?"

I tapped the tan hat on the bar. "You've got a cowboy name. Rhett . . . or maybe Stetson." I narrowed my eyes at him, studying his chiseled features. "Yeah, Stetson. After your father's favorite hat."

He looked at me, then the hat. He grabbed it from the table and sheepishly placed it back on his head. "Is that one or two facts?"

I smirked, giddy at being right and suddenly couldn't wait to show off more. "Just one." I nodded my head towards the belt. "That's one fancy buckle, my guess is it's from the rodeo. You look like a bull rider. Don't bull riders get all the girls? And injuries?" He smirked, telling me I was onto something. This man wasn't going to buy me a drink. "You also live on a ranch. Hell, you probably own it. You drive a truck—a Ford F-250 or something ridiculous like that. It's probably white. And last fact, your drink order."

"My drink order?"

"I guarantee you order the house tap—the most watered-down beer in the joint simply because it's local."

I rested my arm on the wooden bar top, the smile of victory spreading upon my lips. I had him. The look on his face told me I did. He was stone cold, his eyes fixed on the bar top. Bringing his eyes to me, he glared, knowing full well I had won. He shifted in his seat, licking his lips as he searched the bar for something that wasn't there.

"All five have to be right in order for you to win, right?" he asked.

"I'm right, aren't I?"

"You are—"

"Ha!" I laughed, my entire body jerking forward in my chair. I won.

"—on all except one fact."

"Wait, what?"

"So that means . . ." He raised his hand, waving to the bartender, giving her a slight nod. "I'm buying your next drink."

I was stunned.

"What'cha drinkin?" he asked again once the girl came to take our order.

"Rum and Dr. Pepper," I mumbled, my tone low as I grappled with the fact that I had lost. I never lost.

"And I'll have the most watered-down house beer on tap you have." Cowboy smiled, his eyes not once leaving mine.

"You got it." The bartender winked at me.

I was silent as my drink was placed in front of me, and when he brought his mug to his lips he laughed.

"Ah, watered-down to the perfect amount." He smiled, watching as I picked up my drink to sip.

"Are you going to tell me which one I was wrong on? I was pretty sure I got them all."

"I'm not a bull rider," he corrected.

My eyes widened as I turned to look at him, "You mean to tell me your name really is Stetson?"

He laughed, "No, that's my nephew's name. I'm Rhett." Rhett held out his hand for me to shake. "And you are?"

I held back a laugh. "Rhett? I was only half-kidding. You look more like a Stetson. But Rhett? That's a name you only see in romance novels." I touched my glass, almost looking forward to the taste of the alcohol.

Rhett dropped his hand, but the smirk stayed on his lips. "My mom's favorite book is *Gone with the Wind* . . ."

"Ah . . ." I raised my glass to my lips. "Rhett Butler."

"So technically, I got two wrong." I slumped my shoulders.

"Technically, you guessed Rhett first. I'd take it as a win. So . . . let's start over. Hey girl, I'm Rhett. And you are?" He raised his hand again, this time his fingers moving slightly.

I looked quickly at his hand, and then back to his blue eyes, heavy and beautiful as they studied me, the smirk on his lips growing. I sighed and accepted the defeat. Taking his hand, I felt his warmth instantly. Sparks flew up my arm and his fingers pulsed against my skin. This was new. I would be the first to admit I was nervous. I hadn't had this feeling since . . . well, never. I can't recall having it with my ex. But the weight that came with Rhett's handshake, the hunger in his eyes . . . it was intriguing, and I was curious to have more.

Hell, it was one night in a bar, then we'd go our separate ways. Him to his ranch, me to Washington to begin my new life. A few hours in a bar couldn't hurt.

"Kyla," I answered him, a newfound courage bubbling after learning I wasn't going to spend the evening alone. Rhett had found me.

Two

Rhett

WYATT DIDN'T NOTICE HER, neither did Lachlan. They were too busy talking about God knows what. I *was* involved in their conversation, but when she walked in the door, she was all I saw. Her brown hair was straight, falling over her shoulders as she attempted to tuck it behind her ears. She wore jean shorts with a tank top, showing off her flawless skin, but the one thing I couldn't see was her eyes. And I was itching to see them.

I had never seen anyone like her come into The Steel. The bar and grill was mainly frequented by locals. The small town of Alpine Ridge wasn't where tourists gathered, we weren't even on the map, yet here she was. She ordered a simple drink—a rum and coke maybe—and then sat in silence as she drank it. Her gaze would wander around the room, falling on me every now and then, but was seemingly oblivious to my attention on her. When I finally got the courage to approach her I wasn't expecting her to retaliate, but to be honest, that made it more fun.

Her little guessing game made me laugh, and the fact that the only thing she got wrong was my profession made me want to stick around even more. Of course, she would have guessed that I was a bull rider. But bull riding wasn't my world, I was a tie-down roper. I'd rather feel the lasso and jump off the horse—that's where the excitement was for me.

I watched as Kyla drank her drink, slowly, her chocolate eyes on me the whole time. They sparkled, just like I hoped they would, as they danced around the room. The corner of my lip twitched, waiting for her to break the silence. She rolled her lips before she turned and narrowed her eyes in my direction. Finally, she swallowed and drew a sharp breath.

"Your nephew's name is really Stetson?" she asked, her voice heavy from the alcohol.

Giving her a single nod, I caught her gaze. "Yup." I popped the *P*. "After his mom's favorite hat," I joked, leaning into her. My sister had her fair share of Stetson hats, but I knew that wasn't the reason why she named her son that.

But playing with Kyla was becoming fun.

Kyla lowered her eyebrows at me. "And a white truck?"

"A Ford F-250, like you guessed."

"Leather seats?" Her face tilted, her fingers drumming on the bar top.

"Nah, but they are heated."

"Oh." She let go of a smirk as her eyebrows rose. "That's a game changer." She turned her body, giving me a slight eye roll, her voice heaving with sarcasm as she straightened her back—all the warmth from her body that was just mere inches from me fading away.

"It is. Winters up here can get rough."

"Oh, do they? I'm from Arizona, we don't get much winter down there." She raised her glass to her lips, eyeing me from the corner of her eyes. The chocolate brown gleaming with . . . with . . . something. I couldn't read her as easily as she could read me, but there was something there.

Mimicking her, I lifted my mug, smelling the alcohol before tasting it. "I would imagine not. I've been there a few times in the circuit. No offense but it's not my favorite place to ride."

Kyla snorted, lowering her drink as she formed a soft smile and licked her bottom lip. If she kept doing that, I'd be begging to kiss her.

"I don't blame you at all. Arizona is terrible, but . . ." She shrugged her shoulders. "Born and raised in Phoenix."

"So, tell me, what brings you to Idaho?"

I propped my foot up on the rest to get more comfortable on the stool. With one hand resting on my knee, the other on my mug, my body was open to her. I wanted to show her she could open up to me, have fun and talk to me, even if it was just for her time in the bar. *Relax, just a little.*

"Just . . ." she began, "a change of scenery." Her voice and the way she lifted her eyes to me told me there was more to the story. I raised an eyebrow, curious to learn more. There had to be so much more to this woman.

"Arizona to Idaho is a bit of a change."

"Idaho isn't the end of the line for me, Washington is."

"What's in Washington?" I prodded.

"A job." Kyla raised her drink to her lips, pressing them to the glass softly. She sipped her drink, her gaze meeting mine with intensity. Her shoulders tensed as she lowered the glass, her lungs filling with a deep breath.

Her body language was saying more than she knew. I swallowed, my eyebrows twitching as I looked at her. I wanted to begin to peel away those layers. "Just a job?"

She raised an eyebrow and looked over at me, placing her glass back on the bar top. "Yes, Rhett—" she enunciated my name, "—just a job. Like I said, I'm not looking for anything—even in Washington."

"Hey, like I said, that's not my intention at all. I just wanted to—"

"Buy me a round." She smiled, a smile that lit up the room. "So, tell me, if you're not riding bulls, what do you do in the rodeo?"

"Tie-down," I answered simply.

At the change of subject, her attention anchored to me. With her voice steady, she said, "I wish I could lie and say I know what that is but . . ."

"Tie-down roping. I lasso the calf, jump off the horse, and tie it down."

"Oh!" She bounced up, her hair flipping over her shoulders. "Is that where you tie up the legs and then wave your arms in the air once you're done?" She mimicked the motion I do so well.

Lowering my chin I laughed. "Yeah, that's the one."

How can I convince this girl to stay longer than one round?

"Has a calf ever gotten away from you?" she asked, her voice still full of excitement as her hands lowered.

"Yes." I nodded, meeting her gaze.

She leaned in slightly. "How are you scored?" she asked.

"It's a timed event. No scores. Fastest time wins," I answered, leaning in to meet her.

"What's your best time?" She raised her chin, her body tilting even closer to mine. I could touch her knee if she'd let me.

"7.6," I answered, proud of my time.

"Minutes?" her voice raised as her back straightened.

I grunted a laugh. "Seconds."

"Ha, oh, that sounds better. Harder?" Kyla relaxed again as she slumped her shoulders. Raising her hand, she tucked her hair behind her ear. "What's the world record?"

"6.3," I held her gaze.

"And you can't do 6.3 seconds?" Her arm fell on the bar top, her hand hanging off the edge, close to my knee. If her fingers flexed, she would graze my thigh just light enough to tease.

Was she teasing? Taunting? Flirting? Or did she really want to know?

"It's a goal. I've gotten it during practice once, but never in an event," I admitted.

"Do you get to choose your horse?"

"Yes, I ride my own horse. What's with the questions? Is this a quiz? Are you a secret rodeo fan and you know everything, but you're seeing how much I know?" I smiled at her.

"I've never been to a rodeo."

"Never been to a rodeo? There are tons in Phoenix, and you've never been?" I leaned closer to her, wanting to catch her scent, but she slowly moved away.

Scrunching her nose she shook her head. "No, I'm more of a city girl. David and I lived in the city. No ranches or horses near me. So . . ."

"Change of scenery," I parroted from earlier. "Who's David?"

The question slipped from my lips. I didn't mean to pry, but I wanted to know who he was and if he was waiting for her somewhere.

She let out a long breath. "My ex."

Her . . . *ex*. He wasn't waiting. She had left, she wanted that change. I let out a low, heavy breath; one that I knew she caught. Our eyes met—contact so deep I could basically read her mind. She was nervous, she was excited. She had no idea what she was doing. Her eyes lit up as she inhaled, her exhale shaky as she broke eye contact and her eyes landed on something behind me. Our gazes locked again as her back straightened in her seat, a single eyebrow cocking.

"Wanna play darts?" Kyla asked, the same shake that was in her breath now controlling her voice.

I smiled at her and raised my brow. "You any good?"

Biting her lower lip, sending my gaze to her mouth again, she stood. "Guess you'll find out."

I didn't know what the night would bring, but I did know I was going to kiss her before she left this town.

"How are you this good at pool?" I asked, watching as Kyla sank three balls in a row.

After she had lost two games of darts, she suggested we move to the pool table. If her pool strategy was anything like her dart game, I knew she didn't stand a chance against my skill. But she jumped up, grabbed her cue while I stacked up the balls then walked around the table, positioned herself perfectly, moving her hips in one fluid motion before she struck and broke, sinking two balls straight away.

She gave a small bow holding the cue out. "College." She aimed again, missing the shot.

"College?" I swung my cue around, noticing the table. She may have just landed two balls in a row, but she also lined me up for the perfect shot. "Spent your weekend in a bar I take it?" Bending over the table, I gave Kyla one last glance before sinking the ball.

"Not at all." Her smile grew with the playfulness in her voice. "My roommates had a pool table, one that folded up and slid under the couch. We pulled it out a lot and may or may not have had some parties."

Even though she was beating me, we were taking our time, not worrying about lining up the shots, not caring about points—but she was teasing. In every way possible.

She would shimmy in front of me, her hips gently touching me as she passed. If she passed from behind, her palm would trail my shoulder blades, and after the first few shots she grabbed my hat off my head and placed it on top of hers. Raising an eyebrow, I watched every move she made.

I watched as she bent over the table to take her shot, her focus on the table. She seemed unphased by what she was doing to me. I rested my cue on the ground and leaned on it, studying her body as she moved. She swayed her hips and lightly jerked her elbow to hit the cue ball off to the right, taking out the yellow stripe like it wasn't even there. She rose and used her hand to move her hair from her shoulder, giving me the sexiest smirk I had ever seen—winking at me. I told myself it was because she wore my hat with more confidence than I did even though it was two sizes too big, but the wink was just enough to send me over the edge. I needed to kiss her. Kyla was absolutely mesmerizing.

"Hey, Cowboy." Her voice brought me back to the table. "I missed, it's your shot."

She came to stand next to me, raising her chin to look up into my gaze. My hat tilted back, *yeah*, it was way too big for her dainty frame. Her teeth racked across her bottom lip, practically begging me to kiss her.

"Come on, take your shot," she pressed, her lips forming a sly grin.

I exhaled and stepped away from her, not wanting to take things too far, too fast. It had only been a few hours and I wasn't planning on this going outside of the bar. In my mind it was a fun date, going to end with a kiss (or two, or three) and maybe a heated moment in the hall, but then she would be in her car and on her way to Washington. And I would be back on the road—gone for almost two weeks in the circuit. This woman would stay in my head for a long time, that much I knew. But nothing more could come of it.

I lined up the cue and tried with all my willpower to concentrate on the ball while Kyla stood in my line of sight. Even blurry in the background I could see her hips move as she shifted on her feet. Any concentration I had was thrown out the window. I narrowed my eyes and inhaled.

"Hey, Rhett!"

I fumbled and missed the shot as Wyatt came up next to me, his voice louder than normal after a few beers. I stood up straight and glared at my little brother. "Yes, Wyatt, do you need something?" I bit.

He laughed, hearing the frustration in my voice. Without hesitation he leaned his elbow on my shoulder and smiled. Wyatt was a rodeo announcer. He had that charisma, that *voice* you needed to tell the world what was happening on the dirt. But right now, I didn't want to hear it.

"Are you winning?" he chuckled.

"No, he's not. Hey, Wyatt." Kyla gleamed across the table.

"Well in that case, can I play the next game? I happen to be fabulous at pool." He waved his hand around, almost smacking me in the face a few times. He turned his head and gave me a grin. He caught my glare, but decided it wasn't worth it.

"Against me? I've got to warn you, I'm pretty good. I'm Kyla, by the way."

Wyatt's face snapped towards Kyla, really looking at her now. He took her in, his eyes moving from her simple brown shoes to my hat on her head.

Wyatt, being the drunk idiot he was, chuckled. "Hey, Kyla, I take it my older brother is taking you home tonight?"

Kyla gave a nervous scoff, and turned to me. "Um, no. Not that I'm aware of. We're just having a good time."

Wyatt shot up an eyebrow and jerked his head back to me.

"Wyatt," I said sternly. He may only be four years younger than me, but sometimes he needed to have the sense knocked into him.

"What? It's a valid question. She wears the hat, she rides the cowboy."

THREE

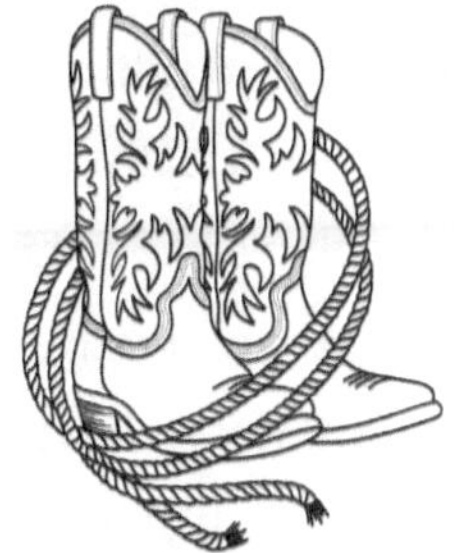

Kyla

I'M AN IDIOT.

I knew the "rule."

You wear the hat, you ride the cowboy.

Rhett froze, his eyes searing into his brother. But Wyatt just leaned on Rhett's shoulder, his smile huge and eyebrows wiggling up and down.

"Where's. Lachlan," Rhett grumbled, his voice heavy with anger.

Wyatt looked to the side, pushing himself off Rhett's shoulder. "Paying the tab. He says it's time to go."

"Agreed. You should go." Rhett didn't even blink as he glared at Wyatt.

I licked my lips, still thinking about the hat perched on my head. The two began to bicker, Wyatt trying his hardest to stay while Rhett tried to push him away. I tightened my lips and backed away from them. My mind began to spin as my hand found the top of the cowboy hat. I removed it and placed it on the pool table.

I wore the hat. Did I want to ride the cowboy?

I glanced up at Rhett and really, truly looked at him. His t-shirt hugged all the right places, showing off his biceps and chest. His hair fell over his ears ever so slightly, and his lips were a tight line as he tried to convince Wyatt to leave. Then there was his ass. Perfect in the Wrangler jeans. At first it was for fun. Touching him lightly as we played, moving my body just the right way to make it so he missed his shot, but now that Wyatt had put that idea in my head . . .

You wear the hat you. Ride. The. Cowboy.

I wasn't really considering sleeping with Rhett, was I?

Nope. Hell no.

That's not what this was. This was just a fun night that was supposed to end with me finding a nice motel and leaving in the morning for the next destination.

"Wyatt," a booming voice came from behind me. Turning, I saw a man wearing a black cowboy hat towering over me. "I turn my head for one second."

"Lighten up, Lach," Wyatt cackled.

"No," Lachlan's voice was toneless. "Sorry, Rhett . . ."

Rhett's chuckle had an edge to it, showing his irritation. "Please get him home." He dug in his pocket and pulled out his keys, tossing them to Lachlan.

"How will you get home?" Lachlan pinched his brow at Rhett, flipping his keys between his fingers. Rhett's gaze landed right on me, and the corner of his mouth ticked up into a smirk.

"Don't worry about me."

"All right." Lachlan turned his body, holding onto Wyatt's shoulder as he passed me. "Sorry to ruin your night, ma'am," he said as he passed, tipping his hat as he and Wyatt made their way for the exit.

"I'll see you in the morning, Kyla," I heard Wyatt call.

I forced back a laugh and raised a single eyebrow to Rhett. "That was . . ." I began.

"I told you someone would make a fool of themselves, should have known it would've been Wyatt." Rhett walked around the pool table to me, coming up slower than I anticipated. It was almost like the table grew another twenty feet as I watched him walk over seamlessly. The space between us filled with tension as he inched closer. Grabbing his hat from the table, he placed it back on my head. "It's not really a thing, you know," he said, his voice low, sending chills down my spine.

"What's not?" I blinked, trying to keep my voice steady. I knew exactly what he was saying "wasn't a thing," but that didn't mean I didn't want to hear him say it.

"What Wyatt said. I just think you look damn sexy in my hat." He winked and turned his back to me. "I believe it's your shot."

I blinked again, a few times, erasing the encounter with Wyatt from my head and I ran the tips of my fingers along his hat. I took one quick look at the balls on the table and instantly had my shot lined up.

A smirk formed. "You sure you want me to take the shot, Cowboy?"

"We can play another round, sweetheart."

I cringed. "Um, no. If we're doing nicknames, that one has to go."

"You can call me 'Cowboy,' but I can't call you 'sweetheart'?"

I shook my head, feeling the hat swivel. He didn't need to know that's what David would call me after a fight. This was just for tonight. He didn't need to know anything about David to begin with.

"Nope. Find another name."

"Game on." Rhett smiled, watching as I leaned over the pool table, not taking my eyes off of him as I sank the ball.

The alcohol buzz had long since vanished as the night carried on. Before I knew it was well past last call. We had almost an hour before the bar was going to close and Rhett had led me to the dance floor. The song was slow, and Josh Turner's voice filled the room as Rhett's hands were firm and warm on my back. He would press his fingers into my skin before he moved, finding my elbow, feathering his fingertips up to my chin. He played with my hair and finally, with his thumb and forefinger, lifted my face to meet his gaze.

The night had gone completely opposite from what I was expecting.

To be fair, my expectation was one drink, track down a hotel for the night, and read a book. But my focus had completely switched to the man who had me wrapped in his arms.

It had been a long time since I was held like this. My ex never did after he proposed. I guess he thought the dating was over and the "wooing" was accomplished. He put a ring on it. He won. But with Rhett, he made me feel like I was the center of the universe here in this dingy bar, in this no-name town. He just made me *feel*. He felt more secure, more open, more . . . whole than David had ever felt.

I knew one thing, if this man asked me to go to bed with him I would say yes. I would put his hat on and make sure I followed that rule.

His thumb roamed my jawline, his fingers tangling in my hair, but even with those distractions it was his eyes that pulled me in. He studied my face as the air between us grew intense. I wasn't sure if it was the song, or if it was just Rhett, but all I knew was that I was immersed in this moment. I was drowning in it and I never wanted to come up for air. I was beginning to feel like a new person—someone I was too scared to really be. But with Rhett I could be whoever I wanted.

"Where are you staying tonight?" Rhett asked, his voice barely above a whisper, interrupting my thought process completely.

I pulled myself from the water and took a deep breath. "Well I need to find a hotel . . ."

"You don't have a place to stay?" he asked, lifting his chin in the air.

I scrunched my nose and lightly shook my head. "I may have skipped that part when I came into town. I wasn't really planning on meeting a cowboy."

"Well, not to sound too forward, but the ranch has a worker stable—"

"A stable!?" I reared back and raised my eyebrows. I knew he was trying to help me find a place to stay—hell, he may even be trying to hint at staying with him—but offering a stable? I wasn't going to let him live this down.

He drew in a shuddering breath. "Housing . . . unit?" he stumbled. "The ranch hands live there. I think we have an open room . . ."

"Rhett, are you suggesting I stay in a large building with a lot of smelly men?" I ran my hands up his chest and onto his neck, lacing my fingers in the hair that was free under his hat. "Would Rhett Butler do that?"

"Okay, okay." He chuckled, the smile on his lips fading as he inhaled sharply. His eyes became heavy, and when his voice filled the space, my knees went weak. He was Strong. Confident. *Smooth.* "Stay with me tonight."

Time stopped.

I filled the small distance between us to take his mouth with mine, feeling each and every tingle as his lips moved against me. We stopped swaying as his hands moved to cup my face, bringing me in for a deeper kiss, his tongue slipping through my lips. Fire filled my body as the heat rose, and Rhett's hands found the right spot on the back of my neck that held me firmly against him.

This wasn't me. This wasn't what I did. I didn't randomly make out with cowboys in the middle of nowhere Idaho. I didn't take invitations for one-night stands. I didn't do this.

Yet here I was, completely drawn to this man, wanting to feel his hands on me . . . everywhere. I wanted his kiss, I wanted to taste him, and I *definitely* wanted his hard length that I felt between us.

Be free for one night, Kyla.

Rhett drove my small car with ease. Butterflies grew in my stomach the longer the car ride became, but I had no fear, only trust—only anticipation. *Want.* I took deep breaths to calm the flutters, thinking about what was coming.

The roads were black, and only a few street lights illuminated the way. As we arrived onto his property, we passed under a worn, wooden archway and the paved road turned into dirt. I could see a larger house, only the porch lights on—but then more darkness before Rhett finally parked the car in front of a small cabin and killed the engine.

"It's not too late to tell me to take you to a hotel," he whispered softly, a slight shake in his voice.

Was *he* nervous?

"Hey, Cowboy." I felt a blush of heat hit my cheeks as I leaned across the center console. "Don't get cold feet on me now. It's just one night." *Yeah, Kyla, keep telling yourself that. It's just one night. It means nothing.*

Rhett let out a long breath. "One night?"

Pressing my lips to his, I gave him a single nod. "Do I get a tour?"

Letting out a small laugh, Rhett's chin fell before he looked at the wooden cabin in front of us. "It's not much. I'm not here often so it's kinda dull, but I can give you the whole tour tomorrow."

An entire tour? I cleared my throat. "Well then"—I unbuckled and pushed open the car door—"let's not waste any more time."

Who was this person? I did not say things like this. Whoever was in my skin, I wanted her to stay. She was taking the *be free* thing way too seriously, and I relished in it.

Rhett followed, his boots loud on the wooden steps before his hand grasped the door handle.

Once he flipped the switch and light filled the room, I didn't see a dull house at all. I saw a home. Rhett claimed he was never here, but the small living room was quaint and decorated in a way that made you feel like you could grab a blanket, a book, and just settle in. There was a television hanging on the wall, bookcases on either side of it, half-filled with books, the other filled with medals and photos from what I had assumed were from his accomplishments.

Before taking in the rest of the house, I made a beeline right to the photos. There was a picture of Rhett with a rope between his teeth, Rhett on his knees in front of a calf with his hands in the air, Rhett on the back of a brown and white paint horse—a large smile on his face as he waved to a crowd. Third place, second place, and even more first place medals sat around the photos, all showing how amazingly talented he was.

"I think this one is my favorite." I pulled a frame from the shelf, looking at Rhett mid-jump off a horse holding onto the rope as he made his way towards the calf.

His hands found my waist and slinked to my stomach from behind me, his chest hitting my back. He was so warm, so solid . . . I could melt in his arms. He kissed my neck before he whispered, "Why's that?"

"You look determined." I leaned my head to the side, giving him better access to kiss me. My knees shook as I tried to stay steady. There I go . . . melting.

"I was. I always aim to beat my fastest time." He kissed my shoulder, using his teeth to move the strap of my tank top to the side.

"Did you?" I set the photo down and twisted my body to face him. He had taken off his hat, his hair only slightly disheveled, perfect for my fingers to run through.

Rhett narrowed his eyes and let out a long sigh. "Not that time. Third place."

"Not bad." I smiled up at him.

This man was stunning. I must have thought that so many times tonight. Just looking at Rhett was enough to send my stomach into knots. His jawline was defined, covered in scruff, with a dimple peeking out on his right cheek when he smiled. His skin had seen the sun, but it only amplified his features. His blue eyes were sprinkled with dark navy specks, and now seeing them up close . . . I could get lost in them. I could get lost in *him*. He raised his hand and moved my hair from my face, his fingertips lightly grazing against my skin.

"Kyla, you're the most gorgeous woman I think I've ever laid eyes on," he said in a low voice as he leaned closer to me. "I can't believe you're mine for one night."

I took a sharp breath, feeling it shake as my heart rate picked up. This man couldn't be for real. "No one has ever really talked to me this way before. I'm not used to it," I admitted, shivers running up my spine as I thought of David and the way his voice sounded as he said he loved me, giving me nothing but broken promises.

"No one?" Rhett repeated, narrowing his eyes. "I don't want to believe that. You deserve nothing less."

He kissed me then, slow and smooth, silencing my thoughts. I moaned into his mouth as his tongue found mine, my mind dizzy in a haze. My entire body was under his control. What would happen if I let him have *full* control over me? Would he be soft and tender, or unlike anything I had ever experienced? If his kisses were any indication, I was in for the best night of my life.

"Rhett," I gasped as his lips trailed down my neck, his tongue teasing as I tried to gain composure. "This isn't normal for me. This isn't what I do. But I want . . ."

"Kyla." He raised his head, his thumb finding my chin as he caressed it gently. "Tell me what you want."

I gave him a shaky breath as I fell into him. He kissed me again before I could get any words out between us.

I broke the kiss, breathlessly calling to him, "I want you to touch me."

He inhaled, his hands finding the skin under my shirt faster than expected as his lips found my shoulder.

"I want you, Rhett. All of you."

FOUR

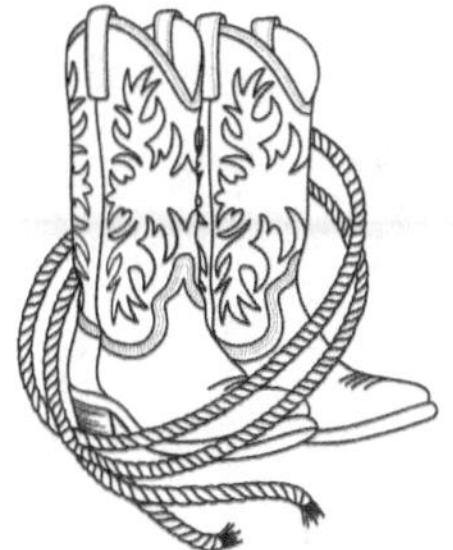

Rhett

IT DIDN'T MATTER THAT I had only gotten two hours of sleep when the other three were spent with Kyla. When she let it slip that no one had talked to her the way I had, I made it my mission to give her the best night possible. I had to show her that she was worth every touch, every kiss, and every single moan. I could still taste her on my lips—a taste I hoped I could have again.

I woke earlier than my alarm, making sure to silence it before it woke Kyla. Facing her, I suddenly wished I could spend the day here with her instead of on the land. Her chest rose and fell softly as she slept, complete bliss on her face. Her cheeks were still flushed, but she was relaxed. Absolutely perfect.

I traced my knuckle up her arm and she stirred, raising her arm above her head as she exhaled, allowing the sheet to fall from her chest. We had agreed on one night, but one night wasn't enough. Washington was her final destination, that wasn't that far from here. Maybe, just maybe, I could keep her for longer than one night.

But for now, I knew Lachlan was waiting for me. The morning was hers to relax while I was out working on the ranch, and then I would show her everything—give her that tour I promised her.

She hummed in her sleep, tilting her face away from me. I trailed my fingers down her arm before kissing her bare shoulder. I dressed silently, slipped my boots on and went to the kitchen, making sure to make enough coffee for her. My thermos full and my hat perched on my head, I took a few moments to write a note to Kyla. I didn't want her to wake up alone thinking I had taken off, leaving her alone in my house.

I didn't want her to feel like a one-night stand.

The morning air hit my lungs as I opened the door, and Kyla's small, red SUV announced to the entire ranch she was inside. I knew the moment I walked in the main house for breakfast, someone would say something. Taking a long pull from my thermos, I stepped off my porch, making the quarter-mile trek to the main house. I focused on the landscape in front of me, trying my hardest to ignore the tug towards the sleeping beauty in my bed.

The ranch was still silent, and the sun hadn't quite made its way over the mountains yet. Soon the glow from the sun would illuminate the valley, creating a picture-perfect world filled with soft-lit gold and greens. I may love the arena, but this was my heaven on earth.

Hartwell Hills Ranch, named by my grandfather Phillip Hartwell, was where I grew up. It's where I learned how to mount my first horse and how to tie-down my first calf. This was home—all five thousand acres of it. The rolling hills flew into the mountain backdrop perfectly, and now, in the beginning of summer, I knew they were covered in the brightest greens Idaho could offer. Behind the main house sat the barn, as well as an indoor and outdoor arena, and if you took the path following the gated pastures, you'd eventually hit a small lake, with a quiet river flowing into the gardens. My mother had claimed that lake when she moved in, instantly naming the river that flowed from it "Lottie's River." I had never called it anything else.

Making it to the main house just in time to fill my thermos back up, I stepped inside and was greeted by the smell of bacon and sausage. My younger sister, Abi, was already in the kitchen, her blonde hair pulled into a ponytail as she focused on the stove in front of her.

"Good morning, Rhett." Abi turned to face me, coffee pot in hand, like a waitress, but instead of filling my thermos she set it down in front of me on the counter, the coffee sloshing around inside. "Wanna explain that SUV I saw this morning? I know it doesn't belong to one of the ranch hands, it's way too nice." Her eyebrows rose and for a split-second I saw Wyatt in her facial features. Fraternal twins, yet they were so much alike.

I shook my head and removed the lid. "Nothing to explain," I answered with a neutral tone.

Abi pinched her brow and hummed. "Sure, there isn't. I'm assuming you need me to help keep her company, or least make her breakfast and show her how to get out of town? I know the drill, but never with you. It's always Wyatt bringing girls home from The Steel."

I let out a long sigh, needing to stop Abi before her comparison to her twin got any further. "Her name's Kyla, and I'd really appreciate it if you hang out with her. Maybe convince her to stay? I won't be out on the land long. I need to pack."

"Not until those cows are in the grazing field." Lachlan walked into the kitchen, his boots hitting hard with each step. "You don't need any more distractions. You agreed to work."

"I'll work." I nodded to him, giving him a silent promise.

He narrowed his eyes and took a sip of his coffee, turning away from me.

My cousin, always quiet and reserved, mainly kept to himself. A part of me knew it was because of what he went through years ago, and even though he claimed he was "fine," losing his family the way he did destroyed him. When his father, my uncle on my dad's side, died, he left Lachlan his portion of the ranch. Lachlan took charge and completely flipped his life around. He and my dad ran the ranch together, more responsibilities falling to Lachlan as my father began to step back more and more. Lachlan Hartwell's entire world centered on Hartwell Hills the moment he signed the deed. This land was his life.

"I guarantee you we will get the cows in the field. I promised I'd help, but I didn't say how long." I lifted my coffee to my lips and walked around Abi, grabbing a fork and stabbing a piece of sausage.

Lachlan huffed. "So, you'll help move 'em and then take off?"

"Damn straight." I bit into my sausage link.

"She stuck around, didn't she?" he asked as his expression dropped, his lips forming a straight line as his eyes bore into me. He was obviously not amused.

"And he wants me to convince her to stay," Abi added, smirking when Lachlan's gaze jerked towards her.

"Wyatt is normally the one who brings girls home," Lachlan taunted, the tight line of his lips forming now the slightest curl.

"Right?" Abi leaned on the counter. "That's what I said."

"I left her a note asking her to stay," I started to explain. "It's up to her if she wants to stay or leave. We only agreed on one night anyway." I stuck the sausage in my mouth, using it as an excuse to stop talking.

Abi pushed herself off the counter and patted my shoulder before turning back to the stove. "I'll keep an eye out for her. Wyatt is supposed to help Stetson with his riding today, maybe while trying to 'convince her to stay'"—she air quoted—"I can convince her to get on a horse."

The front door opened, and the ranch hands began to fill the room. Their normal loud voices were always quieter in the morning, keeping in mind my parents and Abi's son were still sleeping above their heads. Mornings were always more peaceful than anything, but once the sun was up noise was fair game, and most of the time welcomed.

"Morning, Abi," they all began to say as they filled their coffee mugs and grabbed their own breakfast.

Abi's eyes followed them, but her body was still aimed at me. "Morning, guys."

"See you at the stables soon." Lachlan patted my shoulder, grabbing a sausage link before turning his back.

"Nah, I'm coming. Thanks for the coffee, sis." I waved as I followed Lachlan out of the house, catching Abi's nod.

The rhythm of saddling up the horses was what I needed to get my head where it needed to be. I focused on my paint horse, Buckle, as I placed the blanket and saddle on her and she patiently waited. I patted her as she turned to nudge me with her nose before I shoved my thermos in her saddle bag and mounted up to leave the stable. Lachlan followed with his black horse, Onyx, trotting to catch up to me. The sun had now peaked over the mountains, the morning glow making me wish I had thought to grab my sunglasses.

"You left her a note, huh?" Lachlan finally broke the silence.

I turned to my cousin, seeing the other guys getting their saddles ready. "I don't want her to leave. Having a one-night stand is bad enough, but leaving her in my own house so I could go move cattle with my cousin—"

"Boss," Lachlan interjected. "I'm technically your boss when you're on the clock." Lachlan liked to make note of that little fact. "Who signs your paycheck?

"You mean the few paychecks I get out of the year? Didn't know I was on the clock."

"You're not," Lauchlan admitted with a groan.

"My original statement stands. I didn't want her to think I left her alone to help my *cousin* move cattle."

"It shouldn't take too long, once they're in the field you can take off."

"Pretty sure we already established that." I laughed. "Wyatt and I leave early tomorrow to get to Billings. I need to pack. And . . ."

"Make sure that gal in your bed is ready for any other curve balls you may throw at her?" Lachlan chuckled as he jumped off Onyx, making his way to open the gate to let the cattle out.

The ranch hands showed up just in time, slowing their horses down as the cows began to make their way towards the grazing field a few miles away. With one final glance at my house, I wondered if Kyla was awake yet.

"I don't throw curve balls," I finally replied, watching Lachlan mount Onyx.

"She knows you're leaving?"

I nodded.

"She knows you'll be gone for a few weeks?"

I pursed my lips. "I added it to the note . . ." Now that I've thought about it, maybe that wasn't the best way to tell her I was leaving. I scrunched my nose and looked ahead, breathing in the clear air.

"She knows you're Rhett Hartwell—"

"She doesn't know anything about the rodeo, so no, she doesn't know I'm *Rhett Hartwell*," I grumbled. "Like I said in the house, we agreed on one night."

Lachlan looked over at me, a single eyebrow cocked up as he sized me up. "Just watch it. I guarantee you'll be back by noon."

"Perfect." I looked at my watch, it was barely seven. Five hours. I just needed to make it through five hours.

I just hope she'll stay that long.

My mind wandered back to her. Was she still asleep in my bed? With that same blissful, relaxed smile on her lips?

The noise of the cattle brought me back to reality, and I forced myself to focus on the task at hand. Move the cattle as fast as possible and then race back to the house. Don't even think about the gorgeous naked woman in my bed.

Ha . . . yeah right. My mind wouldn't think of anything else.

FIVE

Kyla

I STRETCHED OUT ON the bed, feeling the cool sheets hit my skin, the memory of hours prior still crystal clear in my mind. Rhett was everything I'd never had before. He was one hundred percent focused on me.

I could still feel his rough hands on my soft skin, his lips on my neck, the heat as he filled me. We came together, both of us completely breathless and immersed in each other. Our bodies calmed as Rhett trailed sweet kisses all over my skin, almost as if, even though we had both found the perfect ending, he was ready to make it happen again. That had never happened to me before. Orgasms were few and far between when I was with David, but with Rhett it was an entirely new experience. A part of me couldn't wait to feel that again before I left. Maybe I could extend the one night to be one *more* night.

I reached out across the bed, my eyes flying open when I felt nothing but sheets. I shot up, looking at the empty space next to me. Rhett's warmth was long gone. After getting past the initial shock, I looked around the room. It was dark when we came in, and we were so quick to remove every piece of clothing, we hadn't even bothered to see where everything landed. My clothes were folded and placed on the ottoman at the end of the bed. The boots he had taken off the night before were gone, and his jeans that I had ripped off of him were laid out over a chair.

Did he really just leave me here alone?

By the looks of it, he did.

My stomach dropped and I felt nauseous. Not only were last night's events not in my character, I even told him that.

This just proved why I never did this.

My mind began to race. I was in the guy's house, alone, completely naked, vulnerable, and to top it off I had no idea how to get out of town, or if this place had any cell phone service.

Grabbing the sheets in a hurry, I climbed out of bed, wrapping the white fabric around my body as the queasy feeling got stronger. I vaguely remembered dropping my phone on the dresser last night as I was tangled up in Rhett's arms, not thinking about what would happen come morning. My first thought was to text my best friend, Grace, and beg her to find me a way out of here. She was, after all, the only person I shared my location with. But what I saw instantly changed my state of being.

A small piece of cream paper sat next to my phone. Messy, but legible handwriting caught my eye.

Good morning, beautiful. I'm sorry to leave you so early, but I promised I'd help move the cattle. It won't take me all day. Once we get them moved, I'll come back. I'm dying to see you again. I made coffee, left the pot on. It should still be warm for you, unless you sleep all day. Even if you do, I'll wake you when I get back. Make yourself at home, venture outside if you'd like, my sister is around somewhere. Please stay. I leave tomorrow on the circuit for a while . . . but I'd really love to see you again. I'll kiss you soon. R.

In an instant, the nausea was gone.

My shoulders relaxed.

No one had ever left me a note like this before. There really wasn't any need, but my eyes still read the last line over and over.

I'll kiss you soon. I'll kiss you soon.

Running my fingers over the words, I smiled to myself. Licking my lips, I turned my phone over, tapping the screen alive. I needed to talk to Grace, but before I could even think about dialing her number I was greeted with a plethora of missed calls and texts.

Grace

Did you decide to stay in Boise?

Call me when you get to a hotel.

> Ky, I need you to respond to me. Unless you're driving, then drive.

> Okay you missed a phone call. You never miss phone calls. I'm starting to freak out.

> KYLA RICHARDS ANSWER THE PHONE!

> Oh Kyla . . .

> It's been fourteen hours since your last text, if you don't text me back in fifteen minutes, I'm calling the police and starting a search party.

I knew she was half-kidding, but I hit the FaceTime icon. Keeping the camera off so Grace didn't get a show, I grabbed my pile of clothes and headed towards the bathroom.

"You had seven minutes." Grace's voice filled my ears. "Why is your camera off?"

"Because I'm getting dressed. Hello to you too." I chuckled, throwing my tank top over my head.

"You scared the shit out of me. Where are you?"

"Idaho. On a ranch."

"Be more specific, please."

"I honestly don't know. You have my location," I reminded her.

Grace Flint was, without a doubt, the one person I leaned on. She was the one thing in my life I knew was never going anywhere. When I left David, and didn't know what I was going to do, she let me stay in her one-bedroom apartment. I slept on her couch for months before I finally decided to leave Arizona. Grace knew my every step and I trusted her to keep me safe, no matter where I ended up.

Grace's face turned out of focus as she tapped away on her phone—her eyebrows pinched, biting her bottom lip. I laughed, running my fingers through my hair, suddenly wishing I had a toothbrush. I turned my camera on and lifted my phone just in time to make the best eye contact FaceTime would allow with Grace.

"Idaho. In the middle of nowhere, a town called Alpine Ridge?" she said, her voice calmer now that she could see my face. "How small is this place, all I see is a main street and bar . . ."

"Don't forget the ranch."

"There's a story here." Grace placed her phone down, tilting it up on something to keep me in view. She sat down at the kitchen table, cup of coffee in front of her steaming as she settled in for my response. I held my phone out in front of me as I began to take in Rhett's house.

"There is," I assured her, biting my bottom lip to keep my smile in.

The light filled Rhett's living room, leading into the open concept kitchen. The colors were the same light and dark browns, splashes of red and orange, but as promised, on the very modern coffee maker, there was a full pot of coffee waiting for me. He had even gone the extra step and set a large mug next to the carafe.

"Oh hell," I muttered, picking up the mug. Is this how a woman was supposed to be treated? Or was it just Rhett? My stomach twisted as I inhaled, memories of his smile flashing in my mind.

"What—Are you going to tell me the story?"

"I met a cowboy," I said simply.

"Ky, I need more details." She paused, clearly scoping out the living room behind me. "Are you in his house!?" she shrieked.

"He made me coffee and even left a mug." I lifted the mug into view.

Grace's eyes grew wide as she leaned into her phone, her copper hair falling on the desk. "Excuse me?" she asked, incredulously.

I shook my head. Knowing me, I was taking the simple gesture over the top—making it out to be something it wasn't. I was instantly jumping to conclusions thinking that this was him being a gentleman.

"He probably just did it so I didn't go snooping."

"You said he's a cowboy. He's probably more polite than you think."

Rhett's words from last night rang in my ear, *a woman as beautiful as you deserves nothing less than to be worshiped. Let me worship you, Kyla.* Oh, and how he worshiped. My body hummed at the memory. His fingers trailing down my hips and thighs, finding that most perfect spot as his eyes bore into me. The tension, the build, the release . . .

I looked at the mug, feeling my lips twitch in a smile. I knew I had been silent for far too long. I blinked, trying my hardest to erase the feel of his fingers.

"He left me a note," I muttered quickly, placing the mug on the counter.

"I'm begging you to tell me the story," Grace pleaded, her voice basically a groan when she said "begging."

Taking a deep breath, I filled the mug with coffee, and opened the fridge—thanking the coffee gods that Rhett had creamer—as I started to relay the entire night to Grace, starting with his opening line and ending with the note I had found next to my phone.

"It does *not* say 'I will kiss you soon,'" she said with a swoon in her voice. She had relaxed, her chin resting on her palm as she listened, her eyebrows knitting together as even she seemed to melt.

"It does. It also said to make myself at home and find his sister. I'm honestly not sure if I should just stay here and watch some television, maybe start reading one of his books . . ." Taking a look at the bookshelf I noticed titles like: *Not my First Rodeo, Chasing the Rodeo,* and *Rodeo at Heart.* "Nevermind, maybe I won't read."

"No. Go outside and take a look at the ranch, find him on a horse and then drag him back to his place before you head to Washington." Grace pointed at the screen. "You need this"—her hands began to circle in front of her—"tiny escape. You've been through hell. You don't have to be in Washington until August, right? You have three months before you even start the new job. Stick around the ranch for a while. Spend time with Rhett."

"According to his note, he leaves tomorrow for a rodeo." I waved the note in front of the camera, widening my eyes at her to try to prove a point.

"Then go with him. Experience something you've never experienced before, and then when it's time you can go back to your normal life. Let this be the Summer of Cowboys." Grace moved her hands across the screen as she said the last three words, basically crafting a title for my summer.

"You make it sound so easy, when it's not. I have to get to Washington and find a place to live." I looked down to avoid her all-knowing stare.

"You have three months. What happened to your plan? Your bucket list? Sure, you saw the Grand Canyon, but that's all. Now you're suddenly out of time?" Grace questioned.

I heaved a sigh and fell onto the couch. "You know it was hard for me to leave teaching. Leaving Arizona in general was hard."

Just the memory of leaving my job halfway through the school year stung like a thousand bees. I loved my job. I loved teaching. Seeing the kids' faces light up when the book finally made sense, or the math problem became clear—it made everything worth it. But once things got worse with David, and I knew I had to make a change, the only option was out. I couldn't stay at the school, David would find me there—even if I had security look out for him. The school was understanding, but leaving in the middle of the school year was hard—for me and my students. I would have to recertify my license, but until I could find a new school, I found a tutoring job. It wasn't ideal, but it would do until I could get my feet back on the ground. I had a decent savings saved up, I technically didn't start until the end of August, and my plan was to travel and find who I was again before starting over.

"I just . . . feel like I need to find my footing. All those bucket list things weren't going to happen and you know it," I added quickly.

Grace had helped me put together my "bucket list." The few things I wanted to do before making it to Washington went out the window when the fear of not having a place to live, or food in the fridge—not having *anything* to my name—crept up. Adulting took over and I started the drive. Washington was far enough away that I could start over, but close enough that with a quick flight, I could still feel connected, in a way, to home. I was supposed to be in Washington.

But somehow, I ended up here.

"Rhett leaves tomorrow?" Grace asked again.

Looking at her through my screen, I nodded.

"Drink the coffee, go outside, see the ranch, and spend the day with him. You said he was moving cattle, maybe he can show you the ranch when he's done and then you can adult tomorrow. Just let me know when you leave, okay?" Her voice was soft, going from *Summer of Cowboys* to *Okay, I guess you can be an adult.*

Grace always knew how to calm my nerves and knew what to say even if she didn't agree. She knew when to end a conversation on a positive note, knowing full well I valued her opinion, and she valued mine as well. Grace was always there, and she always would be.

"I'll drink my coffee and then go find his sister. It's still early and I bet it takes longer than a few hours to move cattle."

"Then you have time to make yourself at home. Keep me posted?" She raised her eyebrows, the fun storytelling now over, and her eyes filled with concern. She knew me. She knew what I endured. She knew what I was trying to do. She also knew I was scared shitless.

Giving her a soft smile, a silent thank you, I answered, "Will do."

"Love you."

"Love you more."

Grace waved and then ended the FaceTime. Tossing my phone to the side, I gripped my mug with both hands. I thought about what Grace had mentioned, to experience something new. I wanted to say I checked that off the list last night, but she was right. What was one more day in the grand scheme of things? Nothing. I could leave Idaho tomorrow and start my life in Washington. But today . . . today didn't have to be a checklist day. I could have just one more day.

Six

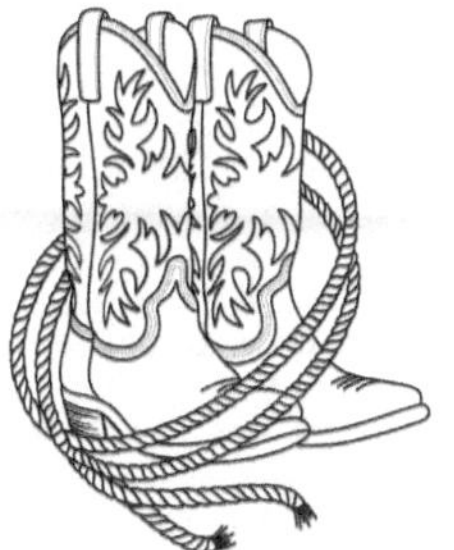

Rhett

Once we had the cattle in the grazing field, as promised, I took off. Lachlan called after me, but I completely missed what he had said. He knew my intentions, he even promised I'd be back before noon. The cattle were where they were supposed to be. I did my job, now I had a girl to see.

It was hard focusing on leading the cows when all I thought about was Kyla, praying she was still at my house. I checked my phone a few times, hoping Abi had texted with some kind of update. Even a simple, "She has emerged!" would have sufficed, but nothing. For all I knew she woke up, saw me gone, and left. It was past noon now. If she had left she would have been long gone by now. But, she had a different feeling about her. Ever since the first moment I saw her. A part of me knew she wouldn't leave.

The barn came into view, and the outdoor arena that sat behind had two horses running in it. I slowed Buckle to a trot and approached the arena. Stetson, my seven-year-old nephew, was on one, and Wyatt was on the other. Wyatt had a huge grin on his face, his backward ball cap hitting the nape of his neck. He loved to ride, just on his terms, but when it came to Stetson, Wyatt was always ready to jump on a horse. On the other side of the arena, leaning against the metal gate I saw Abi, watching her son with pride, and next to my sister . . .

A wave of relief hit me.

Kyla.

Kyla stood on the lowest bar of the gate, her arms outstretched as she held herself on the railing, her smile larger than Wyatt's. She was wearing the same shorts as last night, but had put on a loose-fitting t-shirt, half-tucked into her shorts. One of Abi's beige woven hats sat on her head, allowing her brown hair to fly around the nap of her neck. If I wasn't a professional cowboy, I would have fallen off my horse just from the sight of her. I could feel the shivers run through my arms. They wanted to reach out for her even though I was still mounted on Buckle.

I tightened my grip on the reins.

Remember, to her it was only one night.

"Hey, Rhett," Abi called, waving me over, "I take it the cattle are where they need to be?"

I gave my sister a quick nod, but my eyes were focused on Kyla.

"Hey, Cowboy." She gave me a soft smile. "Thanks for the coffee."

I jumped off Buckle, landing right behind Kyla. Leaving one hand on the gate, Kyla turned her body to face me and our eyes locked. I tried to find the words to talk, but my brain had malfunctioned, and all I could think was *you're still here.*

Returning her grin, I looked up at her, completely ignorant of the fact that Abi was watching us.

"Hey, Rhett," Abi said again, this time louder, with an emphasis on the T's in my name. "I take it the cattle are where they need to be?"

I looked over at my sister, her blonde hair now in a braid hanging over her shoulder. Her hat shadowed her face, but her piercing blue eyes were clearly visible. She and Wyatt shared the brightest blue eyes, and while Wyatt's could be seen across the arena, Abi's could be noticed even in the middle of the night.

"Yes, Abi," I replied. "They sure are."

Amusement rippled through her as she turned back to the arena. "Oh, Rhett, you are distracted."

"That would have been fun to see!" Kyla beamed as she ignored Abi, jumping from the gate to face me. Being on her feet again she was back to being an entire head shorter than I. "I thought it would take you all day to . . . how did you put it Abi? 'Move the herd'?"

"They're still up there, but I need to pack and get ready to leave tomorrow. Plus . . ." I stopped, desperately wanting to kiss her again, but it may not have been the best idea in front of my sister. "I was getting hungry," I lied.

"Hungry." Abi swallowed her laughter as she opened the gate to the arena. "Too bad lunch is over. Kyla and I already ate. And you may have some competition with my son. Kyla is head-over-heels in love with him."

"With a name like a Stetson, how can I not be?" Kyla's eyes caught mine, alight with humor from her little guessing game last night. "He asked me out on a date."

"Oh really?" Tilting my head, I cocked an eyebrow. "Did you accept?"

"Dinner tonight is his mom's famous mac-n-cheese? How could I say no?"

My heart skipped a beat. "You're staying for dinner?" My voice dropped as I stepped closer, making sure only she could hear my question.

Biting her bottom lip, she took another step towards me. "And the night, if you'd let me."

I inhaled, taking in her scent. I knew now whenever I smelled vanilla, I would think of her. "You can stay as long as you'd like." I caught her eye before turning my back, reaching for Buckle's reins. "I believe I promised you a tour. Wanna take a ride?"

Her eyes widened as she looked at Buckle, and then back to me.

"Don't scare her away, Rhett. I like this one." Abi came up with Stetson, hand in hand. "I offered a ride around the ranch, and she politely declined."

"No offense, Sis, but that was *you* offering. Who said I was going to make her ride on her own?" I winked at Kyla, reaching my hand out to her.

She rolled her lips, keeping down the smirk I knew was hiding there. The hint of hesitation was making my stomach twist in knots. I had the mental image of her behind me, her arms wrapped around my waist as I led Buckle around the ranch. She would lean her chin on my shoulder, her soft laugh in my ear. Once the tour was over, we'd go back to my place, and I'd attempt to keep her to myself for just a little longer.

But as she looked at my hand, the image began to fade away.

"You gotta tell me what's going through your head darlin'."

"Darlin'?" she parroted. "That's worse than 'sweetheart'."

"I'll find you a name," I said confidently, the smile on my face fading as I watched her shift on her feet. I could practically hear her brain buzzing. "What's going through your head?"

She sighed and looked down at her feet. "Nerves? I've never *ever* been on a horse before," she whispered.

Reaching out to try to calm her, I lightly touched her shoulder, trailing my fingers down to grasp her hand. I squeezed my fingers around hers, lifting her hand to my lips.

"Buckle's a smooth ride, and you can hold on to me as tightly as you want," I whispered back, kissing her knuckles.

Kyla bit her bottom lip and her gaze went to Buckle's nose. My horse took the opportunity to nudge me, giving a light snort as Kyla watched. Letting out a sharp breath and a small laugh, she looked at Buckle's back, then down the length of her legs. Her entire body was tense.

Letting go of her hand, I stood a single step back from her. Her eyebrows twitched as I lifted my chin. "Let's start over. I'm Rhett Hartwell." I held out my hand for her to take. "And I'd love to show you my home."

She looked at my hand, taking another deep breath before taking it gently in hers, giving it a slight squeeze.

"Kyla Richards," she said sweetly. I raised an eyebrow, her mental peptalk must have worked. "Let's go for a ride, Cowboy."

We rode out to the lake, Kyla's arms wrapped around my waist the entire time. After a few moments she relaxed her body, moving with Buckle instead of trying to remain a solid board, but her arms never left my waist. She listened as I bored her with the day to day life of the ranch. I was even boring myself so I could only imagine what was going through her mind.

Once we reached the lake, I dismounted and reached my arms out to guide Kyla off Buckle with ease. Placing her hands on my shoulders, she moved her leg and slid off Buckle, our bodies centimeters from each other. I held on to her waist, my fingers pressing into her hips.

Her chest rose as she inhaled. "The lake?"

Her hands left my body as she side-stepped away from Buckle, allowing me to grab the reins to lead Buckle to the tie post. I watched as Kyla stood on the edge of the lake, the reflection of the sun on the water made her a mere silhouette. The thought that we didn't stop for a picnic churned in the back of my mind. I still hadn't eaten, and this would have been the perfect time to sit and enjoy Kyla as long as I had her.

Ruffling through Buckle's saddle bag, I pulled my empty thermos and a granola bar from the bottom of the pouch. At least I had that, although I had nothing to offer Kyla.

"Abi said this was 'Lotties Lake'?" Kyla spun her waist to look at me, her hands firm on her hips.

"The river. Lottie's River. My mom claimed it when she married my dad," I answered, taking a few steps towards her. "The river runs into the gardens and that's my mom's sanctuary. It's only fitting the river is hers."

"And the lake?"

"Just . . . the lake." I shrugged, reaching her side. Reaching for the granola bar package, I gave her a quick glance. "Did you eat?"

Kyla quickly looked down at the granola bar and then back at me and a small chuckle left her lips. "I did, but, you didn't. And you said you were hungry."

Tearing open the granola bar, I silently thanked her. "Sit with me?"

Together, we sat on the edge of the lake, Kyla removed her socks and shoes to dip her toes in the water. The calm and silence filled the air as I ate, and Kyla sat. Tilting her head back she closed her eyes to take in the sun. Her chest rose and fell as she breathed, and I was taken back to last night. The memory of her rising and falling against me as her breaths matched my own, her fingers digging into my shoulders as she took control, pushing me to my back to ride me. I felt the heat rise in me, praying she'd give me another chance before she left my life . . .

"Rhett?" I heard her say, pulling me back to reality as I slowly finished chewing.

I raised my eyebrows in response, hoping I wasn't daydreaming for too long.

A smile teased her lips. "You were gone there for a minute, weren't you?"

Shaking my head, I looked over the water. "Just enjoying the view. I'm sorry, did you ask me something?"

"How long have you owned the ranch?" she repeated.

"My grandfather bought it when he returned from the war."

"The war? World War II?"

I gave her a quick nod. "He and my grandmother were high school sweethearts. They got married right before he left. They were both young, but when he got back, they bought this land to build on and create something they both wanted. It grew over the years, and when they passed, my dad and uncle took over."

"A family affair," she said wistfully.

"Most ranches are. My grandfather left it to my dad and uncle, and when my uncle passed, he left his portion to Lachlan."

"Lachlan?" Kyla mused. "He's your cousin. So . . . I got two facts wrong."

Knitting my brow, I looked over at her, confused. "Two facts?"

"You don't own the ranch. Your father does." Her lips twitched as she held back a smile, but I could see it when her eyes hit mine—she was losing that battle.

Shoving the rest of my granola bar in my mouth, I narrowed my gaze at her. Swallowing, I let the smirk that was tugging at my lips loose. "I guess, technically, you did get two facts wrong. Maybe I'm not as easy to read as you thought."

"Three out of five is sixty percent. That's still pretty good." Tilting her body she moved to flip her hair behind her shoulder. "Plus, I can only assume your dad will pass it to you."

"You would be correct there. Abi and I will split it."

"Not Wyatt?"

"Did you meet my brother? He has no interest in running the ranch."

"But you do?"

Taking a sharp inhale before answering, I looked at the lake. I loved every acre of this place and wanted to see it thrive. I knew with Lachlan and Abi it could become more than it was now. There was so much we could do with it, and I honestly couldn't wait until that chance became mine—*ours*.

"I really do," I answered honestly.

"And the rodeo?" she asked.

"I love being on this land just as much as I love tying down a calf. I love the sun hitting the water, I love the way the dirt flies around my feet as I jump off Buckle. I love the quiet and calm that comes from this place every day, and I love the cheers and excitement I get from the crowds in the arena. This is heaven on earth, and the arena is my home away from home." Turning to look at her, I caught her eyes. Her eyebrows were pinched slightly, and her cheeks were a faint shade of red as she bore into me. But then she blinked, and it all went away.

"I love that you love this place," she whispered.

"This place is all that matters."

She shifted, bringing her knees to her chest, and wrapped her arms around her legs. "I don't . . ." she started, her voice beginning to shake. "I don't have a place like that."

"Well." I reached my arm out, gently taking her cheek in my palm to pull her toward me. My fingers threaded through her hair as I made eye contact, connecting with her the same way I did last night. "We have to find you one."

The ride back didn't last as long as the ride out, even though I made sure Buckle's pace was slow. We made it back to the stables in time to see Lachlan putting Onyx in her stall for the night. He tipped his hat at Kyla, said a polite "Glad to see you again ma'am" before he left the stables. We jumped off of Buckle and, together, removed her saddle and brushed her. And by together, I mean Kyla pet Buckle's nose and gave her apples while I did everything. But it was wonderful to have her company just the same.

I checked my watch as we headed into the main house for dinner. We had been together for almost twenty hours. I still had to pack and find a way to convince her to let me see her again.

During dinner Kyla sat between Stetson and myself, with her attention on my nephew, but a part of her body was always touching me. Whether it was her thigh against mine, her hand finding my wrist, or when she decided to try to find five facts about Wyatt—she used my shoulder as an elbow rest. She was comfortable with my family and they were taken with her the same way I was.

My father, Leo Hartwell, sat at the head of the table. His arms folded across his chest as he studied his family. His skin seemed permanently tanned thanks to the days spent out in the sun, and his graying hair and full beard stood out next to my mother. Charlotte—*Lottie* as everyone called her—sat to my dad's right. She had dark hair, not a gray strand in sight, with gray eyes that would capture anyone's attention. She was the complete opposite of my dad. Her personality was bright and welcoming as she spoke. To her, if you were at the table, you were family.

Wyatt and Lachlan sat on the opposite side of us, with Lachlan focusing on his food—only engaging in the conversation once my father asked about the land. Wyatt, however, was completely engrossed in Kyla, his jaw dropping as soon as she got all five of *his* facts right.

"How did she guess the kind of car I drive?" Wyatt asked as we were getting ready to leave. "I didn't drive today, and there were too many cars to guess which was mine . . ."

"I'm a teacher, I like reading people. It's a game I play with my kids at the beginning of the school year. It's fun for them. They think I'm magic because of it." Kyla smiled. "It's definitely not magic, I'm just very observant . . . and you have a Toyota keychain." She motioned towards his waist, where his keys sat hooked to his belt.

Wyatt shook his head. "Observant?"

"It's easier with kids, but it's fun to play with adults too."

"Okay, okay . . ." I touched Kyla's shoulders. "As much fun messing with Wyatt is, I need to pack. Keep me company, Kyla?"

"I'd love to." Kyla turned to face Stetson before she followed me out the door. "Goodnight, Stetson. Maybe I'll see you before I leave tomorrow."

Stetson smiled and pretended to tip a hat, making Kyla melt.

SEVEN

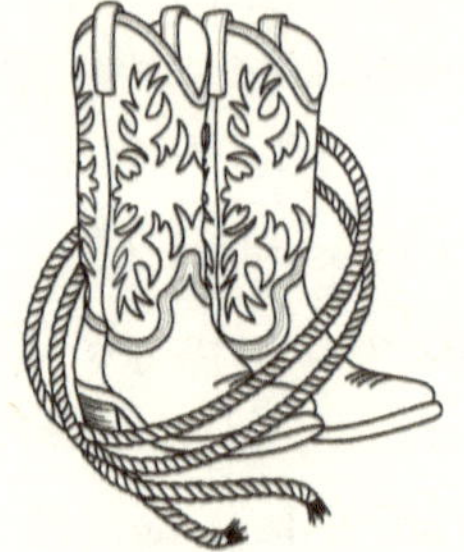

Kyla

EARLIER, BEFORE RHETT FOUND me again, and after I hung up the phone with Grace, I ventured outside and found Abi quickly. I could tell she had been busy, gloves on her hands and buckets of water by her feet.

"Ah," she had said with a large, welcoming smile on her face. "Just in time to get the troughs full. I'm Abi."

She was a ray of sunshine from the moment we shook hands, and she was able to distract me just enough with small tasks that I had almost, *almost*, completely forgotten about Rhett.

Until he showed up. Once he was on the ground in front of me, I turned back into who I was the night before—except I couldn't go there again. So, with a small pep talk before climbing on his horse, I told myself to put an end to it. I had to be logical. I knew what his hands felt like, what he felt like inside of me. I knew I wanted more. It wasn't easy to talk myself out of it.

But then we sat by the lake, and his eyes bore into mine as he said we would find a place that was for me. A place I could love with my entire being. He had said *we*. As in him and I.

I folded my arms over my body as we walked back to his house in silence. I could feel myself closing off, easing back into my normal rhythm as the night came to a close.

Where was the other Kyla? The one from last night? I wanted her to come back.

"I need to get Buckles' things. I'll be in the house soon, okay?" Rhett's hand lightly grazed my elbow as he began to head in the direction of the stable. A chill danced up my arm from the simple touch.

I mimicked his smile, nodding before turning back to his house, watching him jog to the stables. Once inside, I leaned against the door, exhaling through my lips, closing my eyes and seeing Rhett here with me. Nothing could happen tonight, I knew that much. As much as I wanted it, I knew—I just *knew*—I had to be the sensible one here. I'd stay the night and then leave shortly after he did in the morning.

I gathered my things quickly, getting a fresh pair of pajamas from my car before settling onto the couch, pulling my knees up to my chest, waiting for Rhett to return.

The day of cowboys was over. I had to stop pretending to be someone I wasn't and move on. It was fun while it lasted—and I would have a fantastic story to tell later down the road—but . . . it was over. Time to move on and find me again. No more pit stops.

Moments later Rhett came back into the house, giving me a small, fleeting kiss before beginning to pack, moving around his house quickly. My lips tingled from his kiss. I wasn't expecting it, but the way he acted, it seemed like the normal thing to do. A kiss between partners. Heat rose in my cheeks at how little thought it took for him to kiss me. Like it was something he did everyday. Like kissing me was just . . . habit.

Rhett moved seamlessly as he pulled out a suitcase and duffel bag. He was a very organized packer, not to sound cliché, but this wasn't his first rodeo. I watched as he pulled a few button-down shirts from his closet, laying them on top of one another carefully before returning to his bedroom. He came back out with three hats on his head, and one in each hand. He looked adorable with the tower of hats, concentration on his face as he carefully placed each one down as if they weren't just stacked on his head. He pointed at each, silently counting to himself before he mumbled, "I may need more . . . ten days . . . how many rides," then he turned, only to come back with two more hats.

"How many hats do you own?" I scoffed. "And don't they go in boxes?"

He slid on his heel and threw me a crooked smile. "A cowboy can never have too many hats." His smile grew and he lifted his eyebrows before turning back to his room.

I studied him, every inch of him. Remembering the way he fit with me so well last night, and the way he treated me today. I found myself wishing he would almost do something that remotely reminded me of David. But he was simply too perfect. He was going to make it hard to forget him.

He paused, catching me watching him. He smiled again and instead of turning back to his bedroom, he took the moment to pour me a glass of white wine. In one fluid motion he came over to the sofa and handed me the glass, his eyes never once leaving mine.

"You trying to liquor me up, Cowboy?" I took the glass from him, shocked by how easy it was to tease him.

He winked. "It's not rum and Dr. Pepper."

I stopped myself from taking the teasing further. "Listen." I paused, eyeing him for half a second before looking at the wine. "Last night was a—"

"I know, I know. A one-night thing. Just a friend offering a friend a drink. You just relax." He turned back to his things, leaving me in the living room to "relax."

Taking a small, sweet sip of wine, I kept my eyes on him, and once I had caught my breath I pulled out my phone to update Grace.

Me

> Rhett is packing now . . . the day of cowboys is coming to an end.

Those three small dots danced as Grace answered but I could predict her answer, *You could still make it the Summer of Cowboys, not just the day.*

Grace

> You know, you could still . . .

I laughed, not even finishing reading the text as I began to respond.

Me

> I knew you were going to say that.

"I like your laugh," I heard Rhett say from behind me. "It fills the entire room and it's just . . . beautiful."

I dropped my phone and twisted my body, hanging my arm over the back of the couch to get a good look at him. He was folding up a pair of Wrangler's, placing them in the suitcase along with ten other pairs. He still had his work jeans on, his boots tucked underneath, paired with a gray t-shirt, untucked, but still fitting him perfectly, showing off his perfectly toned body.

Sighing, I pulled myself back to the moment. "It's been a long time since someone has told me that," I admitted because it was true. David had told me that while we were dating . . . once. It used to be a memory that endeared him to me, but now it was tainted. That should have been a small clue that he wasn't worth it. In hindsight . . . it's always in hindsight.

Rhett furrowed his brow. "No one told you you're gorgeous? No one asked what you wanted to feel in bed? And no one pointed out your amazing, knee weakening, laugh?" He placed the pair of jeans in the suitcase and folded his arms, his eyes heavy on me. "Your ex must have been a miserable man."

"David," I finally said, my voice softer than it was two minutes ago. "His name was David, and he really was . . ." I trailed off, not exactly sure how far I wanted this conversation to go tonight. How much did Rhett need to know?

But then I met his gaze, his shoulders square as he took a long, deep breath. "Did he hurt you?"

He was still, but his voice deepened as a storm raged in his eyes. Biting the inside of my check, I slowly nodded.

He took a deep breath, and I could see exactly where his mind went. His eyes rapidly blinked as his breathing quickened. He tried to hide it, but the complete stiffness to his posture wasn't letting him hide the anger that began to surge through him. I had known this man for less than twenty-four hours and he was already more concerned for my well-being than anyone else. My own mother told me to be the wife I was supposed to be, she never bothered to listen to me. Rhett's mind went directly to the worst case scenario, but there was more than one way to hurt someone.

"It wasn't physical," I added, making sure to clear the air with him. "He never hit me. Came close the night I broke off the engagement, but he never hit me. It was more emotional—verbal."

"That's worse sometimes," he said, his voice soft and caring. "Getting in someone's head like that? Making you believe things that aren't true. Hell, that will kill you from the inside out."

I turned and leaned to set my wine glass on the coffee table, bringing my knees to my chest. It had taken me years to see that David was crushing me, gaslighting to the extreme—and when I finally decided to act, I was manipulated into staying by my mother. Which only made leaving that much harder. Not only was I letting her down, but I was making David look like the person he really was. The facade that he had worked so hard to build would come crashing down the moment his trophy wife left him. And I wasn't even his wife yet.

"I left," I finally added, "and I'm starting over."

"Moving to Washington?"

"Remember how I said I'm a teacher?" He nodded in response. I inhaled, urging myself to continue. "I still have my license, but I left my school after Christmas, on good terms. They understood and knew what was happening. I'll recertify once I get to Washington," I explained as Rhett walked around the couch, taking the seat next to me. He was careful not to reach out for me, though I could clearly see he wanted to. I would welcome the touch, but I also appreciated the space he was giving me. "Until I can find another school in Washington, I have a tutoring job set up."

"Does he know where you're going?"

I shook my head. "Only my friend Grace knows. I haven't talked to my mom since I left David. I completely broke away. New phone number, new car, new everything. I'll call my mom once I get settled in August."

A line formed between his brow. "That's months away. What are you doing until then?"

Letting out a small laugh I dropped my knees, reaching forward again to grab my wine. "That's the funny part. I had a list of things I wanted to do, wanted to see. I kept enough in my savings so that I could find a place to live once I got to Washington after spending the summer 'finding myself.'" I air quoted. "But now I'm being a rational adult thinking I need to get to Spokane now or there will be no apartments left in August. Almost like everyone is moving to Spokane and they all will need an apartment at the same time I will.

That girl you met last night—the one in the bar who took your hat and played pool and teased the living hell out of you—that's not me. I teach, and overthink things, and do as I'm told, but I figured why not be free for one night? You helped me be free for one night—hell one *day*—and I loved it. But I have to get back to the real world sometime.

"And honestly"—I took a sip of my wine, the sizzle of the alcohol sliding down my throat—"I don't know why I'm telling you all of this. Just because you said some nice things to me and gave me one of the best nights in my life, doesn't mean . . ." I shrugged and took another drink, hiding the blush I felt rush to my cheeks. At this point I was rambling. Rhett didn't need to know any of this. I was better off locking it up. I began to guzzle my wine until I felt Rhett's hand on my arm, forcing me to lower the glass.

"You're telling me because you can trust me, and I think you know that."

I met his gaze. I didn't trust many people with my story or inner emotions except for Grace and my therapist, but Rhett gave me the same feeling they had. He would listen to everything I had bottled up and take it. He wouldn't give me advice, unless I asked, but he would sit and listen. It was an odd feeling to have, especially with a man I had just met. I knew very little about him, yet I felt completely safe next to him. I trusted him.

"Come with me," he whispered softly.

I furrowed my brow. "What?" The word came out more like a laugh, the corners of my lips tugging into an unsure smile.

"You said you wanted to see and do things? Come on the road with me and Wyatt. See things before you overthink again."

It was tempting to say yes. I almost let the word slip through my lips, but the logical part of my brain went into gear, and I shook my head.

"I can't go with you. I need to find an apartment and get my life set in stone before I screw it up even more."

Rhett let out a long breath, his nostrils flaring as he tilted his head. His jaw tensed as he began to look around the room. I tightened my lips, keeping the three letter word that started with a Y in my throat. That couldn't . . . wouldn't happen.

"Then why don't you stay here?" He broke the silence that was growing between us, his gaze moving back to me on the couch.

I blinked. "I'm sorry?" I asked.

"We're only five hours from Spokane. You can stay here while I'm gone. Spend some time with Stetson—I'm sure Abi will appreciate that, she's always busy during the summer months. And you can search for an apartment." He bent his knee as he got comfortable on the couch, his entire body leaning towards me.

I could feel his heat radiating off of him. His woodsy scent swirling around me. Everything he was suggesting felt right, but that stupid logical side of my brain . . .

"Stay here?" I repeated. "On the ranch?"

"In my house."

"You're not serious?" But the way he was looking at me, the way his eyes lit up, told me he was being one hundred percent serious.

What was crazier? Going with him on the road, or claiming his space as my own for ten days?

"Sure I am. Wyatt and I leave tomorrow and then we're gone on the circuit for ten days. You can stay here and make yourself at home."

Stay in his house? Without him? Just pretend that I live here, hang out on the ranch all day until he gets back, and what . . . what happens then?

"Wouldn't that be weird? Wouldn't your family think that's . . . unusual?" I asked, furrowing my brows and biting the inside of my cheek.

Rhett's expression told me it wasn't. It would work out. I should stay. Our eyes were glued to each other for a moment, until he blinked, taking a deep breath and shifting his weight on the couch.

"Only if we make it weird. My family won't question anything."

"Oh, so you've been in this position before?" I half-joked, cocking an eyebrow, trying to ease the heaviness between us.

"No," he stated, his voice toneless. "Sometimes I rent it out as an Airbnb while I'm gone. Ten days doesn't normally warrant that, but I think they would understand making an exception for you." He met my eyes again, and I melted. The blue of his eyes got brighter as he held my gaze.

He cleared his throat. "I don't want to make you uncomfortable. I won't be here to be in your way, and you can do whatever you want. I can tell my family to treat you like an Airbnb guest and leave you alone, or they can keep you company. It's your call but . . ." He reached his hand out to me, gently placing a piece of hair behind my ear. "You're welcome here, Kyla."

"Is this how all men are supposed to be?" I asked, my mind reeling with the idea of him. It was hard to imagine he was real.

"Decent men, I'd like to think." Rhett faintly smiled. "My mama didn't raise me to treat a woman any other way." He leaned across the couch. The fingers that were just in my hair moved and his palm cupped my face. I leaned into him, simply loving the warmth he offered. "Stay here as long as you need."

Sighing, I studied his eyes. I wanted to lean over and kiss him; tell him to treat me like he did last night. To make love to me like no one else had—but that's not why he was doing this. He simply just wanted me to be safe, and I believed that. Instead of giving in to what my body wanted, I placed my hand on his and gently kissed his palm.

"Did you really just see a girl sitting alone at a bar and decide to buy her a drink?"

He touched my bottom lip with his thumb. "Honestly, that's all. I didn't expect you to stay, but I was terrified you would leave."

"I almost did, until I saw your note."

"I'm just glad you could read my chicken scratch." He chuckled, a small smile tracing his lips.

I let out a laugh. For the first time in a long time, I felt safe. I felt wanted. I felt . . . secure. "Okay." I sighed. "I'll stay. Thank you."

He let out a sigh of relief, steady and sure. His calloused thumb made soft, small circles on my chin, sending shivers down my spine. His hold on me was intense, another thing I never experienced. Inhaling, I moved my chin from his grip, trying to force the feeling off my skin.

But then his unsure, shaky whisper pulled me back to him. "Can I kiss you?"

I sighed, that same three letter word screaming to be let out. Instead, I heard my answer. "That's not who I am, Rhett. I was honest with you when I said I don't do that kind of thing. I had to talk myself into being *free*."

"That may be the case, but I really . . . *really* . . . would love to kiss you. Even if it's the last kiss we ever share." His eyes searched my face, the deep blue turning back into that ocean I wanted to swim in.

I hesitated briefly, but as I looked into his ocean eyes, I began to swim. I couldn't—didn't want to—resist. "One last kiss . . ." I leaned in and our mouths met, the taste of his beer still lingering on his lips. The butterflies grew in my stomach as I longed to take it deeper. But simple, sweet, loving, that's all this needed to be.

Our last kiss.

Rhett leaned his forehead against mine and took a deep breath, almost as if he knew that would be our last kiss too. The air between us still felt thick. It made sense in my mind to step back—we both wanted something we shouldn't. It would be better to start a friendship now that I would be living in his house.

"I'll change the sheets and sleep on the couch tonight," he whispered.

"You know." I lifted my head, still not believing that this man was real. "Most cowboys named Rhett are the 'bad boys.' They wear black hats and have long hair. Your name doesn't fit you."

"You must not have met a real Rhett before. I can promise you, my name fits me." He kissed me again, another fleeting kiss against my temple before he stood and disappeared into his bedroom.

Grabbing my phone again, I sent an update to Grace.

I'm staying for the summer.

Grace's response was instant.

Summer of Cowboys—I approve.

Not cowboys . . . just one.

The next morning, Rhett was awake before the sun came up. He moved silently around his room as he dressed, and I rolled to my side in his bed. I was tempted to reach out to him, pull him down with me, and beg him to stay, but I stayed still. Last night, I made it clear that wasn't going to happen again. I had to stick with that. He was a gentleman and honored it. I had to keep my hands to myself.

So I simply watched him. I had known the man for a little over thirty hours and yet I felt like I had known him for a lifetime. I sat up, bringing my knees to my chest. From his bedroom I could see into the kitchen perfectly, and Rhett was focused on the coffee machine in front of him. He had a baseball cap on, not the cowboy hat I had grown accustomed to seeing him in, but the baseball cap fit him just as well. He looked relaxed, ready for whatever was going to come his way.

"Good morning." He smiled once he noticed I was awake. He walked into the room, bringing me a mug of coffee. "I don't know how you take your coffee—if you need a splash of creamer or an insane amount. I guessed . . ."

I looked at the liquid gold in the cup. Coffee was coffee, and it was hand delivered.

"It's perfect," I answered, raising it to my lips. "How long have you been awake?"

"A few hours . . ."

"A few hours? Rhett, you could have woken me up."

"You were too peaceful, I couldn't. I set out some clean towels for you, and let my family know you'll be staying here while I'm away. Abi is excited." He smiled. "And Lachlan knows not to be too much of a hassle."

"They can put me to work. I can earn my keep."

"Well first, you won't be 'earning your keep,' you're a guest. But Abi may have some things she will ask you to do. If not, treat this as a vacation. Maybe take a drive around Idaho . . . check some things off that list of yours."

I smiled. "I hate to break it to you, but I don't think there's anything on my list that I can do here at the ranch." I sipped my coffee, taking in its scent.

"Well, add a few things. Trust me, there is plenty to do here." He shoved his free hand in his pocket. "I have to get Wyatt, but . . ." He pulled out a sticky note and handed it to me. "There's my number. Please, keep in touch?"

I looked at the numbers on the sticky note, and then back up at him with a smile. "Can I text you every day?"

"You better." He gave me the sexiest smile I had ever seen. That temptation to pull him into the bed with me got stronger. "I have to get going," he added, tugging me from my fantasy. "Don't worry about anything here, just"—he spread his hands out in front of him—"relax."

"Relaxing is not really my personality. Good luck out there, Rhett. I'll be rooting for you."

He gave me a wink and then flew out the door, grabbing one last bag before the door shut behind him. It took all of my strength not to beg him to kiss me goodbye.

EIGHT

Rhett

HOURS INTO THE DRIVE and all I could think was, *Why didn't you kiss her goodbye you idiot?*

Kyla sat in *my* bed, wearing nothing but a tank top on her torso showing me her bare shoulders, watching as I made coffee and silently walked around the room. I slept like shit the night before, because I was stupid enough to take the couch when there was a gorgeous woman who wouldn't mind having me lie next to her in *my* room. Then what? I just gave her my number and said, "Have fun, relax"?

Rolling my eyes at myself, I asked myself, yet again, *Why didn't you kiss her goodbye?*

Because she didn't want that. To her, I was a one-time thing.

Wyatt had his eyes closed next to me, his arms folded and head leaning back on the headrest. Not a care in the world. Wyatt had one goal and one goal only, to be an announcer at the National Finals Rodeo—The NFR—in Las Vegas. And even though he had a ways to go, I would be the first to tell anyone he was going to get there. He had that charm. Me? All I had was a lingering thought that I should have kissed Kyla. And how that would have ruined everything.

There was something there with her that I couldn't quite put my finger on. The pull to be near her, even just in the same room, was strong. The pure need to have her in my arms, just to simply feel her warmth, was more than physical. There seemed to be a deeper desire that I wasn't quite sure how to put into words. She was unlike any woman I had ever been with. And here I was, driving hundreds of miles away from her. I wish she would have said yes to coming with me. She could check things off her list. She could *add* things to her list.

Her bucket list.

I wondered what was on it.

Sleeping with a random man in Idaho probably wasn't. Hell, living on a ranch for a few weeks probably wasn't either, but I was suddenly very interested in what was. Taking a quick glance at Wyatt, I saw that he was still sound asleep, and I made a quick mental note to ask her the first time I heard from her. She had my number, but I had to wait for hers.

I'd wait as long as it took.

The trip this time around was packed. We were heading to Montana, North Dakota, South Dakota, Wyoming, and then finally home in time for the Fourth of July. The Fourth was always a time for major rodeos, but racking up the times and money didn't really appeal to me when I knew my family was holding their own shindig at home. I'd rather participate in the rodeo in my hometown than be somewhere else.

After the Fourth, it was back on the road and off to Utah for their biggest rodeo of the year. If I won in Utah, I'd be a shoo-in for the NFR.

This was my life, my world, and I loved it.

We arrived in Billings in record time, the nine-hour drive killing me just as much as it killed Buckle, even with the extra stops to let her walk around. I unloaded her first, pulling her into the stable and making sure she was taken care of before I made my way to the arena. I had been here before, numerous times, but man did I love the look and feel of the dirt—the empty stands that would be filled with a huge crowd, everyone cheering.

Just seeing it empty made me wonder what it would be like to have Kyla in the stands. My family had come to events to watch me ride, but I never had a girl in the stands waiting for me. If she was, I knew exactly what I would do after a ride—I could picture it. If Kyla was here, I would climb the gate and take her mouth in mine, letting everyone see exactly how I planned to celebrate.

I should have asked her to come again this morning. Would her answer have changed?

Wyatt was already up at the booth, his white cowboy hat hard to miss as he talked with Jason, his fellow announcer, both holding a sheet of paper in their hands. I pulled my phone from my pocket thinking maybe he could tell me when I was up, but instead I found a text from an unknown number.

Unknown

> Hey, Cowboy.

I couldn't fight the smile that grew across my face. *Kyla.*

Unknown

> I downloaded this app called the Cowboy Channel, and paid a pretty penny for it. What Rodeos are you in?

I quickly saved her number, thinking of ways I could respond to her, when another text popped up.

Kyla

> This is Kyla . . . btw.

A chuckle left my lungs as a smile spread across my face and I leaned on the railing to respond back to her.

Me

> Not many people greet me with "Hey, Cowboy."

Kyla

> Well, more people should greet you that way. Actually, no, just me.

Me

> Only you, Sugar.

Kyla

> Um no . . . I don't like that one either.

Me

> I'll find one soon. I'll send you the list of Rodeos. Not sure if this one is streaming on the channel though. I'll ask Wyatt.

I swiped her text away, pulling up Wyatt's photo, when another text from Kyla came through.

Kyla

> So far, your nicknames have sucked. You're running out of options. Let me know about the rodeo!

Typing a quick text to Wyatt, I looked up at him in the booth. He reached for his phone, glanced at the screen and then began to search for me in the stands. He found me quickly and then gave me a strong nod, a dorky smile on his face, with a thumbs up before he went back to the schedule.

Me

> It's on the channel tonight, turn on your notifications and watch the rodeo in Billings Montana, PRCA.

She started responding, and I had to force myself to breathe.
I loved watching those little dots dance.

Kyla

PRC . . . what?

Me

Have Abi brush you up on rodeo terms before the show starts. You've got an hour.
There will be a quiz.

I pocketed my phone and pushed myself off the rail, feeling
lighter than I was moments before, knowing the teasing and messages from Kyla was all it took. This place was about to light up, and
she was going to watch. She may not be here in person, but knowing
she was watching me sent shivers down my spine as my flesh warmed.
I could still feel her. All I had to do was close my eyes and she would
be in the stands, not in front of the television or streaming from an
app.

I handed my phone off to Jeff, the rodeo assistant, right before
I slipped the rope between my teeth. The lasso moved freely as I
moved Buckle around in circles near the gates. So far, I had an 8.2,
7.9, and a 9.5 to beat. I could beat the nine—maybe the eight—but

that seven was going to be tough. Circling my wrist, I moved the lasso as Buckle stopped, moving her nose up and down.

She was ready.

I was ready.

"Hey, Rhett!" Jeff shouted as he headed my way, waving my phone in the air. "You have a FaceTime coming in."

I pulled the rope from my teeth. "They can call back, there's one more run in front of me."

"Some gal named Kyla?" Jeff said, looking at the screen again. He cupped his hand over his mouth as the crowd cheered. "She's called twice now."

I looked at the big screen, seeing Darren Harper jump back on his horse to wait as the calf stayed still for the six required seconds. Shooting my eyes back at Jeff, I gave him a quick nod. "Answer it for me." I agreed stupidly. Talking to Kyla before a run was either going to be the best idea I ever had—or the dumbest.

Jeff furrowed his brow, but did as I asked, still holding onto my phone as he held it towards me.

"Cowboy!" Kyla screamed.

"Kyla, I'm up next!" I shouted back, glancing at the arena.

"I know!" Her smile beamed and I swear it lit up the entire place, even through the screen. "Wyatt sent me the schedule."

"How did you get Wyatt's number?"

"Um, his twin," Kyla responded, jabbing her thumb as Abi came into view behind her. My sister gave me a cheeky grin and waved.

"Up next is Idaho native and the top Tie-Down Roper in the nation." Wyatt's voice boomed over the speakers. "Holding the number one spot for the season, for the third year in a row, he's been showing some amazing times in the last few weeks, and I happen to know he had a very relaxing weekend. He's your favorite roper of the night, Rhett Hartwell!" In classic fashion, Wyatt drew out my name as long as he could.

Glancing up at the big screen I saw myself with Jeff holding my phone up to my face. I shook my head and smiled, a deep laugh that no one could hear bubbling up as I turned to look back at Kyla. The men next to the chute started to wrangle the calf for me, waiting for my nod.

"I want to watch! Good luck!!" Kyla shouted.

I winked at her and stuck the rope between my teeth, taking one final breath before giving the go ahead.

The chute opened and the calf burst through. Buckle bounded after I urged her with my heel, the lasso flying through the air. I aimed and let it go, grabbing the calf faster than I thought I would. I jumped off Buckle and ran to the calf, my fingers sliding on the rope. I grabbed the calf, lifted her off the ground and brought her down, wrapping up her three legs as fast as I could, waving my hands in the air right before I stood and walked my way back to Buckle.

Whoever said we aren't athletes had another thing coming. That shit is hard. I got back on Buckle, my breath heavy, and looked at the calf. Six seconds . . . she had to stay down for six seconds, and it would be a qualifying time, and I knew I didn't break that barrier. I let out a deep breath and looked at the screen, finally allowing myself to listen to the announcers as they replayed my ride.

"I've seen Rhett pull faster times at home for sure, but you could definitely tell he was there tonight. Speed, absolute speed." Wyatt's voice rang through my ears. "And with the calf down six seconds, that puts Rhett Hartwell at 8.0, putting him in second place for the night. Now, Rhett . . ."

Second place, not bad. 8.0, not bad at all. Once the calf was up, I turned Buckle and went back to the gate, dashing through to meet Jeff, who still held up my phone. Jumping off the saddle, I patted the other riders back, congratulating him on placing first. Jeff approached, handing off my phone with a smile on his face.

"This one seems interesting," he said, his eyebrows raised close to the rim of his hat, his grin basically to his ears. She definitely was *interesting*.

"Who? Kyla?" I asked, taking my phone. "Just a new friend."

Did I just friendzone myself?

"Okay, so what does all that mean?" I could barely hear her voice as the chutes opened up next to me.

"So far for the night I'm second," I said loudly into the phone, reaching for Buckle's reins. "Not bad."

"Not bad at all, Cowboy. I tried to watch from here but didn't see much other than your ass." I raised an eyebrow and noticed her lips roll, a light blush adding color to her cheeks. "Abi has it streaming though so I can rewatch. Oh, but look at this." Kyla switched her phone camera around to show me Stetson, using a small rope in place of a lasso. "He's been doing that the entire time."

"A roper in the making. Hey beautiful"—I pulled Buckle along, not wanting to hang up, but knowing I had to pay attention to the arena—"I need to go, but I'll call you back from the hotel."

"*Beautiful?*" she emphasized, rolling her eyes at me. "Yes, please call. I have so many rodeo questions."

I chuckled. "I'll answer them. So long, Doll Face."

"Not. That. One."

I ended the call and shoved my phone in my pocket, my cheeks hot as Kyla ran through my thoughts.

After the rodeo ended, Wyatt and I met a few of the guys at the nearest bar. Our schedule was tight, and we needed to be in the next city for two events tomorrow, but stopping for a drink—especially after a time like that—was necessary.

Wyatt bounded to the bar top, patting Darren and Zeke, fellow ropers, on their backs as he shoved his way in between them.

"No girls for you guys tonight?" Wyatt mused, his announcing voice still booming over the crowd.

Zeke glared at my brother over his shoulder. "You know very well that I'm happily married, Hartwell."

"Ya, but Darren isn't." Wyatt looked over at Darren, a cheeky grin spreading as he raised a single eyebrow.

"Doesn't mean I need a girl." Darren raised his mug to his lips. "Do I want one? Sure, but I don't *need* one." He dropped the mug with a bang, small splatters of beer flying out. "Rhett had a bystander on his phone during his run, you should have seen Jeff trying to catch it all."

My lip tugged into a faint smile at the mention of Kyla, which I quickly forced down. I had to keep reminding myself I was officially friend zoned.

"She's just interested in the sport. She's never been to a rodeo before and wanted to see what it was like," I answered, keeping my composure down.

Zeke's interest peaked. "Got yourself a city girl?"

"He does. She wore his hat and he took her home." Wyatt laughed, his eyebrows wiggling up and down.

"You make it seem like something I normally do," I retaliated, waving my arm to the bartender. I needed that beer if this was the way the conversation was going to go.

"Nah, Wyatt, we all know that's you, not Rhett." Darren patted my brother on the back, only giving him more attention.

"Damn straight. Now, who am I taking with me tonight?" Wyatt lifted his hands to his eyebrows and scanned the room.

Darren and Zeke both laughed in response. I just shook my head, thanked the woman behind the bar for my beer and drank, keeping Kyla out of the conversation.

NINE

Kyla

Being in Rhett's house without Rhett wasn't as uncomfortable as I thought it would be. It was oddly relaxing. Abi came to me faster than I expected, handing me a pair of boots and hat before grabbing my hand to pull me out of the house. The day was spent in the sun, where Stetson showed me the horses and how to hold my hand out flat for them to take the apples from me. We chased the goats and made sure the cows had plenty of feed. I was dragged every which way as he showed me everything. The only thing he managed to fail at was getting me on a horse.

Then we gathered to watch the rodeo.

Rhett's parents were welcoming to the random stranger in their house, and almost treated me as a member of the family. Charlotte was the sweetest, warmest woman I had ever met. Her hair fell over her shoulders with a slight curl at the tips, while her eyes matched Abi's with a hint of gray around her iris. I could have sworn she was the same age as my mother, but where my mother made sure to hide every gray hair and always had the most fashionable suit she could find, Charlotte was down to earth in jeans and a flannel top, with mud caked under her fingernails.

The rodeo drew all my attention, watching each new event as all the questions formed in my mind. I was impressed with the bareback riders the most—men riding a bucking horse with no saddle and just a rope to hold on to. As I watched the men basically lay on the back of the horse as it bucked, I wondered how none of them had whiplash.

"Oh, I guarantee plenty of them have," Charlotte had told me. "Lachlan had a few injuries back in the day."

Lachlan came from the kitchen, his sleeves rolled up to his forearms as he reached for his hat, rolling his eyes at his aunt's comment, leaning in to give her a quick kiss on the temple. "Dishes are done Aunt Lottie. See ya tomorrow," he mumbled, leaving the room quickly before anyone could ask him to stay.

"Is he okay?" I whispered to Abi.

Abi shrugged her shoulders, giving me a sly grin as she nodded softly.

Mr. Hartwell—who told me I had to call him "Leo"—was quiet and reserved. But unlike Lachlan, he lit up as he watched his son land second place in his event.

"Still top in the nation." He clapped his hands at the television as the arena prepped for the next event.

"What does that entail?" I turned to look at him, confused as to how he could be leading when he came in second.

"Just like any sport, he's leading the nation this season in wins. He's earned the most and he has the best scores." Leo beamed. "Just wait until you see him on the Fourth—the best event Alpine Ridge has to offer."

"The Fourth of July?" I asked, excitement creeping up until that knot in my stomach formed when I remembered I'd be gone. "I'll be long out of your hair by then," I added, taking another look at Leo as he fell back onto the couch, a new bottle of beer in his hand.

"Where are you planning on going, Kyla?" Leo asked as he took his first sip.

"Oh, Leo, let her be. She's a guest." Charlotte touched her husband's knee, giving him a look of annoyance.

"I'll be off to Washington. Speaking of . . ." I stood, wanting out of this conversation before it even had time to root. I gave Stetson a smile and ruffled his dark hair. He turned and smiled up at me, the rope stopping by his sides. "I should probably do some research into apartments tonight. I'm sure Rhett would like his house when he gets back. Thank you, again, for letting me watch, and for dinner."

Charlotte smiled. "Oh dear, you're welcome to stay as long as you need."

I nodded at her. "Thank you, Charlotte. I'll see you tomorrow?"

"I'll walk you out, it's bedtime for Stetson anyway . . ." Abi stood and followed me to the door with Stetson not far behind.

"But Mama the bull riders are next!" Stetson protested, dropping the rope as he spun to glare at his mother.

"No, bud . . . bed." Abi scowled at her son, who gave us another pout, but followed her anyway. "They're serious, you know," she said to me as I opened the front door. "You're welcome as long as you like."

Stetson wrapped his arms around my legs. "Wanna help me with the pigs tomorrow?"

"Pigs?" I looked down at him and then back up at Abi.

"You're on a working ranch, my new friend. There's way more here than meets the eyes. See you tomorrow?" Abi asked with a smile and a wink.

I gave Stetson a quick hug back and returned her smile with a soft nod. "Tomorrow."

Rhett's house was dark when I stepped inside, memories of the night with him flooding my mind before I quickly squashed them out. I showered and made a cup of tea, then relaxed and readied myself for bed. When Rhett had told me to relax, this is what I pictured—not spending the day out in the sun. But even though it was completely out of the norm for me, a smile spread across my lips as I thought about my day.

In a way, it was relaxing.

The only thing missing was . . .

Rhett.

Before heading to the couch, I grabbed my phone, jumping only slightly when it rang in my hand.

My stomach dropped as those butterflies came back as I saw Rhett's name staring back at me.

He remembered to call.

"Hey, Cowboy," I answered.

"Hey, Bunny."

"Bunny?" I shouted. "That's a huge no from me."

"I'm running out of options."

"Kyla works fine for me, you know." I chuckled, shoving my body into the corner of the couch and lifting my legs up to my chest. "Besides, Lachlan was telling me about something called Buckle Bunnies?"

"Oh god," he groaned.

"So 'Bunny' is out of the question."

"Okay, okay, I'll accept that that was a terrible choice in nicknames, but again, I'll come up with something. So . . ." His voice sighed, lighting up again, and I swear I could hear his smile. "Now that I can actually hear you, and I'm not surrounded by horses and calves . . . what did you think of the rodeo?"

"I actually really enjoyed it." I suddenly wished I had him on FaceTime and not just a phone call. I had the urge to change the phone call to a FaceTime, but then I remembered I was wearing just a t-shirt and shorts, my wet hair not even brushed yet. I wasn't anything to fawn over. If David had seen me like this, he would have handed me a hairbrush. "I do have a couple questions though."

"Hit me with 'em, I've been doing this for years."

I moved, crossing my legs on the couch like I was a student sitting on the floor waiting for the answer. "What does 'breaking the barrier' mean? I heard Wyatt say that a few times."

"The calf has to have a head start, and that's determined beforehand. If you don't give the calf that head start, ten seconds is added to your time," he explained.

Closing my eyes I tried to envision him as he talked about the rodeo. Was he smiling, moving his hands, running his fingers through his hair? Was he lying on the bed? Or was he in the stable with Buckle? What was he wearing? Did he still have his hat perched on his head . . . or had he taken that off long ago? *God, I want to see him . . .*

"That would explain the groans from your family. Have you ever done that?"

"More than I'd like to admit." Rhett's chuckle was deep and airy.

"But you're top in the nation," I added, my smile growing.

He laughed then—the same laugh from the bar. I did a quick look at myself, thinking it didn't matter what I looked like, I wanted to see him, badly—not just hear his voice. Putting him on speaker phone, my thumb hovered over the FaceTime icon.

He answered, bringing me back to the conversation. "I am, but even the top roper breaks the barrier every now and then."

"And even though you came in second tonight, you're still the top roper?"

"Possibly," he confirmed. "It all depends on my earnings. If I earn the most money, I hold my spot. If I hold my spot, I'm headed towards the NFR in Vegas."

"That's the big time, right? The Superbowl of the rodeo?"

"Yes, Kyla . . . the Superbowl of the rodeo. The top fifteen in each event head there in December. I've competed twice now, but never won a buckle. That's the goal this year."

"Then what?" I asked, more out of curiosity than anything else. I knew that Rhett loved the ranch and the rodeo, but there had to be more.

"Then it starts all over again. Another season in the cards and the beginning of a new one next year." He took a deep breath, a long exhale flowing through my speakers. "What's another question?"

"Are you planning on competing your entire life?" I asked rather quickly, already knowing the answer.

"Until I decide to retire. This is my life and I love it."

"Tying down calves," I muttered.

"Would you rather me ride a bull? Did you see that event, or did you lose interest?"

"I left right before the bull riders, but I have questions there too. For starters, why would anyone want to do that to themselves? Abi told me one of the lead bull riders had to retire due to injuries."

"J.B. Mauney retired last year. Hell of a guy, but yeah, bull riders get the most injuries. They wear protection for a reason, but it's a hell of a rush."

"You've ridden a bull?!" I sat up, almost spilling my tea all over his couch. I clenched my teeth and composed myself, setting the mug on the coffee table before settling back down on the couch. "You lived to tell the tale?"

"I grew up on a ranch, Sunshine, of course I've ridden a bull. Wyatt has too. Broke his arm and then he made the decision to stay far away from rodeos . . . until he got that voice for announcing. Lachlan used to ride Bareback."

Sunshine? I scrunched my nose, deciding to let the nickname slide for now.

"Your mom mentioned that. How do those men not leave with head injuries after every event."

"It's not as bad as it looks, really."

"I highly doubt that *Sunshine,*" I teased.

"Yeah I didn't like the sound of that one either. Regretted it the second I said it."

I hummed, holding back a laugh that I knew wanted to come out. "What's on your agenda tomorrow?"

"A few rides tomorrow afternoon, and one big party tomorrow evening," he answered, his voice falling soft like mine was.

I tried to picture him again. Before I was wondering what he was doing, but now I saw it. He was lying on the bed, his hat next to him, his legs hanging off the sides, an arm over his eyes. He had to be tired, and here I was, keeping him awake simply for my own joy.

"Well then, Cowboy, get some rest."

"What?" he laughed. "You don't have any more questions for me?"

"Oh, I have plenty, but you're probably tired. How long was the drive today?"

Rhett let out a long, exasperated sigh. "Too long. Wyatt slept, and we stopped twice to let Buckle out. So, yeah." He paused. "I'm dead tired."

"I'll write down my questions and text them to you tomorrow. Get a good night's sleep."

"Always do before I ride."

"No buckle bunnies?" I laughed.

"Nope . . . no buckle bunnies, *Bunny.* You off to bed? It's pretty late."

I scrunched my nose. "Gotta blow dry my hair first, I refuse to go to sleep with wet hair."

Wait . . . *what?* Why did I find it important that he knew that information? I closed my eyes and lightly slapped my palm to my forehead.

"Oh well, I wouldn't want my pillow to get wet. Sleep well. Talk tomorrow?"

I gave him a sweet "mmhmm" before hanging up the call. I looked at the phone, biting my bottom lip. It was a fifteen-minute phone call. That's all it was to bring that hint of something more to my mind. I lightly touched the top of my phone to my forehead, the small buzz that radiated my screen with a notification giving me a slight jump.

Rhett

Sleep well. Don't forget to blow dry your hair.

Even though there was a small flutter in my stomach from that final butterfly leaving, I tossed my phone to the side of the couch . . . wishing I had hit that FaceTime button.

TEN

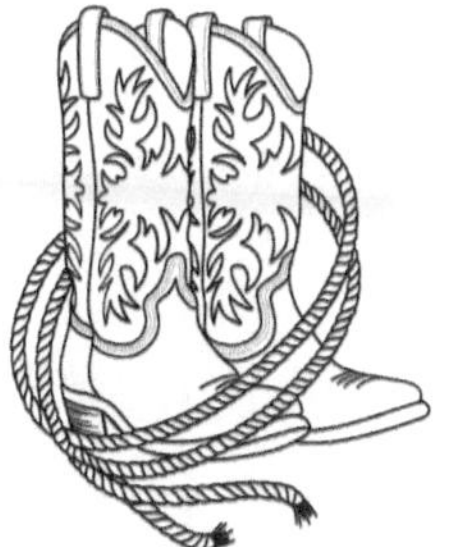

Rhett

Do you get to do a run before the event? Like practice?

This woman. All day she had been texting me questions, and all day I had been ignoring others to answer her. *Why does the calf have to stay down for six seconds? Does the rope ever hurt your teeth? Why do you hold the rope with your mouth? What's a flag man? Are you scored differently than bull riders?*

Glued to my phone, I held it tightly as I felt the vibration in my hand.

Me

No. No practice runs.

Kyla

Why not? Wouldn't that benefit you?

I scoffed and shook my head, that stupid grin appearing again.

Me

I train at home. We have a giant arena.

Kyla

But Abi says there is no "season." I'm just confused as to when you actually have time to relax and . . . sleep.

Me

I'll show you more when I get home, Princess. Stay a little longer and you'll know everything about the rodeo. Even how I relax.

Kyla

Princess? I think you're running out of options. You used that one already.

Me

I have not used Princess.

Kyla

But you have. The first day we met.

The memory of the first time I saw Kyla resurfaced as I pocketed my phone. I let out a breathy chuckle I was sure only I could hear as I reached for Buckle's reins.

"For the past four days you have laughed at that screen more than anything." Wyatt took off his baseball cap and rubbed the back of his neck as he followed me. I guess my laugh was louder than I thought.

I looked at my brother and raised a single eyebrow at him, trying to pretend like I had no idea what he was talking about. "What is that supposed to mean?"

"You wouldn't happen to be texting a certain girl, one who's maybe staying in your house now, would you?" He mimicked my expression, a single brow reaching his hairline, his baby blue eyes boring into me.

I took a deep breath. "She just has questions about the rodeo, she's interested."

"She could ask Lachlan, or Abi . . . hell, she could talk to Stetson. He probably knows more about the rodeo than anyone else on the ranch," he said as he opened the trailer hatch for Buckle. She stepped in, her hooves hitting with a *clank*.

Giving Buckle a pat on her neck, scratching the spot that made her let out a soft breath, I hooked her to the trailer and turned, my eyes staying away from Wyatt. He had made it known he thought it was weird I let Kyla stay in my house, giving her full access to everything. But he didn't know why she needed it.

Just thinking about it made my blood boil. She guaranteed me that he never hit her, that the abuse came in other ways, but that didn't make it any better. Kyla needed to know she was safe. She needed to know she was welcome. She needed the time to herself, and if my house offered any of that, she could stay there as long as she needed. *As long as she wanted.*

It wasn't a secret I had hoped she would stay longer. The secret was that I didn't want to admit out loud I was falling for her. One night—one day—with her was not enough. I wanted more. I wanted all of it. It was a constant reminder when we hung up our phone calls or texted for the last time that day that to her, we were friends. I was willing to be what she needed, and right now that was a friend she could talk to. She needed a home, even though it was temporary, and that, for now, was me.

"We're friends," I added hastily as I locked up Buckle's trailer, making my way to the front of the truck.

"Friends?" he repeated. "I've never seen you turn down so many girls during a trip."

I stopped and glared at my brother. "Excuse me?"

It had been a long time since I took a girl back to my hotel room, maybe even too long—but now with Kyla in the picture, I didn't even think about that. Having Wyatt accuse me of turning down girls was a surprise, seeing as not one had even approached me. Or maybe I didn't notice them approach me.

"They're saying you're not interested." Wyatt clicked his tongue.

I didn't even answer him. I held his stare for a few beats before climbing into the cab of the truck. Once he shut his door and looked over at me, his eyebrows up to his hairline, I finally acknowledged him. "More for you then." Turning the ignition, I took my hat off and placed it on the dash, giving my brother one last glare. "You know for a fact I have never been one to have a different girl every night—that's for bull riders, and apparently announcers."

He barked out a chuckle. "Not every night, but you have been known to have some fun. Everyone can see you're acting differently."

"I'm not acting any differently," I argued.

"Where's your phone? Do you have any new messages lately?"

Not wanting to give him the satisfaction of reaching for my phone right away to see if Kyla had messaged back, I left it in my back pocket and ignored the buzzing that came on cue.

"I'm about to drive." I raised my hand to the road.

"Yeah, but you're thinking about Kyla."

I shook my head slightly, ignoring him completely, making the drive to the stable in silence. Thankfully, Wyatt got the hint and dropped it. Once we got to the stable, he took off to meet with a few of the bull riders, leaving me alone with Buckle, just the way I had hoped.

I led her out of the trailer before glancing over at my brother who was already surrounded by a few girls. He took advantage and wrapped his arm around one's shoulder, probably wishing he was still wearing his cowboy hat versus the ball cap he normally donned after an event. Leading Buckle into her stall, I was suddenly grateful for the time alone.

I had a few more rides before I was back for the Fourth of July, and knowing Abi, she was already busy with planning the rodeo back home. It was tradition, and knowing that a few bigger names had registered, even if the prize money was smaller, made me wish it was July. I counted down the rides in my head: South Dakota,

Wyoming, home. Then a few weeks of relaxing stress as I watched the roping stats and back to it until December.

Relaxing stress. That was a new way to put it. I normally would ignore the stats as I took the few weeks in July to myself, but coming this close to the NFR for the third year in a row—close to the buckle—was starting to wear on me. I had the thought of adding a few more rides to my schedule, to make sure my time and earnings stayed high. Top in the nation was a big deal and I was determined to keep it.

The stress that came along with keeping it, I didn't care for though.

I almost wished I was home with Kyla.

I *did* wish I was home with Kyla.

I took off Buckle's bridle and watched as she shook her head.

"You did great today, girl." I ran my hand down her neck. Removing her saddle and blanket, I grabbed the brush to begin settling her down for the night.

She nodded her head at me once the brush hit her skin. Knowing this was her favorite part of her day I would draw it out—let her enjoy the moment a little longer than normal. I tried to focus on her coat, loving where the white turned brown. She really was a gorgeous horse and I wouldn't trade her for the world. She and I shared a bond. Buckle needed to know my every move and I needed to know hers. Her uneasy stance tonight told me she knew something was up with me as much as anyone else did. Even though I could turn it off in the arena, here in the stable all that was running through my mind was Kyla.

"Hey, Rhett." I heard Wyatt's voice behind me, startling me. I turned and looked at him. "I'm gonna head to—"

"Yeah, yeah just don't stay out too late. We have an event at one tomorrow."

He saluted and gave me a cheesy smile. "Don't forget to check your phone," he sang as he disappeared from the gate.

Lowering the brush, I reached into my back pocket for my phone, just in time to see Kyla's name as she called. It was a FaceTime call. I drew in some air at the thought of seeing her face. Her eyes, her smile, the way she rolled her lips when she was nervous about saying something. Relaxing my shoulders, I answered quickly.

"Hey . . ." I paused, completely out of nicknames. I scanned my brain for anything. She didn't like Sweetheart. Maybe, Darlin'? No, she said that was almost as bad as sweetheart. I was losing this game. "Enter nickname here." I chuckled.

"Oh, that's a good one." She laughed, her eyes beaming. She sat on the porch, her hair flowing over her shoulders as the night air hit her skin. Gorgeous as ever, I studied her through the screen.

"I promise I'll find one," I added softly.

"Which ones have we said no to?" she asked.

I glanced at the phone as I walked away from Buckle. "Princess, Bunny, Darlin', and Sweetheart. But I personally like Darlin'." I smiled, setting the phone on the ledge on the gate, turning my back to return to Buckle.

"Don't forget when you used Sugar."

"I don't think I've used that one yet."

"But you did, through a text."

I rolled my eyes and held back a laugh. "Needless to say, I ran out of nicknames. Did you watch today?"

"Don't hate me but, no."

"I could never hate you. Today must have been good then, huh?" I turned and looked at her.

She gave me a smile before I turned back to my horse. "Stetson and I worked on his reading."

"Tutoring my nephew?"

"He's excited to start second grade and Abi needed him out of the way, so we read The Magic Tree House. Have you ever read The Magic Tree House?"

"Can't say that I have, but I'm not much of a reader."

"You have a ton of books. How can you not be a reader?"

"A lot of those are rodeo stats . . ."

"I did notice that. I'll buy you some books once I get to Washington."

"What kind of books do you read?" I asked, keeping my focus on Buckle.

"Non-Fiction mostly, to be honest—continuing education. I haven't read in a while though. I never really had time to myself to read." She paused, pinching her brow. "You're in the stables?"

"Buckle needs to get comfortable before I head in for the night, then we're on the road tomorrow." I turned, tossing the brush on the floor next to my feet before dusting my palms on my pants. "I have a few rides tomorrow before a bigger event in Cheyenne."

"When do you come home?"

Home. She called it home. Did that mean she was getting comfortable there? Waiting for me to come back?

No . . . I was just reading too much into it. *No, I was just seeing things that weren't real.*

"Six days." I smiled, walking towards the phone.

"I put an application in for an apartment," she blurted out unexpectedly and I swear, my heart stopped. "I can take a virtual tour this week. I may just be out of your hair before you get home."

"At least stick around to say goodbye." I leaned against the wooden wall, my hands on either side of the phone.

She smiled, and I swear the dark stable brightened up. Even though that was damn near impossible, I could feel it. I lowered my chin, hiding the heat in my face.

Remember, that's not what this is.

"How could I leave Stetson on such short notice?" Kyla joked, winking at me.

"Right, Stetson." I raised my head to look at her.

She had a hand resting on her neck, her head tilted just enough that her hair fell to the side, framing her face. The one thing I hated about FaceTime was it felt like she was in the room with me, yet I couldn't reach out and touch her. She was several state borders away, miles and miles in between us, but I still felt this pull. She had to have felt it too, right? It couldn't only be me.

She gave a small hum, a sweet smile growing on her lips before she spoke, softly this time. "I'll stay for a few days after you get back, if that's okay."

My breathing slowed as my heart beat again, the warmth that was in my face radiated. "That's more than okay," I responded.

Her lips rolled as her chin dropped. If I were with her, I'd take her face in my palm and lift her back up to me. I'd kiss her and feel her melt. I'd let her consume me.

"What's on your list?" I asked softly, wanting her attention to come back to me more than anything.

"What?" Kyla responded, her gaze coming back to the screen.

"Your list. You said you had a list of things you wanted to do before you went to Washington. What's on it?"

"Oh, um . . ." She shifted on the couch, her knee coming into view as it came close to her chest. "See the Grand Canyon, which I did."

"And?" I raised my eyebrows. As much as I didn't care for Arizona, the Grand Canyon was a spectacular sight to see.

"It was a giant hole." She laughed before continuing, "I also wanted to lay on the Four Corners, sleep under the stars, hike to Delicate Arch, buy my own coffee maker . . ."

"Buy your own coffee maker?" I parroted, not really believing a simple task like buying a coffee maker would be on someone's bucket list.

"Don't laugh! I've never been able to choose one. David always had to have the top of the line espresso maker. I want a simple drip one. I want yours." Her face turned to the house. "Where did you get that one?"

"I'm not sure, it's kinda old."

"Seasoned. It's seasoned."

I huffed a laugh, trying to get back to her list. "Okay. Grand Canyon, check. Sleep under the stars . . . it's summer in Idaho, you can make that happen—"

"And get kidnapped? No, thank you."

"You should put *ride a horse* on there . . ."

"Stetson would like that."

"Okay, *ride a horse* has been added. Anything else?"

She nodded, but kept silent, those damn lips rolling again, but this time forming a tight line.

"Tell me," I pleaded. I wanted to know more about her; continue to peel away those layers I was finding at the bar.

She blushed and turned her head. "It's embarrassing. And it's just for me."

I raised an eyebrow and curved a corner of my lips. "It's not embarrassing if it's for you."

Shaking her head, slowly at first but speeding it as she looked down, she finally said, under her breath, "Shop for lingerie. Just for me. It doesn't matter who sees them or . . . who doesn't. I've never had something like that for me before, and well . . . now seems like the perfect time to do that. Starting over and all."

My mind instantly went to Kyla wearing a red lace bra and panties, spread out before me as my eyes caressed her every curve. During our night together I didn't care what she was wearing, she was the sexiest thing I had ever had in my bed, and now just the image of Kyla in lingerie, I could feel myself harden. How I longed to make that one come true for her . . .

"Hey, Cowboy . . . did I lose you?"

With the image of her still ingrained in my mind, I took a deep inhale through my nose, I shook my head and forced a casual smile. "Princess, have Abi take you into town one day, get Stetson to get you on a horse, and sleep under the damn stars."

ELEVEN

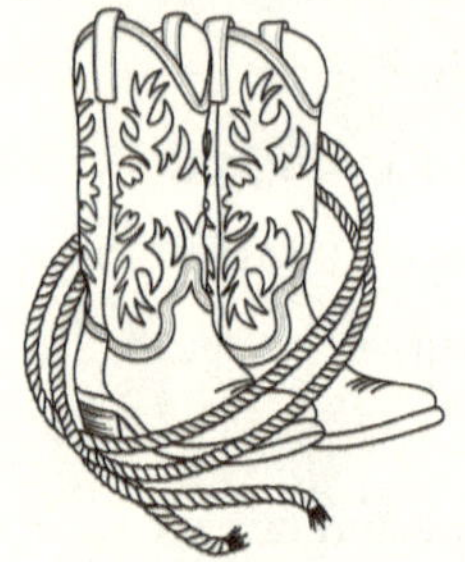

Kyla

"ARE YOU EVER GOING to ride with me, Miss Kyla?" Stetson asked me as he led me towards the stables.

"Stetson, I don't know how to ride a horse. I've only ever been on a horse once and your Uncle Rhett was in control. I would have to be tied to the saddle if I tried by myself so I don't fall off."

Stetson swung his arm back and forth, mine going with him. "Well." The little boy squeezed my hand tighter, pulling at all the heartstrings. "I can teach you what I know. I don't have to be tied to the horse. I'm a pretty good rider." He looked so damn pleased with himself. Sooner or later, I'd have to get on a horse just to make him smile.

Looking down, I hid my face as I felt the blush rush to my cheeks. Rhett's voice from last night ran through my ears, *get Stetson to get you on a horse and sleep under the damn stars.* "I like the sound of you teaching me how to ride a horse, but let's stick with reading for now, okay," I said, looking back down at Stetson.

"But Marshmallow is the perfect horse for you, Kyla!"

"Marshmallow?" I asked, letting go of his hand as he rushed towards the barn.

"I named him!" he called over his shoulder.

Moving into a jog, I caught up with Stetson, who was already opening up the stable door to let the white horse out. Abi came around the corner, carrying a few buckets while wearing the largest galoshes I had ever seen. Along with the galoshes, she had a blue flannel shirt open to reveal a white tank top underneath and a pair of jean shorts hugging her thighs. Mud was caked on the toes of the galoshes, and water sloshed out of the buckets as she set them on the ground in front of her son. She took a breath as she stood up, her cheeks puffed as she used her forearm to lift her hat and wipe her forehead.

"You are not riding today, mister." Abi looked at her son sternly.

"Moooommm . . ." Stetson groaned.

"Your horse—" Abi dropped her chin and placed her hands on her hips, giving her the ultimate mom pose. Even I raised my eyebrows. "Is supposed to be white, not light brown. We are bathing Marsh today."

Stetson sighed, but then reached for a bucket.

"No, get the hose first. You know what to do." Pointing her finger, she watched as her son gave a groan. Stetson followed directions, gathering the hose to spray down his horse. "I swear." Abi came up next to me. "He's going to turn out just like Wyatt."

"Would that be a bad thing?" I asked, crossing my arms over my chest, tilting to look at her.

"Wyatt is . . . not how I want my kid to turn out. I'd rather he'd take after Rhett. Hell, Lach even, just not Wyatt. I love my brother, but he has made some interesting life decisions." Abi raised her arm and wiped her forehead again.

Abi was the constant here at the ranch, but I couldn't tell if she liked the work or not. She let me come and go as I pleased, but was always thankful if I took Stetson out of the house. Each night she would come to Rhett's house with a beer in hand, pulling me onto the porch and into the wooden chairs that sat facing the stars. We would talk and quickly became good friends. We kept it light most of the time, mostly talking about her day at the ranch, my day with Stetson, and my plans moving forward, but heavier topics did come up. Even the topic of David had scratched the surface. She had let me know that Rhett told her the basic gist, that he was—and I quote, "Not worth our time or thought."

Looking at her now I couldn't help but wonder what happened to Stetson's father. Abi was an amazing mother, showing constant love to her son and family, but she was, without doubt, lonely. Wyatt was training Stetson on riding, Lachlan would take him out on the field sometimes, Leo would play with him and teach him things about the ranch . . .there were so many amazing men in Stetson's life, but no one was there for Abi.

"May I ask"—I turned towards her, not knowing where this new confidence was coming from—"your last name isn't Hartwell . . . is it? Where's Stetson's dad?" I said the last part softer than planned, hoping I didn't strike a nerve.

She shook her head, dropping her gaze to the ground. "No, it's Acosta. He . . ." Abi let out a long, sorrowful, breath. "He died." Her expression didn't show that of grief or mourning, it was just . . . blank. My heart broke thinking she had been blocking it out, and here I was throwing it out into the open.

"I'm so sorry," I whispered.

She gave a small hum and looked back to her son. "Thank you. He looks just like his dad with his dark hair, tan skin, and dark eyes. He's got his spark too. That kid was on a horse before he was walking. All thanks to Sye." A smile spread across her lips as she looked at her son. The love could be felt through the air, even though there was hurt behind it.

"Sye?"

"Sylas. That was his name." Her smile faded as she watched Stetson take the hose and spray the horse's feet, leading up to his belly.

"Sylas, Stetson. I love the 'S' theme."

Abi gave a small chuckle. "I did too. We joked that all our kids were going to have names that start with S. Sye liked Simon or Stella for baby number two, but . . ." She paused, biting her lip, and shrugging her shoulders. "He died right when Stetson turned three."

"Ho—" I stopped. I wanted to ask how he passed, but I didn't want to bring up any old wounds. She knew very little about my past or what I had dealt with. It wasn't my place to ask her to open up about her life.

"He was in an accident," she answered anyway. "He was a bull rider."

I stayed silent, not exactly knowing how to react. Rhett hadn't mentioned anyone in his family being a bull rider. I thought back to the first time we had watched the rodeo. Abi had pulled Stetson away right before the bull riders came out, claiming it was time for bed, and I had said goodnight, not thinking anything of it.

"He was getting ready to travel with Rhett and Wyatt, and they were training here. He got on that bull and Wyatt opened the chute. He lasted eight seconds and then jumped off, but the bull was *mad*. Trampled him as he was leaving the arena. He died in the hospital due to his injuries. They were just too much." Abi turned to look at me, her eyes darkening as if she was reliving the moment. "We miss him every day, but he's not gone *gone*, you know." Turning towards Stetson, I could faintly see the light returning to her. "I see him in Stetson every day. I'm glad I have a small piece of him."

She sniffed, the small smile on her lips fading as she rolled her eyes and tilted her head back, a heavy groan leaving her lips. Turning my attention from her to her son, I saw Stetson's jeans covered in bubbles as he began to work the sponge on his horse's stomach.

"It's never a dull day with him," she said smugly. "Hey, bud . . . wash Marsh, not you."

Abi left my side, sticking her hand in a bucket to pull out another brush to help Stetson bathe his horse. Crossing my arms, I watched for a moment before turning my back and leaving the stables, giving Abi the needed time with her son. Reaching for my phone, I brought it to life.

Rhett

Have you gotten on a horse yet?

I laughed, something that always happened after getting a text from Rhett.

> **Me**
>
> It hasn't even been twenty-four hours since you told me to do that. So . . . no.

> **Rhett**
>
> Get. On. A. Horse.

> **Me**
>
> I'm hanging out while Stetson gives Marshmallow a bath. How's Buckle?

> **Rhett**
>
> Buckle is one in a million. And she did a 7.8 today. Still ranking on top.

> **Me**
>
> I read it has to do with the rider and the horse. So, you BOTH pulled a 7.8. Close to that world record.

> **Rhett**
>
> Damn Straight, Baby. Call you tonight.

Baby . . .

Baby.

Baby?

That was a new nickname—one I didn't mind. David had never, *ever*, called me "baby." He stuck with "sweetheart" *after* he had done something to hurt me. But baby? He wouldn't dare call me that. I held my phone, looking back at the stables where I could hear the laughter from Abi and Stetson, when I felt the slight buzz in my hand.

I blinked.

Grace

I saw David.

My heart dropped.

"You saw David?" I asked once I got back into Rhett's house, my palm pressed against my forehead to calm the anxiety building, my phone barely touching my ear.

I hadn't heard from—or seen—David since I left him back in December. He would cross my mind, but I was able to navigate my life. It would take a long time before he was a distant memory, but I was trying. Now, just the single mention that Grace had seen him brought back a wave of hurt and anger and I felt like I was going to spiral.

"At the store," she answered. "I caught his eye and turned. The douchebag followed me out into the parking lot."

"He talked to you?"

She was silent for a beat, but then said, "He asked about you."

"You didn't . . ." I coughed, the ball forming in my throat forcing it to sound like gravel.

"No," Grace added quickly. "No, Kyla, no. I told him I knew exactly where you were, and he would never see or hear from you again."

"Grace, that's . . . that's worse." I held my breath, "That's just going to egg him on."

I could feel the panic rising in my chest. I could *feel* the anxiety begin to boil under my skin, seeping out through all of my pores. I began to pace, the quick intake of air hitting my lungs with each short breath.

Breathe. Just Breathe.

We broke up.

I handed him the ring, told him I was done and that I was taking back my life. I didn't leave in the middle of the night. I just took control of something . . . finally, and he just stood there and watched me leave, clutching onto my ring in his palm. He knew we were over, right? I didn't leave Arizona until May. I had six months of successfully avoiding him. I was in the clear.

There was no need to panic.

None whatsoever.

So why couldn't I get my heart to calm down?

"Ky," Grace said softly. "There's no way he can find you. You changed your phone number. You're off the beaten path. You. Are. Safe."

I took a deep breath, feeling my mind go down a different path than I was before. "Safe until he decides I'm worth his time again," I mumbled, flopping down on the couch. "I know I'm overthinking it. He doesn't care enough to come find me but . . . Grace . . ."

"He won't. He'll have to torture me before I tell him anything." She spoke fast, trying to make her voice as calm as possible. "You're overthinking this because that's what was trained into your brain. That's what he made you believe . . . I shouldn't have told you."

"No, it's fine. I mean, he's in the world, I can't stop that. I'm just ready to stop feeling this way." Swallowing back the tears I knew were going to come, I closed my eyes and leaned my head on the back of the couch.

I tried to focus on the past few days—meeting Rhett at the bar, making love to him, seeing the ranch and meeting Abi. Helping Stetson with his reading. Family dinners. Watching the rodeos, watching Rhett.

I was completely at ease and relaxed here.

There was no way *he* was going to take this away from me.

TWELVE

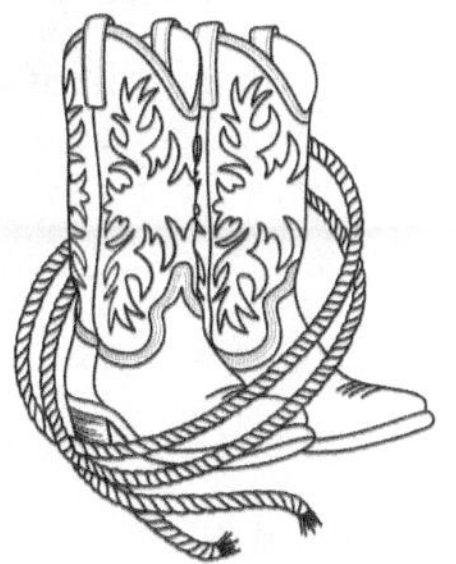

Rhett

"ONE MORE RIDE." LACHLAN'S voice rang in my ears as I walked Buckle up to the gate.

"One more," I repeated. "This was too long of a trip," I admitted, even to myself. Tonight, I'd be packing up my mare, pulling Wyatt away from the buckle bunnies and making my way back to the ranch. Darren, Jaxson, me, then home.

"It's been ten days," Lachlan grumbled.

"Ten days too long."

"You've been gone longer. Speaking of . . ."

"Ha, I knew it." Having a phone call from Lachlan was unusual when I was on the circuit. I would get a few texts here or there, but once I saw his name on my phone, I knew there was something that he needed an extra set of hands for. If I didn't answer, I would hear about it later. "What needs fixed?"

"A fence out in the field, a windstorm blew it over."

"Kyla didn't mention a windstorm." I furrowed my brow.

"Why would Kyla have mentioned it?"

"We talk . . ." I slipped my foot in the stirrup, using my free hand to hoist myself into the saddle. "A lot."

He gave a small *mmhmm*. "She was probably in the house, or at your place. I was on the land. It was a big storm, but to her it was probably just another day. She spends most of her time with Abi, actually. When she's not with Aunt Lottie or reading with Stetson, you can find her with Abi."

I swallowed, the lump falling into the pit of my stomach. Just envisioning Kyla at the ranch made my entire world freeze around me. Seeing her with Stetson, with Abi, cooking with my mother, it all seemed possible. *Keeping her.* I didn't hear the cheers from the crowd or Wyatt as he talked about the event. All I could focus on was Kyla at the ranch.

"She even got Abi to open up about Sylas," Lachlan continued, hitting me with a curve ball I hadn't seen coming. Abi *never* talked about Sylas. "In a way, it feels like she belongs here."

She belongs here.

I swear my heart skipped a beat. A small flutter filled my chest. *She belongs here . . .*

"That's a no score for Darren." I heard Wyatt's voice boom over the speaker. "A no score."

I blinked, a shaky sigh leaving my lips, forcing my attention back on to the event, on Buckle under me.

"That's um . . ." I stammered. "That's big."

"Yeah, I'm not too sure what Abi is going to do once she moves on out. But anyway, that fence, you'll be home for a while after this tour, right?"

Lachlan had no idea what he was saying. This was a normal conversation for him, but a hopeful realization for me. Could I get her to stay?

". . . sometimes they get a runner, a few broken barriers, and next thing you know your standing drops. The no score may bump Darren down a few." Wyatt's fellow announcer, Sam, added to the dramatics. "But up next, we have Jaxson Hue who is currently sitting at . . ."

I closed my eyes tight, willing my heart to beat normally. "Yeah—yes. I'll be home, but now . . ." I looked around for a rodeo hand, someone to force me back to the event.

"One last ride. See ya soon." Lachlan hung up without even saying goodbye, and my screen went black. I tossed it to the assistant.

Trotting Buckle up the gate, I saw Darren leave, his chin down, the rim of his hat clouding his eyes.

"Had a runner?" I asked as he passed, thankful for the distraction to pull me back into the here and now. I needed to stop thinking about what Lachlan had said.

"I need a drink," he murmured back, lifting his chin up.

"Meet after?"

He waved his arm in the air, not answering my question.

I coughed a laugh as I passed him, my hands feeling for the rope on the horn, instantly picking it up and shoving it between my teeth. Jaxson flew from the gate, chasing and roping that calf down for his fastest time this season, and then it was my turn. Back in the moment I took a deep breath as the chute dropped, the calf bolted free, and I took off, stopping Buckle at the right moment for me to jump off to wrangle the calf down, throwing up my hands to signal I was done.

It didn't matter how many times I did this. It was a rush. Every. Single. Time.

She belongs here.

The crowd cheered as I tipped my hat as I climbed back on Buckle and waited the six seconds, but once that calf was free, Buckle bounded back to the gates. I patted her neck and did my best to ignore the little voice in my head.

"Rhett Hartwell giving us quite the show, with a 7.8!" Sam's voice boomed. "You know your brother, Wyatt, do you think he's trying to beat his time?"

"Always, Sam. I've never seen Rhett back down a ride, he knows that his best was a 7.6 and he sure as hell knows he can beat it one day," Wyatt answered.

Damn straight I'm going to beat it.

"Back home he's beaten the NFR World Record at a 6.2, but he knows those calves and how they work. Here he only knows Buckle, but man do those two make the team. Rhett currently holds first place for tonight, let's see if he can hold it there." Wyatt's voice faded as I left the gates, with Buckle's hooves hitting the pavement.

I jumped off Buckle, digging in my pocket for a peppermint to give her as a reward for a great run, and she nudged me with her nose. I scratched her nose, proud of my girl.

"7.8, Hartwell?" I heard a voice come up from behind me. "You ain't gonna beat that 7.6 this year."

Zeke was a friend—a fellow roper—who had been with me almost my entire career. Currently he holds the number two slot for the national standings. He had a mocking tone to his voice, but behind it there was a hint of jealousy. Zeke always strived to be the best. He wouldn't take a fellow roper down by any means, but his comment still stung a tiny bit.

"And who walked away with a broken barrier," I reminded him, grabbing Buckle's reins. "Come on Zeke, you know we aren't in competition."

"But we are," he added, catching up to me and Buckle. "We may be friends, but there's nothing wrong with a little taunting."

"A little?" I side-eyed him. "'You ain't gonna beat that 7.6 this year.'" I quoted him.

"All in good fun." He slapped my back.

"Need I remind you, I'm in first, asshole."

Zeke scoffed, rolling his eyes before taking his hat off. "How's the city girl, the one who's been keeping you from drinks every night."

"Not every night, and she's just a friend."

Except Lachlan's words still ran in my head. *It feels like she belongs here.*

Inhaling and opening Buckle's stall, I shook the thoughts from my mind.

"Yeah . . ." Zeke groaned, leaning against the gate. "Just a friend."

Narrowing my eyes at him, I changed the subject as fast as I could. "How's that broken barrier going to affect your score?" I asked, unhooking Buckle's saddle.

Zeke groaned. "One broken barrier doesn't mean anything in the long run. It won't hurt my chances at getting to Vegas." He smiled, the groan completely vanishing as he gained his confidence back. "At least I got the calf." He chuckled, referencing Jaxson's run. "We meeting at the bar tonight?"

"I'll be there."

"On the phone?"

"Nope. Having a drink with the boys. Then home for the Fourth. You're coming to that right? You signed up?"

"I did, and hell yeah I'll be there." He pushed himself off the gate. "I never miss it. Will the city girl be there? Will I get to meet her?" he prodded.

I held back the glare. As much as I wanted her to be there . . . "I doubt it."

Giving me hum he smacked the metal gate. "Yeah, well . . . see ya tonight."

I gave him a quick wave and turned my focus back to my horse. She bobbed her head as the reins came free, leaning down to the hay that sat on the floor. Giving her another scratch I reached for my phone, bringing it to life to see a text from Kyla, and my lips curved up.

Kyla

Abi . . . has asked me . . .

What? I furrowed my brow and watched as the three dots danced.

Kyla

TO HELP BIRTH A COW!

I let out a laugh and Buckle pulled her head back up to me, turning and nudging me with her nose.

Pulling off my glove with my teeth I responded back as fast as I could.

Me

Go into my closet and grab a pair of jeans and a t-shirt. You don't want to wear your clothes doing that. It's a once in a lifetime experience, Baby. Just add it to that list.

Kyla

Yeah, COWBOY. MY LIST? Never even thought about being a part of something like this.

Me

Go experience it. Then you can tell me all about it when I see you.

Kyla

Oh, I bet it will be quite the story of me staying out of the way.

Oh yeah, I thought to myself as I imagined Kyla in the birthing pen, *she belongs here.*

THIRTEEN

Kyla

"I CANNOT BELIEVE . . ." I stammered as I watched the new baby calf stumble around. "I did that."

Abi hummed a laugh that seemed to be stuck in her throat. "You didn't even get that messy." She elbowed me.

I turned to glare at her, then down at Rhett's t-shirt covered in goo that had come from the mama cow. It didn't take long like I thought it would, but helping bring the calf into the world was exhilarating. Abi pushed the mama's stomach, while I helped pull the calf from her. With each push the calf gave way and eventually fell to the ground. I shouted, thinking the poor thing was dead, but when Abi grabbed my arm and pulled me to the side I just watched. In absolute amazement.

Within the hour the little brown and white calf was on her feet, stumbling around looking for her mother, and soon she began to nurse.

I took a deep breath, the smell of cows, hay, and manure hitting me. What shocked me the most was that I loved it. Closing my eyes I took it all in, still not believing the last few weeks I had experienced. The ranch was an entirely different world than I was used to. It brought a calmness even I couldn't describe.

Maybe this could be a summer destination for me each year. I could rent Rhett's place while he's away on the circuit and just enjoy living simply. Maybe bring Grace and just . . . live. I imagined myself on the porch, with Grace next to me, as we both read or drank wine and chatted about anything and everything.

This could be the escape we both needed.

"Your mind is racing." Abi's voice echoed past my thoughts, pulling me back to reality. "I can practically hear it."

"I like it here," I answered simply.

"Well . . ." She trailed off, her gaze going back to the baby calf. "We like you here too."

"My goodness you are thirsty," I said to the small cow as she grabbed a hold of the nipple on the large bottle I held. "No wonder why your mama won't let you nurse, you have a death grip on this thing!"

"Does she have a name yet?" The deep voice that came from behind me shocked me slightly. I wasn't used to hearing Lachlan.

He was normally out on the land, and very stoic. I turned to watch him carry a hay-bale as he walked past me to set it down on top of the rest of the hay.

"Abi told me I couldn't name her. That she would get a tag and number and that would be that." I noted, turning back to the calf who still downed the milk in the bottle as if it were her last meal.

Lachlan let out a huff. "She's getting attached to you."

"She's a cow." I rolled my eyes, grinning at him as he studied me.

I had never truly looked at Lachlan before. He had broad shoulders that led to his chiseled frame, his skin was tanned from the sun, his face was hidden by a full, dark beard and his black cowboy hat shadowed his eyes. He took the hat off, almost as if he could hear my thoughts, and rubbed his forehead with his forearm. I noticed the ink of tattoos on his arms but didn't study him any further. I met his gaze, his eyes rich and dark as he lifted his chin towards the calf.

"And just like any other animal, cows can get attached to certain people. You seem to have a friend in that calf. So . . ." Lachlan sat his hat back on his head and dusted his hands on his jeans. "Name her."

Looking at the little cow in front of me, I loved the thought that she was getting attached to me. Her brown eyes widened with each sip she pulled, and her ears perched back. She was only a few days old, but it felt like she had been alive for a lot longer. I was amazed with how quickly she seemed to grow. Then again, I knew nothing about cows. All I knew was she was cute, and she liked to follow me around.

Lachlan must have seen it. I would walk the fence with Abi, and she would trot over and follow us, mooing at me to give her some attention. I would scratch behind her ears and laugh as she groaned, but I figured that was just a cow thing to do. She was basically a big puppy.

"What do you even name a cow?" I asked, knitting my brow.

"Anything but Bessie," Lachlan answered, letting out a deep breath as he passed me, bending over to get another hay bale.

"Awe, but Bessie is such a good cow name," I cooed, looking at the brown eyes that were hyper focused on me as she guzzled down the bottle.

"Just remember she will most likely—"

"I don't want to know." I cut him off, knowing they had sold cows off to end up in the grocery store. I didn't want to think about this adorable little calf being sold to become a hamburger.

Lachlan threw the hay on top of the pile, a grunt leaving his lungs. "I was going to say she would most likely become a milking cow, so you're safe to name her."

I twisted my lips and focused back on the calf. "Oh, that changes things."

"Shout out some ideas." He waved his hand in the air, turning his back to me, his voice fading as he went to grab another hay bale.

"Um . . . Juniper?"

"Juniper?" he parroted, raising an eyebrow at me, stopping the moment his back was straight.

"Okay, not Juniper. Um . . ." I started thinking about books I had read with cows in them; of TV commercials with the laughing cow or some milk farm. All the cows that popped into my head were nameless. "Clarabelle?"

Lachlan tossed another hay bale. "Isn't that a cartoon character?"

"I think it's Goofy's wife."

"Goofy's married?" Lachlan dropped his arms to his side. "To a cow?"

"I don't know." I shrugged, pulling the bottle from her mouth, only to have her follow it. "Okay, not Clarabelle."

Lachlan shook his head as he passed me. "I'll let you think of names . . ."

"Josie?" I shouted behind my back to Lachlan. I heard him give a slight grunt as he lifted yet another bale. "I like Josie." I smiled down at the calf who had claimed the bottle again, her eyes now closed as she drank every last drop. "What do you think?"

Lachlan stopped next to me and the calf, one eyebrow arched. "Josie will work."

"Awe yeah." I set the bottle down on the fence post and scratched behind Josie's ears. "You look like a Josie. My little Josie."

"I'll tell the guys," Lachlan mumbled.

I turned back to Josie and leaned into her, letting her bump my shoulder with hers. I started reaching up to pet her again when I could make out the faint rush of dirt and footsteps flying into the barn. I turned to see Stetson trampling through, dirt flying behind him.

"Miss Kyla! Miss Kyla!" Stetson's voice echoed as he got closer to us, not slowing down for anything.

"Stetson!" Lachlan shouted, almost losing his footing as his nephew came up to our side. "Slow it down or pick up a bale."

Stetson stopped in his tracks, freezing as he looked up at his cousin. "Sorry, Uncle Lach, but I had to come see Miss Kyla." My heart rushed, loving how even though Lachlan wasn't Stetson's real Uncle, he still called him by that title.

I gave Josie one last pat and turned to Stetson. He was buzzing with excitement as he caught his breath. Lachlan's gaze met mine before I focused on the little cowboy in front of me.

"You have a cow, my little cousin, *and* my cousin falling for you," he grumbled.

"No one has fallen for me," I retorted, folding my arms over my chest.

"I have," Stetson answered, turning back to me with his eyes wide. "Mama said you were leaving for your new home soon and Miss Kyla, I don't want you to leave."

My lips parted and a small gasp left my lips. Stetson reminded me of some of the kids I taught, and how at the end of the year they didn't want to leave my classroom. My heartstrings tugged. "Oh Stetson . . ." I leaned down to be eye-level with him.

"So," he shouted, "I was with Nana Lottie, and I found this." He held out a small ring in his palm—a simple gold band with a single diamond. Nothing like what David had given me. The ring I wore with him was heavy and large—only there to show status. This ring was perfect in every way that mine wasn't. Simple. Sweet. Delicate. "Nana gave it to me and told me that one day I needed to give it to the girl I loved and wanted to keep around. Miss Kyla, I want to keep you around so . . ." He held his palm out to me. "Here."

"Pretty sure a seven-year-old just proposed to you." Lachlan nodded, reminding me that he still stood next to us.

I glanced up at Lachlan, but then focused back on Stetson, reaching up to place my hand on his shoulder. "Stetson," I began, but the kid shoved it closer to my body.

"Here, Miss Kyla."

I gave him a tight smile and took the ring from his palm, slipping it on my left ring finger. I grabbed Stetson by his shoulders and gave his forehead a simple kiss. "Okay, I'll stay a little longer."

Stetson gave me the biggest grin before wrapping his arms around my neck, his hat hitting my forehead, forcing it to the floor. He pulled away, the same smile on his face as he scooped up his hat and ran out of the barn. I looked back up at Lachlan, who still stood as stoic as before, his hands on his hips as he looked at the ring on my finger.

"I guess I'm getting married."

"You might want to go make sure it's okay with his mother." Lachlan situated his hat before returning to his task. "Oh, and I'll be tagging Josie soon, if you want to help."

"You will not be tagging my cow." I pointed at him, my eyes narrowing at him. "But . . . I should go find Abi and tell her the news. Keep an eye on Josie for me?"

He turned to Josie and gave me a curt nod. "She'll be thrilled you're joining the family," he retorted sarcastically.

I gave him a wave, turning to see Josie had already occupied herself with something else, and I left the barn. The sun hit my skin, making me wish I had the hat that Abi had lent me on my first day, and I shielded my eyes with my hand as I began the short walk over to the main house. Abi was outside, her horse next to her being guided slowly, her blonde hair braided loosely under her cowboy hat.

"I'll have you know," I shouted, approaching her. She spun, giving me a welcoming smile. "You're looking at your new daughter-in-law." I stopped and gave her a curtsy.

"I'm sorry, what?"

I held up my hand to show off my new ring. "Stetson proposed while I was feeding Josie."

"Josie?"

"My cow," I answered, cocking a shoulder to my ear.

"You have a cow and you're marrying my seven-year-old?"

"He said . . ."

I was cut off by a honk, and then a few horses neighing. A black SUV came up the drive to the main house, the dust and dirt flying around it, clinging to the shiny paint. The SUV turned and came to a stop, and my stomach dropped.

I knew that car. I had spent many . . . many times in that passenger seat. *His* pristine Lincoln that he kept in perfect condition. *He* loved that car more than he loved me. I was certain of it.

How the hell did he find me?

I swallowed as I watched him, sitting in the front seat with that stupid smirk on his face. He waved before turning and getting out of the car.

"Abi . . ." I whispered. "That's David."

"David?" Her head jerked towards me. "David David? *The* David?"

"What the hell is he doing here?" I crossed my arms over my chest, determined to stand my ground. There was no way I would give into him, no way I wasn't going to stand up for myself. How the *hell* did he know I was here!?

He climbed out of the car, and I swear, he made direct eye contact with me.

"Kyla." He stopped as he raised a hand to his brow. "Is that you?" I heard him shout as he walked around the car, wearing his perfectly tailored suit. He buttoned his suit jacket as he moved a portfolio under his arms.

That was it. That's why he was here. I wasn't sure if he was here solely for a job, and I just happened to be here—or if he knew I was here and this was his ploy. My bet was on the latter. He had somehow hunted me down, found out I was on a decent chunk of land, and then decided to use his business to try to weasel his way back into my life.

Too bad that wasn't happening.

"He's going to ask you about selling the ranch," I mumbled to Abi before he got into hearing range. "I guarantee you that's his idea."

"What?" Abi whispered back, but the time I had left to answer was quickly taken away when David got closer and closer.

His black suit hugged him in all the right places, places that used to send me into a frenzy. His blond hair was gelled back, with a woosh that flowed from the front to the back. But the sides of his hair were short, nothing you could run your hands through. He *hated* having his hair touched. And his eyes were just as dull as I remembered. Green with absolutely no spark to them.

I hadn't seen this man in six—almost seven months—and the disdain I felt for him was even stronger.

"It is! Kyla!" He quickened his pace.

I cleared my throat and shifted on my feet. "David," I answered.

"I don't believe it." That stupid, corny smile that I thought I loved flashing as he reached out to me, not even stopping when I took a step closer to Abi. Was he expecting a hug?

"You knew I was here," I countered, keeping all emotion from my voice.

"I had no idea. Kyla . . . I . . ." He stammered, most likely trying to remember his line. "I'm here to talk to the owners of Hartwell Hills." His business smile formed once again. "That must be you." He turned to Abi. "Hi, I'm David McIntyre." He stuck out his hand for Abi to shake. She looked at his hand and then at his eyes. Her face was comical. Her lips were twisted up and her eyebrows were furrowed in a pure look of disgust. I was tempted to burst out laughing.

"Hi," she responded, her voice just as monotone as mine, not taking his hand to shake.

David stood in a stupor for a moment before lowering his hand and clearing his throat. "Are you the owner of Hartwell Hills Ranch?"

"Maybe, who wants to know?" Abi folded her arms and pivoted her stance. While most people stood straight next to him, trying to show more power, Abi was calm and collected. A trait I wish I had had—one I would try my hardest to convey.

"David McIntyre, I'm here on behalf of my company—"

"The ranch isn't for sale, David," I interrupted him, forcing him to stop his speech and look at me.

"Now Kyla," he cooed. "I believe I'm here to talk to Miss Hartwell." I looked to Abi who muttered *not my name* under her breath. "And unless you know more about the ranch handlings than she does, I suggest you stay out of this, okay, sweetheart?" My bones rattled at the nickname. His smile made the blow he gave me seem less intoxicating. Thankfully I no longer bought his shit, and by the looks of it, neither did Abi.

I shook my head and looked down at my feet. My arms were still crossed over my chest as I took one more step towards Abi.

David let out a small chuckle, and when I lifted my head, his gaze was heavy on me. "But . . ." he took a deep breath. "I can see you may actually know more than I thought."

What?

"We've only been separated for six months . . . and you're engaged?"

His voice was different. It wasn't the professional one he had approached us with. Now, it was thicker—there was anger lingering there. He stared at me, his eyes burning into mine as his gaze followed my arms to my hand.

Shit . . . the ring.

Looking down at my left hand I lifted my fingers from my elbow and curled them into a fist.

"I—" I began, unsure as to what to say.

"Married actually," Abi answered for me. Both mine and David's head spun in her direction. "To my brother, so if you have anything you need to say or discuss in front of me, it can be discussed in front of Kyla."

"Married?" he stammered, his voice breaking.

Taking a deep breath, I figured, why not? If it got him away, I would say I was married. And since both of Abi's brothers were away, and there was no way I would fit in with Lachlan, David would be none the wiser. He would leave once he found out that they had no interest in his stupid game. I would make sure he knew I was never, *ever* going back to him, and that would be that. I would be free, and he would be gone.

"Yes, we've been married almost two months now." I smiled, hoping I sounded like someone who was desperately in love.

"Two months? We were engaged for two years."

"Well." I shrugged. "When you know, you know. And with *him* …" I instantly thought of Rhett. I caught my breath and swallowed. "I knew."

"Well then." David rolled his shoulders, looking from Abi to me. "Let me meet him. I'm sure he'd love to discuss the ranches' potential and future."

"He's not here," I answered honestly. "He's away on the circuit."

"Circuit?"

"Rodeo," Abi answers as if it was obvious. David had never been near a horse in his entire life. There was no way he knew what the rodeo circuit was. But then again, neither did I until a friendship had formed between Rhett and me.

"You married a cowboy?"

"Damn straight she did. Oh look." A laugh left Abi's throat. "Speak of the devil." Abi jerked her chin forward. "There he is now."

My stomach churned as I lifted my head to see behind the black SUV. Sure enough, there was Rhett's white Ford F-250 hauling a horse trailer up the drive, creating a hell of a lot more dust than David's Lincoln did. He wasn't supposed to be back until tonight—at least that's what he texted me this morning—but he was here now. And David was here. And the nerves started to build faster than I could stop them. I bit my bottom lip and focused on the truck.

Rhett was driving, his hat on the dashboard as he turned to avoid David's SUV before he brought the truck to a stop, the ground settling under the weight of the car. Wyatt jumped out of the car first, giving Abi and I a quick glance before making his way to the horse trailer. Rhett's smile beamed as he rounded the front of the car, his hat now perched on his head. He was looking directly at me, and relief flooded through me.

My breath stammered, my heart shuddered, and I was so glad he was here.

I smiled without thinking, and moved the moment I saw him take a single step. I took off in a run, trying to tell myself this pull was just to fill him in on my little ruse, not that I wanted to be near him. I needed to tell him he was my husband, at least while David was here, but I needed to show David he was. Or else he would never believe me.

"Hey, baby." *Oh, why had he settled on baby?* "I was hoping you would be willing to—"

My mind entirely focused on him, I grabbed his neck and pulled him down to me, my lips crashing into his. I lingered there for a moment, savoring the taste and smell of him. The salt on his tongue and the woody flavor that enveloped him. He smelled the exact same, and I breathed him in. His hand found my waist and he gave a slight hum. I pulled away to see him staring at me, his lips parted slightly, his eyes wide and glazed over.

"I need you to pretend to be my husband for the next fifteen minutes."

FOURTEEN

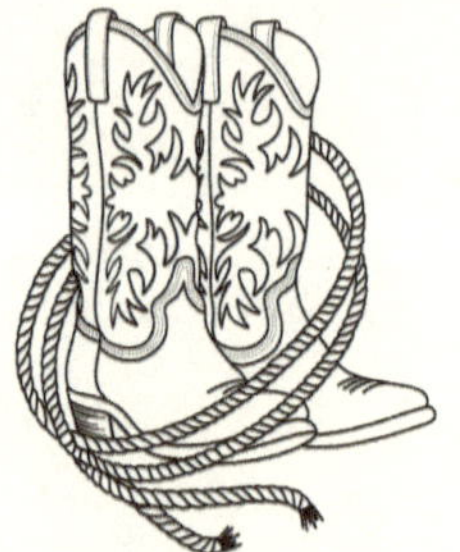

Rhett

OUT OF ALL THE things I expected upon returning home, having Kyla approach me as she did wasn't one of them.

But then her mouth was on mine, and her tongue was separating my lips. She was kissing me. This wasn't a dream. And she tasted exactly like I remembered: citrus and vanilla rolled into one. Her fingers threaded into the hair at the nape of my neck as she deepened the kiss. Or did I deepen it? At this point I couldn't tell. We were both so immersed in it. Resting my hand on her waist I pulled her close to me. This moment could last forever, but with a soft moan and exhale, she finally pulled back.

I blinked, forcing myself to come back to reality.

I wasn't quite sure I heard her right. Did she say *husband?*

Swallowing, I parted my lips. "I'm sorry . . . what?"

"Put your arms around me." Her voice was still a whisper, I felt her hands slip to my shoulders.

I didn't even hesitate as I wrapped my arms around her waist, her body pressed against mine. She could ask me to do anything at this rate and I would give it to her. She felt so damn good. If she was expecting me to let her leave for Washington now, she had something else coming.

"You need to smile, and act like you haven't seen me in days." Her eyes met mine, and I breathed in her vanilla scent.

"I *haven't* seen you in days." I raised the corners of my lips, leaning down to kiss her again.

Kyla stopped me, tilting her head away. "That man next to your sister . . ."

I glanced up and looked at the blond standing near Abi—hands on his hips, his stance wide. Smaller, narrow shoulders began the frame for his entire body, and he was wearing a suit, with a skinny tie visible with his jacket open. His shoes were so shiny I could see them from here, although I knew they would get covered in dirt. He stepped to the side, his head moving from side to side as he never once stopped looking at Kyla and I.

This man would die on a horse.

Raising a brow I looked back at Kyla, kissing her forehead gently. She didn't need to say anything else; I knew exactly who that man was.

"What the hell is he doing here?" I murmured back, lowering my chin so the rim of my hat shadowed us.

Kyla took a deep breath, her hands running down my arms. "He says it's to talk about the future of the ranch, but I know he has other motives."

"Well then." Using my arm to pull her even closer, a small gasp leaving her lips, I kissed her again, the same shock hitting from the first time I kissed her on the dance floor. This woman was going to be the death of me. "Let's go talk to him, *Mrs. Hartwell.*"

Feathering my fingers across her waist, I laced my fingers with hers. She spun, using her opposite hand to hold on to my bicep as she led me toward the house. Abi stood with one hand on her waist, one hand blocking the sun from her eyes, her smile growing wider as Kyla and I approached.

"Hi, there," I started, trying to give my best *I don't know who the hell you are* acting job, "My wife tells me you need to talk to me?" I smiled, holding out my hand to shake his and surprisingly David grasped it and shook. It was a softer handshake than I was used to, so I squeezed a little harder, my way of taking charge of the situation. "Rhett Hartwell, how can I help you?"

He let out a deep breath and then gave the widest, fakest smirk I had ever seen in my entire life. "David McIntyre, nice to meet you Mr. Hartwell. I'm representing McIntyre Holdings, we're a real estate firm based out of Phoenix. I discovered your property a few weeks ago and I haven't been able to get it out of my mind since."

"It's gorgeous, isn't it." I looked around at the tree line and turned to the house.

"Cowboy"—Kyla got my attention with my nickname—"David's the developer for McIntyre Holdings, he's the one who buys and builds the land up."

Furrowing my brow, I looked down at Kyla. *Gotta keep acting.* "You know him?"

Kyla scrunched her nose at me. "He was . . ."

"I'm her fiancé," David answered for her, his voice booming.

"Well, that's awkward because *I'm* her husband." I forced myself to keep the quiet laughter in. I loved hearing the word *husband* possibly a little too much.

David stared at me, his eyes like daggers as they bore into mine. He seemed to read exactly what was going on. I shoved my left hand in my pocket, hiding the fact that I wasn't wearing a ring. I moved my thumb over Kyla's hand, feeling the small band on her finger. Turning to her I raised an eyebrow. She squeezed my bicep.

"That's interesting because she's been engaged to me for two years, and then she disappeared." David's attention turned back to Kyla.

"No, David, I left you. I handed you the ring and told you we were over," Kyla spat, taking a step closer to him.

"Are you here to discuss your past with my wife, or my ranch?" I changed the subject. "Because I'll be honest, neither sound very interesting to me."

That one statement was all it took to get David to look at me. He inhaled sharply, and smiled—back to business. "I'm here to talk about the ranch, I see how much potential it has."

"Bullshit," Kyla muttered. She let go of my hand quickly, spinning to look at me. "I'll be inside. You talk about . . . whatever it is he really came here to talk about." She touched my chest, leaned up and kissed my cheek. "I can't wait to hear about the rodeos."

I watched as Kyla and Abi made their way into the main house, then gave David one last glance over. Turning, I left him standing there, but when I heard his footsteps start up, I wasn't shocked.

"Mr. Hartwell, I'm just as surprised to see Kyla as she is to see me," he shouted as soon as he was closer to my side.

"I'll repeat what *my wife* said." Damn I liked the sound of that, almost as much as when I said "husband." "Bullshit. You think I don't know who you are."

I opened the trailer more forcefully than expected.

"Well sir, with all due respect, you do now." David's voice was sinister, one I would never care to hear again. "I came here . . ."

"I know, I know. You 'found my ranch on a site and have to buy it because it has potential.' Again. Bull. Shit. You wouldn't have known about Hartwell Hills if you didn't know Kyla was here. I highly suggest you get off my land and leave her alone." I took a step towards him. I towered over him, my frame bulkier and heavier than his. I was six-three, and I could tell just by standing near him, David was barely six feet. Three inches was enough to force his eyes to move up.

I expected him to leave. I expected him to turn, get in his Lincoln, and drive off. My fifteen minutes of being Kyla's husband was over and right now, all I wanted to do was go into the house and make sure she was alright. But instead, his eyes narrowed, and his lips formed a thin smile. No—I wouldn't call that smile. A sneer. One fit for a villain.

"No, I won't be leaving. When I do leave, it will be with my fiancé on my arm." The villain transformed into a business man as he rolled his shoulders and straightened his jacket. "I brought this for you." He held out a leather portfolio. "I'm interested in buying your land. Not all, just some—for housing, or a business center. Something more fit for the community."

I looked at the portfolio, not taking it and then back at him. "It's not for sale."

"Everything is for sale."

"Not this."

"I'll say it again *Rhett,* everything is for sale. Take this, look it over, and I'll be back. I'm staying in town until I land this deal, so I have a feeling you'll be seeing a lot more of me. Tell Kyla I say goodbye, and that I'll see her soon." David narrowed his eyes, his true colors coming to life as his eyes screamed. "I do remember the way her body feels, I can guarantee you she remembers mine as well."

I grabbed the portfolio from his hand and took a single step towards him. "After feeling mine, I can guarantee you, she doesn't."

After I settled Buckle in the pasture, I made my way into the main house. Kyla sat at the kitchen island, her hands laced in front of her as Abi cleaned up from lunch. Kyla was silent, her lips pursed together as she concentrated on anything but me. She was nervous, possibly still worried that David was still outside. I looked at them, my eyes moving from Abi to Kyla, until I finally focused on Kyla.

"He wants to buy the ranch," I mumbled, finally breaking the silence.

"Asshole . . ." Abi breathed.

Placing my palms on the counter I leaned into the kitchen is-land.

"No, he doesn't." Kyla shook her head. "He somehow figured out where I was and that was his way in. He has no interest in buying the ranch. He sells commercial real estate for god's sake, not ranches."

"He said he wouldn't leave without you on his arm," I said softly. Just the idea of her with *him* sent my stomach in knots. She deserved so much more than him. She deserved somebody . . . somebody like . . .

"I'm not going anywhere with him," she muttered under her breath.

"Come on." I pushed myself off the island. "We need to talk."

I held my hand out to her and let out a breath of air when she took it. Leading her off the porch we walked in silence to my house, but her hand was in mine the entire time. I used my thumb to twist the ring on her finger. I knew that ring. The simple diamond, the gold band—it was my grandmother's. How it happened to fall on Kyla's finger, I could only imagine. Lachlan had told me she fit in, and the phone calls we shared told me she was comfortable. I could just see Kyla and my mother sifting through her jewelry, Kyla finding the band and slipping it on her finger not even thinking about where it came from or what meaning it held to my family. That was something I could tell her later—after we figured out this David situation.

I opened the door to my cabin and stepped inside, feeling the air hit me. Home. I loved being on the road, but nothing compared to this place. And with Kyla here, it had a different feel to it. Her purse sat on the dining room table and her phone was face down on the counter. There was a vase of daisies sitting on the kitchen island and one single plate and mug sat next to the sink. I took a quick glance into the bathroom and saw her lavender towel on the hook, as well as a blow dryer and straightener on the counter. Not only was she comfortable on the ranch in general, but she was comfortable here.

"I'll pack up and get out of your hair. Maybe when I leave, he'll leave, and you won't have to worry about your ranch," Kyla began, holding her body as she walked into the living room.

"Kyla."

"I can't believe he found out where I was. Grace was telling me she saw him, but that she didn't tell him anything, which tells me he was looking . . ."

"Kyla," I repeated, a little louder.

"I'll call him, talk to him, and tell him to fuck off. Convince him that, yet again, we are done."

"Kyla!" I basically shouted.

She stopped, her lips still parted, but her eyes met mine and I could see exactly how stiff she was. After what felt like forever, her shoulders slumped as she let out a long breath.

"There's more to the story here isn't there?" I asked. "You told me he never hit you, but . . ." I trailed off, making my way towards her. I was tempted to reach out and hold her, just like I had when David was standing in front of us. It felt natural to have her in my arms. "Why did you leave? Why did you feel like you needed to start over?"

Kyla's brow pinched as her jaw tensed, and I swear she stopped breathing. She was silent for a few moments before she exhaled, the color returning to her face. "I'm the black sheep of my family."

"I doubt that," I said softly.

"No, I am. I didn't go on to be a trophy wife like my mother, I actually wanted to do something with my life. So, I became a teacher and refused to let my parents pay for my schooling. I racked up debt and rented an apartment. Can you believe it, Rhett?" She plopped on the couch, then put on an affected, haughty tone I imagined was a mockery of her mother's. "I *rented* an apartment." She grasps at fake pearls at the shock of such a thing. "My mother wasn't proud or happy of the life I was building, but then she met David. She introduced us and at first it was perfect. He was a gentleman and showered me with gifts. He asked me to move in with him after three months and then proposed after six. My mother was ecstatic."

"Well of course she was," I said with disdain. "So, what happened?"

"I didn't really notice it, but I began to feel anxious. Like everything was my fault. I felt overworked and overwhelmed. I tried to talk to David about how I felt, but he would say, 'You need to take time for yourself. Relax . . . enjoy the weekend.' Then the weekend would come, and I would do exactly what he said, but then he'd say, 'You didn't do anything productive this weekend.'" She looked small sitting there, telling me about this miserable time in her life. I just wanted to reach for her, but I wasn't sure that was what she wanted. Her eyes caught mine as she continued. "It would turn into a fight, but it would always stop. He would yell, make me feel small. Then once he saw how it got to me, he'd stop and pull me into his arms.

He'd tell me he was sorry, that he loved me and that he didn't mean it. Then it would be good again—sometimes too good to be true. Flowers, jewelry, chocolates . . . he fawned over me.

"I'd get so caught up in him during those times, he was all I'd see. Grace and I began to talk less and less, and I stopped participating in school events and speaking to co-workers. The only thing that mattered was David. I didn't realize it at first but depression took over, and then the anxiety. So much anxiety."

"Kyla," I breathed, my heart began to ache for her. She must have felt so hopeless. I reached out to her, my fingers barely brushing the hair from her shoulders. She shivered and heaved a long sigh.

"I finally began to see it when loneliness sank in, and I took it upon myself to find a therapist. She helped me unpack every-thing—and I mean . . . *everything*. Things I didn't even know were happening. Like, the way he could make me feel stupid with just a word. He'd manipulate me into believing things had happened differently than I remembered, twisting his or my words to fit his narrative. I was always the problem, or Grace was. Anyone but him. And I believed it . . . I'd agree with him." Her eyes shuddered closed, I could tell this was hard for her to talk about, but I soaked in every bit of the vulnerability she shared with me. "When I finally figured out that it wasn't about me, I wasn't the problem, that I wanted and deserved more, that's when I told him I was leaving."

"Thank god," I breathed, probably harsher than I intended. My internal thought was *good girl,* but given the moment, I didn't think that was the most appropriate thing to say.

"Yeah, well, we had been engaged for two years by then. The wedding was almost planned, and my mother had just lost my father.

David told me I was speaking out of grief—out of fear—and that I wasn't making any sense. But when I defended myself, I told him that I was making complete sense. I wasn't happy, and the only thing I was afraid of was losing was myself because . . ." She paused and took a deep breath. Swallowing, she met my gaze. "Because of him."

I stayed silent, listening to her as she finished.

How long had she been holding all of this in?

"He raised a hand to me that night. He was holding onto my arm so hard he caused a bruise." She rubbed her bicep, most likely the same place where the bruise once sat. I clenched my jaw at the thought of him touching her that way. Taking a deep breath, she continued. "He didn't hit me. He said, 'No, I won't hit you. I could, but I won't. I'm too *nice.*'" She sneered. There was a shake to her tone at just the memory of his words. "I gave him my ring, told him we were over, and then packed up my belongings. I left that night, and he just . . . watched.

"I went and stayed with Grace until I could figure out what to do. I would lay low at first, but after a month or so I started thinking I was fine. I would go to the grocery store on the other side of the city, but I swear I would see similar faces and I got it in my head that he was having me followed. Grace assured me it was all in my head, but I just couldn't shake it. So, after that, I came up with my plan to move to Washington, and it was all going smoothly, right up until you asked me what I was drinking. I never knew it would lead me here, and I never thought I would like it. And now I've pulled you and your family into this."

She didn't pull us into anything. If anything, I welcomed the pull. I had been trying to ignore it, trying to force myself to say she was just a friend, but to me she was more.

Not knowing what to say, I started with the one thing that festered in my mind. "Where did you get the ring?"

She let out a laugh, one I had grown to crave as she slid the ring off her finger. "Your nephew. He proposed to me this afternoon. Right before you got here." She handed the ring back to me.

Staying silent once again, I took the ring and watched as she stood and rubbed her hands on her hips.

"Stetson," I let out a breathy laugh. Of course it was Stetson.

"I'll pack."

"Kyla." I stopped her, holding the ring between my fingertips. "I think you should stay."

She inhaled heavily, lifting her chin. "If I stay, David will stay. He'll push buying the ranch and try to get me back. It would be a complete mess."

"Not if we stay married."

I don't know why it slipped from my mouth, why I even *thought* it was a good idea. I just held the ring in my fingers, watching the small diamond sparkle even with its age and it seemed like a good idea. It would help her finally be rid of David. It would allow me to keep her for just a little longer and maybe show her she deserved more.

Maybe she deserved somebody like me.

FIFTEEN

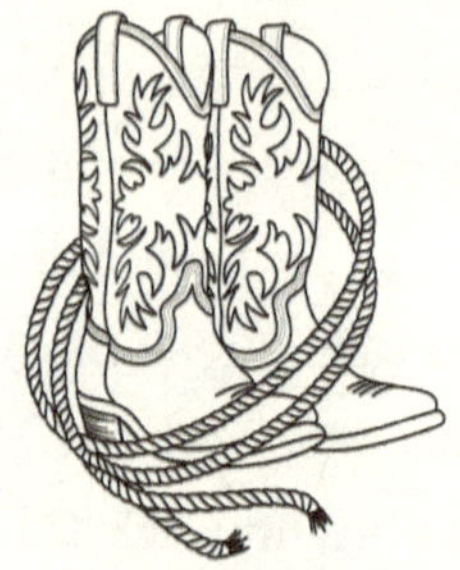

Kyla

"I'M SORRY? WHAT?" I asked, completely dumbfounded by what Rhett had said. "That was just a cop-out to get him to leave. He saw the ring and . . ." I froze, blinking rapidly as I replayed the last hour in my mind. "Abi was the one who said I married her brother and then, almost as if you planned it, you pulled up."

"And you kissed me." He gave me a smirk—a sweet and sexy smile. He raised an eyebrow as he held my stare.

"It . . . seemed like a good idea at the time," I stammered.

"Think of it this way. If we stay 'married,' David won't stay around for long. Hell, he may even leave within the next few days knowing he's not going to get anywhere with the ranch. You and I both know he's not here for the ranch. But if you've moved on, if you're happy, he'll have to accept it."

"You don't know David."

"No, but I know men like him. You deserve better."

I tilted my head. "And what do I deserve? A fake marriage?" I pursed my lips and crossed my arms. The logical side of me was screaming that this was insane.

Rhett winced slightly, shrugged his shoulders. "You deserve someone who loves you. Who lets you shine and become who you are meant to be. Not someone who holds you back, and for now, that can be me."

"Rhett. This isn't logical."

"It doesn't have to be."

I shook my head. "So what? We say we're married and act like a couple every time he shows up. He'll ask for proof you know. He'll call my mother. And then next thing you know we have to prove it to her too, and she's just as bad."

Rhett blinked a few times, his mind working, making me wish I could read his thoughts. I watched as his eyes narrowed, the muscles in his jaw tensing, and then his eyes met mine. He nodded and looked at the ring in his hands.

"Well then—" he began, his gaze thickening. His blue eyes made me melt. "We'll have to show proof."

I swallowed, biting the insides of my cheek to keep my jaw from dropping. He just looked at me, his eyes tense on me. He didn't blink. He didn't move. I didn't even think he breathed.

"Wait. What?"

"Marry me, Kyla," he added simply. "Really, truly, marry me. We won't have to fake anything. It would be real, and David can *see* it's real, especially if you kiss me like you did today, every day." His voice was low and husky—serious. He walked towards me, his scent of wood and leather getting closer with each step.

David didn't smell like that. David smelled like cologne, the deep cologne that stung once it hit your nose. I used to love it, but now it made me want to vomit. The way Rhett smelled, the way he held his body—cocky and confident—if I was being honest, was sexy as hell—the complete opposite from what I was used to. For a moment, he hovered over me, so close we were almost touching. Then he sank to one knee, holding up the dainty ring in between his thumb and forefinger, his gaze under his cowboy hat never once leaving mine.

"Marry me," he repeated.

"Rhett . . ."

"Even if it's temporary."

"It's not really real . . ."

"It will be real."

"Temporarily?"

"Temporarily real."

I narrowed my eyebrows at him, looking at the ring and then his eyes. There was no doubt or fear in his gaze. He was genuine and . . . *real*.

"Kyla," he said softly, as he rose to his feet, his hand reaching for mine. His thumb and forefinger lightly brushing over my chin as our eyes met. "Marry me?"

With a small flutter rising in my stomach, I gave in. "Okay," I whispered, praying that it wasn't as dumb as I thought it was—Marrying Rhett, and turning the ten days into who knew how long. How temporary would this be?

He smiled and moved his hand to cup my face, his thumb trailing the line of my jaw. He leaned down and lightly kissed my forehead, the touch of his lips bringing unknown comfort to the known anxiety that crept through my skin.

"I promise to keep you safe," he whispered, and I felt the shivers trail up my spine.

I was getting married.

I didn't want to believe it, but I was really getting married. One simple lie for fifteen minutes had turned into me standing next to Rhett in the courthouse. He held my hand as the officiant went through the standard marriage ceremony, and a random man I didn't know acted as our witness. My heart fluttered each time he mentioned Rhett being my husband, and me being his wife—but here we were.

I said "I do" softly—half of me dying to shout the words, the other half dying to run and hide again. Rhett said them with confidence as he squeezed my hand a little tighter. When the officiant said with joy, "I now pronounce you husband, and wife," Rhett wasted no time. He cupped my face and kissed me, tingles following the flow of his lips against mine, before he pulled away, leaving me wanting more.

I felt him smile against me, and heard a whisper of a promise. The exact same thing he told me last night. *I'll keep you safe.*

Inhaling in his woodsy smell, I opened my eyes to look at him. My husband.

"Congratulations," the officiant said, clapping his hands together. "Now, we just need to finalize the license . . ."

"How long did you say we've been married for?" Rhett asked as his fingers trailed down my bare arm to my hand and on instinct, we laced out fingers together.

I didn't dress up for this. I just wore a pair of jeans and a white t-shirt. I left my hair down and slipped on a pair of flip flops. Rhett at least tried to look decent and wore a white linen button down that he left open, with a light blue shirt underneath and his signature belt buckle and Wranglers. His cowboy hat and boots just brought everything together. He was dressed as I guess any cowboy would be for a wedding.

Our wedding.

Blinking, I furrowed my brow, trying to remember if I even mentioned that. After clearing my head, I nodded. "I think I said two months."

Letting go of my hand he lifted his forefinger and thumb to my chin, his eyes searching me. "I'll be right back."

Then he left, patting the officiant on the shoulder. They went to the desk, leaving me standing in the small room by myself. I wanted to follow, but I was nervous to hear what they were talking about. I had been told to not eavesdrop on David's business dealings, but to stand and be respectful. I knew Rhett wasn't like that but I still couldn't help my reaction.

Shaking my head and letting out a low grumble, I cursed at myself. Why was I still doing what *he* wanted me to do? I wasn't in his life anymore. He had no control over me. I looked at the ring on my finger, a simple reminder that I could do whatever I wanted. Rhett wouldn't hold me back. If anything he'd let me go when I needed to. But . . . would I want to after all of this was said and done?

I glanced up at him as he talked to the officiant and witness, so relaxed in everything. So calm. My mind began bouncing back and forth. The logical side of me screamed that this was insane and not only did I just ruin my life, but Rhett's well.

Knots formed in my stomach as I tried to hold the nausea down.

"Kyla." Rhett came up to my side and gently touched my elbow, his touch making that feeling fade. "The license is ready to sign."

I smiled at him and nodded, allowing him to guide me over to the table.

"I just need your signature here." I was handed a pen. "And Rhett's here. The witness here."

I looked at the paper before signing it, taking in all the details the cream-colored paper offered. The gold flourishes on the corners, the small print that said bride, groom, witness, county, date . . .

Holy shit, he had the date changed.

"How in the hell?" I looked at the post-dated license. It was dated for April 24 this year—two months ago.

"It helps when you know the officiant and clerk." Rhett smirked, winking at me. "We've been married for a while."

"I can't believe you," I huffed as I signed my name, making it officially official.

Rhett signed his name next to mine, and then the officiant spun the paper and did a fast signature. He gave it one more glance, nodding before he lifted his chin to both of us.

"Let me make a copy and get this in the system and then it's yours. Congrats."

"Thank you." Rhett smiled as he watched him turn and leave. "I have a question," he asked me, leaning up against the counter crossing his ankles. "Are you changing your name?"

I shot him a look. "Do I have to?"

"No." He smiled, "But you can if you want."

"Why would I? This is temporary, right?"

A corner of his lips raised, his eyes focused on me before he blinked slowly, turning his head back to the clerk.

"But . . ." I thought out loud. "If David asks, I did."

"You got it, Mrs. Hartwell." Rhett looked back at me, that light curve of his lips turning into a full blown smile by the time I met his gaze. He scoffed and shook his head lightly. "I think I just found the perfect nickname for you."

"Welcome to the family!!" Abi's ecstatic scream hit my ears the moment I stepped foot in the main house.

She wrapped her arms around my neck and pulled me close, completely taking me by surprise. Rhett had told me he let them know the gist, that this marriage was to trick David to get him off the ranch and away for good, and if and when my mother showed up, to show her that I was serious about my life. I should have known they would have taken it more seriously than I did. I was still in shock that

I was actually married, that Rhett was my husband, and that David was somewhere nearby.

"Um . . ." I gave her a soft hug back. "Thanks, but I need to . . ." I stumbled, looking at Rhett who walked behind Abi's back, removing his hat and placing it on the side table.

Charlotte came up in the hall, giving her son a quick pat on the back. "We're having dinner, to celebrate. Let me see." She reached her hand to me, grasping my left hand and bringing it closer. She smiled, and I swear I saw tears swell in her eyes before she blinked back up at me. "It fits perfectly."

My eyes caught the small sparkle of the ring before I pulled my hand away.

"I'll be right back, I need to . . ." I need to what? *To breathe.*

"It's fine." Charlotte smiled, her voice soft and sweet. "Take your time and we'll see you at dinner?"

I nodded at her, mimicking her smile before turning to Rhett.

"Hey, Cowboy." I cleared my throat. "Give me a few minutes, okay?"

"Sure, Mrs. Hartwell."

I turned, hearing Abi say, "Ooo I like the sound of that on Kyla. Did she really change her name?" and I ran out of the main house and quickly walked towards Rhett's cabin. Once I got far enough away, I pulled my phone out and dialed Grace's number.

It rang and rang, and for a moment, I prayed it would go to voicemail, but then her voice hit my ear and the reality of the last fifteen hours sank in.

"Grace, I'm married," I blurted out.

"Um . . ." she stuttered, her greeting coming to a complete stop. "Come again?"

"David showed up, and Abi told him I was married and then Rhett went along with it, and then we went to the courthouse and *really* got married, and Grace . . ." I opened the door to Rhett's—or was it *our*—house and shut it quickly behind me, leaning up against the door to look at my finger. The golden band shimmered, and the diamond looked brand new, even though I knew it was older. I had a feeling it had a story behind it too, but my brain couldn't focus on that right now. "I married Rhett."

Silence.

More silence.

Did she hear me?

"Grace?" I finally said.

"You're married . . . to the cowboy?"

"Technically."

"Technically? Technically you're married to the cowboy." After a single beat, Grace squealed. "Okay, okay, okay . . ." She was hyperventilating. "I need to know the details. How? When? Why!?"

"How? I told you. Abi told David I was married to her brother, and Rhett rolled with it. When? Today . . . literally an hour ago. Why? To get David off my back. Not sure why Rhett agreed to it." I blinked. It wasn't my idea . . . it was Rhett's, I was the one who "agreed" to it. "Well, I agreed. Rhett asked."

"He asked you to marry him?" Grace exclaimed.

I knew my best friend, and I could guarantee she was pacing her living room, an arm flailing as she spoke. She most likely had a goofy smile on her face and her mind was buzzing. Just like mine was. There was no way I could give her enough details to satisfy her.

"Yes." I sighed, looking back down at the ring on my finger. "And then he took me to the courthouse, and we got married. I'm married. To Rhett."

"Well . . ." She paused. "That settles it."

"Settles what?"

"I'm coming to visit."

SIXTEEN

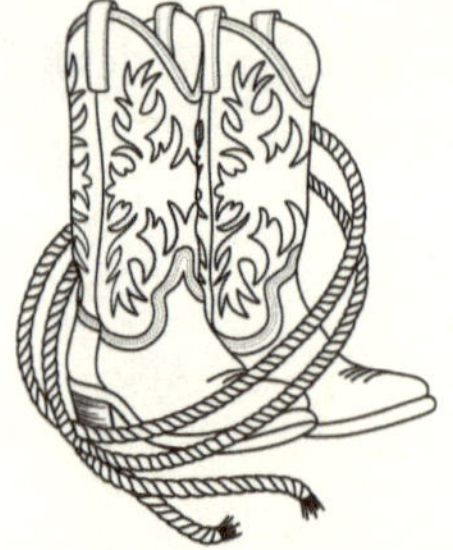

Rhett

I FOUND KYLA IN the bedroom when I finally walked through my front door. She had pulled her hair into a ponytail and changed from the jeans she wore into a pair of shorts and a tank top. And she was barefoot.

Was she okay? Was she uneasy? Was she calm?

I couldn't tell.

I folded my arms and leaned against the doorframe as Kyla dug through a box that sat on the bed. T-shirts and dresses were lying on the white comforter, and shoes were on the floor next to the bed. She pulled out a yellow polka dotted sundress and laid it on top of the others. I just watched.

Where did I even begin? I couldn't really tell her that I was happy to call her my wife, that she was where I thought she was meant to be. I had only known her for two weeks, even though it felt like so much longer, but things felt different with her here. I didn't know how to put all of that into words . . . so I watched as my wife got comfortable in the bedroom. She moved quickly, but once that box was empty, she tossed it on the floor and heaved a sigh, her shoulders slumping.

"Your family wouldn't hate me if I skipped out on dinner . . . would they?" she asked, looking up at me for a split second.

I pushed myself off the door frame and ran my fingers through my hair.

"They'll survive," I responded as I reached out and grabbed the yellow dress, feeling the fabric between my fingers. "Mrs. Hartwell, if we aren't going over there for dinner, what can I make you?"

Kyla let out a nervous laugh. "You? Make dinner?"

"I'm a fantastic cook." Turning, I made my way to the kitchen, praying to the kitchen gods that there was enough food in there for me to make something for Kyla.

I pinched my eyes as I opened the refrigerator.

Score.

Chicken.

"I did go shopping while you were gone," Kyla added softly, her voice getting louder as she approached, taking a seat at the kitchen island. "And then ate with your family almost every night so nothing got made or eaten."

Pulling the chicken from the fridge, I turned to look at Kyla over my shoulder, cocking an eyebrow at her. "So, you *do* need a break from my family?"

"No, your family . . . they're great. Abi has become a friend, your mom is a gem, and Stetson, well . . . he did ask me to marry him." She gave me a soft smile, moving her ring finger, making the small diamond glisten.

"He does know *we* got married right?"

Pinching her brow, she looked up at me through her eyelashes.

"Rhett . . ." She sucked in a quick breath. "What does your family know? I mean, I know you told them that it was because of David . . . but . . . what else?"

Her question didn't take me by surprise. Before I even took Kyla to the courthouse, I sauntered in the kitchen where most of my family sat, and told them I was marrying Kyla. Abi's eyes widened as her arms flew in the air, exclaiming that she took all the credit for this marriage taking place. Lachlan raised his eyebrows, slouching back in his chair to fold his arms, no doubt silently judging me as he stayed silent. Wyatt was still in his small apartment in the bunkhouse, so he missed the news, and my parents . . . they both congratulated me, keeping mainly to themselves. Which was unlike them. My dad would have something to say on the matter later for sure, but I expected more from my mom. Instead, the only reaction she gave was a simple nod.

After dropping the marriage news, I gave them the gist on David, telling them to watch out for him and not to fall for whatever game he was playing. When they all understood, I grabbed a piece of bacon and turned on my heels to go marry the woman of dreams.

My mother though, she was the one who stood to follow me out. Like moms always could, she told me she knew there was more to this than meets the eyes. That there was something there with

Kyla that I had to figure out. It amazed her, but didn't shock her, that I was willing to do so much to protect her—even give her my name—when I knew very little about her. According to her, Kyla was here to stay, and I hoped that her future telling abilities were spot on. Before I left, she gave me a hug, mumbled that she was proud and that she loved me, and then said she would keep an eye out for—and I quote her—"that developer asshat."

Bringing the gas stove to life, I placed the iron skillet on the flame.

"I told them the basic truth," I said smugly.

"So, they know this is fake."

I smirked. "This isn't fake Kyla, we've been married for months." I glanced at her over my shoulder once again.

Kyla twisted her lips. "Okay then, they know it's temporary."

Sensing the unease, I turned to face her, seeing the stiffness in her posture. She fiddled with her fingertips, moving to the ring to twist it in circles. "What's wrong?"

She took a deep breath and put her palms on the counter, her shoulders dropping as the breath left her. "Nothing . . . I called Grace and she wants to come visit, and you were at the main house for a long time and I just . . . started to unpack and it kind of all . . ."

"You're overthinking everything aren't you?" I raised an eyebrow at her.

"How are you not?" she asked softly.

I shrugged my shoulders and then turned back to the skillet which was now hot and ready for the chicken. I listened to the simmer before answering Kyla. "There's nothing to think about."

"There's *a lot* to think about. For starters, there's only one bed in this house."

"I'll sleep on the couch."

"And one bathroom." She eyed me.

"We'll take turns." I held in a laugh. Even now I found her absolutely adorable. I couldn't even fathom what was going on inside her brain.

"And how am I supposed to act around you, your family . . . anyone for that matter?"

"Like you have been. They like having you here, just like I do." The corners of my lips rose as I placed my palms on the counter, leaning close to her.

"And what if David shows back up here, say, tonight? Am I just supposed to kiss you senseless until he leaves us alone? How is that going to be believable? You don't even have a ring. How are you going to pass being my husband in front of him, or my mother, if you don't even have a ring?" Her voice quickened with each rapid question, raising with each word, and I swore I could *hear* her heartbeat. Her cheeks flushed as her hands moved to cover her face. Then it hit me . . . she was starting to panic.

"Kyla, slow down." I tried to keep my voice calm. She didn't need me chuckling at how adorable I thought she was even as she panicked, she needed me to keep my promise. I left the stove and rounded the kitchen island, gently placing my hands on her shoulders. "You'll sleep in the bedroom, and I'll be on the couch unless you would be more comfortable having me in the main house."

"No," she shot, a shaky breath leaving her lips, "I want you here."

I smiled, relieved. "Okay, I'll sleep on the couch. Bathroom is not an issue. My family is not an issue, so don't act any different around them. My mother likes having you around and Abi . . . well she's more fond of you than anyone. She's excited to have you around for longer than you originally planned, and me . . ." I met her gaze and held her there, tried to focus on her breathing, "I'm just excited I get to spend more time with you. We've talked on the phone for the last two weeks, it's no different than that—"

"What about a ring?" she interrupted. "It's going to be pretty hard to convince everyone you're my husband if you don't have a ring."

"Do you want to get me a ring?" I asked.

Raising her hand to her shoulder, she took my left hand in hers and looked at my bare ring finger. Her eyes were concentrated, and her breathing, though still quick, began to slow.

"What about your rodeo schedule, when do you leave again?" she asked, her eyes focused on my hand.

"I don't leave until the middle of July, and I'd love for you to come with me. It's a great time and you'd get to see it firsthand." I watched as her fingers played with mine, finally lacing them together.

"Your dad mentioned a rodeo here, on the Fourth?"

I hummed. "My favorite time of year. And it will be better because you'll be here."

"I won't be in the way?"

"Never," I whispered.

She sighed, running the pad of her thumb over the empty space on my ring finger. She had calmed down, and I wasn't sure if the panic had left her completely, but she was more focused. Steady. Her hand still held mine, grounding her—grounding me—back to each other.

"Kyla," I whispered, watching her intently. I don't know what compelled me to say what I did next, but something told me she needed to know, "I don't regret marrying you if that's where your mind is going. I would do it again in a heartbeat, even without David in the picture."

Slowly, she blinked before giving a small laugh through her lips. "You're just saying that . . ."

"I'm not though. I've thought about you every day since I first saw you at the bar, and now I get to have you a little longer." I let go of her hand, slipping my fingers to the back of her neck, "Do you regret marrying me?"

I had a feeling I knew her answer. I prepared myself for the ultimate drop of my stomach when she said she did, that this was temporary—*fake*—even though the document sitting on the counter proved it wasn't.

"No," she said softly, taking me completely by surprise. "I don't. I would do it again in a heartbeat too, Cowboy."

My heart skipped a beat as her eyes met mine, and gently, I leaned into kiss her forehead, letting my lips linger there a little longer. Taking a deep breath and sitting up straight, her palms running against my chest, she looked behind me to the stove.

"You're overcooking the one side of the chicken," she said with a smile, her voice no longer shaking, no more fear or panic. She had beat whatever it was.

"Oh, shit." I left her sitting alone as I hurried back to the chicken, flipping it to see a semi-charred side. I shook my head and ran my fingers through my hair. So much for impressing her.

"I thought you said you were a fantastic cook?"

"Normally I am, when Mrs. Hartwell isn't distracting me," I teased, feeling the air lighten around us.

"Mrs. Hartwell," she parroted as she stood and walked around the island. "You know, I think I *will* get you a ring."

She leaned against the counter next to me, so close our arms were almost touching. She folded her arms and turned to look at me. I kept my focus on the chicken, ignoring the fact that she was close to me. Despite the fact that I just had her in my arms, I could still feel the flutters that happened in my stomach. She took a few deep breaths, before crossing her ankles, shifting her weight.

"You just helped me through a panic attack—stopped it before it could get worse," she said softly, her eyes on her feet. "Did you know that?"

I looked at her from the corner of my eyes. "Are you okay?" I asked.

Kyla nodded, scooting a little closer to me, as she moved her attention to the stove. Exhaling through her lips, she began. "So, since you're my husband, maybe we should spend the night . . ." She trailed off, her eyes fixed on the chicken as I turned them in the pan. I raised an eyebrow and waited for her to finish her sentence. "Getting to know each other."

Lowing my eyebrow, I gave a small huff.

"What?" she asked. "What did you think I was going to say?"

I shook my head. "I can't think of anything else I'd rather do than get to know you."

So, we talked as we finished cooking and ate. The dishes on the table went ignored as she told me about everything and anything she could think of. She told me all about Phoenix, and how her childhood was extremely different from mine. She talked about growing up in the city, her father owning his own company that led her to David, how her mother was a helicopter parent, while also being incredibly absent. I learned she was an only child, and that she always longed for a sister. She met Grace, her fearless best friend, in high school, and they had been glued at the hip ever since (not including the rough patch that they had thanks to David). Grace had become her sister, and sometimes they introduced each other as such. I smiled, remembering she had said Grace wanted to come visit. I couldn't wait to meet the person that made my wife smile.

Her eyes lit up when she talked about teaching. She loved her students, she loved watching them learn, seeing things click in their brains. She teared up a little when she spoke about leaving the field in the middle of the school year, but simply knowing she could teach again one day helped her see a light at the end of the tunnel. Then there was Stetson, and how she had latched on to him and he to her.

"When he read his first chapter book all the way through, my heart swelled. I do adore that kid," she said as she held her chest.

"I'm pretty sure the entire family adores you, not just Stet."

Dropping her hands to her knees, she cocked her head and looked at me, her lips twitching into a soft smile. I smiled wide, stopping myself from kissing her. This was going to be a lot harder than I thought. I wanted to kiss her whenever I wanted. The thought alone sent chills down my spine. Was it possible to fall for someone you barely knew?

Except now I felt like I knew her.

"Okay so now you." She changed the subject. "You grew up on the ranch?"

I nodded. "I was riding a horse before I could walk."

"And roping a calf?" she asked, raising a single eyebrow.

"Before I could run." I winked.

"And when did you know you wanted to participate in the rodeo?"

"The minute I roped my first calf. I did rodeos in high school—the local dentist was my best sponsor." I chuckled, rubbing the back of my neck as I remembered the moment I took him my paperwork right after he declared I had four cavities. "Then I started going professional after I graduated, entered the PRCA and the rest is history."

"Did you go to college?" she asked, her voice still, almost as if she was worried about offending me.

I shook my head. "No, never wanted to. I wanted to ride and rope and that's exactly what I did. I know that when I retire from roping, I'll be here on the ranch." I leaned on the back of the couch, my arm draped over the cushions as I met her gaze. "We hold a rodeo every July Fourth . . ."

"You've mentioned it several times. Your dad too." She sat up, leaning towards me. "I'll get to be here for it."

Nodding along with her, I followed her excitement. "This year a lot of cowboys are registered, it's gonna be bigger this year. People may even include it in their standing."

"Like to go towards the NFR? How does that work?"

"Livestock events, and some timed, require cowboys to ride in one hundred rodeos to go towards their NFR standing. No one has ever claimed this one," I explained. "I doubt they will, but it's a nice thought to have."

"But this is the Hartwell Rodeo, and you're *Rhett Hartwell.*" She emphasized my name. *Our* name.

I choked a laugh. "I am, and you . . . are *Mrs.* Rhett Hartwell." I leaned in closer, lowering my voice just enough to notice her eyes flutter. I didn't imagine that, she definitely liked the sound of that.

"I am." She sighed, straightening her back and narrowing her eyes at me. "Tell me more about the rodeo, I know I've learned a lot but tell me everything."

Raising my eyebrows, I began to talk about all things rodeo as she sat and listened to me intently. I could get used to this. Having her here with me every night, engaging in what I did for a living—enjoying it. I couldn't wait to see her at her first rodeo, donning that yellow sundress and her own hat. Damn, I needed to see that.

SEVENTEEN

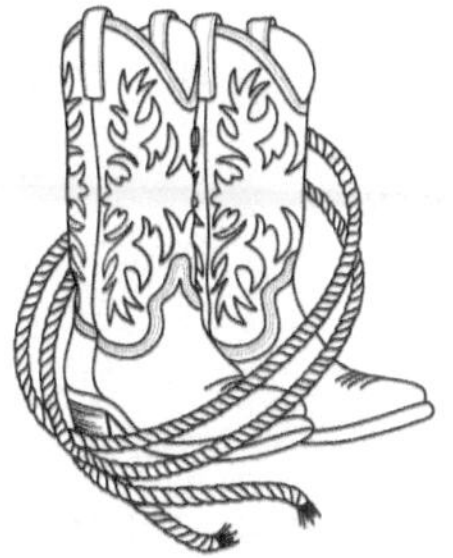

Kyla

Two Days.

Two days had passed since Rhett and I got married.

Two days since he had successfully pulled me out of a panic attack before it had gotten stronger. I was still trying to wrap my brain around those moments. When panic had set in before there was no way out of it; I had to let it pass on its own, which sometimes could take hours—days—and there was always the aftermath. But here I was, two days later, feeling at ease. How did he manage that? Simply by his touch or his voice—what was it about him that grounded me?

I used my thumb to twirl the wedding ring on my finger, the gentle reminder that I had him waiting for me back at the ranch, and that for now David was nowhere to be found.

"What about this one?" Abi pulled my attention as she tapped on the jewelry case. "Gold—like yours?"

When I mentioned getting Rhett a ring, she jumped at the chance to take me into town. Leaving Stetson with Wyatt for his lesson, she dragged me through a few stores until we landed at the local jeweler. The gold band was simple and thin, not something I could picture on Rhett's finger. But as I looked at the rings in the case, I couldn't really picture any of them on his finger.

I sighed in frustration. I was starting to think I'd never find a ring. "What about one of those rubber ones? So, he doesn't have to worry about his ring while he's roping."

"A ring won't get in the way of roping. Plus, he would hate a rubber one." Abi gave me a side eye.

Imagining the thick rope slipping through the well-fitting band and dragging him around the arena, realizing how ridiculous that was, I agreed with her and returned my attention back to the bands. Leaving her looking at the gold bands, I wandered over to another case. A ring sparkled in the lighting, the small diamonds that wrapped around the white gold were extremely flashy, making me chuckle.

I saw something similar as David and I shopped for his wedding ring and the memory came flooding back. He had picked his own band. Sure, I was with him, but any suggestions I threw out were tossed to the wayside. He was in control of that moment, saying, "It's on my finger, I should get to pick what it is." He had picked a gold and black band, the black covering most of the surface with the two thin gold bands wrapping around each one, ending with a single diamond. It had cost more than two months' salary for me, and I was the one to buy it.

It never even graced his finger.

Rhett had told me he would proudly wear whatever I brought back, but I wanted something he would enjoy, and shopping for a man I had just met was hard.

We had spent the last few nights together simply talking. Banter and flirting were thrown in, but it was mostly us getting to know each other. We had a lifetime to try to squeeze in before someone really questioned the marriage, but that wasn't what seemed to fuel Rhett's desire to talk. I could just feel it with him. He wanted to be around me. He would take my hand when we were outside on the ranch, or place his arm over my chair at dinner, scooting closer to me. He would show affection in small ways, opening the door for me, refilling my water glass, or simply leaving a mug next to the coffee maker before he left in the morning. I wasn't used to this, and a part of me thought that if Rhett kept it up, Washington was becoming less and less of an option.

I shook my head. There was no way I could stay here. Married to a cowboy.

This was *temporary.*

Forcing myself to focus, my eyes widened when I finally saw a ring I could imagine on Rhett's finger.

"Abi . . ." I kept my eyes on the ring but motioned for Abi to come closer. "Look."

She looked at the case, and I watched as she scanned the case until her eyes came upon the exact ring I wanted. Her jaw dropped before she covered her mouth with her hand.

"Okay, yes. That's the one."

It was a tungsten ring, a darker shade of silver with an engraving on the smooth outside that resembled a rope. The design was intricate, two strands woven together with detail almost like a Celtic knot. I doubted the designer had meant it to look like a rope, but when I looked at it that's all I saw. A ring fit for a roper. A ring for my *husband*.

"Hey, Tate!" Abi called to the jeweler over her shoulder. "We found it."

An older male approached the other side of the counter, smiling once he looked down at the ring we were both eyeing. "Wonderful." He smiled. "Mr. Hartwell will love it."

"I think so too," I said softly as I watched him open the case.

"Do you want to upgrade yours?" Abi asked, motioning towards my ring.

I looked at it and smiled. The ring David had picked was heavy, gaudy and even though in the beginning I loved showing it off, I grew to hate it. I knew this ring in the long run wasn't mine, but it made me feel settled—made me feel secure.

I shook my head. "No, I like this one, plus, it's only temporary." I sighed, more for my benefit than hers. I didn't want to forget that, and even though I was here spending money on a ring that was just as temporary for Rhett, I didn't want to slip into the delusion that this was—what did Rhett call it—*real*.

"*Temporary* is not in Rhett's vocabulary, Kyla," Abi noted as she gave me a slight eye roll before she turned her focus to Tate. "She'll take it."

We arrived back at the ranch just in time to see Rhett and Lachlan dismounting their horses. I had no idea what Rhett had been up to, but his Wrangler jeans were covered in dust and his white T-shirt was splattered with dirt.

I jumped out of the truck, gripping the bag and made my way over to him, with Abi not far behind me.

"What in the world were you doing?" I asked, a smile growing as I eyed him from his boots to his hat.

"Guiding cattle," he responded simply. "They wandered a little bit."

"And that got you covered in dirt?"

Tilting his head, the shadows of his cowboy hat hit his cheek bones in all the right places, he smiled.

"Ranch work gets you dirty, Mrs. Hartwell," he mocked. He motioned his chin to the bag in the hand, breaking the eye contact we shared. "What'cha got?"

"Your ring," I respond softly.

His smile grew. "Let me go get washed up and then—"

"You can have it once your hands are dirt free."

"It's pretty perfect." Abi folded her arms and looked at her brother. "You don't want to taint it already with the cow shit that's caked between your fingernails."

"I do not have cow shit in my fingernails." Rhett glared at his sister and then turned to Buckle, grabbing her reins as he led her away, giving my cheek a quick kiss before passing. "I'll be right back."

I blushed, feeling the butterflies rise in my belly as I turned to follow him. Giving Abi a quick look and wave behind my shoulder, I caught the sly grin on her face. Catching up to Rhett as he guided Buckle to the stable, I lightly brushed my hand on his shoulders, brushing off some dirt that sat on his shirt.

"Can't stay away, can you?"

My lips curved to a smile as I bumped my hips into him, forcing him into Buckle. He laughed, and god, did I love that laugh. It brought warmth to the air that surrounded us, no matter where we were. Rhett's smile and laugh could turn any situation bright again, even if he was caked in dirt. Being around him just felt so good. So natural.

"Just thought I'd help with Buckle while you wash up," I answered, holding in the *I just really love your laugh and being around you feels good all the time* I wanted to shout.

"She just needs to be brushed a bit—gotta get the mud out of her coat—then I'll put her out in the pasture."

"You're done working for the day?" I asked as he stopped Buckle once inside the barn. He brushed her mane with the palm of his hand. She responded by bobbing her head up and down, a heavy breath escaping her nostrils.

"Oh, hell no, I'm sure Lachlan will find something else I need to do. But in reality, I need to get the rodeo going."

Hooking Buckle's reins up, he left me standing next to her. Still bobbing her head lightly, she took a single step closer to me. I reached up to pet her nose. She blinked and let out a huff, before bobbing her head again.

"I wish I had some apples," I said to her. "I'd give you one, or two . . . or three."

"Oh, here." Rhett dug in his pocket and handed me a small peppermint. "She'll like that more."

Holding the peppermint in my palm just like Stetson had shown me, I waited for her to take it. Her nose moved against my hand and then the wet feel of her tongue swept across, taking the peppermint. While Buckle nodded her head again, giving a soft sound of approval, I gave her nose a pet.

"Here." Rhett came up to my side, showing me his freshly cleaned hands. "Cow shit free."

"You really want to see your ring, don't you?" I held back a laugh. "Your hands are just going to get dirty again as you brush her."

Rhett shrugged a shoulder. "My hands will get dirty no matter what I do, but yes. I really, *really* want to see the ring,"

Giving him a slight eye roll, I reached into the bag and pulled out the small ring box. The black velvet felt cool in my hand, handing it to him. With his eyes focused on mine, he took the box and slowly opened it. His eyebrows raised as he took in the ring, then they furrowed and raised again. So many emotions were going through his face, and I desperately wanted to know what they were.

"What?" I asked softly as he stared at it.

"Nothing it's . . ." His voice broke, the words seeming to catch his throat as he looked from the ring to back at me. "It's . . . it's . . ." Rhett stumbled again as he looked back down. "It looks like—"

"A rope."

"Tate made this?"

I nodded. "Almost custom for you, isn't it."

Rhett closed the distance between us, taking me by complete surprise as his lips met mine in a sweet, soft kiss. He didn't linger, just teasing me with his touch long enough that I could still feel him there. I tasted spice, loving the tingle on my lips that followed as Rhett hovered over me.

"If I didn't know any better, I'd say you had it engraved specifically for me," he said as his lips left, taking the warmth and spark with them.

I licked my lips, wanting to taste him again, even if for a second.

I watched as he took the ring from the box and slid it on his finger. Having guessed at his size, I was amazed to see it fit perfectly.

"Like a glove." He sighed as his eyes met mine again. "Well, it's officially official now. I'm your husband."

"Haven't you been for months?"

He let out a loud, single laugh. "I guess that's true." He shook his head, leaning down to begin to unsaddle Buckle. "Oh hey, I have a question."

"Shoot," I responded.

"You said your friend Grace wanted to come out to visit right?"

"Yep, she didn't specify, but when she sets her mind on something, it happens."

"Tell her to come for the rodeo." His head popped back up over Buckle's back as he removed the saddle and then the blanket. Her coat began to stick up in random places, and once the saddle was on the post, he used his left hand to pat her coat down, his ring catching my eye. "I'm sure—just like you—she has never seen a rodeo."

I scoffed. "No, no she hasn't."

"Tell her to come, I'm sure she'd have a blast."

"I'm sure she would. I'll go give her a call." I gave Buckle one last stroke down her nose. "See ya in a bit?"

Rhett gave me a slight nod as I began to turn away, taking the first few steps out of the barn. "You know it, and Kyla"—the mention of my name made me turn back to him—"I really do love my ring."

EIGHTEEN

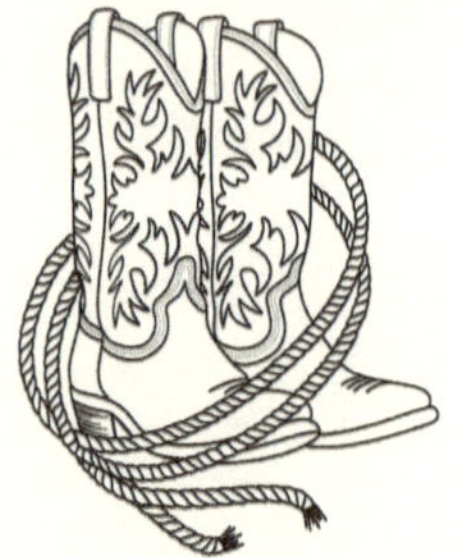

Rhett

WITH A WEEK TO go before the rodeo, the list to prepare was getting longer. I eagerly approached Kyla, basically begging her to come with me to the arena. Not only did I want to show her my turf, but I wanted her to be a part of it. I wanted to hand her a broom so she could dust the stands. I wanted her to see everything firsthand, to experience it. The smile she gave me told me she wanted to tag along. She grabbed the boots Abi had loaned her and a straw hat, before practically running to the truck.

She was so full of enthusiasm, anyone who didn't know her would have no idea the pain she carried. She was doing her best to move on and become who she wanted to be.

My thumb played with the ring that now sat on my finger, loving the fact that for now she wanted to be with me.

The Hartwell Rodeo Arena was built when I was young. It was the one thing in town that had our name on it that didn't sit on the ranch. At first it was small with a few stands for seating and only three chutes, but it has grown over the years. The stands were big enough now to fit the entire town, and more chutes and an announcer box had been added. Our little rodeo was growing each year, and this year was going to be the biggest yet.

"So how do we prep for a rodeo?" Kyla asked as soon as we set foot in the arena.

Lachlan and the ranch hands had done a good job of keeping up with everything during the off-season for the arena, but there was still a list of things that needed to be checked and double checked before we brought the livestock over. Kyla stepped up on the railing and looked into the open area.

"It's smaller than I thought it would be." She turned to look at me, her hair flying over her shoulder.

Removing my hat and pushing my hair back with my fingers before returning it to my head, I rested my arms on the gate next to Kyla. "It's a smaller arena, nothing compared to ones I've competed in, but this one beats them all." I paused, surveying the space. "We have a list of things to do. You ready to get your hands dirty?"

"Hey." Kyla's voice fell, dripping with sarcasm. "I helped a cow give birth. I think I can help prep an arena. But you didn't answer me, *how* do we prep for it?"

"The dirt needs to be groomed, the chutes need to be tended to and we need to make sure there is plenty of feed for the livestock."

Kyla looked over her shoulder at the empty cages. "Because all the livestock that's here is going to want to eat it." There was sarcasm in her voice, hiding the laugh that she so desperately wanted to let loose.

Scoffing, I opened the gate, forcing Kyla to swing with it, letting out a small "Whoo" as she moved forward. "We'll bring the livestock over a few days before. It's going to be a long day so I hope you're ready for that."

"When I think of the Fourth of July, I see fireworks, parades, and barbeques." She jumped off the gate. "You guys don't do that at the ranch?"

I shook my head. "Nah, my mom will make a large breakfast for everyone, but then it's all-hands-on-deck getting the rodeo put together. Then at six that night the stands start to fill, and the show starts at seven-thirty. Once the rodeo is over, the firework show starts on the opposite end of the arena. Lachlan will help get that set up during the rodeo."

"Do we have a rodeo clown?" Kyla spun on her toe, the dirt forming a small circle as she looked back at me.

"Yes, we have a rodeo clown—we have to. Who else is going to sit in the barrel when the bull riders have their eight seconds of fame?"

"Yea, about that." She spun back around. "Why do they sit in the barrel, just for comic relief?"

"Rodeo clowns are more than just comic relief. Sure, they offer that, but their main job is to distract the bull if anything happens."

"No," Kyla corrected me, "that's the bullfighters." She pointed her finger directly at me. "Abi told me that."

"And," I added, "a rodeo clown is a trained bullfighter." I cocked an eyebrow, grabbing the handle to the chute and opening it for Kyla. She stepped in and turned, waiting for me to close the gate.

She was quiet for a moment before she turned, giving me a side eye. "Have you ever fought a bull?"

"More times than I'd care to admit." I smiled.

"Glad you haven't broken a bone."

"Who says I haven't?" I took a few steps towards her, lowering my chin to meet her gaze. "I've fallen off more horses than bulls, and I can tell you it's not the best experience."

"Says the man who literally jumps off horses for a living."

"Don't forget lifting a calf off the ground," I added.

"Yeah, 'cause that's hard," she said sarcastically.

"Next time—what did you name her? Josie?—Next time Josie takes off, I'll let you wrangle her up, lift her off the ground and tie-up her legs. You'll discover it's just as hard as riding a bull." I stepped closer to her still, closing the gap that was between us.

Kyla stood still, folding her arms over her chest, tilting her head, and giving me a smirk. I blinked, forcing myself to keep it together. She was gorgeous—everything about her stood out to me in a way that no one had before. Her smile, the way her hair fell off her shoulders, her captivating eyes, the curve of her hips. I simply couldn't believe she was my wife. Even if it was for a season, I got to call her my wife. I still hadn't truly kissed her since our wedding day, even though I desperately wanted to.

Would she let me kiss her here?

"You're not roping that calf, Mr. Hartwell, no matter how hard you try, that calf stays with me."

I cocked an eyebrow. "Is that so, Mrs. Hartwell?"

She gave me a single nod, her lips curling as her hands moved to her hips. Her fingers drummed on her shorts, the ring giving the smallest glint in the sun. Her shoulders wiggled as she moved her neck, her eyes not once leaving mine.

Every part of my body was telling me to turn, to tell her about the long list of prep, but then she licked those damn lips.

Closing the gap completely I cupped her face in my hands, pressing my lips to hers without thinking. She shuddered for a moment before relaxing into me, giving a soft hum as her fingers found my waist. I kept the kiss simple, memorizing the way her lips felt against mine—soft, full and tasted just like the way she smelled, like vanilla.

I wanted to deepen it, hold her closer and take her in, take her back to the moment at the bar, remind her that this was real. That what I felt was real . . .

She broke the kiss, and our eyes met for a split second before her blink broke the connection. Letting out a breath of air, she looked down at our boots.

"I promise I won't rope Josie, but . . ." I said, moving back into the conversation as if nothing had happened; even though my voice was heavy, and my hands were still on her neck. Just as casually I ran my thumb along her jaw. "I'll teach *you* how to rope a calf."

She laughed then, her hands still firm on my waist as her shoulders dropped, her body completely relaxing into me. "I can barely stay on a horse," she whispered, her eyes raising to meet mine.

Her cheeks were pink, and her eyes were glazed over, a look I hoped I could recreate again. A small reminder of the night we first met. Everything about the way she looked at me, and the way she held herself told me she enjoyed that as much as I did.

I felt a corner of my lips curl up. "I'll teach you," I repeated, bringing my lips to hers once more, a small fleeting kiss she accepted. "It did get added to your list, right?"

"That's right." A sigh left her lips. "It did."

"Well . . ." I locked her gaze, feeling her melt against me, I dipped my chin and my lips once again met hers. *Vanilla.*

As if my family knew I wanted more, I heard the gate behind us bang shut and boots crunch against the ground. Kyla broke the kiss and stepped back, her gaze flying over my shoulder. She let out a puff of air, and then gave a small smile. I turned and saw Lachlan and Wyatt walking towards us.

"Sorry to interrupt," Lachlan started, "but there's a lot to do."

"You're not interrupting." Kyla smoothed out her tank top and adjusted the hat on her head. "Just point me in the right direction and tell me what I need to do."

"I was thinking about letting her drag the dirt. She would like that," I suggested seeing Lachlan raise an eyebrow. "I'll be with her."

Wyatt let out a laugh and walked past me, slapping my shoulder on his way up the steps to the announcer box. "I'll go grab her the keys, I'd love to see this."

Kyla spun to face me, her hat almost falling off her head. "I get to *drag the dirt.*"

"Well, you get to drive the tractor." Kyla's eyes widened at my response. "Another thing to add to your list, Baby."

"I'm in." Kyla smiled, the pink still radiating off her cheeks.

"Look at that dirt." Kyla jumped off the Ground Hog tractor and took a few careful steps off to the side. "I'd say that dirt has been perfectly *dragged*."

"Perfectly . . . dragged," I repeated, jumping off the back. "I'd say this is your job from now on."

"You gotta document this for me. Grace won't believe I did this." She pulled her phone from her back pocket, unlocked it and held it in between us. "Take a photo for me?" She waved her phone, urging me to take it.

"Of the dirt?"

"Of me *and* the dirt. I know it's dumb, but Rhett, I've never done anything like this before. I drove that thing!" Kyla pointed to the blue tractor, bending at the waist with a cheesy grin on her face.

I was tempted to pull her in for another kiss, but instead I readied her phone. "Go stand next to the Ground Hog." I took a few steps backwards, watching as Kyla ran up to the tractor and struck a pose, her hands on her hips, tilting them towards the tractor. She smiled, brighter than I had ever seen. She was happy, she was excited, it poured out of her—even through the small screen. And the best part was seeing the diamond ring on her finger.

I snapped a few photos and made my way back to her, handing her the phone back.

"Here, take one with me," she said, taking me off guard as she switched the camera on her phone, stepping up on the foot ledge of the tractor, using her free arm to pull me in closer to her before holding the phone out and taking a selfie.

In a flash the moment was over, and Kyla had let me go, but for a brief moment she was in my arms again.

"Grace is going to get a kick out of this."

"She's coming out, right?" I asked, grabbing her waist to lift her off the tractor, knowing very well she could jump down, but I simply wanted my hands on her again. I always wanted my hands on her.

She nodded. "Yes. She bought her ticket and she's flying in on the second, staying for the rodeo and then she'll fly home. She still needs to find a hotel."

My attention focused on her as she began swiping through her photos, a curl forming on her tight lips. Once she got to our selfie, she zoomed in, and her cheeks turned pink. She bit her lip as she zoomed back out. The spark to her eyes was still there as she held the screen on the photo. I made a mental note to remind her to send it to me. I wanted that memory forever.

"I bet my parents wouldn't mind her staying in the main house. Otherwise she can stay with us at our place." I finally broke the moment, reminding both of us of the topic at hand.

Kyla stopped what she was doing on her phone, dropping it slightly as she looked up at me. "Our place?"

I shrugged my shoulders. "Well yeah. Where else would she stay?" I could basically see her reeling. We had one bedroom, and I knew her mind was instantly going to us sharing the bed. Her eyes met mine as she stilled. I cocked a grin as I lifted a hand and ran my fingers through her ponytail, gently laying it over her shoulder. "Come on, we gotta put this thing back and then head to the hay bales. Think you can keep up with Lachlan there?"

She blinked, snapping herself out of whatever trance she had fallen into. "I've seen Lachlan with hay bales, and I opt out of that activity, but . . . can I park the Ground Hog?"

I laughed, shaking my head at her. "Yes, Kyla, you can park the Ground Hog. Hell," I held my arms open, tipping my back slightly, "I'll even film you parking it so you can send it to Grace."

Kyla dropped her jaw. "I have an even better idea!"

The next thing I knew I was talking to Grace via FaceTime, all while we watched Kyla park the tractor, with guidance, into the stall.

NINETEEN

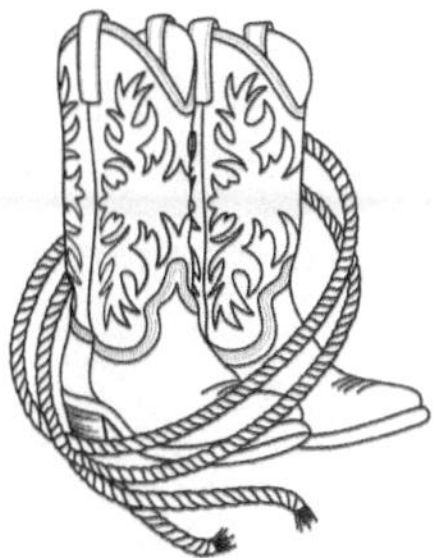

Kyla

I DIDN'T KNOW WHAT it was about the arena, but I completely broke out of my comfort zone. I was trying and doing things I never imagined I would do—adding more things to that list Rhett loved to remind me of. Working the Ground Hog, as Rhett called it several times, was close to being the highlight of the day—the first being the kiss.

The unexpected kiss from Rhett that left me wanting more once the day was done.

That kiss was meant for me. It was mine, and I decided to hold onto it.

It had to have been that kiss that gave me the green light to let go. I wouldn't have driven that tracker if not for that freeing feeling that followed the touch of his lips, just like in the bar. And now look what it's turned into. Everything about Rhett helped build that courage in me. The way he cupped my jaw as he pressed his lips to mine, and the way his hands felt on my hips as he helped me back to the ground with ease. His eyes focused on me as his voice reminded me what to do with the tractor even through Grace's laughter.

It all sent chills up my spine.

A few days later, I found myself in my Buick waiting at the Boise airport for Grace to land. Rhett had offered to drive me, but with work still to be done at the arena, I told him I would do just fine on my own. I could still see his raised brow, his hand reaching up to tip his hat and the wink he threw in my direction before heading out with Lachlan.

My stomach flipped just thinking about it.

Chills, stomach knots, everything about Rhett made my body and mind react. Even the simplest memory.

Once prompted, I drove to the pickup area and basically jumped out of the car once I saw Grace. Her copper hair was up in a tight ponytail, and she looked comfortable from flying, wearing shorts and a T-shirt. Her sunglasses resting on top of her head screamed that she came right from the Arizona summer. Even her skin was tanned. She squealed as she ran towards me, wrapping her arms around my neck, pulling me in as close as possible.

The hug felt good, felt like home in a way. Solid and warm, her cinnamon scent rushed into my mind, flooding me with memories of when I slept on her couch. Grace was that comfort, my best friend, and she was here.

"I've. Missed. You!" she exclaimed. "It's just not the same when we aren't in the same state."

"I know, but—"

Cutting me off, she pulled away. "Let me see." Grabbing my left hand, she studied the ring on my finger. "You really *are* married!?"

I let out a small huff. "I told you I was. It's simple . . ." I looked at the ring.

"Are you happy?" she asked, dropping my hand to hold both of my shoulders.

I sighed, hoping to show her relief. "I'm safe," I responded. "We haven't seen David since, so it's probably all for nothing."

She shook her head. "No, it's not for nothing. Now." —wrapping her arm around my shoulder, she led me to my car—"meeting him on FaceTime was fun and all, but I cannot wait to meet the cowboy in person."

"Rhett," I corrected her. "Only I can call him *Cowboy*." I held back a smile.

"Is he still playing that nickname game?"

"No, he's settled on one," I admitted, secretly loving the nickname he had used since we were married.

"What's that?"

"Mrs. Hartwell."

Instead of taking Grace to the ranch, I took her straight to the rodeo arena, where I knew Rhett, Lachlan, and Wyatt would be. They were transporting the livestock today and I was just a little bummed I was missing out on the action. I saw all three men, plus Abi, leading the bulls into the gates. The only person not on a horse was Lachlan.

Reaching into the back seat, I grabbed my straw hat and the extra I snagged for Grace. I plopped it on her head, her ponytail keeping the back end of it up slightly. Grace let out a small chuckle, giving me a strange look as she went to adjust her hair.

"Trying to get me to fit in completely, huh?"

"Trust me." I raised my eyebrows. "You'll want it."

Grace laughed and then looked towards the arena pinching her eyebrows as she watched. "What are they doing?"

"Moving the livestock for the rodeo," I answered, confident in what I was saying. *Hell yeah, I know what I'm talking about.*

I caught sight of Rhett trotting on Buckle next to a bull, leading it into his area. The sun hit his face just right, the rim of his hat only hiding his eyes. His shoulders broadened as he guided Buckle past the bull and into the corral, turning only once Lachlan had shut the gate. Once the bull was safe, he took off back towards the truck where Wyatt was waiting to release another.

"I take it, that's your *husband?*" Grace said, forcing my gaze from Rhett back to her. "He knows what he's doing for sure. Guiding a bull does not look easy."

I laughed, linking my arm with Grace's. "Come on, I want you to meet Abi."

"Abi?" she parroted. "I thought I was meeting Rhett."

"You will, but Abi is phenomenal and you're going to love her." I began to lead her toward the stock gates, but decided staying out of their way would probably be a better idea. Sure, they had a good grip on the bulls, but you never know what could happen. "On second thought, let's go meet the calves, I'm sure they brought Josie."

"Josie?"

"My calf."

"You have a calf?"

"Damn straight she does." I heard Rhett's voice as hooves approached us. I smiled as he got closer, feeling Grace's posture stiffen.

He smirked down at us as he slowed Buckle, tipping his hat in Grace's direction.

"Nice to finally meet you, Grace." His smooth voice rolled off his tongue.

"It's nice to meet you in person," Grace smiled, "Not on Face-Time." She slid her arm from my grip to shake Rhett's hand. He reached over and shook, his smile only growing. "Gonna tell me about the calf Kyla has adopted?"

I shook my head and met Rhett's gaze. He winked, forcing me to take a breath.

"She helped bring her into the world, so it was only appropriate. Let me get Buckle settled, I'll be right back." Rhett gave me another wink before turning Buckle, running to the gates. I watched as he dismounted and grabbed her reins leading her towards Abi.

"Soooo . . ." Grace drew out the word, almost singing. "You're not moving to Washington anymore, right?"

I pinched my brow. "No, that's still the plan." I only half-believed myself.

"And leave that!?" With her palm facing the sky, she reached her arm out towards Rhett. "My dear Kyla, if you move to Washington, I will gladly take your place as Mrs. Hartwell."

"I'm sorry . . ." I blinked, trying to register what she had just said. "What?"

"What did I miss?" Rhett came jogging up to us, his blue button-down shirt flying off to his sides. His silver belt buckle shined, making it hard not to notice.

"Absolutely nothing," I responded, turning to Grace and glaring at her. A silent plea to stop wherever she was going with the conversation.

"I'm going to convince Kyla to stay here," Grace blurted out, ignoring me completely. "Washington has nothing on this place."

Rhett folded his arms and widened his stance, looking at my friend as if she was *his* new best friend. "Please do, I'll forever love you if you could convince her to stay." His gaze met mine as his smile cocked to one side. "I'm quite enjoying her company."

"So, you two really got married? Like it's official, you are actually married," Grace asked Rhett as he handed her a glass of wine.

It was her third time asking that question. The first was in the airport, the second was during dinner and now here, in Rhett's cabin as we settled on the couch. It was as if she couldn't believe it, not until she had heard it a million times, or had seen it for herself. Her eyes were focused on Rhett as he nodded.

"Do you need to see the marriage license?" he asked, taking a seat next to me on the sofa across from her. He relaxed, his arm draped on the back of the couch as he sat close to me, with his knee touching mine and his fingers finding their way into my hair. He wasn't afraid of a little PDA, even if it was just in front of Grace. She knew every single detail of this charade, yet he still acted as if he was my husband. I welcomed his warmth though, even finding myself leaning into him a little.

"I mean, maybe," Grace said softly, taking a drink of her wine. "Not that it's hard to believe, it's just so crazy to think about. Did she tell you how long she was engaged to David?"

"Too long," I mumbled, raising my own glass to my lips.

I could feel Rhett's gaze turn to me and from the corner of my eye I saw him raise his beer to his mouth. "She did, well . . . he did. Two years?"

"Two years too long," I reiterated.

Grace scoffed. "I still can't believe he showed up. Have you seen him since?"

I shook my head. "Nope. Like I said, all for nothing."

"Well." Rhett let out a long breath. "Not for nothing."

Grace narrowed her eyes and nodded. "Honestly, I agree with the cowboy."

My jaw dropped slightly as I turned to look at Grace.

"What?" she exclaimed as she took another drink. "I'm just saying, I've never seen you like this. Never. And I've known you for a long time."

"Like what?" Rhett asked, bringing his forefinger to my jaw to close my mouth. I turned to him, trying to give him a glare, but when his smile hit, I couldn't help but give him a smile of my own.

"Relaxed. Content. Her shoulders aren't tense, and her breathing is normal. She's not worried about what she needs to do, or what she's going to say." Grace looked over at me and exhaled, a subtle look of ease crossing her features. "Happy. It's been a long time since I've seen you happy, Kyla. She used to be this way all the time. It's been too long, Kyla, and I really love seeing you like this."

"And that has something to do with her marrying me?" Rhett asked.

"I think it has everything to do with marrying you." Grace met my gaze and scrunched her nose. "But, I still need to see that marriage license."

Shaking his head giving a small chuckle, Rhett placed his beer on the coffee table and stood. "I'll go get it."

I watched as he disappeared into the room, making sure he was out of earshot before leaning towards Grace.

"What are you doing?" I whispered.

"Nothing, just noticing the things that you aren't."

I flopped back on the couch. "I never said I wasn't noticing them. I just . . . know it's not going to last."

Grace leaned forward this time. "Okay, but let me ask you something, why can't it last?"

Why can't it last?

I didn't answer her. I wanted to tell her that the thought of staying had entered my mind more than once, that staying with Rhett was a possibility, even though it wasn't a logical one. But the part of me that was louder was saying over and over again *it's only temporary.*

I opened my lips to tell her just that, defending the logical side of me when Rhett came bolting out of the bedroom, our marriage license in his hand.

"Here it is." Rhett handed Grace the cream piece of paper from behind her shoulder. "Proof that Kyla *is* Mrs. Hartwell."

"Mrs. Hartwell." Grace smiled at me as she took it. "Oo, love the date you guys got married."

Rhett took his seat next to me, his arm once again draped over the couch.

I rolled my lips. "David asked when I got married, and I blurted it out."

"And I"—Rhett looked over at me, a tight lip smirk growing—"made it happen."

I quickly turned my attention back to Grace, "He doesn't know where I've been, so he assumes I've been here the whole time. The marriage license is just in case he asks for proof."

Shaking her head lightly, she leaned forward and dropped the license on the coffee table. "Knowing him, he would want it, so"—she gave Rhett a wink—"good call. So . . . when's the rodeo?"

TWENTY

Rhett

THE DAY BEFORE THE rodeo was hectic, so I was grateful Kyla had Grace to keep her company. And by keeping her company, I meant sitting in the stands watching as we worked. But the moment the Ground Hog was brought out Kyla jumped from the stands. Even if it wasn't the arena that needed it, she was still excited to drive it around.

While Lachlan directed her where to go, I leaned on the gate, watching in awe as Kyla seamlessly drove the tractor. The fact that she caught on to driving the equipment only engrained it further in my brain that she was meant to be here.

"Hey, Rhett." I heard Grace come up behind me. She took a single step onto the gate, lifting herself to be taller than me.

"Hey, Grace," I responded, squinting to shield the bright ray of the sun. Grace was fixed on me, a crease on her forehead as she eyed me up and down. I felt it coming. The interrogation. The warning from the best friend. I bit the inside of my cheek, hard enough to draw blood, as I waited for her to turn.

"I see the way you look at her," she finally said. "You're really falling for her, aren't you?"

"Is it that obvious?" I winced, my finger and thumb began to spin the new ring on my left hand.

Raising her eyebrows, Grace tightened her lips and nodded.

"Is that bad?"

Shaking her head quickly she used her arms to stretch herself out on the gate. "Nope. It's great. I meant what I said. I haven't seen Kyla like this in a long time, and I am one hundred percent confident it's all because of you. So . . . try to keep her. She may not admit it yet, but this isn't temporary. I think she's falling for you too. She just won't admit it to herself."

My gaze turned to Kyla, as she drove the Ground Hog. Lachlan waved her back, and she laughed—a beautiful, genuine sound I could hear even over the loud engine. *A happy Kyla.*

"You think so?"

"I don't think, I know," Grace finished, jumping off the gate. "Listen, I'll support whatever it is you two decide to do. I'm on your team here. Just know"—she pointed at me, her eyes narrowing—"if you hurt her, I will cut off your favorite appendage with a dull wooden spoon."

Well, that was . . . terrifying.

"Is that even possible?"

"Anything is possible, Cowboy. Anything." Grace narrowed her eyes and pointed at me. "Never underestimate the power of a best friend."

"I can't believe I let him talk me into this," Abi grumbled as she knelt in front of Stetson, straightening his helmet for the tenth time. "How many concussions did you and Wyatt get from this?"

I laughed at my sister, watching the grin on my nephew's face grow as the time for Mutton Busting grew closer. Looking around the arena, I was amazed with how full the stands were. Almost every seat was taken and the hustle and bustle behind the chutes was just as crazy. Cowboys from all over had signed up to join in on tonight's Fourth of July rodeo, and with the barrel racing and bull riders, it was going to be a fantastic show. Even the fireworks at the end are going to be a hit.

There wasn't a better way to celebrate tonight.

The only thing missing down here was Kyla.

"A fair few," I remarked as Abi stood, her eyes heavy on her son. "You've fallen off your fair share of horses, Abi. At least he'll be close to the ground."

Abi turned her head and glared, her blue eyes stabbing into me.

"Oh, come on, Mom!" Stetson grumbled. "Don't embarrass me. I'm ready for this." He began to bounce up and down, his fists in front of him as he hyped himself up.

"See! The kid's excited." I motioned at my nephew. "I bet he'll make it all the way across the dirt. He'll win that first place ribbon."

"He'll get a ribbon no matter what," Abi grumbled, folding her arms in front of her chest.

"Sure, but he wants to hang on the longest."

Mutton Busting was the perfect event to start off any rodeo. Who wouldn't love to watch kids hold on for dear life as a sheep ran across the dirt. The kid that held on the longest "won" even though they all got a ribbon of some kind. It was an event that I had participated in numerous times, and I couldn't wait to see my nephew give it his all.

"First sheep and then bulls," Abi grumbled under her breath, running her hand down her face.

"No Hartwell is a bull rider, and I doubt Stetson is going to be the one to start that."

I knew Abi's mind was going to her late husband. The bull riding was what pulled Sylas into this world. At one point, she loved the event, but now she wouldn't stay to watch it. Thinking her son would follow in his dad's footsteps wasn't settling well with her.

"Nah, I want to do bareback like Uncle Lachlan!" Stetson shouted, raising his arms in the air.

"Oh, like that's any better," Abi snapped.

"It is, actually." I shrugged my shoulders, agreeing with Stetson. "He'll get Rookie of the Year."

"Oh Lord." Abi raised her chin to the sky, closing her eyes to exhale a deep breath. Her mom brain was moving a million miles an hour, taking in all of the things that could go wrong.

Pulling Abi close to me for a quick hug, I turned my eyes to the crowd. I knew Kyla was up there with Grace and my parents, but I wanted her down here with me. She had seen what I do from far away enough times, it was time to pull her in—completely immerse her with the rodeo world.

"Hey." I rubbed Abi's shoulder. "I'm going to go—"

"Yeah, yeah . . ." Abi stepped away, waving me off. "Go find Kyla."

"Bring Miss Kyla here!" Stetson jumped.

"I'll try." I patted his helmet and took off towards the stands.

Knowing where my family always sat, I didn't even have to think about where to go. Kyla was most likely seated right next to my mother, probably leaving a gap for Stetson when he returned. I glanced up at the stands, caught a glimpse of my mom quickly, and froze when I saw the yellow dress next to her.

My breath completely stopped when I saw her. She stood next to Grace, a white cowboy hat on top of her head, white boots donning her feet. The yellow sundress fit her like a glove, with a tie around her waist showing off all her curves. Her brown hair fell from the hat, drifting just past her shoulders with a slight curl, and was blowing slightly in the wind.

You're really falling for her, aren't you?

I had already fallen. There was no doubt in my mind.

I had fallen for Kyla.

I scooted past Grace, who thankfully saw me and made it possible for me to get to Kyla, before I grabbed her wrist and pulled her to me.

She gasped, her free hand reaching up to hold on to her hat as she came in contact with my body. The simple feeling of her against me was everything I could ask for. This woman had been the only thing that occupied my mind since the first time seeing her at the bar, and the smile that grew on her lips made me want to take her right here. Let everyone in the area know she was mine.

"Hey, Cowboy." Her laugh was like a drug as she placed her hand on my chest. I was addicted to the sound of her laughter and the feel on her palm against me. Nothing would ever be enough. I held her gaze as her smile grew. "Aren't you supposed to be down there?" She pointed to the arena dirt.

"I had to come get my girl." I ran my hand down her back, feeling her body loosen. "Come watch down where the action is."

"You sure?" She arched her back and pushed away. "I won't be in the way?"

"Trust me, no one will mind." I knocked the rims of our hats together before taking a step back, turning to Grace, my hand still firmly planted in hers. "It's okay I take her away, right Grace?"

"Please! Keep her as long as you'd like." Grace smiled, giving Kyla a wink as she passed.

"Good evening, Hartwell Rodeo Fans!" Wyatt's voice boomed overhead, making the crowd around us cheer. "Glad y'all could join us tonight for the annual rodeo, and the sold-out crowd makes this the biggest yet. I'm Wyatt Hartwell, up here in the box watching all the action from a safe distance as we track times and scores, and of course, we're starting the night off with Mutton Busting. All the kids are ready and raring to go. They are jumping around and cannot wait, so, first up is Heather Cart, a four-year-old from Boise!"

"Four years old!" Kyla shouted as the crowd cheered again.

"I was three." I turned back to her. "Come on, you're not going to want to miss Stetson."

"A 77 for Heather, not bad for a first run! Up next Gavin Jones. He won best time last year if I remember right, so let's see what he's got for us tonight . . . Oooo, 75." Wyatt was having way too much with this.

The noise from the crowd faded a tiny bit as we made our way behind the stands, back to where Abi stood with Stetson. Kyla had kept up with my pace, removing her hat as we quickly walked. She had two steps to my one larger step, and I had to force myself to slow down—to focus on her hand in mine as the crowd by the gates got thicker.

"And here we have my nephew, Stetson Acosta, who may be up for Rookie of the Year. I'm shocked my sister finally let him compete, but let's see what he's got and *whoo* there he goes!" Kyla let go of my hand and ran towards Abi, coming up next to her to watch Stetson, placing her hat back on her head.

The world disappeared as she jumped and clapped for Stetson—excitement radiating through her as she became immersed in the world around her.

The noises and crowds faded around us, and all I saw was her.

"An 89 for Acosta, sticking to the Hartwell rodeo genes!" Wyatt cheered, a small laugh to his voice.

Taking a breath to ground myself, I took a step towards Kyla, placing my hand on her lower back.

"Did you see that!" she screamed as she turned back to me. "He made it halfway!"

"My heart has never pounded so hard." Abi let out a deep breath, her hand to her chest. "This boy is going to get himself killed."

"89, Abi! 89!!" Kyla jumped.

"Miss Kyla!!" Stetson's small voice carried as he ran up, wrapping his arms around Kyla. His helmet was still on, but his left pant leg had ridden up past the top of his boots. The kid looked as if he were adrenaline in a bottle, ready to explode. "Did you see me!"

"I did, Stetson!" Kyla hugged him back as best she could while his arms were around her legs. "You were great. I can't believe it!"

"That sheep was not happy," he shouted, letting go of Kyla to turn to his mom. "I think I won."

Abi, who looked ten times more relaxed now, bopped her son on top of his head. "I think you did too."

"Mutton Busting now, bareback in ten years," I remarked.

"Ten years!" Abi screamed. "Make it twenty."

I laughed, slipping my hand in Kyla's, the electric feeling seeping through my skin. She turned to me, her eyes full of life and a smile on her face.

"Come on. Saddle Bronc is first, then Steer Wrestling, Bareback . . . then Tie-Down. You gotta meet a few guys." I leaned down to talk in her ear, her scent filling me. Vanilla with a hint of . . . lavender? That was new. I inhaled, taking her in.

She leaned, turning to look at me. Her lips close to mine, all I had to do was close that three inch gap and I would be kissing her. My breath hitched at just the thought of her lips on mine again. Glancing down at her lips, the light lip gloss made them shimmer, more enticing then I think they've ever been. All she needed to do was roll them together, and I wouldn't be able to stop myself. Instead, she smiled.

"I so badly want to kiss you," I whispered, admitting that truth my brain was crying out, leaning in a little closer.

She took a deep breath, her chest moving as she breathed in and out. She stiffened slightly, her eyes darting quickly as she looked at me. She tightened her lips—almost like she was holding in something she wanted to say. Had she ever been told someone wanted to kiss her? The words she had spoken on our first night rang through my ears. *No one has ever talked to me this way before; I'm not used to it.*

Resting my cheek against hers, I felt her sharp intake of breath. "Has anyone ever told you that?"

A shaky breath leaving her, she slightly shook her head.

"Mrs. Hartwell," I whispered in her ear, gravel filling my voice, "I'm just getting started."

TWENTY-ONE

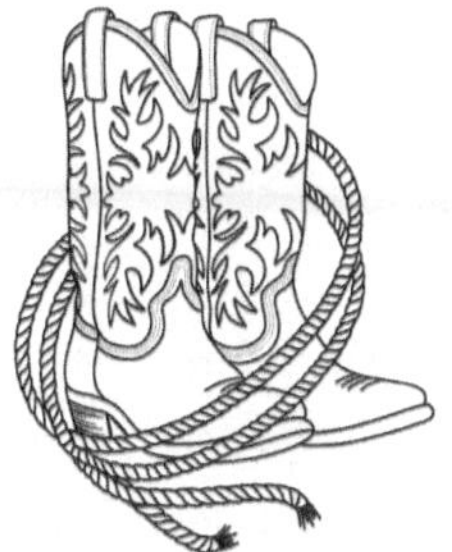

Kyla

RHETT FLOATED BETWEEN EVENTS—HELPING cowboys, attending to Buckle, getting steers in the chutes. And I followed him, trying to hold myself together after hearing his voice in my ear.

I'm just getting started.

I had to figure out what was going through my head when it came to him. I loved the way he made me feel when we were together. I craved the sparks that flew between us and the complete mode of confidence that surged through me. I was an entirely different person. I was, as crazy as this sounded, becoming who I wanted to be.

How I wanted to feel.

Rhett made me feel . . .

Different.

The morning at the ranch was short lived, and even though Rhett assured me the Fourth of July was a busy day, I still missed his presence the moment breakfast was done. His mom, as promised, made a large breakfast, complete with everything you could imagine to eat. Once everyone had their fill, they made their way to their jobs for the day. Rhett and Wyatt left for the arena while Lachlan and the ranch hands went to get the daily tasks done. Abi, Grace and I stuck to the stables, helping Stetson with his chores and a few Mutton Busting runs at home before he was itching to get to the rodeo.

Abi dragged us into town to invest in my own set of boots and hat. Telling me they were more for fashion than work, she supported the decision to buy the white pair. I saw Rhett eye that yellow dress, and these would be perfect to match it, and the second he saw me in the stands I knew he liked what he saw. Just being scooped in his arms made my stomach twist. It even made me forget that I had seen David while we were in town.

He made it a point to come up to us while we shopped, saying, "I'll see you at the rodeo," before forcing me into a hug. Abi grabbed my arm and pulled me away, my nerves rising as he got further from us. From the moment we got back to the ranch—from the moment Rhett pulled me into his arms—I was watching for him, my mind consumed with the worry of what would happen once he showed up. I tried to spot him in the crowd, to no avail, and then once I was with Rhett that feeling seemed to vanish.

And he told me he wanted to kiss me. The memories from the day we got married, the time he kissed me in the rodeo arena, the heat that came with every kiss, flooded through my veins. I wanted to tell him he could kiss me, but we were walking a fine line, and I didn't quite know what side to step on.

I knew which side I wanted to be on. It was telling myself I deserved it.

Stepping up onto the gate, I raised myself above the rest of the crowd to watch Rhett as he rode. Buckle shot out after the calf as Rhett swung the rope in the air for a matter of seconds before he roped the calf, jumping off the saddle with ease. I watched his every move. The way his arms flexed as he raised the calf in the air, his legs kept him balanced as he worked quickly to tie the legs. The way he raised his arms in one quick motion, standing and jogging back to his mare, fixing the hat on his head. The way his jeans pulled against him as he mounted. The way he looked over towards me, and winked. . .

The way he was everything.

Summer of Rhett Hartwell . . . my husband.

I didn't even hear the commentary Wyatt was saying about his run. I was too enchanted by what I was watching firsthand. Rhett guided Buckle back to the arena and his eyes locked on mine. He jumped off, handing the reins off to someone else, before making a direct path towards me, only taking four or five long steps before his boot hit the metal rail and he rose. Removing his hat, he dipped his head and his mouth found mine instantly.

The kiss was deep and raw as his hand found the back of my neck, his tongue forcing my lips apart as he drank me in. I moaned against his lips, reeling in the feeling of him. I grew dizzy, fearing I would fall off the gate if it weren't for his hand on me and my hand firm on the railing. The sounds of the crowd disappeared, the cheers and the roars—there was only us. The warmth, the buzz, the sensation of feeling . . . *whole.*

He broke the kiss and smiled, his nose gently brushing against mine as he pulled away. "Worth the wait," he murmured as a corner of his lips tipped up when he bent to kiss me again, a sweet kiss that was just as knee weakening as the hungry one.

"And if ya'll didn't know." Wyatt's voice came back into my mind as Rhett jumped off the gate. "That is my brother's wife. Ladies and Gentlemen, Kyla Hartwell attending her first Hartwell Hills Rodeo!"

My eyes were still locked on Rhett as he backed away from me, his chin motioning up toward the small "big" screen that sat next to the announcer box. I turned, only to see an image of myself, and I felt the heat rush to my cheeks, but instead of shying away I gave the crowd a small wave. I glanced at Rhett again, shaking my head slightly before eyeing the rest of the crowd.

"She has swept my brother off his feet and from my guess, she'll always be here now to give him an award-winning kiss. That run put Rhett in the lead, actually beating his best time of 7.6 with a 7.2."

My jaw dropped as I turned to Rhett.

He beat his time.

He tilted his head, and held his arms out, giving me the cockiest smile that warranted an even cockier one from me. He knew he beat his time the moment he raised his arms in the air after roping the calf, and the first thing he wanted to do was kiss me. Grabbing the reins, he waved to the crowd as he walked off, making room for the next rider.

Jumping off the gate, I made my way towards him at the end of the arena. He led Buckle with her reins as they walked slowly towards the back as another roper was getting ready to take his turn. The moment I got close enough to him, I ran, wrapping my arms around his neck, my hat falling from my head.

"You beat your time!" I exclaimed into his neck. "You beat it!!"

"I did." He chuckled. "I had to get a winning ride to get a winning kiss."

"Well." I arched my back, leaning away from him. "You still haven't won, technically. There are other ropers to—"

I was silenced when his lips met mine in another deep and sensual kiss.

"I beat my time and kissed my girl," he muttered against my lips. "I won."

My girl . . .

I raked my teeth against my bottom lip. "You did win, didn't you?"

"I believe you dropped your hat," I heard a voice from behind me, making me pull away from Rhett slightly. David stood there, holding my hat in his hands. "It's new, isn't it? Don't want to ruin it. Don't know why you picked a white one when brown would've been more practical."

Rhett reached out and took my hat from him, placing it back on my head. I turned in his arms, standing off to his side, looking at David as he stood still in front of us. He had on a pair of jeans and a short sleeve button-up shirt. On his feet—to my surprise—was a pair of brown boots. I had to give him some credit, he was trying to blend in. That is, until I saw the ostentatious Rolex on his wrist, which left him standing out like a sore thumb.

"Enjoying the rodeo?" Rhett asked simply, his eyes beating down on David.

I felt his arm tighten around me as he pulled me closer. His body tensed as he held his ground, attempting to look like he wasn't going to shoot David where he stood.

"Yes, actually. It's my first rodeo . . ."

Rhett snorted. I looked up at him and gave him a small smile. I could feel that confidence Rhett offered leaving as David's presence lingered there. The anxiety he always created wanted to beat it out so badly, and I was worried I would let it. I inhaled and swallowed, focused on Rhett's arm around my waist.

"Not ours," he retorted. "We met at a rodeo. Brings back amazing memories, doesn't it, Baby?"

Baby.

David knitted his brow. "I honestly can't picture Kyla willingly attending a rodeo," he condescended.

"Well, to be fair," I retorted, "you never let me go anywhere. I'm shocked to see you here."

David's eyes flew to me, and they narrowed. Normally, if I said something like that he would argue right back, telling me it was my fault I never went anywhere, but instead, he replied to me as if there was nothing wrong with the conversation.

"I told you I would see you here, this is the biggest event in the town. And I hear there are fireworks tonight." David forced a smile.

"There sure is. We put on quite the shindig." Rhett moved his free arm. I noticed Buckle's reins for the first time since I found him.

He tugged her a bit closer, only a few steps until her nose was right next to Rhett.

"Another reason to be interested in your ranch, Mr. Hartwell. Too bad you've been knocked off the leader position." David stuffed his hands in his jean pocket and turned to the screen.

He was right, Jaxson had beaten Rhett by point one second, knocking Rhett to second place. Rhett didn't seem at all phased by it. In his words, he had already won.

"Can I help you, David? Or are you just here to ruin the moment?" Rhett snapped.

"I'm just enjoying the festivities." David looked around. "May as well take in the town while I'm here. I always get to know the area of places I intend to buy. This will make a great tourist destination." I bit the inside of my lip. He did travel to places he wanted to invest in, that wasn't a lie. But wanting to buy the ranch, that was a different story. Even if it was a cover, he was playing the part very, very well.

"We prefer our town to stay like it is—small," Rhett added. "If you'll excuse us, David, I have to get my mare settled in her stall before the bull riders go up. I hope you enjoy the rest of the rodeo, and I highly suggest you stay out of here, the livestock can get a little rowdy."

Rhett's arm slid from my back, latching onto my hand to pull me away from David.

"Kyla," David said suddenly, causing us both to stop. "Could I talk to you in private, please?"

I looked at Rhett and saw him furrow his brow. Before he could even open his mouth, I placed my hand on his chest, making sure that ring was in David's line of sight.

"I'll meet up with you, okay?" I gave him a soft smile, hopefully relaying that I was okay.

Giving David one more glance, Rhett gave me a nod, kissing my hand before letting go to lead Buckle away. Once his back was turned, he looked over his shoulders, his eyes dark from the rim of his hat. I folded my arms and looked back at David.

"What?" I asked bluntly, wanting this conversation over before it even started.

"I want you back."

"Tough shit," I snapped. *Good start, Kyla.* "In case you forgot—"

"You married a cowboy. Yeah, Kyla, a ring on your finger doesn't prove that."

"I have the marriage license if you'd rather see that," I said sarcastically, thanking god Rhett had the courage to make the marriage legal.

David shook his head, his eyes closed tight as if he was searching his brain catalog for the exact words to say. "I was an idiot," he began, his voice softening as he took a single step towards me. "I waited for you to come back, to come *home,* but figured out that you weren't . . ."

"So, what, you had to track me down on your own?"

"Not like you made it easy," he bit out, turning his head, his tone changing. The softness he had mere seconds before was gone. "You were actually hard to find."

"You're admitting you looked for me?"

"Why wouldn't I have looked for you? You're my fiancé, Kyla. We were supposed to get married this summer. Instead, I find you married to some hick." He raised his arm in the direction where Rhett had gone. I could still see Buckle in the distance, Rhett holding tight to her reins as he talked to another man.

"I married a *cowboy*. That cowboy swept me off my feet from the moment we met. He made me feel loved and cared for and *worshiped*." I glared at him, pausing only to relish in the way his eyes flared when I spoke. "He loves me, David. That's more than can be said about how you felt."

I was even shocked with what came from my lips. David took a deep breath and took a single step towards me. I held my ground. His entire demeanor changed once I finished. There was a fire behind his eyes, one that was burning to take over. His line from earlier, *"I was an idiot, I want you back"* was all a part of his ploy. He took another step, a breath hissing through his lips as he got closer.

He lowered his head and as soon as his cheek was close to me, he whispered, "I know you haven't been here for as long as you're saying. I know your *marriage* isn't real. It's just to get me to back off, but I won't be. You're mine, Kyla."

I pulled my head away and looked at him, pinching my brow. My heart faltered, my breath stopped. He had me. He had me backed into a corner and I didn't know what to do from here. That courage I had found was gone—vanished—just like his fake smile and care. He knew exactly what to say to get a rise out of me and I hated that he was going to win.

I clenched my teeth to keep my jaw from quivering. I couldn't let him see that he was getting to me. That the fear was still there. It still lingered no matter what I did, still made my stomach twist and the anxiety boil. I tried to force myself to think about the time I had spent with Rhett. Those were the moments when I felt safe and secure—the moments where I could be myself. But David reminded me it wasn't real. It was only a temporary feeling.

But I couldn't let him see that. I took a deep breath and swallowed, pulling the courage I knew was in there somewhere.

"I met Rhett at a rodeo in February in Arizona, he invited me to come with him and I had such an amazing time with him that I agreed. We got married in April after realizing we never wanted to be apart. Come to terms with it. I was never happy with you, but I am insanely happy with Rhett."

Pinching his brow, David locked eyes with me.

"I know what you're doing," I continued, rolling with it. "Rhett knows what you're doing. You're not here to try to buy his ranch or enjoy festivities. But David, this game you're trying to play, it's not going to work."

David inhaled, raising his chin to look down at me. "I'm not the one playing a game, Kyla. You're the one who dragged Rhett into this. You're the one playing the game. Not me."

"You're not going to twist this to be my fault." I defended myself, willing the tears to stay back.

He didn't deserve anymore from me.

"I'm not twisting anything." He backed away and then smiled. The man actually smiled at me, turning back into the perfect person he wanted everyone to see. "It's good to see Grace made it out to visit you. I'm sure your mom will be next; she'll have to meet her *son-in-law* at some point."

"My mother hasn't spoken to me since I left you."

"With good reason. She supported our marriage, not whatever this is." He sighed, his hand waving around as he looked at the rodeo. Lowering his head, he closed his eyes, his fist clenching at his side. Silence for a few beats, David finally opened his eyes, fake tears pooling in them. "I still love you, Kyla. You still mean the world to me, and I will be leaving here with you."

I was an idiot.

You're the one playing a game.

I still love you.

I will leave here with you.

I shook my head and began to turn my body, "No, I think I'll stay here with Rhett."

TWENTY-TWO

Rhett

"You sure I can't kill him?" I asked Kyla as we stood next to a pen holding some horses while we waited for the fireworks to start. She wasn't gone for long, but the five or ten minutes she had been alone with David was enough to start a fire in me. "Or at least punch him?"

"I'd rather you not stoop to his level," she said softly, reaching over the bar to pat a horse on the nose. "He's just trying to rile me—*us*—up. He says he knows this marriage isn't real." Her voice was low—hesitant.

"Yeah well," I grumbled, trying to keep my composure together. "He riled me up for sure. I didn't think I'd see him here."

Kyla sighed, keeping her attention on the mare that had come up to her, no doubt looking for an apple. She had been quieter since she told me about her talk with him. I could see the wheels in her head turning, her brain overthinking as anxiety rose. It was the same look she had the night before I left and after we were married. Nerves were settling as she took a deep breath, leaving the horse to adjust the hat on her head, pulling the rim down so I had to tilt my head to see her eyes.

"I saw him," she admitted, almost as if she didn't want to. "While we were out this afternoon. I knew he was going to be here." She lowered her hand and let out a long breath. "I hate that even after all this time, after all the therapy and starting over, he still gets to me."

I kept quiet, not truly knowing where to place myself in this. I wanted to protect her, offer her things she never had before. In the short time that we had spent together, she was becoming more than I thought she would. I was able to see things differently when she was around. Heat flooded through me with just a single touch and when we kissed . . . the spark was undeniable.

"Kyla." I reached out and gently took her hand in mine. "I want to . . ."

She turned, her gaze focused on our hands as our fingers laced together. My brain was completely blocked. Frozen at the gate. I heard her breathe, slow at first, but becoming deeper the longer our hands stayed fused together. I tried to will the words to come. To tell her exactly what I wanted for her, for us. But since those words were refusing to come, I told her the opposite.

"I don't want you to leave."

"To end the night." I heard Wyatt's voice over the speaker. "Turn your gaze to the east, the fireworks will be starting in just a moment . . ."

But instead of focusing on the east, where everyone had turned, I looked at the beautiful woman in front of me. Her jaw was tight, and her brow pinched. Her eyes—as much as I hated to see it—were wet with tears.

"Stay here, where you're wanted and where you can let loose and be free. I don't want you to leave," I said again, pulling her closer to me still.

She furrowed her brow, a shaky breath coming from her mouth. "I don't want to leave . . ." she finally muttered.

"Then don't."

"Aren't you leaving on the circuit again?" she protested. "What am I supposed to do when you're not around? It's different with you. The moment you left me alone with David, it felt just like it did before—like I was stuck, and he knew he had me. I could tell by the look on his face. He knew it."

"He doesn't have you. He never did."

Kyla tipped her head, scoffing as she glanced towards the east. "Yeah well, he thinks he does. He said he's not leaving this place without me. With you back on the circuit, I guarantee you he will think he can 'win me back.'" She air quoted with her fingers. "I don't want to be alone here while you're gone. Not while knowing he's here."

"Come with me," I blurted out.

"Come with you? To rodeos?"

"Yeah, why not? It's gotta be on that bucket list of yours now, right?"

"Well, I just saw one . . ."

"This one doesn't count. Wait until you see Cheyenne, or Days of 47. Hell, the Western Stampede. I have a great line-up coming up, and Kyla, I'd love to have my wife there with me."

My wife.

I loved the sound of that.

I lifted her left hand and kissed right above her ring, bringing a soft smile to her lips.

"No tutoring Stetson. No watching Josie get branded . . ."

"What!?" Her eyes widened.

"No David," I continued. "Just you and me on the road."

"Josie is getting branded?"

"Come with me, Kyla." I placed my hands on her waist, feeling the heat of her body under the yellow sundress.

Just looking in her eyes I could see her calm. The tension in her shoulders released and the breath she was holding left her nose. She closed her eyes as the air left her, and she leaned towards me. Keeping my hands firm on her waist, I could feel the weight of everything lift and she was able to breathe. She gave me a soft laugh before she ran her hands up my chest, settling on my shoulders. I loved the feeling of her weight on me, even if it was for a brief moment.

"Okay." She smiled. "I'll go."

A firework boomed overhead, causing Kyla to jump slightly. Laughing at herself, she rested her body against mine, breathing for the first time since I had left her alone.

"But really," I said, running my fingers down her spine, "are you sure I can't at least punch him?"

"No punching."

Lifting a hand from her waist, I used my thumb and forefinger to bring her gaze back to mine. I ran my thumb on her lower lip. Her heated eyes met mine and the glow from the fireworks lit up her skin. Breathtakingly beautiful, she had managed to stop the panic and anxiety before it even began to settle. She was more confident than she gave herself credit for.

"Kiss me," she said, her voice heavy. "Mr. Hartwell."

I smiled, lowering my lips to hers. The sweet taste of her lips against mine, the thrill each kiss brought. This woman . . . Grace was more than right. I was so far gone.

The following morning, I woke before Kyla and Grace, watching as they both staggered out of the bedroom as if they had been drinking the entire night. Granted we got back from the arena later than planned, and Grace had all but disappeared before the fireworks. It took Kyla a few laps around the arena to find her already waiting for us by the truck. Besides asking her if we had seen David, she was just as quiet as Kyla had been, dragging her into the bedroom the moment we walked into the house.

Grace grumbled next to me, reaching for a coffee mug.

"Good morning." I chuckled.

Pinching her brow, she turned to look at me. "No talking before coffee."

"Grace." Kyla yawned, rolling her eyes as she watched her friend pour the coffee into a giant mug. "We need to drink our coffee quickly and then head to the airport. What are you up to today, Cowboy?"

"Well, Mrs. Hartwell." I smiled at her, leaning up against the counter. "Lachlan and I are moving the livestock back. I'll be gone most of the day." I took a drink from my mug, she didn't need to know what else I had planned for the morning before heading to the arena. "Miss Grace"—I turned to Grace, who still looked like she wanted to murder someone as she gripped her mug with both hands—"it was great to meet you, I'm sure we will see each other again."

"You know it. I think I convinced her . . ."

"I hope so." I winked at her, wishing I had more time to stay with them, but one quick glance at the clock told me I was already late. I didn't even know if David was going to be there, but I had high hopes he didn't travel far. "I'll see you at dinner."

"Okay, have fun!" Kyla called after me as I placed my hat on my head and headed out the door.

The trailer was already attached to the truck and Wyatt was lazily waiting for me. I double-checked my back pocket for the envelope before patting him on the shoulder. He wasn't happy we had roped him into helping transport, but he would do his part—even if it was a waste of time for him. However, he didn't ask questions when I pulled into the only hotel in town instead of going to the arena.

He gave me one quick glance, his eyebrow raised to his hairline, as I parked. He pulled his hat down over his eyes and rested his head against the seat.

"Just don't do anything stupid, " he grumbled.

"I'm not," I answered, turning off the truck.

Wyatt gave me a deep groan. One I quickly ignored as I made my way into the hotel.

I noticed David instantly. He was sitting at a booth in the attached restaurant, with a small cup of coffee and a plate with eggs and toast in front of him. He was looking at his phone, already dressed in a suit and tie. He lifted the mug to take a drink.

It would be a shame if it spilled.

But I promised I wouldn't do anything stupid.

Pulling the envelope from my pocket I slid in the booth cross from him, taking my hat off and placing it on the table.

"I hope you're having a decent morning, David."

Licking his lips, he set the mug back down, reaching for the cloth napkin. "Ah, Rhett, just the person I was hoping to see this morning."

"Yeah, I'm sure of that. You were going to head over to the ranch, weren't you?"

"Yes, I was hoping to." He smiled that same business smile I had seen before.

Don't punch him.

I hummed. "Well, let's save the gas, shall we. Let's get one thing clear. My ranch isn't for sale. It will never be for sale, and you are going to give up on this little charade of yours. Kyla may not be brave enough to say it, but that doesn't mean I won't."

"I'm not sure I know what you're—"

"No, I'm not done talking." I stopped him, keeping my voice steady and calm. *Smooth.* I slid the envelope towards me, slowly pulling out my marriage license. "As you can see here, Kyla and I are married. Been married since April. I don't know where you think she's been, but I can assure you she's been right here with me." I held the license up, making sure he had enough time to really take it in. "So, here's what's going to happen." I put the license down and relaxed in the booth, my arm draping over the green vinyl. He reached forward and grabbed the paper, reading it over once more. "I have to go to the arena to move the livestock, Kyla is at the ranch, and you? You are going to leave. You're going to check out of the hotel, get in your fancy car and get the hell out of my town. I don't want to see you again. If you ever come near Kyla, I will call the police, and trust me, they like me a hell of a lot more than they like you."

Lifting a single brow, David's gaze met mine. Clearing his throat, he used the folds on the license to neatly hand it back to me.

"I've told you, Mr. Hartwell, everything is for sale. I also told you I'm not leaving here without my fiancé. I don't care what this fake piece of shit paper says. It's a game she's playing, and she's roped you into it."

I barked out a laugh. "Nice pun."

That caught him off guard. He blinked before he scoffed out a smile. "It's all a game, Mr. Hartwell."

I shook my head. "Kyla's not playing a game. You are. Kyla is starting to see she deserves more than the bare minimum, and I plan to give that to her. You, David, are the bare minimum. She's happy, she's finally feeling free. But trust me"—I took my marriage license and slid it in the envelope, sliding myself out of the booth—"if you don't take my advice and leave, it's not going to look good for you. I'm sure Kyla would gladly punch you."

"Is that a threat?"

"No, just a statement. After all you've put her through, I wouldn't imagine her saying anything less."

"And what if Kyla isn't happy? She told me so last night. You must be—"

"If you think I'm going to believe anything that comes out of your mouth you have something else coming. I told her I wouldn't do anything stupid, so I'm leaving it at that. You have your proof that she's my wife and I'd greatly appreciate it if you left us alone."

I picked up my hat and placed it on my head, seeing a single slice of bacon left on his plate. I reached down and grabbed it, popping it in my mouth.

"Have a great day and a semi-safe drive home." I tipped my hat, chewed the bacon, and turned my back to leave.

TWENTY-THREE

Kyla

SAYING GOODBYE TO GRACE was harder than I thought it would be, especially with how she was acting. Grumpier than normal, she assured me it was due to one-to-many drinks at the rodeo, and since she refused to open up about anything, I trusted her.

I gave her a hug and didn't let go, practically begging her to come back soon.

"I mean, wherever I am, please come," I reiterated.

"You'll be here," she said back, giving me a final squeeze before grabbing her bag. She blew me a kiss and stepped into the terminal, turning back one more time to give me a wave.

You'll be here.

She was so certain.

I pulled up to the arena just in time to see Rhett leading horses into the trailer. I pinched my brow when I noticed he wasn't on Buckle. Of all the times I had seen that man on a horse, it was his Paint horse. But today he was mounted on a simple brown coat. Once Wyatt shut the trailer, he pulled the horse in my direction, a smile crossing his face as soon as we made eye contact. Giving me a wink, he turned, directing the horse back towards the pens.

I climbed the stairs to the stands and sat in the first row I came to, shoving my hands between my thighs.

You'll be here.

I noticed Abi step out of the truck first, her boots hitting the ground with a thud and her blonde hair flying under her hat. Stetson rounded the corner and ran after his mom, the dust from the ground trailing after him. Wyatt was still by the trailer, making sure the horses were locked in. Then there was Lachlan. Mounted on his black horse, his black hat on his head as he rounded the bulls, he wore a smug look on his face. He made eye contact with me and nodded his head, breaking the eye contact when I gave him a wave.

I could very easily get off the stands and find a way to help, but just watching them work was . . . relaxing.

You'll be here.

"Hey, Mrs. Hartwell. How was the drive?"

The sound of boots clanging on the metal forced me to turn. Rhett walked up the steps towards me. I didn't even notice him get off the dirt, he just appeared. My breath caught as he sat down next to me, leaning back on his elbows on the seat behind him, his knees apart. I caught his scent and turned to look over my shoulder at him.

"Good. I miss her already," I admitted spinning on the stands so I was straddling the bench. I lightly reached out and ran my fingers against his knee.

"What's on your mind, Mrs. Hartwell?" he asked, a calmness to his voice he knew I needed.

"There wouldn't happen to be rodeos in Arizona you can piggyback on? Maybe a day with Grace?" I asked, half-joking, half-hoping he would instantly add another day to the already long trip. But to see Grace again, even though she was just here, would be amazing.

"There's always rodeos in Arizona." He winked, his lips curling to a grin. "We can make that work. It's not too late to get on the board, but that also lengthens the time we're gone."

"That's fine," I said quickly.

"You're not worried about getting to Washington or anything?" Rhett dipped his chin and raised an eyebrow.

Washington?

I met his eyes for a split second, taking a deep inhale. Holding it for a few beats before letting it free. What was in Washington? Technically a job, which would give me a salary, a means to get back to teaching. But that was it. It was a way to "adult" and have the "logical" side of my life happy. But here—*here*—with Rhett's knee lightly touching mine as the summer breeze hit his hair just right, that eyebrow still cocked, the logical side of me wasn't screaming like it normally did. I watched as the Hartwell Family moved around the arena. Laughs filled the air as Stetson ran after a calf that broke free before making it into the trailer, even Lachlan smiled.

I started to roll my lips, but stopped and parted them slowly, releasing a slow laugh.

What about Washington . . .

Washington was logical, but here I felt a sense of security that was stronger than the logic Washington would offer.

I heard nothing but Grace's voice.

You'll be here . . .

I smiled and turned to Rhett. "No, not really," I admitted, not only to him but to myself. Washington didn't seem like it was real anymore. "I like it here."

"If we add Arizona," Rhett said as he looked at the computer screen with an atlas next to him on the kitchen island, "it would add two days to the trip, but they are still accepting cowboys, so . . ." With a smirk and not lifting his chin, a single eyebrow rose as he caught my glance. "Shall we go to Arizona?"

I leaned on the kitchen island and mirrored his smirk. "Are you sure?"

That eyebrow raised higher. "We met there, remember?" He winked. "Let's add it to the list." Pulling his attention back to the computer, he used his fingers to type away, silent as his eyes ran with the screen. "Done. Registered. Now . . ." Turning his body he grabbed the atlas.

"Who uses an atlas?' I pushed myself off the counter and walked around the kitchen island, coming up next to him. "Google Maps exists for a reason." I was tempted to run my hand across his shoulders, touch him like I knew he would want me to. That part of me still craved him nonstop, but the logical part stopped myself. He shook his head at me as he plugged in Google Maps on his computer. I smiled and reached for the atlas, sliding it towards me. "You know," I said, my mind instantly turning to the one thing it should after seeing the city of Phoenix on the map, "my mom is in Arizona."

Why did my mind even go to the subject? I was avoiding my mother—I hadn't seen her since I left David—but there was this sudden, strange pull to reach out to her. To tell her about Rhett, about the ranch and the happiness I found here. Would she accept it? Or, like David, know it was all a farce? I could just imagine driving up to her lavish house in Phoenix—Rhett's white truck dusted with mud getting tracks on her pristine driveway. Would she open the door and hug me, welcome me home, and say she was happy I was safe? Or would she roll her eyes?

He cocked his head and turned to me. "Should we pay her a visit?"

I shook my head. "I'd rather not but . . ."

At the end of the day, she was my mother and I wanted her to accept me.

"Kyla." Rhett turned, slipping his arm around my waist, pulling me towards him. "Are you wanting to go visit your mom?"

I pressed into him, feeling his heat as my hands found his shoulders.

"It's probably better she finds out through us and not through—"

"David," he finished for me.

I sighed as the thought of him mentioning my mother at the rodeo resurfaced. Bringing Rhett to meet my mother would most likely add fuel to their fire.

"Do you want me to meet her?"

"Well, you're my husband." I raised my shoulders and rolled my lips. "You should, shouldn't you?"

The corner of his lips tipped up, creating a small dimple I hadn't noticed before. His eyes searched mine, landing on my mouth. He was going to kiss me; I could sense it. Deciding to bring my courage back, I leaned forward and kissed him sweetly before he could even make his thought a reality.

"I should," he said softly against my lips.

"What if she doesn't want to meet you?" I argued, closing my eyes, dropping my forehead to his shoulder.

I felt his hand touch the back of my head, his fingers making small circles on my scalp. "Then I'll shake her hand and bring you back home. I don't know if you've figured this out yet, or not, Kyla, but I quite like having you here, and you admitted it yourself, you like it too."

"Home?" I raised my head, his fingers still tangled in my hair.

"Home. Here. With me. Maybe once your mother sees your smile she'll come around. She'll see how happy you are with somebody like me—"

"Somebody like you, huh?" I cut him off. "You're so sure of yourself, aren't you?"

"Damn straight. I knew from the minute I saw you in the bar that you needed me." He smirked, knowing very well that he was using his charm to get my brain to stop spinning. Biting my lip, I couldn't help but grin when it started working.

"Uh huh, sure. I think your exact words were 'I'm coming over before my friends do something stupid.'"

"I'm glad I did, aren't you?"

I glanced at my left hand on his shoulders, the small ring still sitting there, having not once left my finger since he slipped it on after he proposed.

"I'm glad," I admitted. "I just hope my mom will be at least a little happy."

"I'll cook her dinner. She won't be able to resist my chicken."

"Oh, Cowboy." I laughed. "She has a chef."

"Your mother has a *chef*?" Rhett blinked his eyes a few times, arching his back slightly.

"Oh yeah. She and my dad were loaded, and when he passed, she began to indulge in things." I stepped away from him. "She barely lifts a finger now.'

"Should I bring a tux?"

I let out a cough and turned from him, grabbing my cell phone from the counter. Rhett in a tux? As fabulous a sight as that may be, I closed my eyes just to picture him. Jeans covered in dust, sleeves rolled up to show off his perfect forearms, scruff on his chin, his hat perched just right—a cowboy that didn't belong in a tux. Handsome. Rugged. *Perfect.*

"I'd rather you not. I'm attracted to the rugged cowboy I met in the bar. I don't particularly want to ever see you in a tux." I smiled.

"I would suggest our wedding day for that but—"

"You wore Wranglers," I finished his sentence. "I better call my mother. Give her a heads up, talk to her." I looked at my phone, knowing I wouldn't find her contact there, but also knowing I knew her number by heart. I took a deep breath and typed the first few numbers, the rest flowing easier as the seven digits morphed onto the screen. "Okay . . . wish me luck."

"You don't need it." Rhett smiled as I walked out onto the patio. "You're stronger than you realize."

I gave him a soft grin, not sure it resonated as I intended. The look he gave me in return proved he could sense the anxiety I felt as I lifted the phone and listened to the ringtone.

"Hello?" My mother's voice hit me like a ton of bricks. I hadn't heard it in so long. She sounded the same, not a stitch different.

"Hi, Mama." My voice cracked.

I heard a gasp and then her voice was low. "Kyla?"

Giving Rhett a final soft smile, I stepped out of the house, not sure why I was wanting privacy for this phone call.

Kyla

Well, that could have gone better.

I sat on the porch after hanging up the phone with my mom, impatiently waiting for Grace to text me back. Once my mother heard my voice—once she got over the shock of me calling her—she retreated back to her normal ways. David had, of course, contacted her to tell her where I had been and who I was with. And—as expected—she didn't believe any of it.

She had assured me she didn't want to meet Rhett, that she wanted nothing to do with these decisions I was making. She was upset with me. She wasn't happy I left. Her exact words were, *"It's what we do—we put up with it. We make it work with the men who keep us."*

Keep us.

I didn't want to be kept. I wanted to be loved.

The conversation didn't last long, but it still left me in tears on the porch.

What the hell happened to that confident Kyla from earlier today? Why was this happening again?

I held my phone tightly in my hand, hoping that Grace would text back. Or call. It would be better if she called.

I sniffed, running the back of my hand on my cheek, wiping away my tears and taking mascara with it.

Maybe it was best she wasn't answering me.

Dropping my phone next to me I leaned on my elbows, shoving my face in my palms.

"I take it"—I heard from behind me, forcing me to look up, dropping my hands from my face—"she doesn't want to meet me?"

I spun around, finding Rhett leaning in the doorway, his legs crossed at his ankles, with his arms folded over his chest.

"I don't know why I thought that was a good idea. I knew she would react that way." I sniffed, turning away from him so he didn't have to see how ridiculous I looked.

"There was hope she wouldn't." Rhett sighed, moving so he was sitting down next to me, his arm sliding around my waist, gently pulling me into him. I welcomed his warmth. Closing my eyes, I leaned into him.

"She told me I was being childish, that I was being selfish and not thinking of what this *marriage* . . ." I said the word the exact same way my mother did. Snarky. Rude. With a hint of disgust in her voice. ". . . would do to those around me. Obviously thinking of her and David. That's all she ever really thinks about," I muttered the last part, knowing it was all too true, but hoping he didn't hear it enough to comment on it. I still hated that I was dragging him into the mess that was my life. He didn't need this.

But, I felt like I needed him. What he said earlier was right. It may have been a way for him to get me to calm down in the moment, but there was truth behind those words.

Somebody like him.

He sighed, and pressed his fingers into my shoulder. "If what you told me about your mother is accurate, she's more controlling than David."

I nodded. "She can be, but it's not her fault. My dad was that way. She was married to a David." Slowly I turned to him, using the back of my hand to rub my eyes once more. "Not a Rhett."

He chuckled, his forehead pressing against mine. "Ah, well not everyone is going to be as lucky as you are."

I knew he was trying to defuse the situation, trying to make me smile—to break the tears. Just knowing this man was next to me made the phone call with my mother less daunting. Yet again I found myself feeling calmer in his presence, just knowing he was there if I needed him. I had never ever felt this way, was never given a chance to.

I leaned my head on his shoulder, sniffing softly as I felt his fingers move on my shoulder, pressing in and out, acting as a grounding force. Just sitting with him made me forget about wanting a text back from Grace. Even when my phone dinged with her response, I just kept my head on his shoulder, relaxing in the quiet he brought with him.

TWENTY-FOUR

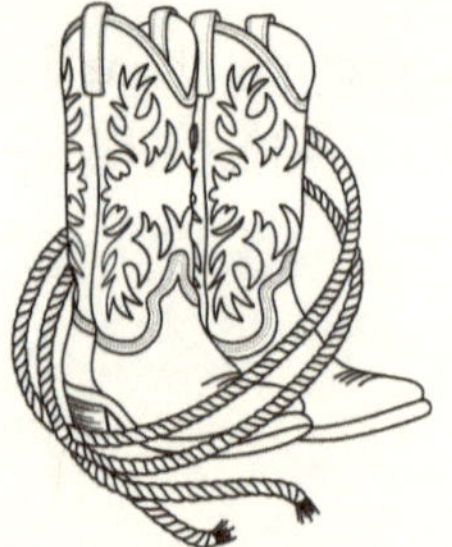

Rhett

KYLA YAWNED, STRETCHING HER arms over her head as she left the cabin. It was still dark, the light from the porch illuminating her as she made her way over to me and the truck. She looked comfortable, ready for the three-hour drive we had ahead of us wearing leggings and an oversized t-shirt. Her hair was in a messy bun, and she looked gorgeous.

"Morning, Mrs. Hartwell." I sauntered up to her, shoving my hands in my pockets to keep myself from scooping her up. "You ready for a few weeks on the road?"

"Actually . . ." She looked up at me and gave me a sexy, sleepy smile. My mind was suddenly taken back to the night we met. After we calmed our breaths she lay in my arms, and she had the same smile on her lips. She was relaxed, she was calm, and I still couldn't believe that in this moment she was mine. "I'm really looking forward to it. Just tell me I have enough time to get coffee."

I pulled my hand from my pockets and lightly reached out for her. Stepping into my embrace, she leaned her cheek on my chest. "I made some, did you see the thermos?"

She hummed, rolling her forehead before lifting her head. Her eyes were closed, but she softly spoke. "I think so? Honestly, I wasn't paying attention. I just knew to get dressed and come help you pack up the truck. Buckle's ready to go?"

"Yup. She's settled and ready for the drive. First ride is at 3, and then again at 7:30."

"Two rides today?"

I kissed her temple. "Then a hotel and all day on the road tomorrow to Montana."

"I've never been to Montana." Kyla yawned again.

"Bucket list?"

She chuckled. "Bucket list." Raising her head she put her chin on my collar bone. "What is there to see in Montana?"

"Everything," I replied.

Closing her eyes she relaxed into me. "Wyatt still sleeping?"

"He's not announcing these ones, he'll fly out to Billings and meet us there." I rubbed her back, feeling the way her body melted into my touch. "Today and tomorrow is all ours, Mrs. Hartwell."

"Believe it or not, I like the sound of that."

And I *loved* the sound of that.

I couldn't wait to get Kyla all to myself for the next forty-eight hours.

The days leading up to leaving were quiet. David hadn't shown his face at the ranch like he told me he was going to—which told me he had taken me seriously—and Kyla's mom had been sticking to text messages. She responded, but kept it simple and blunt. She had finally agreed to one dinner, that was it. I had even made sure to pack the marriage license just in case her mother needed to study it the same way David had.

I was preparing myself for the worst, ready to defend this union as much as I could.

I wanted Kyla to stay with me, I wanted her. And with how her body had eased into mine, I had a feeling she wanted it too.

Yawning again, Kyla sighed, her arms wrapping around my waist to tug me closer. I pulled myself away slightly, forcing her grip on me to loosen as I began to lead her back to the cabin. Everything was set and ready for us to climb in the truck and go . . . right after we got the coffee.

"We'll have time for me to change before the rodeos, right? I packed the sundress you like so much. I have to be hotter than those buckle bunnies you claim you know nothing about."

I stopped and pulled her back to me. I didn't even make it three steps before needing to be near her again. Her hands hit my chest as she looked up at me. Placing my hands on her lower back, I gracefully lifted my fingers under her t-shirt, pressing my fingertips into her skin.

"You're the only bunny I'll have my eyes on, Mrs. Hartwell."

Tilting an eyebrow, she shot me a glare. I knew the line was cheesy, but I gave her a grin all the same.

"You sure do like that nickname, don't you?" she grumbled before placing her forehead on my chest.

"It's the only one that fits."

"You promised coffee." She pushed off me. "And you didn't answer my question."

I laughed, following her into the cabin. I grabbed my hat and placed it on my head, watching as she found the two thermoses and filled them with coffee, yawning yet again.

"We'll get checked in at the hotel before I take Buckle over to the arena. Then the events start."

"Perfect, I'm sure you don't want the other cowboys to see your wife looking like this." She moved her head, making the bun wobble on her head. She turned and handed me my thermos, her eyes growing wide. "Do I have time to say goodbye to Josie before—"

"Kyla, your cow will be fine."

"Lachlan better not brand her." She glared at me as she came up, allowing me to place my hand on her lower back as we made our way back out to the truck, turning to lock the door behind us.

"He won't . . . probably."

After dropping Kyla off at the hotel, I went straight to the rodeo arena. I set Buckle up in her stall, making sure to give her hay and a peppermint, and once I knew she was settled I left to walk around the grounds. The rodeo was attached to a fair, complete with carnival games and a Ferris wheel. There were lines of vendor booths selling their crafts or clothes, and even a few face painting stations were set up. I caught a glance of flowers that adorned one vendor's booth, reaching for the brightest bouquet of sunflowers there.

I paid, holding the bouquet close to me, wishing Kyla was here.

She wanted to change and freshen up, assuring me she would meet me at the arena before my ride, but that didn't stop my eyes from searching the crowd, hoping to find her among the strange faces. Would she even think to find me here, or would she head straight to the arena?

As if she knew I was thinking of her my pocket buzzed, and Kyla's photo lit up my screen.

"Hey, Mrs. Hartwell," I answered, my eyes starting to look for her more than before.

"Hey, Cowboy," she responded. "So, I have no idea where to go. This place is a lot busier than I thought."

"I was just wondering if you were going to find me here. It's packed." I turned in a circle, thinking that she could be closer than I imagined.

"I don't think I could find you even if I tried. Meet me by . . ." Her voice faded, but then I saw her.

Kyla stood at the end of the vendor line, wearing a stunning lavender sundress, her white cowboy boots, and her hat perched on her head. The sun hit her just right . . . she was radiant. Even standing fifty feet away from her, I lost my breath, still in disbelief that she was my wife.

She looked around, the dress's skirt flowing around her thighs. Her eyes squinted as she searched for me.

"How 'bout this. Look for a cowboy wearing a tan hat and red button-down shirt, holding sunflowers." I took a step towards her, knots growing in my stomach as I got closer and closer to her.

"That's oddly specific. How about I head over to the arena."

"Or, you can look for the cowboy."

"You're close aren't you. You can see me?" She spun, her hair flying as she moved.

"Maybe."

"Rhett." She smiled and damn, my knees went weak.

"Kyla." I smiled back, getting closer to her. "You look gorgeous."

I could see her cheeks turn red as she went on her tiptoes, scanning the crowd. "It's not the yellow one, but I thought you would like this one just the same. Where are you?"

"I think this may be my new favorite dress of yours."

"Where"—she spun, her back to me now—"the hell are you!"

"Here." I came up to her side, dropping my phone to give her a kiss on her neck. "For you." I swung the sunflowers around and held them in front of her.

Arching her back, she looked over at me, taking the sunflowers from my hand, the heat in her cheeks deepening as she completely turned to face me. Her eyes danced as she brought the flowers to her nose, a small sigh filled the air between us, and when her lips lightly touched mine, I melted. Cowboys didn't melt, but here I was, turning into a puddle in front of her.

"You're stunning," I whispered against her lips, pulling myself back to her as I lifted my hands to cup her face. A faint blush moved across her cheeks as the butterflies in my stomach fluttered. It was involuntary when it came to her, everything was out of my control. Lightly trailing my thumb across her cheek, I found the will to form words again. "Just . . . wow."

Giggling softly, she lowered her chin and smiled. "Thank you." She sighed, her voice shaking slightly. "You're handsome as always. I thought this was a rodeo, not a fair."

"Most rodeos take place at state fairs, this just happens to be a county one. Buckle's set up and I have an hour. Walk with me?"

Lifting the sunflowers to her nose she hid her smile. I moved my hand to find hers, gently taking her palm. Her fingers clasped around mine quickly, and the sparks and heat flew up to my shoulder and down my body.

"Where are we going?" she asked, her body relaxing in mine as she stepped closer.

"We're at a county fair, let's get a terrible, overpriced corn dog, some funnel cake, and then head on over to the arena. Families have their own section—great seats." I squeezed her hand.

"You mean I can't stand down there while you take your ride and kiss you after?"

I let out a laugh. "Don't you want to enjoy the rodeo?"

"I want—" The loud ringing of her phone made her pause. Stopping to look at it quickly, she lifted her head back. "My mom."

Tugging her along, I pulled her attention back to my grip on her. "Don't answer. Remember, today and tomorrow are ours."

Silencing her phone she twisted, slipping it into the small bag on her shoulder before turning back to give me the sweetest kiss on my lips.

"Let me treat you like my wife."

She hummed. "Starting with an overpriced corn dog."

Three corndogs and two funnel cakes later, I ushered Kyla over to the seats. I didn't want to leave her alone in the stands, but Zeke's wife instantly linked arms with her and assured me she would be in good company. Jaxon and Zeke were already there waiting for me, ready to go. First was the Mutton Busting, where we got to rile up the sheep and hype up the kids, then we stood back and watched the Saddle Bronc and Steer Wrestling. But once it was Buckle's and my turn to run—the moment I roped that calf and mounted Buckle—I looked towards Kyla. Her smile was all I needed to know she was having the time of her life. The moment the rodeo was over, and the crowd dispersed I grabbed Kyla and headed to get Buckle in her trailer.

"Wait, I want to see Jaxson!" Kyla shouted as I tied Buckle up. "Can't we say 'hi' to the guys?"

"Jaxson will be at the rodeo tonight, so will Zeke, and I guarantee you they will drag us out for drinks later."

She turned, the dress flying as the dirt crunched under the heel of her boot. Her white boots were already covered in dust and dirt, but they still looked perfect.

"I like the sound of that. So," she began even though I had already started to make my way towards the cab of the truck. "Did this one qualify for the NFR?"

We both settled in the cab and buckled up, Kyla shifting in her seat to face me.

"It does, and it's a good time too."

"Still top in the nation?"

I turned the truck on and turned to her, smiling as I removed my hat and placed it on the dash. "Still top in the nation." Shifting the truck in gear I leaned across the console, wiggling my eyebrows at her as her smile grew. "You ready for the next one?"

TWENTY-FIVE

Kyla

I WAS LOVING THIS. Every second of it. Even if I was just sitting in the stands, watching the rodeo was thrilling. Watching *Rhett* was thrilling. I relished in the way he made me feel, enjoying the way his arms felt around my waist as he enveloped me. All the fears and anxieties that seemed to follow me simply weren't there when I was with him. A part of me wanted to feel like this forever.

But . . . why couldn't I? Why did I have to let the background thoughts of this temporary marriage shadow the way my heart fluttered when I saw him. He had said it himself several times. It *was* real. And right now, I wanted nothing more than for it to be real.

Rhett placed third in his second run, and after Buckle was settled, we raced back to the hotel to change and get ready for the night out. Rhett kept his Wranglers and boots on, but quickly removed his shirt covered in sponsor patches, only to replace it with a simple green t-shirt. It fit him just snug enough, showing off the way his chest was formed. Just looking at him made me want to reach out and touch him, slip my fingers up his shirt to feel his skin against mine. Biting my bottom lip I began to sway, watching him with anticipation.

"If I didn't know any better, Mrs. Hartwell, I'd say you were ready to hit the town." His laugh hit my ear.

I stopped my sway and bit down harder on my lip. "It's been a minute since I've been out. Plus, I'm still on a high from the rodeo."

"It was a great rodeo tonight." He smiled, reaching for his hat before coming to slip his hands around my waist. He pulled me closer to him, our hips meeting as his heavy eyes met mine.

"Third place is amazing, Cowboy. And yes." I grinned, tilting my head. "I am actually really, really looking forward to going out. Who's coming?"

He smiled, and *god* his smile. I couldn't get enough of it. It had only been four—*was it really only that long?*—weeks but it felt like longer, it felt like more. Not just because of the little kisses we shared, but because of the moments we had spent together. The way he made me feel whole. Grace's words still rang in the back of my head. The simple "*You'll be here*" played like a broken record over and over in my head, only fading when I was in Rhett's arms.

"Zeke, Jaxon, Darren. And I need you to do me a favor."

"What's that?"

"I need you to guess things about them."

I let out a laugh. "I mainly do that to break the ice you know."

"Perfect." He kissed the tip of my nose and if his arms weren't around my waist, I would have fallen. He stepped away, his hands leaving my waist slowly, as if he knew I needed the extra support after the nose kiss, but the warmth left as he turned to grab my shoulder bag and hat, placing it on my head before passing to the front door.

Opening the door, he turned and held out his open palm to me. "Ready, Mrs. Hartwell?"

I looked at his empty palm, his wedding ring giving off the tiniest bit of shine. Licking my lips, I slid my hand in his, feeling that jolt of electricity that always came with him.

"Are you ready to get your ass beat at pool again, Mr. Hartwell?"

"How?" Zeke's elbow hit the table with a thud as he pointed at me. "How can you possibly guess five things about me without even knowing me?"

"I'm telling you"—Rhett leaned back in his chair, one hand resting on his knee, the other draped on the back of my chair—"she guessed all but one for me."

"And with Wyatt . . ." I looked over at him. "I got all five, right?"

"That's true."

"Wyatt's easy though. Listen, chick, you don't even know me." Zeke narrowed his eyes to me.

"Did you just call my wife '*chick*'?" Rhett glared at his friend.

"Hey there, Cowboy, calm down." I placed my hand on Rhett's knee, giving him a reassuring look before turning back to Zeke,

"How about this. I get five things right, and the next round is on you. I get any wrong and you can call me *chick* for the rest of the night." I folded my arms in front of me and looked at the cowboy across the table. I smirked, hoping he would fall for it. Thankfully, Rhett had already told me some fun facts about his friends.

"Chick is a good one, I never thought of that when I was trying to find nicknames," Rhett mumbled under his breath, grabbing his pint from the table bringing it to his lips.

"Chick is a terrible nickname," I snapped. "Ready?"

Zeke lifted his chin and met my gaze, "Hit me."

Rubbing my palms together I wiggled in my seat. I looked over at Rhett, whose eyebrows were lifted as his gaze firmly planted on my waist. He liked that little wiggle. I felt the heat rush to my cheeks. *Not the time, Kyla. Get a free drink.*

"You drive a Toyota." I smiled.

"Okay there's one. But what kind?" Zeke narrowed his eyes.

"Tundra. It's silver and the guys give you crap for it. Everyone else drives a Chevy or a Ford, but you have the Toyota."

"That still counts as one."

Rhett snorted as his nose bent down into his pint. "I say that's two because she got the color."

"You've won your fair share of rodeos, Rhett here is actually your biggest competition." I never once lost eye contact with Zeke. He furrowed his brow.

"True." Zeke admitted, "But anyone could guess that."

"I bet your real name is Ezekial. Your mom probably named you from the Bible."

"That's not impressive. Is anyone with the name Ezekial *not* named from the Bible." Zeke dropped his arm on the table, causing our drinks to rattle.

"And last—"

"No, you got two more."

"—your drink order."

Rhett snorted, again, forcing me to turn.

"Nah, that doesn't count. I ordered the beer while—"

"While I was in the restroom." I finished the sentence for him.

Zeke slid his pint across the table and held it close to his chest. "Still don't think that counts. You can smell it."

"The whole place smells like beer, Zeke," Darren, who had been the quietest, finally said. "I'm getting a kick out of this and hope she does me next."

"She's not 'doing' anyone," Rhett mumbled.

I slapped his knee and turned back to Zeke. "Your drink order."

Zeke shook his head. "Okay, what beer did I order?"

"You ordered the Crimson Cascade." I smiled, cocking an eyebrow and flipping my hair over my shoulder. I felt Rhett's fingers grace the nape of my neck. Shivers ran through me, but I held my stare on Zeke.

"Damn!" Darren cheered.

Zeke lifted his pint to his lips and took a long pull. "Best beer in the joint." Setting the mug on the table, he leaned in and looked at me. "How much did Rhett tell you?"

I gave him a cheeky grin. "Not much." I leaned across the table. "I'm just good at reading people.

"He had to have told you my order."

"Nope." I shook my head. "I saw your license. Colorado. It's the only Colorado-brewed beer here so of course you had to go for it. Darren ordered one brewed in Montana and Rhett stuck with the—"

"Most watered-down beer in the joint. Simply because it's local." Rhett finished my sentence for me. "Next round is on Zeke."

After successfully guessing facts about the other two cowboys, we made our way to a pool table, only to be ditched the moment a few girls approached Darren and Jaxson. Once they saw those girls take their hats, they were lost to us. Zeke had played a few games with Rhett, both winning one until he excused himself to call his wife back home. Once he was out of sight, Rhett grabbed my hand and pulled me onto the dance floor.

The live band had stuck to country songs, slow and smooth and set the mood as the night went on. Being in Rhett's arms as he swayed me back and forth . . . my memory went straight back to that first night. The one where I told myself to be free. The one where I told Rhett I wanted him. I took a shaky breath, having no idea how I ended up here, but not regretting a single moment of it.

The moment the notes for Josh Turner's "Your Man" started playing, my heart basically skipped a beat. This was the song he first kissed me to. I blinked, wondering if he remembered that as vividly as I had. After all, it wasn't *that* long ago.

"Do you remember the first time we danced to this song?" I asked, my voice heavy.

"I do," he responded, dropping his chin. "I'll never forget that night, Kyla."

I ran my palms on his shoulders, my fingers lacing on the nape of his neck. "I don't think I ever will either. I felt so . . . so . . ."

"So, what?" Rhett's voice lowered, urging me on. He didn't finish my sentence like David would. Rhett wanted me to speak. He wanted me to say it. He wanted me to be in control.

"So free," I mused. "I know I say that a lot, that I was never this way before and I'm not sure how to act and how to be, but it's true. I'm not sure how else to say it other than I felt free."

Rhett was silent, his eyes heavy on me. He studied me, his eyes roaming as his hands traced up my back, his fingers pressing into my dress, sending chills up my spine. He felt the same way. I knew he did. He didn't have to tell me; I didn't have to second guess it. It was the way his hand always found mine. The way he always tried to find time to kiss me even if it was simple, the way he jumped in and was willing to become my husband. Rhett was falling.

And the more I thought about it, the more I thought about *him*, the more I knew I was too.

Even if it was ridiculous. Even if it was too quick.

It just felt . . .

Real.

"Rhett . . ." I muttered, not even loud enough for me to hear.

"Kyla." Rhett's voice stopped me, making me look up at him. "I don't want this to end."

"The song?" I asked, knowing exactly what he was talking about. And it wasn't the song.

"The song, the night, us. All of it. I don't want any of this to end. Kyla . . ." His hand lifted from my side and landed on my neck, his fingers threading through my hair with ease. "I've been falling for you since the moment I saw you. Just having you with me I can feel myself falling further and further. Please, I don't want this to end."

My voice crept up my throat before I could stop it. "I don't want it to either."

"Stay with me," he whispered, his smooth buttery voice sending shivers down my spine. "No more thinking this is temporary, because I can assure you, for me, it's very, very real."

"It's real," I repeated. "I think I was just telling myself it was temporary to not fall . . ."

"Kyla."

"I've fallen, Rhett. When I'm with you I . . . I never want it to stop."

"You'll stay?"

I looked up at him, the heat in his eyes all too real, making me forget the thought that had bubbled in my mind the second I told him I had fallen. "I know we're married, but I want to know you, I want to date you. When we get back from our trip, let's go on a date. A real date."

"Can I kiss you anytime I want?" he asked, a single eyebrow lifting.

"Rhett Hartwell, you can kiss me every minute of every day. I'll welcome each one and count the minutes until the next," I admitted, using my hand to bring his lips close to mine.

He kissed me, the taste of him flowing onto my tongue and his scent wrapping around me. His hand cupped my face as our bodies swayed to the music, Josh Turner still crooning as everything else in the world vanished.

Breaking the kiss, I leaned my forehead against his. He let out a long, heavy sigh before lifting his chin and looking at me.

"So, what do I call you? I can't really say you're my boyfriend, but if we are really making this official . . ."

"I'm your husband, and you're my wife. Mrs. Hartwell."

"Husband." I kissed him again. "I really, really like the sound of that."

"And Mrs. Hartwell . . ."

"The best nickname you've ever given me."

"You're staying?" he asked again, almost as if the kisses and admissions weren't enough for him.

It was going to be strange, and a lot of work to cancel everything I had set up for me in Washington. Grace was going to be excited; I knew that for sure. My mother, well, she'd get over it. It was going to take time to really truly feel at home on the ranch, and then find a job in the town. But just thinking of everything made me excited. It made my heart jump and the chills Rhett created grow stronger.

It wasn't exactly what I had planned, but maybe Rhett was right. I needed him. I needed this.

"I'm staying. I'm yours, Rhett Hartwell."

"Thank God," Rhett growled before his lips crashed into mine for the most amazing, knee shattering, heart pounding kiss I had ever had.

TWENTY-SIX

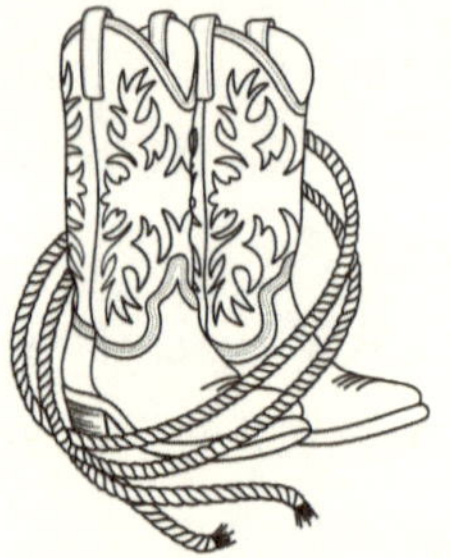

Rhett

I'M YOURS, RHETT HARTWELL.

That wasn't the first time she told me she was mine, and it wasn't going to be the last. Kyla was staying. She was going to stay my wife. She was mine.

I kissed her, as often as I could on that dance floor. I loved feeling her body move against mine, swaying and hearts pounding. Just the feel of her brought me back to life.

Kyla was my wife. Kyla was mine. And I was, without a doubt, in love with her. But I couldn't tell her that yet. She wanted to date—that much I understood—but I knew it was going to be said sooner rather than later. Just having her near me made my heart pound faster. Everything was clear when she was with me. Everything was *her*.

We danced until they called last call. Jaxon and Darren had long since left with their buckle bunnies, and Kyla and I made our way back to the hotel. She yawned, stretching her arms over her head before she climbed in the passenger seat. I reached behind the seat and grabbed the blanket I had draped across the seat. She settled herself, positioned the seat of her chair back a tiny bit, but when she raised her legs and laid them over the console, her calves and feet resting on my lap, that took me by surprise.

"I wish you had one of those older trucks, with the huge seat. I would sprawl out and let you rub my feet for me," she muttered, her eyes half closed.

I managed to buckle up, making sure she semi-buckled too, before turning the engine over and popping the truck in gear.

"I have one," I stated, "back at the ranch. An old Chevy that by some miracle still runs."

"Is it white?" she asked.

"Nope. Red."

"Well, when we get home can we take a ride in it? I'd love to just sprawl out and—"

"Relax?" I finished her sentence.

She hummed a yes then closed her eyes fully, and the cab of the truck grew silent. I opted for the radio. Low, old country songs. George Strait, Brooks and Dunn, Toby Keith—soft sounds that would lull her to sleep. I rested my palm on her calf, moving my thumb in low circles over her skin, simply loving the way it felt. It wasn't until we got back to the hotel when she finally moved.

She climbed out of the truck, using my shoulders as balance, allowing me to slip my arm around her waist as we walked into the hotel and to our room. The moment I opened the door she plopped on the bed, boots and all still on.

"Kyla, Baby." I chuckled, taking her boots off for her.

"I'm just tired."

I laughed again, catching her lips curl in response. "I know, crawl up and get settled."

I turned to go to the bathroom, brushing my teeth and readying myself, only to stop when I saw Kyla, still in her lavender dress tucked under the covers in the king-sized bed. Her eyes were closed, and she was breathing deeply. Perfectly peaceful. Brushing her hair from her face, I leaned down and kissed her temple, the sweet hum that came from her sent my heart beating a million miles an hour.

I'm yours, Rhett Hartwell.

Not missing a beat, I climbed in the bed, laying on my back, trying to just relax. I hadn't been in bed with Kyla since that first night we slept together, and like many things with us it felt like it was so long ago. I breathed deeply, cooling my body down, trying not to assume anything. She was sleeping, she was tired, but she inhaled and shifted her body, rolling to face me. She draped her arm around my waist as my arm went up to wrap around her shoulders. She cuddled closer, yawning as her cheek rested against my chest, her legs tangling with mine.

"I love hotel beds," she muttered. "They are so soft. So comfy. I could live here."

"Kyla," I whispered, my fingers tracing the outline of her sleeve.

"I missed this," she said softly. "It was only one night in your arms, but that was the best sleep I'd ever gotten. Just . . . hold me?"

"I'm here." I kissed the crown of her head. "I'm not going anywhere."

I pressed my fingers into her shoulder, closed my eyes, and listened to her steady breathing, barely believing that she was in my arms, and she was mine.

"How far away is the next city?" Kyla asked as she climbed into the cab of the truck the next morning. We had just gotten Buckle situated in her trailer and the truck packed up to head to the next rodeo. Kyla was back in her jean shorts and loose tank top. Her hair ran down her shoulders with her hat perched on her head.

"Billings," I said, buckling up. "About ten hours."

"Ten hours, all today?"

"Well for us, fourteen hours. We gotta let Buckle out to rest a few times, she can't go that long."

"A fourteen-hour road trip. Just me"—she smiled and leaned over the center console—"and my *husband*." She kissed me before flopping back in her seat and securing her seatbelt. "I hope you are ready for amazing music that you are most likely going to hate, and me being the passenger princess."

"You mean passenger queen." I smiled, shifting my body to her and winking.

"Ha, no, I am not a queen. Princess, yes, queen, no."

"A rodeo queen."

"Oh, that means I get to carry the flag. I should probably learn to ride a horse first."

Kyla's phone rang from her purse. Giving me a sexy smile, she bent to grab it, unlocking it and sighing, the fun demeanor that was there seconds before now gone.

"It's my mom." Kyla sighed, her eyes glued to the screen.

Raising an eyebrow, I turned to look at her. "And?"

"She wants to know when we are planning on being in Arizona. And shit—" She locked her phone and placed it face down on her lap. "I still haven't told Grace we're coming. Or that we . . ." She smiled, the stress from her mother's text leaving as soon as she thought about us. "Made *us* official. She'll be excited about that."

"Well, I'd hope so. She told me she was going to convince you to stay."

"She didn't have to convince me, I had to convince myself," Kyla admitted, swiping away the text from her mom to open Grace's text thread. "She's either going to be mad that I waited until now to tell her, or excited to start planning an actual wedding."

"We had an actual wedding, it may not have been fancy, but we had one. After we"—I leaned over and wiggled my eyebrows—"date, if you decide to still want to be married to me, we can have a bigger party. One you deserve with a white dress and all."

"I think it's safe to assume I'll still want to be married to you." She finished her text message and then dropped her phone in the cup holder. "What are we going to do for fourteen hours?"

"Drive," I responded.

We were only three hours into the drive and Kyla had resorted to looking at the atlas I had shoved in the back pocket of my seat.

She followed the road we were on to Billings, finding small towns we could stop in and let Buckle out of the trailer, or simply where we could stop and enjoy each other.

"I thought you said no one uses atlases anymore," I teased.

"Well," she grumbled, "I forgot my kindle."

I laughed, turning my gaze to watch her as she followed the roads. She frowned slightly as she studied the map, her finger following the roads we had to take. She pinched her brow, grabbing her phone. From the corner of my eye I saw her open our schedule.

"This is a long time on the road," she began. "I mean, I knew it was going to be a long trip, but can Buckle handle this?"

"With resting time, yes. She's stronger than you think." I grinned over at her. "Speaking of, we should probably let her out soon."

"What's the furthest she's traveled?" Closing the atlas, Kyla shifted in her seat, facing me.

"She's gone across the country before."

"How long has Buckle been yours?"

"I helped birth her."

"Really?" Kyla's voice raised a few octaves. "Like Josie?"

"Kind of like Josie." I chuckled. "I broke her, trained her, changed her shoes, and walked her when she had colic. She's mine just as much as I'm hers."

She listened, a small *mhmm* leaving her lungs as she turned back to the road. "We're coming up on a rest stop, ready to let her out?"

Agreeing, I followed the signs to the rest stop, the tires crunching on the ground. The moment I parked the truck Kyla jumped out, putting her hat back on her head. She dashed to the building, while I went straight for my horse. Buckle was ready to get out of the trailer, her head bobbing and legs dancing as I approached to untether her. Leading her out, I patted her neck and led her off the side, the clank of her hooves getting the attention from other families that had stopped.

A buzz came from my pocket as I led Buckle to the grass. Knowing I probably shouldn't ignore it I yanked it from my back pocket.

Lachlan

> He's back. That developer you told us about. He wants to talk to Uncle Leo about buying some of the ranch. I thought you told him to leave.

I let out a frustrated groan. David was at my house. Still trying to weasel his way in.

Me

> Get. Him. Gone. He knows the ranch isn't for sale.

Lachlan

> Your dad seems to think a part of it could be.

Fuck.

Me

> You've got to be kidding me.

Wish I was, Rhett. I know you have a route, call me when you get to Billings. I'll hold him off as long as I can.

Forcing the anger down, I locked my phone and shoved it back in my pocket. Reaching up, I pet Buckle's nose, hoping the feel of her under my palm would calm me down, but all it did was cause more anger. My ranch. My home. This guy was trying to ruin more than my wife's life, he was trying to ruin mine now as well.

"Hey, Cowboy." The sweet, soft voice pulled me from my haze as I turned to notice my wife walking up to me.

God she was gorgeous.

It still baffled me that someone treated her the way David had. Why would anyone even think they could? Why would anyone want to darken her shine?

The feeling of telling her everything ate at me, but I knew where her mind would go. She would retreat, back down, and fall back into what she was before she started to find herself. She didn't need that anxiety right now. She didn't need to know my problems when she was flourishing in front of me. I wouldn't—couldn't—break that. I could keep this in. All of it.

She approached me with confidence and ease, bringing a lurch to my stomach once she slid her hands on my waist. Her touch calmed every thought in my mind, replacing it with only her. Gently, she kissed my jawline and then turned to Buckle.

Buckle's head nodded a few times, most likely demanding attention. Kyla chuckled and reached out to scratch behind her ear.

"Hey girl," she mused.

Seeing Kyla interact with Buckle brought an idea to light, one that wouldn't just erase the text messages, but shift my focus completely. *Her list.*

"I have an idea."

"What's that?" Kyla asked, leaning her chin on my shoulder.

"Let's ride a bit." I looked down at her and smiled.

"We have one horse and riding behind you wasn't all that comfortable," she grumbled, her chin digging into my shoulder.

"Not me, you." I squeezed her. "Let me teach you how to ride."

Kyla may have been growing in confidence around me, but once Buckle was saddled and ready to go, she was as stiff as board. Her arms were folded across her chest and her feet hadn't moved an inch since I began to get Buckle ready. When I walked Buckle up to her, her arms dropped to her side and she took a single step back. I grinned, thinking my wife was absolutely adorable.

"I've been on a horse exactly once," she stammered, "and you were driving."

I chuckled, remembering the day by the lake, "I know, but if you're staying—"

"I am. No *if,*" she corrected me, filling my body with heat.

My gaze hit hers as I leaned forward to give her a fleeting kiss. "Then you need to learn how to ride, and there's no better horse to learn on then Buckle."

Taking a deep breath, Kyla nodded, closing her eyes and shaking her hands out on her sides. "Go on then. Let's do it."

"Foot in the stirrup," I directed, my eyes not once leaving her as I pointed to the stirrup. Kyla followed my directions, mounting Buckle with hesitation as she grabbed onto the reins and sat still, seemingly afraid to move.

I looked at her hands, her knuckles turning white as she gripped the reins.

"Relax." I smiled, holding in my urge to laugh. It was adorable to me how she was acting, even though I knew it shouldn't be. I had helped people ride before, I wasn't a trainer by any means, but I could at least help them learn how to move forward and stop. But with Kyla, I found myself wanting to jump on Buckle and help guide her—take care of her in a way I hadn't with other students. She probably would have welcomed it, but I refrained. "Squeeze your knees here." I put my palm on Buckle. "And she'll move forward."

Kyla followed my direction, and Buckle lurched forward.

"Oh!" Kyla gasped. I began to walk next to Buckle, gripping onto the muzzle to be a gentle lead, keeping the mare in line. Buckle was a calm horse, she knew my cues and, given that Kyla had squeezed just a little harder than I thought she would, was going faster than anticipated. "Did I do something wrong?"

I chuckled. "Nope. You're doing great." I dropped my hand on Buckle's muzzle. "Use the reins to turn her, she knows to follow. Tug left or right, depending on where to go."

I watched as she got comfortable with the reins, her body language relaxed and she smiled. Kyla was smiling.

"To stop—"

Kyla straightened her back, pulling on the reins, and Buckle came to a stop. She turned and scrunched her nose, a tight smile on her lips. "I knew that one," she said, proud of herself.

"You're a natural." Shoving my hands in my pockets, I motioned her forward. "Go forward. Walk her around. I'll walk next to you, then I'll show you how to make her run."

Twisting her lips and narrowing her gaze, Kyla used her knees to move Buckle, starting the motion just as easily as it would be to ride a bike. She *was* a natural, even though she claimed she wasn't. She even began leading Buckle ahead of me, so focused on the horse under her and where she was going, she didn't notice I wasn't by her side. And I just watched, in awe at my wife who had come so far from the woman I met weeks ago. The woman that said she wasn't brave, she didn't do things like this, yet here she was, meant to be on a horse. Meant to be with me.

"Look at you!" I shouted once she got a little too far. "Didn't even notice I wasn't there."

She turned her head, her hair flapping under her hat, a look of fear on her face at first, but she relaxed, and her fear turned into a smile. She wiggled her back as she turned forward again, a little happy dance. Pulling the reins she turned Buckle full circle, and walked back to me. And I watched as Buckle slowly walked up, her head bobbing and Kyla's full face and bright smile came into focus.

I still couldn't believe that she agreed to stay. That she agreed to remain my wife. No more temporary. No more marriage of convenience. Nothing but real feelings and real love. Something I had never truly felt before.

I couldn't wait for my life with her.

I couldn't wait to fall even harder than I already had.

TWENTY-SEVEN

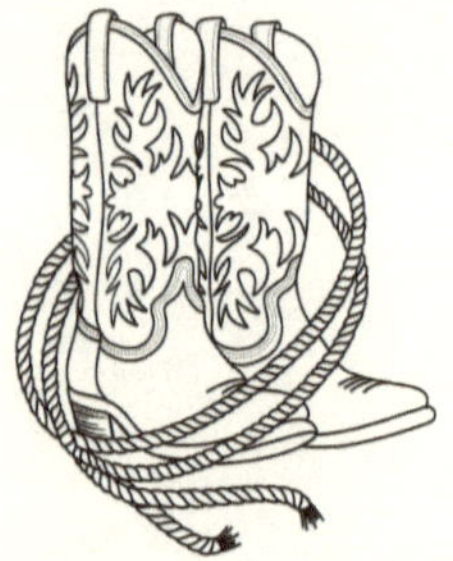

Kyla

"AND THAT'S ANOTHER BROKEN barrier for Hartwell, adding ten seconds to that 6.2—" Wyatt's voice boomed over the speakers, and I watched as my husband walked back to Buckle, his head down giving a defeated shake. "That would have beaten the NFR record, but did you catch his foot in the stirrup?"

That was his third broken barrier since Billings. His first I thought was a fluke, those things happen, but then the second . . . and now this one.

"It caught. He would have flown right off that horse if he wasn't holding on to that rope. But he still pulled a 6.2—"

Something was going through Rhett's mind. Something was pulling him away from his game.

And I had no idea what.

After he taught me how to ride, after his first broken barrier, I noticed every time his phone buzzed his eyes would flutter shut. He would read the message and instantly lock his phone back up, never responding to whoever was contacting him. Tension would course through him, strong enough it filled the air. But then he would turn to me, smile and give me a kiss. And when we would stop, he would let me curl into him, but his breathing was never steady. I doubted he was getting any sleep.

He was quiet, but he still held me as tightly as he had before. Our connection was still strong, but was it strong enough to break whatever was hurting him?

"It's not like Hartwell to break those barriers but he can't seem to shake whatever funk he's in. That 16.2 takes Hartwell to—" Wyatt's announcing partner—I had completely missed his name—stated the obvious in telling the entire arena that Rhett was now in last place for the night.

Tune them out Rhett, I thought, hoping he could read my mind. His chin lifted, searching for me in the crowd. I caught his gaze and scrunched my nose, trying to give him a *don't sweat it* smile, but since I was sweating it myself, I knew my reaction wasn't coming off the way I had hoped. He pinched his brow and jerked his head, motioning for me to leave the stands and find him. Not wasting a single second, I left my seat and made my way towards him.

We met halfway to the trailer, and Rhett was already peeling his sponsored shirt off.

"Hey, Cowboy." I tried to sound upbeat, giving him a winning smile, even though I could see it in his expression he wasn't feeling it.

"I wasn't in the ride," Rhett grumbled. He didn't make eye contact, he didn't reach out for me, he just opened the trailer and led Buckle in. He latched her reins and scratched behind her ears, flinging his shirt over his shoulder before leaving the trailer.

He began to walk right past me, his head still down, his hat covering his eyes. Darkness crowding him.

"Do you want to meet the guys?" I asked, following him to the front of the truck.

He shook his head, not saying a word.

I rolled my lips as Rhett opened the door to the cab. I hated how stiff he was being—how quiet. I had never seen this man act this way. He was normally the one to smile at me, ground me as my anxiety took root. There had to be more going on through his mind than just three broken barriers. Did those times really hinder his standing that much? Did three broken barriers make or break him?

"Don't we need to wait for Wyatt?" I asked, trying to get him to talk.

He shook his head again, a force behind it as he sat his hat on the dash. "No," he bit out. "He's not going to Arizona."

Right.

Arizona.

Arizona was our next stop.

To meet my mother.

I hugged myself, rubbing my arms up and down as if I was cold, but under the setting Colorado sun I was anything but. I was just . . . nervous? A small ball of anxiety grew in my stomach as I watched Rhett hang his shirt up on the hanger in the back of the cab, completely void of emotion. I hated him like this. I hated the way he seemed so closed off.

"Rhett," I whispered his name, seeing his shoulders rise as he took a deep breath. "You know how you tell me I need to tell you what's going through my head?" I moved, reaching out to touch his arm.

He let out a long-exasperated breath, a huff moving his lips as he turned to face me, instantly pulling me into him. I breathed him in, getting used to his scent. He wrapped me in his arms, and held me close, his breathing falling into beat with mine. After a few moments of silence—I couldn't exactly tell how long we stood there—he finally relaxed. He lifted his head and pressed his lips to my temple.

"I'm fine," he mumbled, lowering his chin as he softly kissed my bare shoulder. "I'm just not focused."

Arching my back slightly, I raised an eyebrow at him. "I can tell. So." I raised an arm to cup his chin. "How do we get you focused?"

Leaning his forehead against mine he inhaled. "I just need—"

I kissed him softly, stopping his words.

"Time," he finished, his eyes opening slowly.

Moving my fingers to the nape of his neck and threading his hair into my hand, I parroted, "Time."

Time was impossible to find.

We drove through the evening, Rhett focused on the road, with me drifting off in the passenger seat. The roads were quiet, and Rhett stuck mainly to the backroads as we ventured across the borders. His hand found mine and our fingers linked together. The tension in his eyes was lifting. It wasn't gone, but his shoulders seemed to relax the further we got from the broken barriers.

When my eyes weren't closed, I focused on him. I studied the way his hands moved on the steering wheel, and the way he settled into the seat. The complete ease he had, even though there was something haunting him. I didn't want to believe it was just the broken barriers that were running through his mind. He had told me that he could make up those times—those runs simply wouldn't count towards the NFR. So I knew that couldn't be the only thing. There was something else. Something he wasn't telling me. Something that was taking his attention away from what he found important.

But, he drove, letting the road and the night sky take away anything that may have been holding onto his thoughts. Every now and then he would take a deep breath, knitting his brow as he checked the GPS I had talked him into keeping on.

"Where are we going?" I asked, once I noticed him turning off the path the GPS had set for us.

"You're supposed to be asleep," he answered softly.

"I've been awake. Where are we going, Cowboy?"

Cocking a grin, he turned to me, a single eyebrow raised slightly. "You'll see."

"You're crossing into Utah?" I sat up in my seat, trying to make out the dark terrain outside the windshield.

"Just a *corner* of Utah." He smiled.

My eyes widened. No matter what was going through his mind, he still was thinking of me. Still thinking of that stupid bucket list I had. He taught me to ride a horse and now, he was taking me to the Four Corners. Next, he'd have me sleeping under the stars.

We approached the Four Corners hand in hand. It was dark and there were no lights shining down on us, only the light of the moon. I looked around for any sign of a security vehicle—a sign of anyone really, but no one was around. It was just a slab of concrete surrounded by benches and a few buildings. It wasn't much to look at but still. Four states met here, and I could lay in all four.

"Now . . ." Rhett turned, a playful smile on his lips. I loved that smile, I hadn't seen it since we left the arena, but it warranted one from me as well. "They're closed, so—"

"We could come back in the morning you know," I whispered, a sudden rush flying up my spine thinking we were breaking the law, moving closer to Rhett.

"Now, where's the fun in that?"

"We're supposed to be getting you focused, not breaking and entering."

"We're not breaking and entering." He pulled me into his side. "We're walking and laying."

I hid back a laugh, loving that he was making this come true for me. His grip on my hand tightened as we came up to the borders. The four large names of the states made a square as their borders came together, and all I could do was stare at them. I wasn't sure why a circle that lay on the ground was something that got my heart beating faster, but looking up at Rhett and seeing his eyes heavy on mine, made it all the more worthwhile.

Rolling my lips I dropped his hand and went to the ground. Making sure to lay my back right in the middle I sprawled out spread eagle, each part of me in a different state. Rhett stood, his hands in his pockets as he looked down, a soft smile shining down on me.

"Your right leg is in Arizona, your left leg is in New Mexico, your right arm is in Utah and your head and left arm are in Colorado. You are in four places at once." He tilted his head and bent down to squat next to me. "I knew I couldn't get you to Delicate Arch this trip—"

"This is better." I reached out to him, pulling him down to lay next to me. "Until we get caught."

"We won't get caught." Rhett drew out the words, a low rumble filling the space between us. He kissed my temple lightly. "I made sure there were no cops around."

I turned to look at him, giggling as I moved to hit him lightly in the chest, but before I could, he grasped my hand, his lips finding my fingertips. Our fingers laced together as they hovered above us, the small diamond on my ring glistening as the light of the moon hit it. It wasn't even a full moon, it wasn't even that big of a diamond, but it shined.

"Did I ever tell you about this ring?" Rhett said, breaking the silence that hung in the air.

My lips twitched. "No," I responded softly, loving how he was basically reading my mind. "Tell me."

"It was my grandmother JoAnn's." His eyes met mine, a fire behind them that seemed to replace the tension from earlier. "My grandfather proposed to her right before he got deployed." He kissed my fingertips again. "He had no money to his name, absolutely nothing, but knew he needed to marry my grandmother. He proposed with this simple ring, promising her to replace it once they had more to their name, but she wouldn't accept anything else. My grandmother always said it was the ring that held them together for so long, she would look at it, and remember his simple promise that he would come home to her. The day he got back, they promised each other so much more, and then they bought the land. Without this ring, Hartwell Hills wouldn't be what it is. She wore it up until my dad married my mom. My mom wore it for a few years before she got into the dirty work, and she didn't want to ruin it. It's been cleaned and waiting for you ever since."

"Waiting for me?" I questioned, lifting my head to look at him.

"I know it's not a romantic story like you were probably expecting, but I don't think it belongs with anyone else." His voice dropped, "It's yours."

On instinct, I rolled on top of Rhett, my hair creating a curtain. His arms moved as he brushed my hair to one side. He didn't even blink before his mouth was on mine, a kiss deep enough to make me moan against him, wanting more right here in four different states. His fingers trailed my jaw, cupping my face as his lips moved in sync with mine. We kissed like we never had before, a hunger behind it that wouldn't fade. His kiss was crumbling me, and he was picking up all my pieces.

We kissed, and my hand found his skin under his shirt as he sat up, his lips moving to my neck. Wrapping my legs around him I had to remind myself we were in public. I could give him everything right here—feel the tension lift from his body. But whatever that feeling was, left for the moment, and for that, I wanted him more. I was his and he was mine. Whatever he was going through, whatever *I* had gone through . . . none of it mattered.

"Thank you," I said against his lips. "You're making everything come true for me."

"Thank you," he responded, his eyes darkened, heavy, and full of need as he bore into me. "For being my wife."

TWENTY-EIGHT

Rhett

I HAD ZERO PLANS of going to the rodeo today. I contacted the arena and removed my name from the board, knowing that the last thing I needed before meeting Kyla's mother was another broken barrier.

Lachlan was making sure I was completely up to speed on everything happening at the ranch. David had made his presence known, and my dad seemed to like entertaining the idea. I tried reaching out to my father, but he simply responded with, *"You're not aware of what's happening behind the scenes, Rhett."* Which only made my blood boil hotter.

I needed to get that out of my head, and back into my rides, and I knew that wasn't going to happen today.

Time.

I just needed time.

I sent a quick text to Lachlan the morning after we arrived in Phoenix, asking him not so nicely to leave me out of any group or single texts that revolved around the ranch today.

Me

> Just give me today to get my head on straight, then we can tackle this. You own it, I don't yet. Leave me out of everything until I get home . . . please. I need this.

Even though the ranch was the forefront of his mind and should be the forefront of mine, I couldn't help but admit that the ranch wasn't all that was taking up brain space.

I glanced at the bathroom door where Kyla was getting ready for the day, the memory of just hours before wafting through my brain on repeat. She found so much joy in just sitting on the small "X" on the concrete—simply loving the fact that she was in four places at once—and then she thanked me. She thanked *me* for making her dreams come true. Her kiss felt different last night. Where her kisses were always something I craved, last night she had more desire, a deeper pull than she had in the past as her lips and tongue danced against me, her hands finding every inch of my skin that brought me alive. I only stopped because she reminded me we were in the middle of nowhere and should probably find a hotel. I had every intention of kissing her again once we got into the hotel, but instead, after seeing her curl up on the bed and instantly fall asleep, I climbed in next to her and enjoyed the time being with her.

I didn't need time.

I needed time with her.

My phone buzzed in my hand, pulling me back to the cloud that hung in the room.

Lachlan

> I'll text you whenever I damn well please. Get your damn head on straight and stop breaking the fucking barrier.

I could practically hear his voice through the words. *I'll text you whenever I damn well please.* A laugh escaped my lungs as I reread the text, not even giving him the satisfaction of a response. He knew I meant what I said, and I knew he would outright ignore me.

"I like your laugh," I heard Kyla say as she stepped out of the bathroom.

I had said that to her not too long ago, and now, here she was—*mine*—saying it back to me. She wore a sexy smile showing me just how much confidence she had gained since becoming my wife. I knew I wasn't the reason for her newfound confidence, but *fuck*, I loved watching her glow.

"I haven't heard it in a while." She came up to me, her hands falling on my shoulders as she ran them to the base of my neck, her fingers linking together.

I almost pulled her on my lap, wanting to feel her straddle me, but I refrained.

"I laugh," I defended, pulling out the teasing nature I knew existed with her.

"You haven't for the past few days. You gonna tell me what's going through your head, *darlin'*?"

"Darlin'?" I parroted, a full laugh gaining one from her as well. She tilted her chin as she laughed, her cheeks flushed, making me forget about everything completely. She was gorgeous when she laughed.

"Princess, Darlin', Bunny, Sugar . . ."

"I don't think I ever called you *Sugar.*"

Twisting her lips and raising an eyebrow, Kyla smirked. "You've called me a lot of things."

"But you have a favorite?"

"I have two, but that's not what we are talking about right now. What's going through your head?" Kyla moved her hands, cupping my chin, a small flush radiating through her skin when I kissed her palm.

I wanted to tell her everything. That I was nervous that no matter what we did, her ex would be in our lives forever—always there to threaten us. That he would succeed in taking a piece of my land and never ever let it go. Nerves that Kyla wasn't mine; that her happiness could get taken away with the quick swipe of a pen on a paper, and that all of this meant more to me than I let on. But none of it mattered more than her. If he didn't stop, I could lose more than a corner of land. I could lose *her.*

"Absolutely nothing a day out with my wife won't fix," I said instead of dropping everything.

Her eyebrows knitted. "What time is the rodeo?"

"I bowed out," I told her, kissing the tip of her nose. "I told you I needed time, and I want that time to be with you. I have an idea."

I grinned, dipping my chin but keeping my eyes firm on hers. She raised an eyebrow, tilting her head. "But you gotta trust me."

"I . . . trust you . . ." She drew out the words, arching her back away from me as an eyebrow rose.

"Good." I kissed her, just enough to leave a tease on both our lips. "Because I know you're going to love it."

Kyla folded her arms across her chest and pushed herself into the seat. She glared out the front window, avoiding me completely. The hesitant look she gave the store in front of us told me everything I needed to know. She didn't want to do this. Even though she had told me it was just for her, now that she was here, with me, I could see the nerves building in her body.

"You brought me to a lingerie store. You're skipping out on a rodeo to let me shop for lingerie?"

"I'm skipping a rodeo to spend much needed time with my wife, who happens to want to buy herself lingerie. So, what better way to spend time with her."

"The purpose of lingerie shopping was for me—"

"And it still is for you," I reminded her, moving a strand of hair that had fallen over her shoulder, "I can stay in the car if you'd like."

"No," she said quickly. "You should come in." Kyla unfolded her arms and took a deep breath. "I mean, you need to enjoy them too . . . right?"

I held back a smile. "This is for you, not me." I met her gaze, concentrating on her breathing, "After this we will go buy a coffee maker. This is for you, Mrs. Hartwell. I promise."

Biting her bottom lip, she turned to look at the store one more time before making the jump out of the truck. "Okay, but"—she turned to look at me over her shoulder—"you're coming."

Soft music filled the room as we both entered the store. Kyla released my hand as she turned and made her way to the racks of red and black. The small twinge of nerves that floated through her was still present in every way as she gently reached out to touch one of lacey sets, but with the way she held herself, a passerby would never be able to tell she was slightly hesitant. A plump woman approached her, a smile on her face and as Kyla raised her arms so she could wrap a tape measure around her, I turned to the other half of the store.

Silk nightgowns and lacey covers adorned the walls, and my mind couldn't help but wonder what Kyla would look like in all of them. How the white silk would lay against her skin, until I could slowly raise it over her to take her in. How the black lace would stand out, even if the dark room covered her from my sight. My chest tightened as I imagined the way she would feel, the only thing guiding me was the memory of our one night. Her soft skin, the shivers I caused, the breaths that came from her lips as she moved...

Maybe it wasn't a good idea for me to come in with her.

Blinking away the heat that I could feel rising in my body, I turned to find Kyla, but all I saw was rows of lace and silk. A quick glance outside told me she hadn't left, so the other option was . . .

"Excuse me," I asked the woman I had seen helping Kyla. "My wife?"

"Oh, she went into the dressing room." She smiled, pointing me in the direction of a room off to the side. "Second door on your left."

"Thank you." I tipped my hat to her, heading into the small hallway.

The five dressing rooms were empty, except for one. I gave the second on the left a quick knock, leaning against the door frame.

"Mrs. Hartwell," I mused. "I take it you found something?"

"A few things, Mr. Hartwell. I'll be out soon. Are you okay out there?" Her voice sang in my ears and I felt that heat rise again.

I swallowed. "Can I join you?"

"The point of lingerie—"

"Is for you to feel damn sexy, not to surprise me. Can I join you?" I interrupted, trying to remain quiet and calm, waiting for her to make the first move.

I heard her exhale before the door gave a small click and opened. Keeping it slightly closed, I snaked into the small room, all thoughts leaving my mind the moment I saw Kyla. She was wearing a purple lace bra, black butterflies trailing up her breast into the straps, and purple boy shorts covered her own thong, hugging her hips and curves in all the right ways. Her breasts were plump at the top of the lace fabric, almost begging to be free—to be touched. She was flawless.

I forced my hands into fists.

"Holy . . . shit . . ." I murmured, losing my breath as I took in the sight of her, feeling myself harden as my heart rate picked up.

Kyla gave me a soft smile and a sexy giggle before turning back to the mirror. Her hands trailed down her stomach as her eyes focused on the boy shorts.

"I have others to try. Felica was great in helping me pick out some sets. I have a red, black, yellow—"

Before I could stop myself, I found my hands gliding along her lower back, my fingertips light as feathers as I traced her hips, resting on her waist. I met her eyes in the mirror, closing the distance between us, wanting—no *needing*—her body against mine.

"Rhett . . ." she warned, breathlessly. "We are in a dressing room."

"That's right, *Princess*, and my wife is wearing the most perfect lingerie I have ever seen in my entire life." I leaned down and kissed her bare shoulder, a smile spreading on my lips once I heard her breath shake.

"Rhett . . ."

"I don't think you know how sexy you are, *Darlin'*." I kissed her neck, moving her hair to the side, lightly biting down on her skin. She gasped, making me want to bite harder—but remembering where we were—I held back, using my lips to kiss where I had bit.

"Rhett." Raising her arm she cupped the back of my head, her fingers grasping onto my hair as her back pushed into me.

I trailed my hand along her stomach, reaching her breast, cupping her in my palm.

"I love it when you say my name like that. I love every sound you make, *Sugar*." I spun her to face me, pressing her up against the mirror. Our bodies met, flush against each other and I wish I was as bare as she was. I wanted her skin against mine.

Her breath hitched, a high gasp of air as her eyes met mine.

"Cold . . ." she whispered as my lips came close to hers. A shiver escaped her as I felt her warm breath on me.

"Let me warm you up, *Baby*." I kissed her, hard and strong. There was no time for sweet and gentle when she looked and sounded like this. My kiss was electric, but hers was just as hungry, kissing me back as she moaned into my mouth.

My hands trailed along her entire body, feeling her shiver as I cupped her breasts, her ass, enjoying everything about her. The way her skin felt against my hands pulled away everything my mind was trying to hold onto. Everything left, and all that meant anything, was right in front of me.

"Oh, my god, Rhett . . ." She leaned her head back, hitting the mirror with a soft thud. I kissed her chin before kissing her throat again, gently nipping to hear her gasp.

My fingers slipped under the lacy boy shorts, feeling her own thong underneath, feeling her heat there as I inched closer and closer to her center.

"You are *so perfect.*" Lifting my chin, I kissed her again, simply loving her moan. "*Mrs. Hartwell.*"

She breathed me in, her hands moving up my chest, finding the nape of my neck and hair all too easily as she pulled me back to her mouth. The kiss—*this kiss*—was one for the record books. The heat and need that grew between us was anything but temporary. She wanted this as much as I did. The proof was in the way her mouth claimed mine, as she took control of the situation. Her tongue moved against mine and I suddenly wished her mouth could travel other places. Everywhere, just as mine would.

I slowly reached up, unclasping the purple bra, ready to move to take her when a small knock at the door startled us both.

Kyla pulled away, bringing her arms to her chest to keep the bra on her, as her lips formed a tight line, her eyes wide on mine. I grinned, raising my eyebrows at her, the fact that we were almost caught only adding to the rush.

"Doing okay in there?" Felicia asked through the door.

"Yes." Kyla's voice shook. "Perfect. Thank you."

"No problem, don't be afraid to let me know if you need anything."

We both listened intently as her footsteps faded. Once Kyla's eyes met mine once again, I cocked an eyebrow.

"We're getting this set," I hummed, my fingers slipping through the loose strap that still hung on her shoulder.

Rolling her lips, she finally formed a smile. "I can't believe you did that."

"You loved it."

"That may be but . . . go." She kissed my lips gently as she pushed me away with one hand, the other still firmly holding the purple lace in place. "Let me pick the others." Her free hand reached out for me, her thumb trailing my swollen lips. Her eyes were still heavy, her lips still raw.

I bounced my eyebrows once, reaching for the door handle. "I'll be waiting out front." I winked, loving the small giggle she let loose as I left the dressing room, my body reacting once again to the heated sigh she let out.

TWENTY-NINE

Kyla

M Y MOTHER'S HOUSE LOOKED exactly the same as it did when I left.

It was completely different than Rhett's cabin. His was welcoming and homey, blending in with the background of the ranch. Even with the modern interior, Rhett's cabin had become more home to me than . . . *this*. And I grew up here.

It was a large brick house, the largest on the street. The red brick walls clashed with the xeriscaping in front. The front door was black—my father had said it was to distinguish us—and stood out against the white pillars and shutters that surrounded the front door and windows. A few palm trees looked extremely out of place amongst all the rocks. Her Lexus sat in the driveway—freshly washed and shined, I was sure. Just looking at it made me want to run away again.

I met David in this house.

He first kissed me in the backyard during a party.

He proposed to me during Christmas dinner.

So many things were tied to him just looking at it.

"Hey." Rhett's voice pulled me back to him. He grasped my hand and brought it to his lips. "You ready?"

"No," I grumbled.

Slinking his arm around my waist he pulled me to him, giving me a kiss. A deep one, not quick and simple, one that drew all my thoughts from my head, the same way it had in the dressing room earlier. Once he broke the kiss, he raised his chin to kiss my forehead.

"A kiss for luck," he muttered against my skin.

"I'm supposed to kiss *you* for luck."

He shrugged his shoulders. "It helps us both. So"—he dipped his chin—"you ready?"

I looked at my husband, honestly happy he hadn't bothered to shave. I wanted him to be *him,* not polished and fake to appease my mother. He wore his signature hat and boots, complete with Wrangler jeans. I was shocked he changed his shirt from the blue button down to a nice, tailored black one. He still tucked it in to show off his belt buckle, and the first few buttons were left undone, showing the deep red shirt underneath. His hair was messy under the hat, but honestly perfect. His hands were rough as they traced my jawline.

My mother was going to have a hay day when she saw him.

"We should probably ring the doorbell," he muttered.

Taking one last sigh I turned, my hand firm in his as I reached forward and rang the doorbell.

I don't want to do this . . .

I do not want to do this . . .

The front door flew open, and my mother stood there. Her dark hair was shorter than I remember, and her gray eyes seared into mine. She wore a simple white tank top and black flowy capris. Her sandals told me she was trying to be comfortable yet classy at the same time. She forced a smile, her eyes roaming to Rhett beside me, before clearing her throat, turning back to me.

"Hi, Mom," I said softly.

"Kyla," she mused. "It's so . . . wonderful . . . to see you, my baby."

I tightened my lips, keeping down a retort. Instead, I turned to Rhett. "This is my husband, Rhett Hartwell."

Rhett smiled, like the gentleman he was, and raised his hand to her, giving her his best smile. "Nice to meet you, Mrs. Richards. Kyla has told me all about you."

I let out a soft sigh, watching as my mother eyed his hand, slowly reaching hers out to shake. "It's a pleasure . . . I'm sure," she replied. "Come in. Sandra made Kyla's favorite for dinner."

"Mom," I mumbled following her into the foyer. "You didn't have to."

"Of course I did. It's been too long, Kyla." She waved her arm as she walked into the sitting room right off from the foyer.

"This place makes my parent's place look small," Rhett bent down and whispered in my ear.

"Trust me." I turned to him, our lips only centimeters apart. "I'd rather be on the ranch. I didn't even think my mom knew what my favorite dinner was." I gave him a small kiss in the corner of his mouth.

Rhett gave a small "mmm" as we made our way into the sitting room with my mother. She came back from the kitchen, carrying two wine glasses, handing one to me and keeping the other for herself. She glanced at Rhett.

"I'm sorry I don't keep beer in the house." She sneered, a tight smile forming on her lips.

Rhett gave a small laugh, looking down at his feet before meeting my mother's gaze. "That's alright, ma'am. I'm more than happy to share the glass with Kyla." With his left hand he reached smoothly to take the glass from me. My thoughts instantly went to Nicholas Cage taking the glass from Abigail in *National Treasure*—all too smooth.

My mother gawked at him as he took a sip, and her jaw dropped. I smiled at my husband, reaching out to grab my glass from him, stopping myself from kissing him right there. I loved the bold move he took, even if it lost him points in my mother's eyes.

"I know where glasses and wine are, I'll get you a drink since my mother forgot her manners. Red or white?" I asked Rhett.

"Oh no, no. Sandra!" My mother turned. "Can we get a glass of merlot for Rhett?" Turning back to Rhett, she gave him the same tight smile. "So." She gave a breathy sigh as she sat on the sofa, motioning for us to sit across from her. "You own a ranch?"

"My family does, but yes. I will own a portion of it," Rhett answered, taking the glass from Sandra once she arrived.

"A portion? David made it seem like you owned the entire acreage."

Rhett tensed. "My family does," he repeated.

She hummed, that tight smile still there. I took a deep breath, placing my right hand on Rhett's knee and using my left to chug the wine that was left in my glass.

"Kyla," she snipped as she watched me place the empty glass on the table in between us.

"Well, I'd love some more." I turned to look at Rhett, whose eyes were wide, a single eyebrow cocked. "Oh, what?" I smiled at him. "You've seen me chug more than that."

"Kyla." My mother's voice was stern.

"When will dinner be done?" I asked, my voice shaky.

What the hell was wrong with me? I was nervous to be here, sure, but the anxiety that was creeping up seemed completely out of place. I squeezed Rhett's knee, hoping he would get the signal that there was something going on.

I thought back to the time he had seen me in any kind of spiral.

Our second night together, when I told him I wasn't that kind of girl, the anxiety was creeping in then. But he was respectful, asked for a final kiss and then slept on the couch.

The day David got back. I had begun to pack in a panic, thinking I needed to leave in order for him to not have David breathing down his back. He proposed that night.

After we got married when I began to list off all the reasons this wouldn't work, he stopped the panic before it truly set in.

The Fourth of July he asked me to come with him.

The dance floor. He asked me to stay.

I inhaled and looked over at my husband. I wasn't sure if he had intentionally done it, but each time he was able to pull the anxiety away. So, why should now be any different?

Next to him I felt stronger, braver . . . calmer. Next to him I felt loved.

"I'm sorry, Mrs. Richards," Rhett began, his eyes heavy on me. "You said you made Kyla's favorite?"

"Chicken alfredo, with garlic bread and Italian salad," she answered. "How does your *husband* not know that? David knew."

"David claims to know a lot of things." I took a deep breath, looking back at my mother. The anxiety towards her was still there—not as strong—but there. I just wouldn't—couldn't—let her know. "I'm sure he told you he wants to buy the ranch, and it was just a coincidence I was there?"

She laughed, reminding me of Emily Gilmore in the early years of *Gilmore Girls.* The Emily Gilmore who judged every ounce of her daughter's being. I half-expected her to say, "*Now Kyla, that's absurd,*" but her laugh just faded.

"Hold on." Rhett held out a palm in front of us, stopping my mother before she could say anything. "You still talk to your daughter's ex?"

"Well of course, I did introduce them after all. David is a decent person, he just wants what's best for Kyla."

"And what's best is keeping her from her friend and making her think she's not worth anything? That's what's best for her?" Rhett raised an eyebrow. "If that's what you think is best for your daughter, I think you really need to evaluate your relationship with her and her ex. Decide who is more important."

"I'm sorry, Mr. Hartwell, but what business of yours is it to speak about my relationship with my daughter?'

"You mean my wife?" Rhett shifted on the sofa. "Kyla deserves only the best and it's my mission in life to give it to her. Ever since the day I first met her I've wanted nothing more than to see her be happy and shine. She was open and honest with me from the very beginning, so I know more than you think. It's *entirely* my business since it's my job to make sure she's satisfied in life."

"Satisfied?" She chuckled, her eyes landing on Rhett as they widened. "You don't know the kind of *satisfaction* she would have had if she married David."

"Mom," I whispered, but I went unnoticed.

"She would have been set for her entire life," she spat, her glare deepening at Rhett. "She would never have to set foot inside a public school again. And now she's *married*—if you really *are* married—to a cowboy who rides bulls for a living."

"We're married, and I don't ride bulls. I'm not an idiot. And I'll have you know, with me, she doesn't need to lift a finger ever again. But I know she would want to find a teaching job, she wants to work and I'm not going to stop her from doing that."

"Mom," I whispered again, feeling the tension in the room build and build. The anxiety was beginning to fade, and, to my surprise, it was being replaced with anger.

"David told me he doesn't believe the marriage is real, and after meeting you—seeing you together—I don't think it is either." She bore into him, judging every piece of him.

"You've seen us for all of fifteen minutes. I can go get the fucking piece of paper to show you—"

"I don't need that fake printed paper to prove anything. You are someone Kyla never would have been with, not in a million years. She's never even ridden a horse."

"Yes, I have," I muttered, trying to think back on my time just days ago on Buckle.

"I met Kyla in Flagstaff in February. I fell in love with her the moment she turned me down, and then proceeded to figure me out just by looking at me. She knocked me off my feet, so much so that I knew I couldn't leave the state without her, and to my surprise, she felt the same. We were married April 24th—best fucking day of my life. You don't need to believe it in order for it to be real." Rhett leaned forward, his elbows on his knees, his stare fixated on my mother.

"If you think for a moment I believe this charade . . ." My mother began to shake her head forcefully. "I know my daughter, you don't. And if you think—"

"Shut up, Mother!" I finally screamed, both of them turning their gaze to me at the exact same moment. "Don't claim to know me. You don't know me. You may have been a helicopter parent, but you didn't think to watch me through the day. You just made sure I was right where you wanted me. You never bothered to figure out what was going on with my life. You thought David was good for me? David?! Do you have any idea what he would tell me? I know you do because dad would say the same things to you. I would watch you crumble and pick yourself back up again, making sure your *friends* saw what you wanted them to see—a perfect marriage. Well, guess what? They all knew what dad was doing, because I'm pretty sure their husbands were doing it too. He may have never hit you, but he scolded you. He made you feel small. He made you feel like you didn't matter. And then he would use his charm to apologize his way back in, only to do it a mere seconds later. But that was okay because you were 'taken care of.'"

I stood, my mother mimicking my actions. She held onto her wine glass firmly, and I half expected it to shatter.

"Do you want to know what this man makes me feel?" I gestured to Rhett, who was looking at me as if he had never seen me before. "He makes me feel whole. He makes me feel adventurous. He makes me feel comforted. He makes me feel wonderful. He makes me feel pleasure." I blushed—blurting that last part out and my mind instantly going back to the dressing room, and the way his hands felt on my skin . . . then back to our one night we shared. *Let me worship you, Kyla.* I cleared my throat. "He makes me feel worshiped, loved, free . . . alive." My voice cracked on that last word. "I love him, Mom, and nothing that you or David *think* will change that. He's my husband, he's not going anywhere, and neither am I." I felt Rhett stand, his hand on my lower back, slowly tracing my spine. "If I would have known this is what tonight was going to turn out to be, I wouldn't have come back to Arizona. I love you, Mom . . . but, I need to be alive."

My mother's face was quickly turning red, but I wasn't going to give her a chance to speak to me or my husband again. Before she could open her mouth, I turned to Rhett, giving him a gentle nod and then we turned, making our way out of the sitting room and out of the house. His hand was warm in mine the entire time we walked to the truck. He opened the door for me, kissed my temple and shut the door. I took one last look at the house, and after hearing Rhett open his door and climb in . . . I broke.

Every tear that had been welling up since the moment I walked into the house had decided to fall.

THIRTY

Rhett

"**I**'M SORRY..." Kyla stammered as soon as we walked into the hotel room.

During our short time with her mother, it shocked me to see Kyla stand up to her mother the way she did. I was even more shocked when Mrs. Richards just took it. The look she gave her daughter was daunting, I could see her breaking as Kyla said every word. Almost as if a switch flipped and she finally—*finally*—listened to her daughter. But she must have been too proud to say anything because she willingly let us leave. It even occurred to me that the entire time we were there, I never once got her first name. She was Mrs. Richards. Nothing more.

I knew she wouldn't accept me, or our marriage, but I was hoping she would listen to us. I didn't even imagine she would still be in contact with David. If Kyla hadn't stood up when she did, I would have lost it—gotten louder than I already was. My skin was boiling when she said "just by looking at us," she could tell the marriage was fake, and that she assumed Kyla was using me to hide from David. That she was only playing a game. And now here she was, thinking she had to apologize.

After all the tears she shed. After holding everything in for so long, breaking . . . she thought *she* had to apologize.

"Why are you apologizing?" I asked, locking the door behind me.

She sniffed and sat on the bed. "I shouldn't have done that."

"Kyla." I put my keys on the dresser and went to stand in front of her. She sat with her knees tight together, her hands under her thighs. Her eyes were heavy from the tears, swollen as she swallowed. I took a deep breath, taking in the sight of my wife. I kneeled, placing my palms on her knees. Biting her bottom lip, she met my gaze. "You have nothing to apologize for. If anything, I need to apologize. I shouldn't have spoken to your mother like that, I should have kept my mouth shut, but she was hurting you. She was talking about you like you weren't even in the room, she was just . . ." I closed my eyes, taking another deep, grounding breath. "What you're feeling—felt—is real. The tears, the words, everything was real. I'm proud of you for saying what you felt, standing up for what your heart is telling you is real. I'm real, Kyla, with you—always. You don't need to be sorry for anything, ever, when you're with me."

Her bottom lip quivered, and more tears welled in her eyes. She blinked and let out a long sigh. "A part of me really wanted her to like you."

"Me too, but I don't think that's going to happen anytime soon." I stopped, thinking of the words she had screamed just an hour prior. *I love him.* Did she mean that? Or was that just . . .

"I meant it," she whispered, almost reading my thoughts.

"I know," I responded, desperately wanting to tell her how I felt. Ever since I had met this woman I've wanted to protect her, let her know she was safe and cared for. I gave her my home, my family, my name, and here I was still searching for something else I could give her. If three little words was all she needed, then I would be happy to oblige. "I . . ." I began. "Tell me how to make you better."

She gave me a soft smile. Pulling her hands from her thighs, she placed them on mine. "Just hold me? All that crying . . . just . . . takes a lot out of me."

She didn't have to say anything else. I stood, kicked off my boots, and then climbed over her on the bed. She followed me, scooting up on her elbows until we reached the pillows. Turning to her side, she laid down facing me, allowing me to wrap my arm around her waist, pulling her close to me.

"I'm here, I've got you," I said softly, not exactly sure what to say.

Sighing, she nuzzled her nose into the crook of my neck, giving me just enough space to lean down and kiss the crown of her head. Her free hand found my chest, and I reached up and grasped it with mine. She breathed deeply at first, but soon she calmed and fell asleep.

I laid there all night, thinking there was nothing I wouldn't do for this woman.

I sat at Grace's kitchen island, the coffee mug still warm around my hands, while Grace and Kyla talked on her back porch. Kyla woke up in my arms, gave me a sweet kiss before getting ready to have breakfast with Grace, and even though we were here now, I felt like a knife could slice through the tension between us. She told me she was better, but I didn't fully believe it. I had hoped that Grace's famous French toast (which was delicious) and mimosas would help, but I was also worried it would only alleviate some of the anxiety. She would smile and laugh with Grace, but when her eyes met mine she would blink them away, and it had me worried that I was causing the fear to grow stronger inside her.

My phone buzzed on the counter, dancing away from me as Lachlan's name lit up my screen.

Heaving a sigh, I answered, "Hey, Lach."

"He's back again. I swear Rhett I'm going to punch this guy."

"Go for it." I sighed. "I won't stop you."

"Uncle Leo is convinced we need to sell. Your mother, thankfully, is saying no. They've said they would wait for you to get home to make the final decision. Abi looks like she's about to lose her mind." I could hear his distress, and could picture him pacing back and forth in the barn. This ranch was his life, there was no way he would lose it.

"Calm down, it's not going to happen. Dad is just seeing the financial side of it. I'm sure David offered him a pretty penny." I raised my mug to my lips, glancing at Kyla and Grace on the porch. Kyla laughed, lifting her chin in the air, making my heart lurch.

"Oh, he did, and your pops think getting rid of five hundred acres is worth it."

"He wants five hundred acres?" I stammered, my attention going from Kyla back to Lachlan.

"He wants to build real estate and a business complex, he even mentioned apartments. He says it would bring appeal to Alpine Ridge—get more people to move here. Fuck this Rhett, the town doesn't want this. Your parents aren't the only ones in control here." Lachlan's voice was growing louder, deeper as he began his spiral.

"I know, I know. Fuck..." I ran my hand through my hair. "And Dad's going for it?"

"Says it would be a good investment. David wants the back end—away from the stables but the fields would share a fence line to it."

"The cattle..."

"Yeah, Rhett."

"Listen, I'll call my dad and talk. Once he learns David's not in it for business, he'll understand." I looked at my wife again, beaming with joy as Grace talked to her. "I can't have that asshole there any longer. Get him off the property."

I hung up before Lachlan could respond. Placing my phone screen down on the counter, I turned just in time to hear the sliding glass door open, and watch the two laughing ladies stroll in. I spun in my chair, putting on my best "just looking at social media" face, hiding the fact that Lachlan had just managed to put a dent in my day. I reached for Kyla and when she stepped into my arms, her hips knocked my knees out of her way so she could press her body into mine, and I felt my world stop spinning. She gave me a light kiss on the lips.

"You almost ready?" I asked softly, knowing full well she'd rather be with her friend.

She hummed in approval and gave me another small kiss. "I just need to use the restroom." She grabbed my hat from the counter and placed it on my head. "Give me a minute?"

She left, leaving Grace and I alone in the kitchen. I turned to look at her, not knowing exactly what to say. I knew she helped Kyla overcome what plagued her, and I couldn't thank her enough for that.

So, I settled with, "Thank you."

"For?" she asked, raising an eyebrow.

"Talking with her, comforting her."

"Me?" She placed her palm on her chest. "I didn't do anything. I just listened to her tell me what happened and then called her mom some very choice words. *You* comforted her."

I scoffed. "I didn't do anything."

"You were there. You held her, you let her know she was safe without really telling her she was safe. She just knew. I've seen her take days to recover from an attack—anxiety or panic. You, Rhett. You just"—she waved her hand—"you seem to take it away."

I blinked at her, my breathing stuttering as her words rang over and over in my mind. *You seem to take it all away.*

"Okay, I'm ready." Kyla came back in the kitchen, sounding as if nothing had happened the night before. The tension that I must have created myself completely gone as her smile lightened up the room. She wrapped her arms around Grace's neck for one last hug, closing her eyes and enjoying the moment with her friend.

Grace squeezed once more, before pulling her away. Kyla walked around the island and stood in front of me again, cupping my face in her palms. Beauty. Confidence. Self-worth. It all radiated from her.

"Ready?" she asked, raising her eyebrows as her thumb traced my jaw line.

Staring at her in awe, I nodded, moving my face slightly to kiss her palm. "Yeah," I responded. "Let's go."

THIRTY-ONE

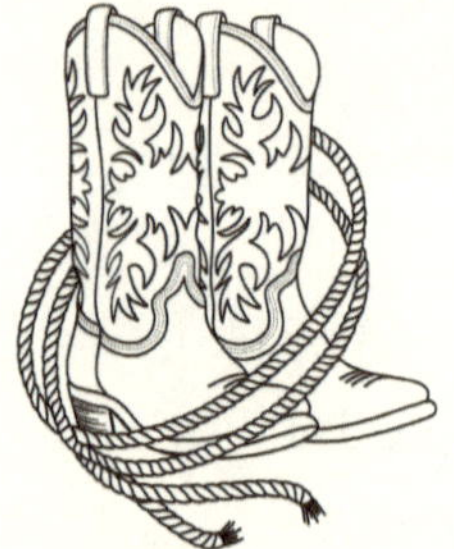

Kyla

MY MIND WAS REELING. Rhett's thumb glided over mine as he held my hand in the cab, the gentle reminder that his hands were firm on me last night. I could still feel his fingers pressing into my shoulder and his hand intertwined with mine. I could still hear his heartbeat, calm and steady as it lulled me to sleep.

I've had panic and anxiety attacks before, and the recovery would always seep into the next day. My head would hurt, my heart would still beat faster than normal, and my eyes would be puffy. I would be drained of everything. David had caused many of those attacks. I would call my mother for help—motherly advice, if you will—only to be told to listen to my fiancé, take his words and just let them roll off my back. Then I would break. I felt as if I had no support, no love, no care from the two people who should be giving it to me. Whenever I would break David would shake his head and make himself the victim by telling me I was overreacting or overthinking. My feelings were never valid. And I always believed him. I was the problem. I was the reason for all the bad things that were happening to me. Then, once I apologized for how I reacted, he would pull me in for a hug and tell me it was okay, that I just needed to understand where he was coming from.

His words would ultimately cause another panic attack.

The last one I truly had was the day before I left. I finally found the courage to go through with it, but the simple idea was daunting. Grace was there to calm me down, and help me sift through the emotions afterward, telling me they were justified, but the recovery time was still there.

Last night, once the tears had stopped flowing and I was in Rhett's arms, the panic—the fear—lifted. He calmed the storm that was brewing inside me. He parted the clouds and cleared my mind, taking the tears away by simply saying a few words that rang in my ears all night long.

Tell me how to make you better. I'm here. I've got you.

I woke up feeling refreshed, although slightly nervous about why I felt fine when I gently kissed Rhett and showered before we left for Grace's house. Then the moment Grace and I sat out on the porch, the truth came flowing out.

"I'm not sure why . . ." I sipped my mimosa. *"But he made it all go away, just by being there."*

"Do you think it's from the way he reacted to it? He didn't blame you or turn it back on you. He said it was okay and then was there for you. No words were really needed?"

I looked back into the house, seeing Rhett sitting patiently on the kitchen island. "Just being near him . . . it's like he pulls everything away and just—"

"Calms the storm?"

"Exactly." Funny how Grace always knew exactly what I was thinking. "I didn't wake up with a headache, I didn't think about what was said or done, I was just . . . awake—in his arms. Comfortable. Calm."

"And that's . . ." Grace's voice drew out.

"Different. He was there, unlike anyone else. He was defending me in front of my mother, then took my hand and led me out of the house, and then just . . . I've never had someone react that way before. I had to explain myself. I had to talk about it again moments after it happened, but Rhett—"

"He just wanted to make sure you were okay."

"I apologized," I admitted.

"Figured. You apologize for a lot of things you don't need to."

"Then he apologized, told me he should have never riled my mother up, and just . . . made sure I knew he had me." I smiled. "I never realized that's what I needed."

"Summer of Cowboys."

"Summer of Rhett. I also—" I swallowed, ready to admit the next part out loud to someone. "I may have said I love him to my mother. And then I told him I meant it."

"We're here." Rhett pulled me from my thoughts as we pulled up in front of a large arena, the biggest I had seen since my time with him—and Billings was pretty big.

"It's *huge*." I leaned forward, my hand slipping from his as I tried to see the entirety of the arena from the cab. I looked over at Rhett, my eyes wide.

He wiggled his eyebrows and winked. "Come on, let's go get Buckle settled and find Wyatt."

The arena was bigger on the inside than on the outside. I felt like I was stepping into the Tardis as Rhett led me around. Someone was using a truck to drag the dirt, making me wish I was in the small arena in Idaho running the Ground Hog. The big screens sat overhead on both ends of the arena, and were currently showing ads for *the Cowboy Channel*. There were so many seats, I wasn't even sure where to start looking. What would it look like once it was filled with people?

"Tie-down ropers are here." He pointed to the chutes. Normally I sat off to the left, close enough that I could see the whites in his eyes as he rode, but here the seats were higher up. He wouldn't be as close, and it would be harder for me to jump out of the seat to go meet him for a hug and kiss after his ride.

"How am I supposed to watch you? I won't be able to see anything." I sighed, turning my head in all directions. "I won't be able to get to you after your ride."

He pulled me close, the feel on his body on mine only a reminder of last night. "You'll be there, with easy access to the chutes." He pointed behind him, having me spin in his arms, holding me tight to his chest. "You're right above the announcer box so"—he kissed my temple—"throw peanuts at Wyatt."

I shook my head, chuckling as he made a joke at his brother's expense. "I'll make sure to throw peanuts while you're doing your run."

"Oh, in that case don't throw peanuts at Wyatt. He needs to be on top of his game."

"So do you." I twisted again and placed my hands on his shoulders. "Are you okay? Focused? Had enough time?" I asked softly as I ran my hands through his hair, the feeling only making my breath twitch.

"I'm fantastic. I'm at the Days of 47 Rodeo, I have my girl in my arms, and am one step closer to the NFR. I'm fantastic." He stopped and furrowed his brow, lowering his chin, the brim of his hat shadowing his eyes. "I should be asking you if you're okay, you've been quiet."

"I." I kissed his lips. "Am." I kissed him again. "Perfect."

He raised an eyebrow, clearly not believing me.

"Really," I assured him. "I am. I wish I could explain it—"

"Try," he said softly as he gently moved my hair behind my ear.

How did I even begin to tell him that I felt peace in his arms, that he—just him being near me—took the clouds that sometimes crept into my brain away? I bet he didn't even know he was doing anything, but he gave me confidence. He gave me the freedom that I so badly needed. How did I tell him that he was quickly becoming my everything?

When I looked at him, things became clear. The depth to his eyes grounded me and pulled me away from whatever was coming. It didn't matter that David was an issue, it didn't matter that my mother would never accept our marriage. All that mattered was him and me and . . . us. I told him I was falling for him, but I truly believe, now, that I had fallen.

I opened my mouth to tell him exactly that but closed it as soon as I saw his eyebrows pinch, and kissed him instead.

"I don't want to talk about anything before your ride," I answered, taking his hat from his head and gently placing it on top of mine. "How about we go out after the rodeo? We can talk and—"

"You took my hat." He cocked a grin, a glint in his eye.

I flashed a teasing grin. "I did."

"We won't be going out tonight if you're taking my hat."

"Noted, then . . . we'll have to order in."

"And talk?"

I nodded. "And talk. Now"—I slid my hands down his arms—"show me the arena, I saw a mechanical bull and a churro stand."

He laughed, lifting his chin in the air. "Okay, okay, let's go get a churro."

I lasted four seconds on the mechanical bull, Rhett lasted eight. Being the show off he was, he hopped on twice for another eight seconds. After an amazing barbecue burger and draft beer, I was sitting in the arena right next to the announcer box, watching as the Steer Wrestlers took the calves down by the horns. I was close enough to Wyatt that I could call out to him but refrained. He was in his element and since I had normally kept my focus on the other cowboys, it was a fun change to see how he reacted.

"Whoo-eee!" he called. "He almost got that one, but that little guy was just too fast, so a no score. Now, here at Days of 47, the only gold medal rodeo . . ."

I chuckled. Listening to him, I could have sworn he was faking a slight southern accent.

Once the Steer Wrestlers were done, Wyatt took his hat off his head and turned to me, a large smile as he walked up.

"What do you think?"

"Of the rodeo or . . . ?" I sang.

"Me." He held his arms out, pride flowing through him.

I shook my head. "Just get back to announcing. Tie-down is next."

"You're becoming a rodeo pro. Next thing we know you'll be going for queen." He gawked, putting his hat back on his head and returning to his microphone.

The Rodeo Clown began to make his appearance, walking around the crowd as my stomach began twisting in knots waiting for Rhett to take his time on the dirt. This was—making myself chuckle at the thought—not my first rodeo. I had gone to plenty since the Fourth of July, but this one just felt different. There were more cowboys, more livestock, more kids holding on for dear life to sheep as they ran across the dirt. This was a major rodeo. If I was nervous just sitting in the stands, I couldn't imagine what Rhett was feeling.

"Wyatt," I called, knowing the clown had a few more minutes in the spotlight. "Wyatt!"

He turned, grabbing his drink and heading over to me. "Yes, My Queen."

"First of all, don't call me that. Rhett never even used that nickname. Second, this rodeo is huge. Do you think Rhett has a chance?"

Wyatt scoffed, "Rhett works best under pressure."

"So, are you saying all those broken barriers . . . ?"

"Not enough pressure." He winked at me.

I rolled my eyes. "Just hype your brother up, okay? Make sure he gets to the NFR."

"If he lands tonight, he rides tomorrow in the Gold Medal—that's the one we want to count to the NFR."

"Then hype. Him. Up." I popped the P. "As your sister-in-law—"

"Ah, pulling *that* card are we?" Wyatt gave me a cheesy smile.

"Yes, I am, as your sister-in-law I demand you hype him up."

Shaking his head he tossed me a laugh. "Okay, you got it. I'll hype him up. He's fourth."

I nodded and inhaled, holding my breath for five seconds before letting it out through my round lips. I bet I had more anxiety than my husband.

Jaxson was first, then Darren and a rider named Stetson who made me think of Stetson back at the ranch. I made a mental note to call them after Rhett's ride. I knew they had to be watching, and knowing that made me miss them. I missed Stetson and Abi, even Lachlan despite his grumpy ass. I missed all of it. And then, that same feeling of calm rushed over me. Home.

"And up next is Rhett Hartwell, riding his mare Buckle. Rhett went through a rough patch the past couple of rides, but tonight it's different. He's got his girl—his new wife—right behind us, and she's told me I have to hype him up." Wyatt chuckled.

The fellow announcer laughed. "Are we allowed to hype up a rider?"

"Being rodeo announcers means that is literally our job, but she happened to pull the sister-in-law card, and I feel as if that was a direct threat so . . . You hear that, bro? You better be fully hyped up."

Rhett was on the big screen, his rope waving in the air next to Buckle, shaking his head back and forth and he chuckled. I wish I could be close enough to hear that laugh, but then he gave a quick nod, and the calf was let out of the chute, and he took off. As always, I watched his every move, reveling in the way his muscles flexed once he jumped off Buckle and lifted the calf. I was suddenly very upset he took his hat back.

"A 7.0 for Rhett, putting him in the top slot tonight, I guess you can say you did your sister-in-law proud by hyping him up because that worked. That was one hell of a ride!" The announcer cheered.

I smiled, and leapt from my seat, rushing to the gate closest to where Rhett would be. No one stopped me, not even the guards that were standing close to Wyatt. Rhett saw me, his eye catching mine as he jumped from Buckle and made his way towards me. I was stopped at the railing, not willing to jump the several feet down to the ground. I was unable to go any closer, but Rhett took the chance and climbed the bars to me, reaching me so fast I could barely make sense of it. He took my neck with a free hand to pull me in for the deepest, strongest kiss we had shared in public.

I love this man.

"And that—in case anyone had any doubts—is my sister-in-law. This will be her second time appearing on a rodeo screen, but I'm sure she's completely oblivious to everyone watching her and my brother."

I pulled back at Wyatt's words and looked at Rhett before my eyes drifted to the big screens. I laughed, remembering seeing myself on the screen on the Fourth of July and how I almost shied away. This time, all I did was smile at my husband and lean down for another kiss as the world watched us.

"Okay you two, up next is Zeke Laraway, so let him have his moment, yeah?"

Rhett looked up at me and gave me a smile that reached his eyes. I mirrored him, reaching down slightly to grab his hat and place it on top of my head, not even caring that the cameras were still focused on us.

"Wearing my hat again, Mrs. Hartwell?"

"See you after the rodeo," I whispered, suddenly extremely happy I had gone back to the hotel room before the rodeo began.

THIRTY-TWO

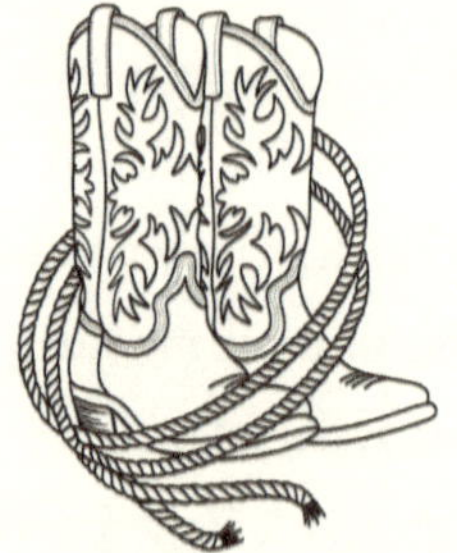

Rhett

I PULLED KYLA INTO the hotel room later that night, and pressed her against the wall the second the door was closed, taking her mouth with mine. I could kiss her all night long, kiss every piece of her. She moaned against my lips, her fingers sliding into my hair, forcing my hat to fall to the ground. Her tongue danced with mine as my fingertips found her skin. I lifted her tank top up slightly, just enough to let me see that purple lace bra hiding underneath, bringing the heat in all the right areas, and I felt my cock get harder and harder with each touch.

But then she pulled away.

"We said we would talk after the rodeo," she said breathlessly.

I growled, giving her another kiss. "But then you put my hat on."

"I promise we won't break the rule, but we should probably talk." Her breath hitched as I kissed the crook of her neck. "Rhett . . ."

"We'll talk, we'll talk," I repeated. "But I just need," I rumbled, "you."

Kyla let out a heavy breath. "Rhett, trust me, I need you—want you—too. But . . . I need . . ." she gasped between each word, only making it harder for me to stop, until finally she pushed me away, her arms flying straight out in front of her. "I need to talk to you."

Letting out a deep sigh I dropped my head, feeling her lips kiss my hair. I raised my chin slightly, raising an eyebrow to look her in the eye.

"Okay, let's talk." I gave in.

Her hands found my face, lifting me to her. "Thank you," she whispered before kissing me again. "I still don't know how to put everything into words."

Earlier she had said she was feeling perfect, but the small differences in how she moved told me otherwise. We still hadn't talked about what happened with her mother, what *was* happening with David. With only two more rodeos until we returned to Idaho, it had to be talked about eventually. I could feel the tension in her body, but according to Grace she was more comforted than she had ever been. She said she didn't know how to put what she needed to say into words, and all I could think to tell her was . . .

"Try," I said softly.

She ran her hands down my arms, grasping my hands in hers, lacing our fingers together.

"Panic attacks aren't rare for me. In fact, they are more common than anything else," she began, bringing our joined hands to her heart. I kissed her fingers, "Normally I would have one and have to take time to recover, only to have another thrust upon me. David mostly—"

"I hate him," I interrupted.

"Hey now." She sighed.

"Sorry." I kissed her. "Sorry," I whispered.

"David would put it all back on me. Tell me I was overreacting, overthinking—that I was the problem and I fully believed him. My last *true* panic attack, before yesterday, was when I made the decision to leave David. I was terrified of what he would do, and the recovery was bad. Ask Grace. It took days . . ." She leaned her head against the wall, making me realize we were still in the same position we were in when we came inside. We didn't move, so caught up in the moment, but now this was just as important. "That was the longest time I ever needed to recover from something like that. I wasn't expecting to break after speaking with my mother—"

"You didn't break." I released her hands and cupped her face. "You didn't—"

"I know, I know." She placed her hands on my wrists, "But it sure felt like it. All the raw feelings just burst out of me and I just couldn't hold it in anymore. The tears just wouldn't stop coming . . . until you took me in your arms."

I furrowed my brow.

"Grace has held me through many attacks, but it's nothing like what you did. Nothing. You told me I was real, you told me my feelings were valid, and then you . . ." She let out a breathy sigh. "You held me." She kissed me softly. "It was as if the anxiety and panic vanished when I heard your heartbeat. This morning, when I woke up, I expected a headache and pain but all I felt was calm. All I felt was *you*."

I searched her eyes, pulling in every word she was saying. That me simply being there was enough for her. If only she knew all I ever wanted for her was to be safe, to be loved . . . Knowing that I was giving that to her, made my entire being worth it. Kyla was . . . she was . . .

My whole heart.

"Kyla I . . ." I began, like her, finding it hard to find the way to form the words.

"Everything I said in front of my mother was true. I meant every word. You make me feel so much and I just . . . Rhett, I think I'm falling for you harder than I thought. You're becoming my everything, Rhett. I'm absolutely in awe with the way you make me feel and I know . . . I know . . ." She paused, drawing in a shaky breath. "Nothing outside of you and me matters."

You and me.

"You and me?"

"I don't think I've ever been more certain about anything."

"I love you," I said, knowing that nothing else mattered at that moment than letting her know. "I've loved you since the moment I saw you. I've wanted to keep you safe, hold you close and just . . . be yours."

She kissed me then, her fingers lacing through my hair as she pulled me closer to her. I could taste her, feel every part of her, sense her need to have me just as much as I needed her. The heat radiated through us as we tangled together and I used my hands to raise her arms above her head without stopping the kiss. I glided my fingers down her arms as she kept them up, reaching the hem of her shirt. Breaking the kiss, I pulled the fabric over her head, her skin burning once the tips of my fingers trailed down to the clasp of the purple lace.

"Kyla." I kissed her neck, feeling her hands move down to my shirt as she began to unbutton the top, slowly working her way down. "I'm yours . . . if you'll have me."

"I want all of you." She breathed, heavily.

I stopped, pulling my head up to look at her. She met my gaze, her hand still working the last few buttons on my shirt until she finally was able to pull it off, letting out a small hum of disapproval once she saw my undershirt.

"Cowboys wear way too many layers, don't you get hot under the sun? Running and lifting the calf . . . I think I need to see you do that with less clothing on," Kyla bit her bottom lip, yanking my shirt over my head. The moment her hands met my torso I sucked in a sharp breath, remembering the feeling of that first night together. This was more heated, more passionate, more intimate, more *everything*. More love flowed between us than I had ever felt in my entire life.

I raised an eyebrow. "I'm thinking you'd like to see me rope a calf wearing nothing at all. I'm right, aren't I, Mrs. Hartwell?"

Her eyes shot up to mine, her hands working my belt buckle. "Call me that again."

"*Mrs. Hartwell*." I kissed her. "I love you," I whispered, "Mrs. Hartwell."

"Hey, Cowboy." She lifted her chin. "As much as I'd like you to take me against this wall—"

I lifted her by her ass, her legs wrapping around my waist, and I turned, leaning my head down to kiss her shoulder, moving us towards the bed. I laid her on her back, climbing over her.

"You are fucking perfect," I grumbled, watching her skin come to life in the moonlight. "I will worship you for—"

"You keep saying that." She laughed, her hands working my pants down my legs. "You've worshiped me before. How about I worship you?"

With little effort she flipped me on my back, straddling me as her hands glided over my body.

"You're the man who makes me feel alive. Let me show you how much you mean to me. Rhett, let *me* worship *you*." Her voice was heavy as her body moved against me, and I moaned. The more she did that, the harder I would come and god damn . . . I wanted to feel her.

"*Kyla,*" I moaned, reaching my hands up to cup her breasts, but she moved, her body gliding down mine. She bent down and kissed my stomach, my navel, the sides of my hips. "I want you."

"You have me, Rhett. All of me."

Then the world went fuzzy—dizzying—as we took turns giving into each other, worshiping over and over until we cried out and shook. The feeling rushing through us like never before. It was electric. That spark you hear about came to life between us and the pull was indescribable. The connection was so deep I couldn't believe it was real. That *we* were real. That she was mine and I was hers. Curled up in each other's arms after our breathing finally steadied,

Kyla nuzzled into my neck, giving me a quick kiss before she drifted off to sleep. I was not far behind her. Sleep found me gently, my body and mind feeling absolute with her next to me.

Kyla shifted, a soft hum leaving her lips. We had slept in, far later than we should have, but the sun crept through the hotel curtains, hitting her shoulder just right. She slept against me, her legs tangled in mine, using my chest as a pillow. I tried not to stir, not wanting to wake, but also desperate to have her again.

I didn't lie when I said I had loved her since the first time I saw her—truly I did. If love at first sight was real, that was me. I fell hard and fast for her and now, she trusted me enough to love me back. It didn't bother me that she hadn't said those words directly to me—hell, it was early—but I knew she meant them. And that was enough.

She would be safe here, and I think she knew that. She was loved and cared for, *worshiped* and appreciated. And now I could show her that every single day.

I traced my thumb on her shoulder, drawing slow, soft circles and making her skin slightly twitch under me. She stirred again, a deep breath leaving her. She needed to sleep, I needed to sleep. But I needed to go tend to Buckle and get ready for the event tonight. This was our last night in Utah, then off to Cheyenne and back home. *Home.*

I couldn't wait to take Kyla home.

My phone buzzed somewhere on the other side of the room. In our rush to have each other, we had left everything on the floor. Our clothes, boots, and even my hat were tossed aside as if they were nothing. I would have ignored it if it wasn't a constant buzz. Kissing Kyla's forehead, I slowly untangled myself from her warmth, grabbing my pants to dig for my phone.

Abi's name lit up the screen, and I furrowed my brow. Lately I had been hearing from Lachlan, not my sister.

I cleared my throat softly and answered.

"Hey, morning."

"Morning, bro." Abi's voice was loud and I almost shushed her, but looked back over at Kyla. She was awake already, her eyes focused on me. She shifted, her hands gliding under the pillow, a soft hum leaving her. She looked relaxed—pure bliss covering her features as she lay in bed.

A corner of my lips tipped up. I *so* didn't want to be on this phone call.

"Good morning, Abi. How can I help you?" I asked as I stood, fully aware that I was going to be ignoring my sister the moment I sat on the edge of the bed. Kyla's hand found my waist and it trailed up my back.

"Oh nothing, just figured I'd call you and wish you luck on the event today. Gold Medal Wednesday."

I shuddered as Kyla's hands roamed my back, slowly finding their way lower.

"Yup," I answered. "Gold Medal Wednesday." With my other hand I reached down and grasped Kyla's, guiding her closer and closer to where I was suddenly very, very hard.

"Oh, and I thought you'd be interested to know that David officially gave Dad an offer yesterday."

"What?" I snapped, causing Kyla to jump and her hand to pull away.

She scooted up in the bed, the sheet falling from her body. "What's wrong?" she asked. "Is Stetson okay?"

"Stetson is fine." I angled the phone away and looked at my wife. "It's . . ."

God, she didn't need to know this now, but then again, if I told her, it may take some of the weight off my shoulders. She was open and honest with me last night. I reached up to cup her check, and she smiled, leaning into my hand.

"It's a pretty good one too," Abi continued.

"It's not going to happen." I sighed, keeping my eyes on Kyla.

"What is it?" she whispered.

"Oh, I know it's not," she sighed. "He said he'd give us a week to think on the offer, then he'd come back with papers ready to be signed because he knew we wouldn't say no." She chuckled as I heard movement in the background. I could picture her moving around the kitchen, getting Stetson ready for riding lessons or feeding a few of the ranch hands. Abi was always on the move. "Does he really think he's fooling us?"

"No, I don't think he does. He's trying to get under our skin, he's playing a game."

Kyla's jaw dropped and her mouth slightly formed the word, *David.*

I nodded.

Letting out a long-exasperated sigh, Kyla plopped back onto the bed, her brown hair flying over the white of the sheets. She stared at the ceiling, her head shaking lightly.

"Listen, don't . . . just don't do anything until I get back. I just have tonight, and then Wyoming . . ."

"And then a twelve-hour drive home. Trust me, Lach and I are on douchebag alert." Abi let out another laugh. "Stetson, no, go get your boots. Tell Kyla we love her and we'll see you soon. We're watching tonight. Do *not* let this get to you, okay? No more broken barriers."

"No more broken barriers. I'm grounded now," I admitted, placing my hand on Kyla's thigh. "Bye, Abi."

"Bye!"

I hung up the phone and tossed it on the floor. It hit with a thud as I climbed my way back to Kyla, lying on top of her, my arms creating a cage around her shoulders. She let out a sigh, her hands moving to find my skin again.

"You've had more on your mind than you've let on," she said softly.

"I have," I admitted. I kissed the bridge of her nose.

"You gonna fill me in?" Her fingers brushed my checks, her thumbs finding my lower lip. "I think you'll feel better if you do."

Dropping my forehead to hers, I closed my eyes. "It's David . . "

THIRTY-THREE

Kyla

Pissed didn't even begin to describe how I felt. I knew David was going to be an issue, but I honestly hoped he would have given up by now. The fact that he was still at the ranch, still trying to weasel his way in, pissed me off. And from what Rhett said, he was succeeding at it.

Rhett tried to calm *me* down when it should be the opposite. He began to rub my shoulders, the coldness from his wedding band finding my skin. He assured me that David wouldn't get away with it, that even though his dad saw the benefit, nothing would come of it. He promised me that David would be gone, and it would be me and him, from this moment on.

He kissed me, apologized for keeping it from me for so long, and then urged me to join him in the shower.

I sighed. As amazing as that sounded, I needed a moment.

I fell back on the bed once I heard the shower start. I was tempted to grab a pillow and scream into it. No matter what I did *he* would always be there, wouldn't he? There was no way around him. I left, he followed. I got married, he told me it's a game. I found a way to move on, he called my mother. I found a place to call home, he tried to take it from me. I wanted to be wrapped in Rhett's arms, I wanted to feel his warmth and hear his voice in my ear. I wanted that more than anything right now and he was still finding a way to take that from me.

I was done with that.

He was done taking things from me.

I decided that *days* ago.

So why in the world was I letting it get to me?

Slapping my hands down on the bed, the thud of the comforter echoed through the room. I let out a long groan.

"Get over yourself, Kyla," I scolded myself as I shot up, the sheets falling from my skin. "And go join your husband in the shower."

I climbed out of the bed, feeling the cold air hit my skin, but the pure thought that soon the warm water, and Rhett's hands would be all over me, warmed up my blood. The bathroom door was slightly open, as if he was hoping I'd join. Slowly opening the door, I silently stepped in, the steam already feeling hot against me. Moving the curtain aside, I did something I never did with David. I peaked.

And all the anger that nestled its way into my chest lifted as I took in sight of my husband.

He faced the shower head, his brown hair wet as he ran his hands, covered in shampoo, over his head. His back was perfectly defined, taking my breath away just looking at it. And his ass, my knees wobbled just looking at it. He didn't move, didn't even know I was there, just kept his face under the stream of water. He was so in the moment—letting the water wash away the worry that came from this phone call this morning. He inhaled, his muscles flexing.

I reveled in the fact that this man was *mine*.

I stepped in the shower, reaching out for him, my fingers grazing his hips softly.

"I was hoping you'd come in," Rhett said softly, spinning to face me. "I'm so sorry, I didn't mean to upset you."

I was upset, even still, but not at him. Never at him.

"I don't think I could ever be upset at you." I wrapped my arms fully around his waist, our bodies becoming flush against each other.

"Oh, I bet down the road you'll find something. We have plenty of years ahead of us for that."

"I love the sound of that." I leaned my chin on his chest, gently kissing his neck.

He hummed, taking a step back into the stream so it crashed into me. The heat only stung for a moment before I melted into the hot water. Kissing my forehead, his hands trailed along my spine, and I felt his lips curve against my skin.

"I'm sorry I didn't tell you," he whispered. "I should have before, when Lachlan first called me, but I didn't want you to have it on your shoulders, along with everything else."

"But it was on your shoulders. Is that why you were getting so many bad runs?" I lifted my head, to take him in. Eyes heavy on me, he took the moment to kiss me.

I felt his chest rise as he took a deep breath, breaking the kiss. "Part of it. It was all I could think of there for a minute. But you, Kyla, you pulled me back to what I need to focus on."

"That calf."

"You. Us."

He moved, his hands cupping my face as he brought me up to him for a kiss. That electric pull buzzed, bringing butterflies to not just my stomach but every single part of me.

"And the calf. . ." he smiled against my lips.

I laughed, using a fist to gently punch him in the shoulder. I was so gone for this man.

"Gold. Medal. Wednesday." Wyatt's voice boomed through the loudspeakers. "Everyone here is in for a treat, the gold medal winners tonight are one step closer to the NFR in Vegas—every Cowboy's ultimate goal—and you're here to witness them do their best to get the highest scores and the best times. But first let's introduce our cowboys!"

A truck drove around the arena with the Saddle Bronc and Bareback riders, as well as the Bull Riders and Steer Wrestlers. The tie-down ropers rode out with the barrel racers and my eyes instantly caught on Rhett. He wore a red shirt tonight, rather than his signature blue shirt, and he looked like fire. He waved to the crowd once Wyatt said his name, standing to remove his hat to wave again. His hat was black tonight, which threw me off, but also made me weak. I had only seen him in brown and tan hats, but that black hat. I twisted my lips, hoping he would let me wear it.

The Bareback and Saddle Bronc riders were first, followed by the Mutton Busting and Steer Wrestling. Each event had a medal ceremony after, and the gold medal winner did a small interview on the stage. It made the night different, more exciting as the winners got to step up on the podium. I loved it—every single second of it.

I pulled my phone from my pocket and snapped a photo of the arena, and sent it to Grace.

Me

Wish Rhett luck! Tie-down is up next!

Those little dots danced on the screen.

Grace

Good luck, Mr. Hartwell, let me know how he fares. Ground looks a bit worn. You should go comb it.

Kyla

Drag it, ha . . . they will before the barrel racers.

"Kyla!" Wyatt called from the announcer booth. I looked down at him as he waved me over.

"I just got a text. They are expecting Rhett to place tonight so they want you ready to get on the stage once he's done being interviewed."

"They think he'll get gold?" I asked, leaning forward on the railing.

"If not gold, silver. I don't doubt he'll place, so get over there."

I widened my eyes. The chutes were under the announcer box. I could leave my seat and go to the chutes to find him—not easily like the other arenas—but I could always find him after his ride. The winner's podium was on the opposite side of the arena. I looked at the stand and then over to Wyatt.

"How?"

Giving a chuckle, Wyatt went over to his partner, said something in his ear and then motioned for me to follow with a wave of his arm. I didn't even hesitate; I leapt from my chair and started to follow Wyatt. We walked behind the stands, a few of the cowboys passing us. I saw Jaxson and Darren, and both gave me a quick hug before Wyatt grabbed my wrist to pull me along.

"Go get on your horses," he grumbled at them.

They both shook him off and tipped their hats to me.

"Be nice," I said to Wyatt as I caught up to him.

"I am nice." Wyatt smiled.

"Wyatt Hartwell, you are not where you're supposed to be." I heard a deep southern drawl come from behind us, and when I turned, I saw the man it belonged to. He wore a tan cowboy hat and denim button-down shirt. His dark-wash Wranglers made the gold belt buckle stand out, his black boots only adding to his look. His tawny skin was smooth, not a scuff in sight, and his eyes were dark. So dark they were almost black. He looked important. He looked official. He looked like he lived and breathed rodeo. "Tie-down is about to start right after that interview and you'll need to announce."

"Yeah, yeah, Cash. I'll be there. Gotta get my sister in-law to the other side." Wyatt sneered.

"I'll take her." The man smiled, his eyes flicking to me. "Kyla, right? I've heard Rhett talk about you. I'm Cash Callahan." Cash held out his hand.

I took it and shook. "Kyla Hartwell, nice to meet you."

He winked and his smile faded as he turned back to Wyatt. "I'm heading that way to meet up with Quinn. Get your ass back to the announcer booth would ya?"

Wyatt rolled his eyes. "See ya soon, Kyla. Don't let this guy talk you into barrel racing."

I watched Wyatt walk away and turned back to Cash. "Why would you talk me into barrel racing?"

"I'm a trainer, come on, Little Miss, let's go find that husband of yours."

Little Miss? There was another nickname Rhett never tried to use, and I wasn't quite sure how I felt about it coming from Cash Callahan.

"You're a trainer?" I asked, brushing the nickname off my shoulders, and making small talk as we rounded the corner. I heard the cheers, telling me they just finished interviewing the Steer Wrestlers and that Wyatt would be announcing Tie-down any second now. As much as I was looking forward to seeing Rhett, I was suddenly annoyed I was missing his event.

"Yes, ma'am."

"Did you do any events before?"

"Saddle Bronc, but I've retired."

"Did you ever get to the NFR?"

"Nope. Got bucked off and broke a leg. Took surgeries and a lot of recovery time to heal. I've never been on that dirt since." He opened the gate, gesturing to let me step in first.

"You stopped riding?"

"Didn't say that, did I?" Cash smiled at me again. "They'll want you here," he said as we stepped into a crowd. "Go ahead and have a seat, and when Rhett is on the stage, you'll meet him after."

I nodded and stood still around a few others.

"Nice to meet you." Cash tipped his hat.

"Thanks." I smiled at him before folding my arms over my chest, turning back to the arena.

"Enjoy the show." Cash gave me a final nod before leaving the gate, making his way over to a girl and her horse.

Enjoy the show? How could I when I was so far away from the chutes? I couldn't see Rhett. My mind went to last night. How I kissed him once he climbed the gate to me, taking his hat even though the big screen was focused on us. Would he even know I was over here? He would look for me—he always did—but I wouldn't be there to catch his gaze.

Wyatt's voice boomed over the speaker, and I listened intently as I watched the screen above me.

Jaxon first . . . a 8.0.

Darren next . . . 10.5.

Zeke . . . 12.2.

A few names I didn't recognize all ranged between 7 to 12 seconds.

A few broken barriers and a few runaway calves.

My stomach started to churn.

Rhett . . .

He was flawless as always. Buckle knew exactly what to do and he landed with an 8.6 time.

I jumped and shouted, wishing I was there to see him up close. I saw his head search the crowd. He was too far away for me to notice facial expressions. He disappeared into the chutes again and after a few more runs, the top three were named: Jaxon, Rhett, and a man named Riley. Wyatt and his team were busy sharing facts about each roper as the three made their way across the arena. Once Rhett got close enough, I locked my gaze on him, willing him to notice me.

That pull worked its magic.

He tilted his head up, caught my gaze, and then broke out in a run, closing the space between us, pulling me in for a quick hug and kiss before he took his place next to Jaxson on the stage. The entire time Rhett was on the podium, giving waves to the crowd and a quick interview, his eyes were on me. Those winks, those grins, those looks of pure joy were all for me.

I could see it in his face that the cloud that had been following him since Lachlan's first phone call was gone. He looked calm and proud to even be on the stage, confidence was radiating off of him.

I love that man, I thought to myself.

After another win in Cheyenne, our final night before returning to the chaos that would be Hartwell Hills Ranch, was spent under the stars. Rhett had somehow talked me into camping out, promising me he'd set up a tent but that he'd count it towards my bucket list. I gave in with the added promise he'd take me to breakfast before we would hit the road for home. Once the sun had set, and the stars shined brighter than I had ever seen them, I curled up to him on the grass, his thumb running up and down my shoulder, a calming motion that settled every nerve in my body.

Bravery seeped out of pores as I looked up at the moon. I would never have thought this before, never have yearned for a man that way I do now, and the little voice inside my head told me to jump, told me to go for it and show him exactly how much I wanted him.

"Hey." I moved against him, noticing his eyes were closed once my gaze found him. "You awake?"

He hummed in response, his eyebrows rising.

"Have you ever . . ." I said softly, my hand running down his chest, "made love under the stars?"

His eyes opened slowly as his chin dipped to look at me. He kissed me, his hand raising from under his head to cup my cheek, pulling me closer to him.

"Make love to me, Rhett," I whispered against his lips. I climbed on top of him, his lips finding mine with ease as he sat up, his arms linking around my waist.

"Are you sure? Kyla . . . I will." His voice was heavy, sleepy almost, but the need fueled him just as much as it did me. "Let's move to the tent . . . we can . . ."

"No." I kissed him. "Right here. Under the stars," I repeated, kissing him again.

He gave into me, his hands sliding up my shirt, causing my skin to chill. His lips found my skin as his hands began to explore my body. I felt his calloused fingers against me, slipping under my bra straps, the rough feel of him completely enveloping me. I wanted his hands everywhere; I wanted *him* everywhere, but if we were staying right where we were, we had to remain a little decent. Which was a shame really. Rhett would be a sight to see in the moonlight.

Our tongues danced with one another as I moved against him, my hands working his belt buckle with ease. I chuckled, arching my back slightly, remembering the first night I fidgeted with this same buckle, laughing once he had to take it over. Who knew a few nights of removing it would help me become an expert.

"What are you laughing at?" He smiled against my skin, his mouth moving to my neck.

"Just this damn belt buckle." I gasped feeling him bite my skin. "There you go, biting me again." I chuckled, my voice breathy.

He kissed the spot he bit. "What do you want me to do, Kyla?"

"Make love to me," I repeated for the third time, still not believing I was telling him to.

"Under the stars," he moaned, kissing me fiercely.

And our bodies began to move, blending together as all the pleasure radiated through us as we made love under the stars.

THIRTY-FOUR

Rhett

A PART OF ME didn't want our trip to end, I was almost tempted to jump on a few more rodeos to extend it, but Kyla reminded me of the reason we needed to get home. She kept me up to date on what Lachlan was saying, making sure we all were on the same page. The plan we put together was simple. Once we got back, we would call David to the ranch, sit him down, and refuse the offer.

Simple.

Easy.

Right?

I hoped so.

We got back late and the big house was dark, but Lachlan appeared to instantly help get Buckle settled. Kyla gave him a hug, which I think shocked him, before she gave me a quick kiss and headed inside. Lachlan raised his eyebrows and looked at me.

"She's staying?" he asked.

I watched as she opened my—*our*—front door and vanished inside. I nodded, a smile forming. "Yeah, she's staying."

"Congrats," he grumbled.

"Thanks," I responded sleepily, making my way to the back of the trailer. "Wyatt got asked to go to a few more rodeos, he was happy too. I think he lasted one drive with us."

"We won't need him for this meeting anyway, he doesn't have any interest in the ranch." Lachlan stepped in the trailer, making himself known to Buckle, who began to bob her head up and down. "He'll go along with what we say."

"Wyatt does like it, but he's not going to stay here." Once Buckle was out of the trailer, I grabbed her reins and led her to the stables. She moved slowly.

"Are we talking about my twin?" Abi's voice came up from behind me. I spun to see my sister, her arms crossed over her chest, her hair falling over her shoulders. She was wearing her pajamas and her pair of slipper boots. "He's a lost cause."

I chuckled. "No he's not, he's just not ready to stop yet."

"He's gonna get himself in trouble." Abi yawned. "Where's Kyla?"

"She went inside. She's tired. It's been a hell of a drive." I led Buckle into her stall, giving her a scratch behind her ears.

"We're home for a while. No rodeos until September."

"So." Abi leaned up against the gate. "I'll talk about the elephant in the . . . barn." She waved her arm around. "We're calling him up tomorrow to get him here. He gave us a week to accept the offer. We have two days."

I groaned. "I'd rather take a day to come home. I bet Kyla would like that too."

"So, take the day tomorrow to settle, and then we set up a meeting with him?"

"It's a damn good offer." Lachlan folded his arms and looked at Abi. Her gaze went directly to our cousin, a sigh leaving her lungs.

I left Buckle's stall, closed the gate behind me, and gave my cousin a glare. I hated that he admitted it was good. It felt as if he would go along with it too, like he would have no issue walking away from everything he's worked towards.

"Not gonna happen." I sighed. "We'll call him tomorrow, set up a meeting and get him the fuck out of here." Brushing my hands on my hips I began to walk out of the barn. "I'll talk to dad tomorrow, before we call him."

"Yeah. Tomorrow. We'll talk to dad." Abi sighed. "Get some sleep."

"I'll get Buckle fed," Lachlan added. "No need to thank me."

I waved my hand behind my back as I left the barn. Leaving my truck and trailer right where it was, I trudged to my house, wanting to be with Kyla more than anything. I hated that this was brought up right before trying to relax for the night. The one thing that would fix it was in my house, hopefully already in my—I sighed—*our* bed. All I needed was her in my arms and then I could deal with this in the morning.

I rubbed the back of my neck as I took a step into the front room, setting my hat on the table and kicking off my boots. Kyla had turned the kitchen light on, and a half full glass of water sat next to the sink. A soft smile and a sense of calm filled me as I looked at the normal things that would happen in every day life. Things I would get to see more and more.

Slowly making my way into the bedroom, I saw Kyla curled up. She hadn't even bothered to pull a blanket over her body. I removed my jeans and shirt, leaving me in my boxers and T-shirt, before grabbing a throw and softly crawling in next to her. I covered her first, draping what was left of the blanket over my legs, before I wrapped my arm around her waist and pulled her close.

She hummed and scooted closer to me. "Took you long enough."

"I got cornered by Abi and Lachlan."

She hummed again. "Are they okay?"

"Yeah." I closed my eyes. "We'll talk tomorrow. For now . . ." I sighed, kissing the crown of her head. "I just want to sleep."

"Me too. It feels so good to be home."

Home.

A blissful morning, that's what we had.

Kyla woke up and turned to face me. She kissed my neck and chin, bringing me to life in more ways than one. We made love slow and sensual—no rushing, no hard moments. Creating pleasure every way we could with our hands and mouths before finally coming together. We showered together, and found that we were still having a hard time keeping our hands off each other. The water had turned cold before Kyla finally convinced me we needed coffee.

She dressed while I made breakfast, and I absolutely loved it once she came up behind me, wrapping her arms around my waist. We drank our coffee, ate our breakfast, and just . . . were. We checked my standings—noticing I was still top in the nation—on the way to the NFR. We read a text from her mother and agreed we would call her *after* we handled David. Then Grace called and we ended up on FaceTime with her.

We planned out our next rodeo road trip and Kyla sent an email to the job she had lined up, with only a small amount of anxiety. Going back and forth between writing the email and calling, she finally decided to write the email first, and then call. Once the email was completed, she slammed the laptop shut and moved over to wrap her arms around my neck, burying her head in my shoulder.

I knew she was here, I knew she was staying, but that final step made it real.

After lunch we decided it was time to head over to the main house, show my family that we were indeed alive, and Kyla was indeed staying. She laced her fingers through mine as we left the house, not letting go for a second as we began to take the walk over.

I could get used to this—Kyla's hand in mine, the feeling of her ring against my finger. She was my wife. She had been in my life for two months, but it already felt like a lifetime. And we had more time. We had all the time in the world.

"So," I started, using her hand to pull her closer to me. I used that same hand to lift above her head, resting my arm on her shoul der. She didn't let go of my hand. "Are you serious about changing your name?"

"I mean . . ." she sang. "I do like the ring of Mrs. Hartwell, don't you?"

"I love it, just as much as I love you." I kissed her temple and she hummed. "But I don't want to force you into changing it if you don't want to. Kyla Richards has a good ring to it too."

"Not as good as Kyla Hartwell," she said as she leaned into me closer. "We are staying married right?"

"I plan to." I leaned over and kissed her temple.

"Me. Too. So let's talk about those dates we're supposed to go on. We're home, and we're here for a few weeks, right? What's the first date gonna be?"

Before I could answer her, I saw it, the black SUV that sped up the dirt path to the main house. Kyla didn't stop walking; her hand didn't squeeze mine, and her breathing stayed steady. She was calm—at least on the outside. I hoped I could portray that, because my heart was going a million beats per minute.

We had a plan.

And he was ruining it.

The SUV stopped as soon as we reached the front of the house, and he wasted no time. David opened the car door, shutting it quietly as he rounded the front of the car, that fake smile plastered on his face.

"Mr. Hartwell." He sneered. "You're back. I was so hoping you'd be here today. I've been having quite the time with—"

"David," I cut him off. "I'd like to say it's good to see you but—"

"It's great to see you too. I've been watching your progress with Steer Wrestling—"

"Tie-down," I corrected.

"You have a lot of failed attempts." He tsked his tongue once. I tightened my grip on Kyla's hand, grateful she still held on, if for nothing else, to stop me from punching him. "And second place in Utah? I still hope you have a shot getting to the NFR."

"He's still top in the nation David, we just checked. We *will* be going to the NFR," Kyla spat.

We. I loved knowing she would be coming with me. Even in this moment, just that knowledge brought a sense of grounding.

David's gaze went from me to Kyla. I could see his face twisting to find the right expression. He finally settled with a calm, longing gaze. I hated his eyes on my wife. He had no right.

"I saw you traveled with him. They had a blast showing you in-between the runs. They know more about you two than I think you do." He brushed his bottom lip with his thumb, his gaze frozen on Kyla as his eyes moved up and down.

"Well, that's what happens when your brother is an announcer." I cocked my head and glared.

"He liked to share the fact that you are newlyweds."

Fucking Wyatt.

"But you're not, are you?" His voice dropped as he looked to Kyla's left hand, no doubt eyeing the ring.

"Cut the shit," I snapped, finally dropping Kyla's hand, and taking a single step towards him. "Get off my property."

"Why would I do that when I was invited?" David chuckled and wiggled his shoulders, presenting himself again, as if he didn't just question our marriage. "I have a meeting with your dad. We want to discuss the offer I made on a portion of the land." His smile grew, reaching his eyes. His teeth were abnormally white, making me think he got them whitened just for this. *The prick . . .*

"How many times do I have to tell you—"

"And how many times do I have to tell you?" he interrupted. "Everything—"

"David . . ." Kyla sighed, folding her arms against her chest. "You know this sale isn't going to have the outcome you want."

"That's not up to you, is it, Kyla. Technically, it's not even up to your *husband*. It's up to his father, and that's who I've been in contact with. In fact"—he shifted his feet and nodded his chin towards the house—"I'm going to be late, so if you'll excuse me."

"I don't think so." I stepped in front of him, "I have just as much say as Lachlan does, and I know you don't have a meeting planned today—"

"What are you going to do, Rhett? Threaten me again? Shove a fake piece of paper in my face to get me to back off? It didn't work two weeks ago, and it's not going to work today. I'm here to talk to your father and cousin about purchasing a corner of your land. And when they sign, I'll be in your life forever and then I can guarantee you, I'll have my fiancé back." He stepped closer to me, his voice low, and a devilish glare spread across his face as his eyes darkened.

"Wait what? You threatened him?" Kyla asked, placing her hand on my shoulder.

"Sure did," David answered for me, his eyes flickering towards her for only a second before returning to me.

"I didn't threaten you. I told you to get out of town."

"What do you mean fake piece of paper?" Kyla asked, squeezing my shoulder as she stepped forward.

"A marriage license. One dated for April 24th, signed by you and Rhett. So even if you are legally married, I know for a fact it's just to piss me off." He twitched his eyes to look at Kyla, leaving them on her for a second before turning back to me. "It's not real."

"Come on David . . ." Kyla groaned, the warmth from her hand leaving my shoulder.

"Do you even want to know how I know it's not real?" David spat, a twitch in his jaw as he clenched his teeth.

I squinted. What the hell was he getting at?

"Come on Kyla, ask me."

"David. I told you—"

"I know. You said you met Rhett at a rodeo in Arizona and fell for him so hard and fast you traveled with him. We all know the bullshit you're spinning—both of you. But do you want to know how I know it's not real? That you two weren't really married on April 24th. That you were married just weeks ago. Right when I showed up."

"Enlighten me," I urged, "Tell me the reason."

He licked his bottom lip and raised his eyebrows. "What were you doing on April 24[th,] Rhett? You have to remember, it's all over the internet. All you have to do is search your history with the circuit. April 24th, you were in Tennessee, claiming the top spot in the Benton County Rodeo. Don't you remember? You almost beat your time."

My eyes widened.

Fuck.

"That's how I know you weren't really married on April 24th."

I stared at him. Not exactly knowing what to say or do, because the fucker was right. I was in Tennessee that day. I did several runs that day. I landed my best time of the season, well, so far, that day. And since Kyla and I were married June 24th, but she had told him we were married two months prior, I just picked the day to put on the license.

Fuck.

I could feel Kyla's eyes on me before she turned back to David. She was silent.

He laughed.

Laughed.

"I also know," he started, "that you"—his gaze turned to Kyla—"weren't here in April. You were in Arizona, still living with Grace—moping. You didn't leave until May, and for some reason you decided that this shit hole town in Idaho was the best place to settle." David took a deep breath and straightened his posture. I looked at Kyla, her eyes just as wide, shock spread across her face. "Now, if you'll excuse me. I have a meeting with your father and cousin that I don't want to be late for." Once again, he wiggled his shoulders, straightening his suit jacket, preparing for the role he was about to play.

But I wouldn't let him play it.

I put my hand on his shoulder, stopping him in his tracks. He turned and looked at me, his eyes darkening.

"Get your hand off of me," he growled.

"Rhett?" I heard Lachlan's voice from behind me. "What's going on?"

I ignored him. "Get the fuck off my property, before I call the police."

"And what are they going to do? I've done nothing wrong."

"You're trespassing. You're not welcome here and you know it."

"Rhett," I heard Kyla say, feeling her hand on my lower back. "Let's just go in . . . have lunch . . . decline his offer and then it will be over. It will all be over."

"No offense, Kyla." David looked over my shoulder at her. "This doesn't concern you. So why don't you be a good fiancée and go get your things, and get in the car. I'm sure your mother will be happy to know you'll be making the right decision."

That's it.

Pure rage possessed me as I pushed him back with a stronger force than intended, and balled my hand into a fist, readying myself to swing.

"Don't you *ever* speak to my wife again."

"Or what? You'll punch me? I can easily take your 'marriage license' to court. You falsified a record, *Rhett*. I suggest *you* get the hell out of my way so I can complete this deal, then I can take my fiancé home and be out of your hair. That is, until I build on your land—"

I swung, shocked when he dodged it, stepping off to the side with that sadistic smile on his face.

"Can't even throw a punch. It's a damn good thing you can rope a calf." He raised his fist.

"So, you do know my event," I joked, cocking a grin as my fist tightened.

"No, Rhett . . . David." Kyla grabbed my arm, taking a single step forward.

"Rhett, he's not worth it. He'll call the police." Lachlan's voice rang in my ear, but I didn't exactly hear him. My focus was one hundred percent on the asshole in front of me.

I swung again, using all my strength to fly towards him. He was so quick to move the first time, but this time my fist made contact with his chin. Pain radiated through my fist as I held it as tight as I could, not letting the shoots get to me. It wasn't my best punch, but it got him to react.

"Motherfucker," he grumbled, his fingers brushing over where I hit. He spit, most likely hoping blood would fly from his mouth, but only the clear salvia landed on the grass. "Now I hope you do call the police. I have reason to press charges against you."

"Oh, come on," I taunted. "You're not going to throw one at me?"

"Rhett, no." Kyla stepped in front of me at the same time David's face twisted, and his eyes turned red. His body reeled as he leapt forward, his fist flying through the air.

He didn't even see her because his eyes were glued to me.

But I felt it. I felt it more than she did . . . once his fist came in contact with her jaw.

THIRTY-FIVE

Kyla

PAIN.

That's all that swept through my body as I flew back, hitting a hard chest as my vision blurred. Heat seeped through my jaw, and I tasted blood. I had never been hit before—not once in the entire span of my relationship with David had he ever hit me. And now, stepping in front of the man I was in love with caused me to catch my first ever punch.

And it hurt.

Rhett's arms flew around my waist, holding me steady as I still struggled to gain my balance. I could hear him screaming at David and heard a struggle. I'm not sure from what, but there was definitely something going on.

My hands flew to my jaw, and I moved it, still tasting the blood.

I blinked and tried to steady myself, my eyes focusing as I saw David walking to his car, his hands in a fist at his sides and his stride full of anger. Lachlan was walking behind him, more force to his demeanor than anything. And then there was Rhett, spinning me and taking my face in his hands, gently, as his eyes searched my face.

"Kyla . . . Kyla . . ." he repeated my name over and over.

"I'm okay," I finally mumbled, not even believing my own words.

"Yeah, I don't believe that for a second." Rhett wrapped an arm around my shoulders and led me into the main house. "I'm sorry," he whispered as we moved. My jaw pulsed with each step, but I kept moving, my fist grabbing onto Rhett's shirt.

"Why did you hit him?" I grumbled.

"I . . ." He sighed. "I don't know . . . Come on, let's get you inside, you need ice."

Once inside the house, the AC hit me like a ton of bricks. The house was quiet except for the noises from the kitchen. I was praying it was Abi—I didn't really need to see Charlotte right now. Not knowing exactly how she would act. I just wanted ice on my jaw, and a drink. A stiff one.

"What the hell—" I heard Abi, and my heart rate calmed.

"Well . . ." Rhett began, drawing out the word.

"David showed up."

"You called him?" Abi turned to Rhett.

"He said he had a meeting with dad."

"And he hit Kyla? She's bleeding." Abi's voice became frantic.

"He was aiming for me." Rhett turned my body and gently pushed me onto the stool, taking my face in his palms.

"I stepped in," I mumbled, a pain tearing through my jaw. "I'm surprised it didn't break my jaw. It hurts." I winced.

"Abi, can you get me some ice?"

"On it." Abi moved fast, a whir behind me.

"I'm sorry, Kyla," he whispered again.

I closed my eyes, wanting to tell him it was okay, that I was okay, but my mind began to spin.

"It's okay," was all I managed to choke out.

"Here's the ice." Abi handed a towel to Rhett, who took it without even moving his gaze from me. He placed it on my face with care and leaned forward, his lips meeting my temple.

I could feel the tears welling up in my eyes, the pit in my stomach growing with each moment that passed. I wasn't going to cry. I was stronger than this. I had my clarity right in front of me. I was home. I was safe.

Except I wasn't . . . was I?

I'm not even sure if Rhett heard him out there, or if he was more focused on punching him, but David admitted to following me. He knew where I was and for how long I'd been there. I wasn't sure how he knew, but . . . he knew. He knew every move I had made since I left him all those months ago. No amount of peace or clarity that Rhett offered would be able to change that fact.

No matter what I did—no matter where I went—David wasn't going to give up. He wasn't going to stop chasing and manipulating.

I looked up at Rhett, allowing the tears to fall.

"I'm sorry," I mumbled, dropping my chin when I saw the look in his eyes. Worry and regret filled him, taking over the calm that normally came with him.

"Kyla." his voice was shaking. "You don't have anything to be sorry for, it's my fault."

"Did you really threaten him?"

He shook his head, his forehead touching mine lightly. "I was an idiot. The day after the rodeo I went to the hotel and shoved the marriage license in his face. I told him to get the hell out of my town. I didn't think he would memorize the dates on it."

I rolled my eyes, "Or research you."

He met my gaze, his eyes boring into mine. There was a sheen over the bright color as he forced himself to stay grounded. He was failing. Just as I was.

"I should have warned you he would. I should have known he would. You're a big name. You're Rhett Hartwell for god's sake. I'm sorry I even asked."

"Hey." He dropped the ice on the counter and gently kissed me. "Please stop apologizing."

Before I could say anything else, the front door swung open and heavy boots slammed on the floor. Lachlan came bursting into the kitchen, stopping in the door frame. Rhett turned to look at his cousin, his hands still firm on me.

"We need to talk to your dad," he stated, his voice stoic.

Rhett turned back to me and nodded. "You okay?"

I nodded. "I'm going to go home." I shook. "Call Grace."

"Keep ice on your chin." He stood and kissed my forehead again. "I'll be there as soon as I can."

My lip quivered as I watched Lachlan and Rhett leave the kitchen. Grabbing the ice from the counter, I stood, not even acknowledging Abi as I left the main house.

How the hell did I get here? I was supposed to be in Washington by now, in my own apartment, starting a new job, and studying for my teaching certification. But I was here, in Idaho, married, and being stalked by my ex. Was that even what this was? Was he stalking me? How the hell else did he know where I was? Where I had been? Remembering that feeling of being watching in Arizona, believing it was all in my head. . .he was. . .he had to have been following me.

I knew it was all a ploy. He never wanted to buy the ranch, he just wanted to get under my skin—force me back to Arizona and back to where my life was miserable. He would twist it to make it my fault I left, make me feel bad about it until I would apologize for leaving him. I wouldn't go back to teaching, I would just be his trophy wife . . . just like my mom was.

If I lived my life here, if I made Hartwell Hills my home—which if I was being honest with myself I so desperately wanted to—nothing good would come of it. It wouldn't end with just denying David's offer. He would take it to the next level by taking Rhett to court for falsifying a legal document. There was even proof that it was false. But he wouldn't stop there. If there was something he could do to make him come out on top of everything, he would do it.

I knew the answer. I simply shouldn't—couldn't—stay here.

Tears began to fall once again as I opened the door to the cabin and sat on the couch, my back straight, trying not to clench my teeth as the pain radiated from my chin. I lifted the ice, gently placing it on my face. It was more of a dull pain now, and the taste of blood had vanished. I could feel the slit on my tongue now, but at least I knew I didn't lose a tooth—I had just bitten my tongue. That was the worst that had happened.

If only that was true.

I stood from the couch, dropping the ice on the sofa as I went for my bag, digging in my purse for my phone. There were a few new messages from my mom, a text from Grace, and an email from . . . my new employer in Washington.

Blinking quickly to stop the tears, I opened the email first.

Kyla, thank you for reaching out to us! We are excited for your new path, but please know if you ever decide to move to Washington. Just reach out to us, the job will be yours.

I swallowed. At least something went right in the last hour.

I still had a job waiting for me. I could just . . . move on.

Closing the email, I opened Grace's text thread, ignoring the message waiting from her.

Me

> David showed up . . . shit hit the fan really fast. I can't stay here. I have to leave. Back to the original plan. The Summer of Cowboys has officially come to an end. Update you soon. I need to pack and . . . talk to Rhett. Love you.

My phone rang instantly, but I ignored it. I placed it on the counter, face down, not wanting to acknowledge what I was doing.

It was for the better, I told myself over and over. This was for the *better*. If I left, so would David. He would either go back to

Arizona, or follow me to Washington. He would stop the game he was playing—stop trying to buy some of the ranch. The act would end. He would win, technically, but so would Rhett. He wouldn't have to worry about the ranch anymore. This wouldn't be clouding his focus when he should be focused on Tie-down. He wouldn't have to worry about where I was, or if I was happy. He didn't have to worry about me at all.

Starting now.

Starting now, I wouldn't be anyone's problem.

THIRTY-SIX

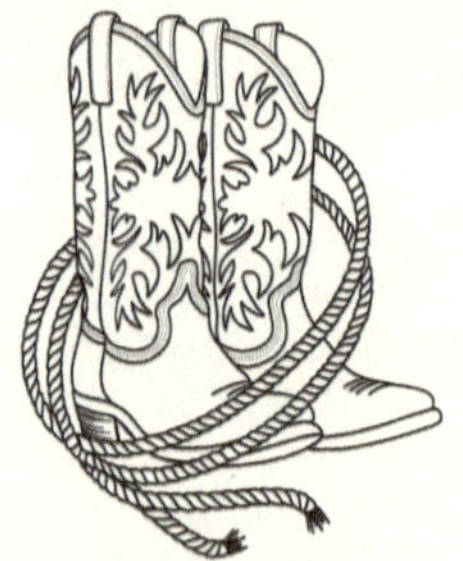

Rhett

"JUST PLEASE TELL ME you weren't really thinking of accepting that man's offer?" I said as I barged into my dad's office, Lachlan close behind me. From his window I saw Kyla making her way over to the cabin. She was hurt, and she was hurt because of me. I took a shaky breath. "You know what he's trying to do, right?"

"He's trying to buy some land—"

"No, he's playing a game. He doesn't give a shit about the land."

"Uncle Leo," Lachlan groaned, leaning his head back and crossing his arms. "Did you not see what went down out there? He hit Kyla."

"I saw." My dad's eyes met mine. "Listen—"

"It's bullshit!" I screamed. "And the fact that you were going to entertain the idea while I was gone . . . Dad—"

"It was—*is*—a good offer, and it could be helpful, but when it comes down to it . . ." He blinked and let out a long breath. "I wasn't going to accept. Your mother would make sure of that. I know you guys had a plan to get him here and decline, but I was already planning on doing that."

"Then why entertain him in the first place?" I argued.

"Because Rhett, it was a damn good offer. We don't need the five hundred he was after and you have no idea what's happening behind the scenes. Ask your sister." My dad's hand flew in the air as he gestured to the kitchen where Abi had been. "It would have been a good business call to take it."

"But, you're not?" I asked, a heaviness hitting my chest like a ton of bricks. What was going on with the ranch that I didn't know about? Was Lachlan aware of anything? I looked at Lachlan and then back to my dad. "What's going on?"

He heaved a sigh. "Nothing we can't handle. I entertained the idea of selling, but not to that man."

I swallowed. "You called David here for a meeting?"

"I did, I knew you were home and I figured we'd get it all out of the way." Dad leaned up against his desk, crossing his ankles. "He was early. I didn't think it would turn out like it did."

Closing my eyes, I ran my fingers through my hair. "If he comes back around you call the police."

"You hit him, Rhett." Lachlan pointed out. "He has cause to press charges against you."

I glared at my cousin. "And he hit my wife."

"And if and when he comes back—because you know he will." My dad stopped me. "We will handle him. You should go make sure your *wife* is okay. She looked pretty shaken up."

"She is." I ran my hand down my face. "She doesn't need this."

My dad lowered his chin, his eyes meeting mine as he bore into me. "This was never supposed to last, right?" He paused, inhaled, and narrowed his eyes. "Is it still . . . temporary?"

I kept my chin down but lifted my gaze to him. Lightly, I shook my head. "It's not temporary. She's staying. We're married."

His eyebrows lifted. "Can't say we didn't call it."

"I love her, Dad. I want her to stay, I *need* her to stay. I know it hasn't been long—"

"I knew the day I met your mother . . . and Rhett, you're a lot like me, so it doesn't surprise me. We all love Kyla, she belongs here. But David—"

"Won't be a problem," I promised. "Next time he comes around—"

"Just don't punch him again," Lachlan groaned. "I'll give Jarret a heads up." He pushed himself off the windowsill and pulled out his cell phone to call the sheriff. He left the room, a distant "*Hey Jarret, it's Lach,*" echoing in my ears as he walked down the hallway.

"It's a good thing he and the sheriff are on good terms now, huh?" My father cracked a joke, trying to lighten the mood in the room.

Ignoring his comment I shook my head. "I need to get back home, make sure Kyla is okay." I rubbed the nape of my neck. "Once she's settled, I'll come back. Apparently I need to be let in on a few things around here?"

My dad raised his eyebrows, and gave me a swift nod. "Yeah, we can talk about it after you make sure she's okay."

I left his office and made the trek to my house, forcing myself to push the last half hour out of my mind. I wanted to take Kyla in my arms. I needed to see she was okay. I needed to be calm and available to Kyla. I needed to protect her and make sure she was safe. She was the priority, not me. Not the ranch. Not David and his fucking offer. Nothing else mattered.

Only . . .

I opened the front door and saw a suitcase sitting by the sofa. I saw the towel with the bag full of ice—now water—sitting on the coffee table, and Kyla's phone buzzing, face down on the counter. I moved, determined to figure out what the hell was going on, when I saw Kyla in the bedroom with her clothes on the bed, another suitcase open. She rushed from the bed to the bathroom, beginning to gather her things in there as well.

She hadn't been here long, but she did make herself comfortable and she was . . .

Packing.

She was packing.

"Kyla," I said softly.

"Oh, hi," she said as she passed me, nonchalantly, as if what was happening here was normal. "How are things with your dad?"

"Kyla, what are you doing?"

"Oh um . . ." She stood up straight, flipping her hair from her shoulder. "I'm . . . uh . . . I'm packing."

"Why?"

She sighed. "Because I can't stay here."

I pinched my brow. I felt my heart stop. She was . . . she was . . . *no.*

"What?" I asked breathlessly. "You're . . . you're . . ."

"Let's face it, I can't stay here. If I leave, this will end. David will give up on his whole endeavor and, well . . ." She dropped her arms and hit her thighs. "It will be better this way."

"Kyla, no. You—you're staying. You said you were staying."

Her expression faltered as she turned, closing her eyes to take a deep breath. "No, Rhett. I can't."

My phone buzzed in my pocket. Not taking my eyes off my wife, I reached in, pulled it out and looked at the screen. *Grace.* Grace was texting me.

Grace

> What the hell is going on, Rhett? Kyla's not answering her phone and she's saying she's leaving. What the hell?

Locking the screen, I lowered my arm. I watched as my wife zipped up the suitcase and began to walk past me. I stepped aside, not quite sure what to do. I knew what I wanted to do. I wanted to grab her wrist, pull her to me and remind her that just last night she said it was good to be home. That just hours ago we fell asleep in each other's arms—made love in *our* bed. I told her I loved her; felt the way she shuttered when the words hit her ears. She knew how I felt—how *she* felt—but all I could do was watch as she was getting ready to walk out the door.

I looked at the room in front of me, now seemingly empty without her things. It may have just been her clothes, hairbrush, toothbrush, but all those things made it real—made it home. And now . . . it was empty.

"Kyla." I turned. "You don't need to leave."

"Yes. I really do. If I had just stuck to my original plan none of this would have happened. I should have never stopped at the bar. I should have gone straight to Washington." Her words were quick as she listed off things she never *should have* done.

"Are you telling me you regret it?" I stumbled, remembering the first time I saw her at the bar. The moment I saw her, I knew she was it for me. "Do you regret all of this?"

"No. Yes." She stopped, closing her eyes and taking a deep breath. "No. I don't . . . Rhett, I don't regret you. I could never regret you. I regret bringing you into this. I regret bringing David into your life. I regret asking you to be my fake husband just to try to get him out of the way." She came up to me, placing her hands on my chest. I felt the weight of them, and my heart pounded. She tapped her fingers in rhythm with my heartbeat. She could feel it, yet she didn't stop it. "I don't regret the summer we had, so many things were added and checked off that bucket list. You made so many things come true for me, but . . . it's not the right time for us. I have to go. I *have* to. All this will end—"

"Kyla." I wrapped my arms around her waist, pulling her close to me. Maybe if she was next to me my heart would stop pounding. "I don't regret marrying you. I'd do it again in a heartbeat. I love you, Kyla. You are my everything—my whole world. Please . . . let's talk this through. Let's not make any rash decisions."

"There's nothing to discuss," she stammered. "I need to leave, Rhett. I've already called the agency. They're still happy to have me on board until I can get in a classroom. I've told Grace, and I booked a hotel in Spokane for tonight."

I shook. My whole body was shaking. This was happening. She was leaving me.

"I had a wonderful summer, Rhett, but . . . please . . . David will follow me. He won't stay here. Once I get to Spokane I'll get a new number. I'll keep in touch with Abi, and I'll get a restraining order against David."

"No, I don't like this. You belong here, with me. You belong with somebody . . . like me. Kyla, this is ridiculous—"

"Honestly." She stopped me. "It's for the best. This was always supposed to be—"

"Mrs. Hartwell," I whispered, "this was never temporary. Not for me."

Kyla blinked, a tear dropping from her cheek. She sniffed and lifted a finger to swipe the single tear away. She had gotten a lot stronger at controlling her emotions, I'll give her that. Either that or I had missed her crying while I was talking to my family.

She took a deep breath and then took one step away from me, forcing my arms to loosen. "We'll need to end the marriage," she muttered. "I looked and we can't annul it, so, divorce—"

I bit the inside of my cheek. "No."

She placed her hand on my cheek and leaned in to give me a chaste kiss. The last one we would ever share.

No, I refused to believe that.

"Please, don't fight me. I'll be fine, you'll go back to being the Rhett Hartwell I met in the bar. Just, give me this. I'll—" She swallowed. "I'll miss you."

Then she dropped her hands from my chest. My arms went limp, and she stepped away. She didn't even look at me when she grabbed her phone and left the cabin. I looked at where her phone had sat, my heart completely stopping when I noticed the ring sitting there. I didn't even notice her taking it off.

I was frozen in place as I heard the engine of her car turn over, the gravel under her tires moved and faded in the distance. I listened until I couldn't hear them anymore—I didn't want to believe my ears. I didn't want to believe she was really leaving . . . that she was . . .

My phone buzzed again, pulling me back to the silence that was my cabin. I blinked and looked down to see Grace's text message.

Grace

Rhett, please call me. What's going on? Where's Kyla?

She was gone.

THIRTY-SEVEN

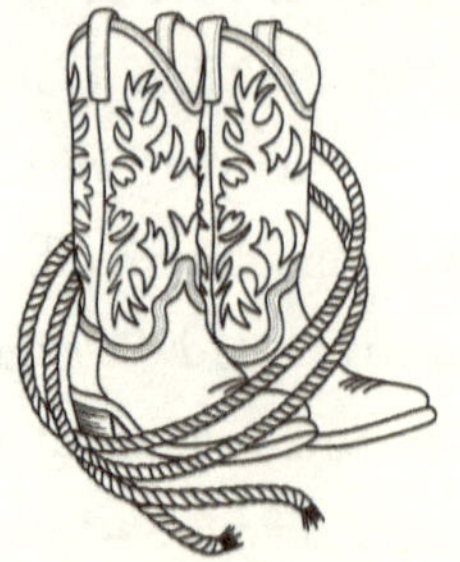

Kyla

"OKAY, SO I CAN offer month-to-month for now, with the possibility of a six-month lease to a year, depending . . ." Helga, the complex manager of Spokane Sea Apartments, spoke really fast as I looked around the small apartment.

It was a basement unit, and the only thing I could find in my price range. Staying at the hotel wasn't going to cut it any longer. It was dark and dreary, but it had a room, a kitchen, and a bathroom. A larger wall spanned from the kitchen to the sliding door to the porch. I didn't even have a TV to mount there.

I wonder if Abi would send me a photo of Josie I could blow up and mount . . .

I exhaled a shaky breath.

I really didn't need to think about the ranch.

"Depending on what, exactly?" I asked, bringing myself back to reality.

"Credit check and if you pay the rent on time for the first few months. We start out all residents on month-to-month, and then we graduate to leases," she explained.

"Month-to-month works great, for now. My job is just down the road so the commute will be great. It's the perfect location. And it's . . . cute."

I looked up at the ceiling, noticing a wet stain in the corner. It most definitely wasn't cute.

"Well, it's available, if you're interested. We can get paperwork drawn up and get you moved in. There's no credit check until you move to a lease." Helga smiled.

I took a deep breath in. "Yeah, yeah . . . I'm excited." I choked on the word.

"Perfect, well, Miss Richards—"

I stiffened and lost a breath. *Miss Richards.* My thumb went to my finger . . . my bare finger.

"—follow me and we'll get everything started. All I need is the prorated month's rent and then it will be due on the first of every month." She waved her arm for me to follow. "Sound like a plan?"

"It does," I forced out.

It didn't. But I didn't have much of a choice in the matter.

I was right about one thing, it *was* close to my tutoring job and the nearby markets. I could walk places and then come home and relax until I did it all over again. Plus, the rent was cheap. I would be able to save until I could find something better.

This is what starting over looked like.

Days later I sat in my new, empty apartment, on the new Ikea sofa I purchased just hours before. I had a twin-sized bed in the bedroom and a night stand next to it as well as a coffee table and my sofa . . . and a single pot of water that was boiling for my mac and cheese.

I longed for bookshelves to line the walls, and a leather couch with blankets hanging over the sides to curl up on with a warm cup of coffee. I didn't even have a coffee mug yet. Or a coffee maker. I closed my eyes and imagined a woodsy feel to the kitchen, making meals that filled the apartment with the best smells. I wanted the king-sized bed with the fluffy comforter and pillows galore. I craved that homey feeling. One that made me relax the second I walked in the door.

Basically, I wanted Rhett's house back.

I groaned and my head fell back on the sofa. It wasn't the first time Rhett had crossed my mind since I left. The entire drive to Spokane I had to convince myself not to cry. I told myself over and over again it was for the best.

Just keep telling yourself that, Kyla.

Grabbing my phone from the couch I turned it over and unlocked it, pulling up Grace's text feed, desperately needing the distraction.

Me

> I need more blankets in my apartment.

The dots began to dance.

Grace

Your apartment needs more than just blankets.

Me

Maybe . . .

Grace

A photo of a certain cow. A certain horse. A certain cowboy . . .

I locked my phone, not even bothering to finish reading the text message. It was silent for a few seconds before another text appeared.

Grace

Sorry, that was inappropriate. You ok?

Me

I'm doing fine.

I lied.

Grace

FaceTime tonight?

Me

Yup. Same time.

Thumbing through my other texts before swiping the messages away, I tossed my phone on the couch beside me.

I was moving backwards. There was an unease settling in my chest and whatever this emotion was. It felt like fear, but I didn't want to call it that. It was almost as if the confidence I had grown over the last months had disappeared. I was back to being a ball of emotions, waiting for something to happen to unravel me. I was supposed to feel better once I got here. I was supposed to feel free. I was supposed to figure out who I was and what I was doing with my life. Instead, I just felt completely stuck.

I wasn't supposed to be *stuck*.

I emptied the box of noodles in the water and leaned against my counter, folding my arms and glaring at my phone.

Maybe you should just . . . text him? He'll help clear your mind . . . he always did . . .

"Nope," I said to no one. "Maybe I just need to get a dog."

But then I remembered my month-to-month lease said no animals.

What I needed was to find a way out of whatever *this* was and start to push myself forward. I hadn't made a single plan all summer, which was not who I was. I made plans. I made lists and all that time without them—as amazing as it felt—messed up any "future" I had here.

A list.

A plan.

That's what I needed to do.

I needed to figure it all out on paper and then things would start to go up.

Placing the wooden spoon over the water I ran to my purse to grab the only sheet of paper I could find and a pen. Flattening the receipt out on the counter I leaned over and wrote:

Get apartment.

Crossed that off instantly.

"Check," I said.

Find new therapist—transfer records.

Restraining order—research how.

Register car in Washington.

Get new phone number.

Get a divorce.

I stopped and looked at the three words on the crumbled receipt. Get a divorce. Moving my fingers to feel for a ring that wasn't there anymore, that pit in my stomach grew as the words seemed to get larger on the page.

Dropping the pen, I ran my fingers through my hair, holding the back of my neck.

"Oh hell," I grumbled, feeling the pit rise into my chest, the tears forming in my eyes.

I missed him.

I missed the way he felt against me. I missed the way his hand would find my hips. I missed the way his eyes would peer into mine, seeming to read my emotions. I missed the way his lips felt against mine, I just missed . . .

I missed all of him.

"This was such a terrible idea." I pushed myself off the counter and turned back to my mac 'n' cheese. I swirled the noodles, drained the water, and went for the milk and butter. Tossing them on the counter, I could feel the pit rise higher than my chest, to my throat, to my vocal cords, and I wanted to scream.

Biting my lip to force the scream down, I spun, dashing for my phone. I needed to hear his voice. I needed to apologize. Tell him I wanted him. Why did I even think leaving was a good idea? Here I was forcing myself to believe that I was doing the right thing, and I was completely wrong.

I grabbed my phone right as it began to vibrate.

Rhett . . .

My heart thumped. It would be just like him to call me right when I decided to reach out to him again. Almost as if he knew I needed to hear his voice. But when I turned my phone . . .

I swallowed.

It's for the best. Snap back to reality, Kyla. No more daydreams . . .

"Mom," I answered, sitting down, trying to catch my breath.

I had never texted her back after we had gotten home—I mean, back to Rhett's place. We had agreed we would once we handled David. I didn't know if David had been "handled," or where he was at this particular moment, but it occurred to me that I never called her back. And apparently, she had run out of patience waiting. I braced myself for the worst.

"Kyla, I . . ." she stammered. "Hi."

"Hi, Mom. I'm sorry I didn't call you, or text you. It's been busy here and well . . ." I looked around my apartment. If only she could see me now. I rolled my eyes. "Things just—"

"Kyla, dear, I'm calling to say . . . well . . ." She paused, and I heard her take a deep breath. "I've been thinking."

I furrowed my brow. "About?"

"About what you said."

I tightened my lips, not exactly knowing what to say.

"You said a lot of things that stuck with me while you were here with . . ." *Pause. deep breath.* "Rhett, but it's just opened my eyes. Honey, we need to talk."

"Mom I"—I fell on the couch—"don't really want to talk about Rhett—"

"David called me."

"Of course he did."

"He told me you weren't really married to him."

"I was—am. I *am* married to Rhett."

"I know, that's why I told him to go fuck off."

My jaw dropped. I don't think, in my twenty-eight years, I had ever heard my mother swear. Ever. Not once. Not even shit or damn, and now I was getting *fuck.*

"I'm sorry . . . what did you tell him to do?"

"Kyla, you were right, and I was wrong. Your father was a terrible man. I was only there to help his image and to create a certain status. I grew to need this life. The status, the money, the lifestyle . . . everything—it was what I needed to survive. And that required me to put up with your father's bullshit and just take it. I put on that happy face, I pretended to love and care for him in public when I was screaming on the inside. I wasn't a good mother—grooming you to be basically the same thing as me, not knowing any better, but wanting you to have the same security I had my entire life."

"It wasn't security, Mom—"

"I know that now, but back when you were growing up it was so easy to overlook. David had that status, he had the means to give you the life I had. But that's not the life you need or deserve. It's not the life you wanted. As much as I don't want to admit this, I saw the way Rhett was looking at you. I saw the way he created a fire in you, helped you be able to stand up for yourself and do things that I never could.

"I'm . . ." She faltered, if only for a second. "I'm proud of you, Kyla, for taking over your life. Taking it back and becoming who you are meant to become. You're finding happiness that I could never find, and I . . . am so proud."

"Mom . . ." I began to cry. She was saying all the things I wanted her to say for such a long time. She was accepting who I was—who I wanted to be—but it was the wrong time. It was all the wrong time. I shut my eyes tight and willed the tears to stay inside.

"I was hoping I could try to fix things with Rhett. He's in your life now—he's your husband, and I would like to get to know him, and you. I want to know who you are now. I was hoping we could plan a trip. Maybe Thanksgiving or Christmas."

"Mom. I left him," I blurted out, opening my eyes and allowing the tears to rain down my cheeks.

There was only silence. I could hear muffled noises in the background and then finally a quick breath. "What?"

"It wasn't real, Mom. I left David and met Rhett on my way to Washington. He offered me his home while he was away and then when David showed up, I freaked. I asked him to pretend to be my husband, but then he proposed. We are legally married, but once we got back from the rodeos and David showed up, I thought it would be better for him if I left—better for me. So, I need to file for divorce."

"So, he's *not* your husband? David was—"

"Wrong. David was wrong, Mother. Rhett was—technically still is—my husband, and god, Mom, I love him. Everything I said to you that night was true. Every. Single. Word," I emphasized, pointing at the air in front of me as if she could see me. "David was—is—wrong. In every way. He doesn't love me. He doesn't care about me. Not the way Rhett does . . . did." I stammered.

"Did?" she said the word louder, almost as if it shocked her. "He doesn't care about you anymore?"

"No, I'm sure he still does, but I'm the one who left him."

She was quiet again and my mind started spinning a million miles an hour. What was she going to say now?

I told you so. You should have known better. This is your mess to try to clean up . . .

"You love him?"

Her question made me blink.

"Yes."

"Then why the hell did you leave him?"

"Because it was for the best."

"I don't care if you thought it was for the best. If you truly love the man—if you have the kind of love that's in those books and movies—then why make the idiotic decision to leave him?"

"Mom!" I shouted. "I don't really—"

"I called you because you were right, about everything. I was a terrible mother, but I want to try to make it right, and if I have to start it with some tough love then . . . so be it." I could almost picture her, standing up from whatever cushy chair she was sitting on to point at me, her eyes glaring into mine as she lectured. "You're a smart woman, Kyla. You were determined to teach even though we begged you not to, and you were smart enough to figure out that you were in a toxic relationship. You got yourself out of it and you found something that made you smile. Made you—how did you say it?—alive. I saw a change in you while you were here and as much as I didn't want to see it, it was clear as day. You were confident. You were brave. Kyla, you were alive."

Alive.

"That's how he made me feel," I whispered.

"Well then there's one answer to this, and I think you are avoiding it—just like you're used to doing. Just like I did. Don't ignore it Kyla. If you love him—"

"I do." I choked.

"Then don't avoid it."

THIRTY-EIGHT

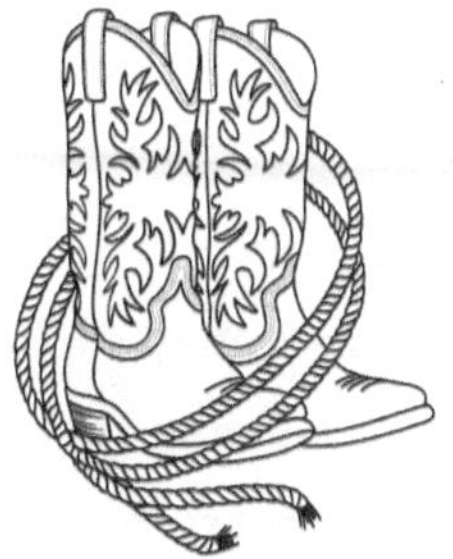

Rhett

"Shit . . ." I groaned as I jumped off Buckle, pulling the rope close to me again. For the fifth time in a row, I watched as the calf ran away from me.

"Well!" Abi shouted as she watched me, leaning against the railing. "Sixth time's the charm?"

"Don't start, Abi," I grumbled, slipping my foot in the stirrup and lifting myself back on to Buckle. "Wyatt!" I called down the arena. Wyatt waved behind him and walked after the calf, lassoing her to bring her back to the chute.

I needed the practice runs, but when I couldn't even catch the calves from my own damn ranch, how the fuck was I supposed to keep my composure when that timer was going?

"Need me to rile her up more?" Wyatt asked as the calf traveled through the chute.

"No, I can't catch her as is."

"We can try Josie," Abi called, sarcasm rippling through her.

"NO!" I heard my nephew shout from next to his mother. "That's Aunt Kyla's cow. If Uncle Lachlan can't brand her, then Uncle Rhett can't rope her."

Abi looked down at her son for a moment, then raised her gaze back up to me. Her eyebrows knitted, she huffed and rolled her eyes.

"Kid's not wrong. No one touches that damn cow." I turned Buckle and trotted up to the chute. Wyatt watched me, waiting for the nod, and once my hat tipped, the calf was out. I launched Buckle, the rope flying through the air . . . only to miss again.

"Fuck it." I forced Buckle to a stop, jumping from the saddle and hunching my shoulders. I left Buckle and the rope in the middle of the arena as I made my way to the gate. Taking off my hat, I wiped the sweat from my brow, making direct eye contact with Abi and pointing at her. "Don't say a single word."

She tilted her head. "I wasn't gonna."

"Can I ride Buckle?" Stetson called, already halfway out to the arena.

"I don't give a fuck."

"That's a lot of f-bombs in front of my son, cowboy."

"Don't call me 'cowboy,'" I grumbled, the anger still rising. "Wyatt, I'm going to The Steel. You coming?"

"Hell yeah!" Wyatt dashed passed his sister, "Abi—"

"I've got the calf and the horse. You guys go get drunk and call me when you're done. Or maybe I'll make you walk home." Abi opened the gate and let me walk through, pushing her way past me to follow her son. "You seriously good with Stetson riding your horse?"

I nodded. "Yeah, and don't worry about us, I'll drag Lachlan along."

A few hours later I sat at the same round table I had been at weeks ago, with the same watered-down beer in front of me—Wyatt to my left and Lachlan to my right. They were talking about god knows what and my eyes traveled to the bar.

Had it really been only been two months since I first saw her there?

I could still see her, clear as day, in my mind. The white tank she was wearing, tan shorts, her brown hair down and laying against her skin. I remembered all the small touches and teases she did when we decided to start playing pool. The first time she ever plopped my hat on her head.

"Hey." Wyatt's hand waved in front of my face, forcing me to blink away the vision of my wife. "She's not over there."

"Wyatt," Lachlan grumbled, bringing his glass to his lips.

"What?" Wyatt shrugged his shoulders. "He needs to stop the moping if he plans on getting to the NFR."

"I'm still leading the boards." I glared over at my brother. "I'm not worried about the NFR."

"You couldn't even catch a calf in our arena. And when Lachlan kept telling you about that asshole, you kept breaking the damn barrier. Face it, Rhett." Wyatt grabbed his ball cap by the brim and twisted it backwards, his blonde hair poking out of the front. "That girl had you whipped, you couldn't focus on what was right in front of you. The buckle. The thing you've worked towards for years."

"I think he wants to get punched." I looked over at my cousin, who simply raised an eyebrow and took another long drink from his mug.

"I won't stop you."

"He's drunk. He's always an ass when he's drunk."

"I'm not that drunk," Wyatt bit out and pointed at me. "I'm just speaking the truth. Listen, I liked her too. She was a blast to have around the rodeos and she made you smile, but—"

"Exactly. She made me smile. It wasn't her that made me break the barriers."

"Technically it was me," Lachlan mumbled.

Not taking my eyes off Wyatt, I pointed to Lachlan. "Exactly. I love that woman and I'm trying to figure out how to get her back. Until I do, I'll be roping calves and finding rodeos to ride." I dropped my hand, hitting the table with a thud.

"Did I just hear the good news?"

A voice came to my side and without even looking I knew exactly who it was. Why he was still in my town was beyond me. He should have left right after he hit Kyla—right after I hit him—yet here he was, ruining my night. More than it already was.

"Kyla left you. No wonder why I haven't been able to get a hold of her."

"She's been gone for almost a week." Wyatt glared at David. "You're just now figuring that out?"

"I had a feeling she would leave after what happened. She never was one to take to"—he tilted his head back and forth, almost as if he was turning the pages to the dictionary in his head—"confrontation very well. It takes her a moment, but she'll come around."

I furrowed my brow and looked up at him. It was the first time seeing him since that afternoon. I hated to see that my punch didn't even cause a mark—unless he had covered it up somehow. Rolling my eyes, convincing myself he did just that, I took a long drink.

"Well, maybe not here," David added. "I did, however, have a nice chat with your father today. He declined my offer, so I'll be heading out tonight."

"Thank fuck," I said into my mug. "Arizona will be lucky to have you."

David gave me a smirk, his eyes narrowing. "Maybe I'll see you at a rodeo, I know Kyla likes them now. I'd love to take her to see what piqued her interest." His smirk turned into a fake smile that almost reached his eyes. "Nice meeting you gentleman, sorry things turned out the way they did. We could have been great business partners."

"What?" I egged him on. "You're going to show up and threaten to ruin my life and now you're just . . . leaving?"

David's eyes narrowed. "I never threatened you. In my memory, you threatened me."

I raised my mug. "Yeah, I'm not getting into this. You knew exactly what you were doing."

A tight smile formed on his face. Smug, false victory spread all over him. "I got what I came for. You won't have to worry, Rhett, your false document is safe with me. I take it she's filed for divorce?"

"You didn't win," I argued back, stopping myself from jumping to my feet to hit him again. He didn't deserve that kind of attention from me—from anyone really. I locked eyes with Lachlan, who simply gave me a single shake.

"Oh, I think I did. You, on the other hand" —he motioned towards my beer, my ring standing out against the amber liquid—"need to accept defeat. You're better off roping the cows." David flicked his eyebrows once, the smug smile never once leaving. "Again, nice meeting you gentleman."

And with that, he left.

I watched him, a small jump in his step as he walked away, thinking he had won. *Cocky asshole.* Right before he reached to door, I shouted, "Go fuck yourself!"

He stopped, turned his head to give me that same tight, devilish smile, before straightening his shoulders and leaving the bar. He was gone.

"I really hate that man." I turned back to my cousin and brother. Wyatt had now completely shifted his focus to the bar. When I followed his gaze, I saw two blondes sitting there with cocktails in front of them, one of them making eyes with my brother.

He gave her a smile and stood. "Well guys, don't wait up for me tonight." He patted my back and headed over to the bar, the two girls coming to life once he got closer.

"Who wants to bet he tells them he's a bull rider?" I watched as he slid his hand over one of the girls shoulders.

"He doesn't fit the bill," Lachlan answered. "That kid is proud to be an announcer. Hell, if those girls keep up with the circuit, they've heard his voice."

"Yeah . . ." Slouching my shoulders I leaned my head down, taking in a deep breath, smelling nothing but the watered down beer. Even *that* made me think of Kyla. Everything made me think of her in some way.

"You really gonna go after her?" Lachlan asked, catching my attention.

Lifting my head I met his gaze for a second before turning back to my brother. He was already in deep conversation with one of the gals, his fingers running through her hair.

"You have no idea how much I want to," I admitted.

"What's stopping you?"

"She told me not to."

He raised his eyebrows. "Pretty sure she told you no when you offered to buy her that first drink, and look what happened."

I didn't respond. If I could, I would head to Washington right now, lasso her up, and bring her home where she belonged. But her words *"give me this"* kept ringing in my ear. I wanted her. I missed her, but did she miss me? Maybe I was just what she said, her Summer of Cowboys. Maybe she didn't even bat an eye when I crossed her mind.

But she sure as hell was stuck—engrained—in mine.

No one was ever going to top Kyla Richards.

Before I could stop myself, I leaned over, pulling my phone from my pocket to pull up her text thread. I didn't look at Lachlan and I didn't force my thumbs to stop moving. All I did was type.

Me

I miss you, every day. I love you.

Send.

"Give me that." Lachlan reached forward and grabbed my phone. "I don't need you checking your stats all night long."

"Checking my stats is the least of my worries," I mumbled under my breath, lifting my mug to my lips, ignoring the fact that I basically just drunk texted my wife.

THIRTY-NINE

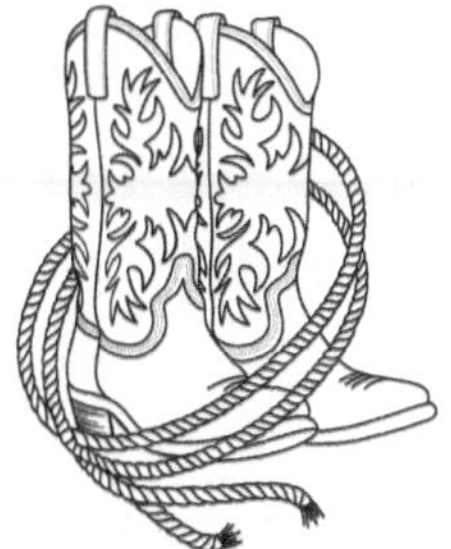

Kyla

"Okay, so . . ." I looked at Ben, the small soon-to-be sixth grader who sat across the table from me. He hated reading. Absolutely hated it. The fact that he had to do summer tutoring just to catch up made him hate it even more. His previous tutor had quit because apparently, he was "unteachable."

My first meeting with him, I sat and figured out what he wanted to read—what he was interested in—and now, here we were, reading *Percy Jackson*. "What happened? Tell me about what you just read to me."

I finally convinced him to read out loud. He stammered and needed help with a few words, but overall, he did it, and he did it well.

"He won the game of capture the flag, and . . ." He inhaled, his brows knitting as he remembered the book. "Percy was claimed by that god."

"What god?"

"Poseidon," he answered, confidence boosting through his voice.

"Good, how?"

"The trident shown over his head?" he said, more of a question than fact, even though it was right. "They didn't think it would be one of the . . . Big Three?"

"Yes, see, you understood that; you retained it."

He closed the book and put it on the counter. "That didn't happen in the movie."

"No, the movie is different than the book. What was different about the book versus the movie?"

"In the movie they knew he was already that dude's son. In the book it was a secret."

"Which do you like better?"

"I like the book better, it's more of a surprise?"

"So you're liking the book?"

Ben looked at the green cover in front of him and rolled his lips. Then a corner tipped up and he smiled. "Yeah, I think I am."

I grinned, remembering the joy that came from teaching. I loved seeing it click. "Do you think you could read three chapters before Friday? And write me a few paragraphs on what you read?"

Ben rolled his neck and looked at the book as if it would burst into flames and then slapped his hand on top of the cover. "You're reading it too, right?"

"You bet. I love *Percy Jackson.*"

"Three chapters?"

I nodded. "Three chapters."

He inhaled "Okay. I'll read three chapters."

"And . . ."

"And write you a paragraph."

"In complete sentences, please," I added.

"Before Friday." He stood, sliding the book along the table.

"Perfect, see you in a few days, bud."

"See ya Friday, Miss Richards." Ben waved, and turned, taking off once he saw his mom.

Unteachable my ass.

After speaking to Ben's mom and meeting with a few other students, I helped lock up for the day before pulling my phone out to text Grace. Rhett's message still sat in my inbox even after three weeks. He hadn't sent another one, and he hadn't called. He was truly giving me the time I asked for. I had read his text several times over the past three weeks, but I could never get myself to respond. I had typed out so many things. *I miss you too. I love you. This is only temporary. I want to come home.* But nothing seemed to suffice.

My mother's words rang through my ears since we talked, don't avoid it—don't avoid him. But there was still that looming fear that I wasn't good enough. In order to be good enough for him, I had to figure out my life instead. And that required time.

As much as I wanted to respond to his text, I couldn't bring myself to do it.

Ignoring his text thread, I clicked on Grace.

Me

> Heading home. You free tonight for Face-Time after my appointment?

Grace

> Of course, have a good appointment with Lauren.

I smiled, still astonished that I looked forward to therapy appointments. I reached out to my therapist in Arizona, happy to hear that she would still see me even from Washington—telehealth at its best. I filled her in on everything that had happened since our last visit months ago and we agreed on a focus.

Me.

I was always a focus, but now that the anxiety attacks weren't as prominent, she helped me on my journey to find my true self. Where that Kyla was, I had no idea yet. I didn't feel at home in Washington. I didn't feel whole here. Things weren't bad, per se. I loved the tutoring job and was in the process of getting certified to teach in Washington. I kept in contact with Grace so I didn't feel alone. Hell, my relationship with my mother was even getting a little better. She was trying at least to hear me and talk to me.

But something was missing.

And I knew exactly what that something was.

A small cow I helped bring into the world.

A little boy who needed help reading.

A single mom who loved time alone, even though she loved her son.

The man who loved me.

The clarity I found being in his arms.

A large part of me knew that I wouldn't be happy until I was back there with him, but I couldn't be that burden on him. And that louder part drowned out all voices that told me to run to him.

I really wish I could figure out how to put that voice to bed.

I walked up to my apartment, fishing for my keys in my purse, yanking them from under my copy of *Percy Jacson at* the same time I flipped my hair off my face, bringing my attention to my front door.

Then . . . I froze.

What the hell?

"Kyla, sweetheart." David stood at my front door, holding a small bouquet of roses, his eyes wet with . . . tears? "You're home."

"David, what the hell are you doing here?"

"I found you." He took a step forward, his voice heavy with dismay. "I'm so sorry, sweetheart."

"Sorry for what?" I took a step back, wishing I had pepper spray or something to shove him away.

I knew this David. This was the David that figured out he upset me, the one who was going to offer gifts to make up for his manipulation. He would say he loved me repeatedly until I gave in and fell into his arms. The fake tears told me everything. I couldn't help but wonder how long it took to prepare this particular speech.

"Everything, Kyla." He took yet another step forward. "I miss you, sweetheart."

"Stop calling me that," I snapped. The first time Rhett had called me that I remembered the chill it sent down my spine. His nicknames had become a game, a sweet thing just between us until he settled on that final one: *Mrs. Hartwell.* But when a normal term of endearment came from David, I wanted to vomit.

"I always call you 'sweetheart.'" He tried to form a smile, a single tear falling down his cheek. "I saw . . ." He cleared his throat and swallowed, locking his gaze with mine. "I saw Rhett a few weeks ago at the bar. He said . . ." He inhaled a shaky breath. I shook my head and slightly rolled my eyes. How did I ever fall for this? He exhaled through his lips. "He said you left him and my heart, it burst. I knew then that I could get you back."

"What makes you think I'd go back to you?"

"We're engaged. We love each other. Kyla, I'm so sorry."

"Again, I would love to know what you're sorry for?"

He blinked, a tear falling on his cheek. "Everything."

"Do you have a list of what everything includes? Or is it just in general? And why the hell are you crying?"

"I'm crying because I thought I'd never see you again."

"Oh bull!" I shouted, a chuckle escaping me.

"Kyla, you left my heart to burn, only you can bring it back from the pile of ash that's left." He put his palm on his chest, pounding where his heart would be.

"The . . . pile . . . of ash that is your heart? You realize that makes no sense, right."

"I've missed you."

"Really? That's the dumbest thing I think I've ever heard come out of your mouth. A pile of ash . . . " I repeated, ignoring him completely.

"I love you," he cried, holding the flowers in front of him.

"Again. Bull."

"Kyla." He tilted his head, the flowers lowering down to his waist.

"No. No, I'm done with this. I've been done with this." I pointed at him and walked forward. There was no way I was going to crumble, not after I felt what true love felt like. What it meant to mean something to someone. David's love was always fake, it never had meaning with it. I was his trophy. I was his way of proving his status, and the minute I began to fight my way out of the darkness, it had to become all about him. It was always about him.

"You never loved me. You never cared for me. You never ever listened to me. You made me feel like I was the problem. You made me *believe* I was the problem. You made me feel like I didn't matter to anyone—ever. Not even my own parents. Since you've been out of my life, I've *come* to life. I've found someone who loves me—who *truly* loves me. I've been fixing my relationship with my mother. Haven't you noticed she's stopped calling you? That's because she finally believes me." I took a single step towards him, courage flowing through my body. I felt my hand form a fist, and I let it clench. "How did you find me anyway? I mean, I can only assume you were stalking me."

"I hired someone, but you made it harder than I thought. The first bit you were just with Grace, that made his life easy, but then you really left."

"You hired someone? I wasn't imagining that? I didn't even mean that much to you to come to Grace's to try to work it out? I mean, not that it would work out, but you couldn't even try to find me yourself? You had to hire someone? You really only do the bare minimum don't you?"

David furrowed his brow as I spoke, taking a step backwards, faltering.

"You, David, are nothing more than a gaslighting, manipulating, arrogant asshole who will say whatever it takes to get whatever it is you want. You wanted the ranch—supposedly—so you said all the right things to twist Leo into selling. You want me back to be your arm candy, so of course you're going to say you love me, that you miss me, that you're 'sorry.' But David . . ." My cheeks flushed and the fire rose in my belly. This was what I needed. This was everything and I was relishing it. "This is me figuring out what I need and what I want. This is me stepping on the pile of ash you claim is your heart. Go find someone else to manipulate. I am done with you."

His eyes went wide as I pushed passed him, my shoulder bumping into his as he stood his ground. I inserted the key into the lock and turned.

David gave a loud huff from behind me, sniffing once before the act was over. "Do you really think he's going to want you after you left him? He knows you came running back to me. He knows it was all a game to you. Do you really think he *loves* you? Well, let me tell you something Kyla—"

"No." I spun back around. "You can shut the fuck up. Your words mean absolutely nothing to me. He means everything, and yes, he does love me. He will love me no matter how long we are apart for. He's given me more in the three months I've known him than you've given me in the two years we were together. I love him. You, David, can go to hell."

I wanted to punch him. I wanted to see him fly to the ground.

But instead, I held my ground and turned back around, opening my apartment door only to slam it in his face.

My apartment was dark and cold, and I leaned against the door to take it all in.

My heart was pounding. My breathing was fast.

I felt like Rapunzel the moment she stepped out of the tower. *I can't believe I did that.*

And it felt good.

Not only had I stood my ground and told him off, but I finally figured it all out. I finally accepted what I wanted and what I needed. Saying it out loud made it true, made it real.

Taking a deep breath, my exhale shook, and tears began to flow from my eyes. I was shocked to discover they weren't tears of sadness or heartache. They were tears of joy. Of victory.

What I needed—what I truly wanted—was Rhett.

My head rested against the door and I smiled, letting the tears fall down my cheeks and everything became clear. I could hear shuffling outside, the start of a car engine . . . tires whizzing away. David was gone, and I was finally . . . me.

Lifting myself up off the door, I dug in my bag for my phone. Rhett's text was still sitting there, but I reached for Grace instead.

Me

> I have the best story to tell you, and Grace . . . . I'm going home.

Her response was instant—those three dots only dancing for a moment.

Grace

THANK THE LORD!!

My smile and tears only grew when a FaceTime came in before I could even respond. My heart jumped. I was going home.

FORTY

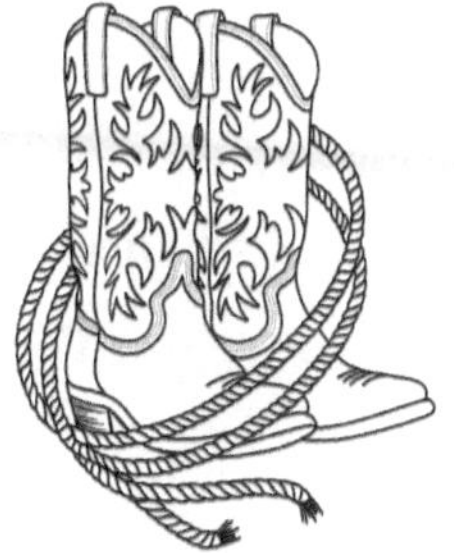

Rhett

"LABOR DAY IS COMING up. You ready?"

I looked up at my sister from the small cow we were preparing to brand. Why she decided this was the opportune time to ask me about a rodeo I was seriously considering dropping, I had no idea. I furrowed my brow and held the calf, determined to remain on task before Lachlan said anything. Branding day. Lachlan branded while I did the vaccines. Abi knew I was stuck in this corner.

"I guess." The calf moo-ed once I removed the syringe, right as Lachlan touched the iron to her rear. She shook but then seconds later was fine, running off to the pasture.

"Still on top?" she asked.

"Second." I grabbed the next calf and waited for Lachlan again.

"Second's good."

"Yup. Second's good." I raised my eyebrow at her.

"When do you leave?"

"Not sure," I responded smugly, praying she'd drop it.

"Wyatt left yesterday."

"I'm aware."

"You normally leave with him."

"He's not announcing at the Labor Day rodeo I'm riding in. He's at Cour de 'Laine," I corrected her.

"Well yeah, but last year you drove together—"

"What'cha getting at, Abi?" Annoyed, I stood and locked eyes with my sister. The calf I was supposed to be vaccinating was shaking its head. Lachlan let out a low grumble before turning back to the fire. He was just as annoyed as I was.

"I guess what I want to know is why you haven't left. Why are you still here?"

"Does it matter?"

"Kinda."

"Abi."

"I guess what I'm trying to ask is—"

"Spit it out, Abi. Before I brand you." Lachlan waved the branding iron in front of her, the smoke coming from the red metal.

"The Labor Day rodeo is in Washington."

I rolled my eyes and avoided eye contact. That was a huge reason as to why I was thinking about canceling it. I didn't know what would happen if I knew Kyla was close. I would chase her, and she made it very, very clear to leave her be. The message left on read was the defining moment I needed.

I loved her, but she didn't love me.

"I'm well aware of where the rodeo is," I groaned, releasing the calf. Up next was the small brown and white calf that was supposed to never be branded, yet here she was in the line up.

Josie.

Ignoring Josie completely, I reached for the one behind her.

"Just get out of your head and go get her already!" Abi shouted, slapping her thighs, her voice and slap echoing through the small barn.

"You really think this is the best time to have this conversation?" I glared at my sister, my voice rising.

"Yes," she bit back, "because the rodeo is in two days, and you will need to get Buckle situated before you go find Kyla. You know where she works, and David's out of the picture, right? She hasn't filed for divorce yet. Just go get your wife." Abi's voice was getting louder and louder with each fact she stated.

I had hoped that David was going to be out of the picture soon, but without talking to Kyla I didn't know if he was. Grace had sent me texts every day with a small update on Kyla. I knew there was the intention of filing for a restraining order, but I had no confirmation it had come to fruition. I could only hope.

It took all my strength to give her the space she wanted. To not chase her.

She didn't want to be chased.

"Abi, it's pointless. She told me to give her space," I reminded her while reminding myself to calm my voice and not take any anger out on my sister.

"Did she use those words exactly?" Abi asked, taking a seat on a bucket near me. Lachlan glared at her, but then went on his way of branding the next calf.

I gave her a quick glance, shaking my head. She knew everything. I told her *every detail* that happened. I loved my sister, but she needed to stop pushing this. She needed to move on. I was trying to, and it would be a hell of a lot easier if she didn't keep bringing her up every chance she got.

Josie moo-ed in the background, her hooves getting louder and louder as she approached me. Her nose hit my elbow. I ignored her.

"Hell, Rhett just go get her!" Abi raised her chin as her voice lifted.

"Just go get her. Like she's mine to control?" My heart twisted, hating the fact that she wasn't mine. Not anymore.

"Yes! Go get her! You belong together. It's clear to everyone but you, obviously."

"I won't push her, Abi. She told me in no uncertain terms to not follow her."

"Well, she's being difficult."

I leveled a glare at her. "I bet that's what David told himself, that she was his and she belonged with him. That she was being difficult." I could feel my voice begin to shake, but I stopped it. Taking a breath, I looked away from my sister. "I . . . I want her more than anything. But I won't become him trying to get her back."

"I see your logic, but . . ." Abi began.

I groaned, not wanting to be in this conversation. Lifting my chin, I began with, "She said to not fight her. To go back being Rhett

Hartwell. To give this to her. And, she hasn't reached out to me once. I'm giving her what she wants."

"Then why are you still wearing your ring?" No longer shouting, she opened her palm to motion towards my hand.

I looked down at my hand, the rope engraved wedding band still felt natural on my ring finger. It was the one thing I had left of her.

"Because—"

"You love her."

"We've established that Rhett is in love with Kyla." Lachlan's glare on Abi deepened. "But I honestly would love it if Rhett stayed here and skipped the damn rodeo. Nick is sick and he's going to get every ranch hand in the bunkhouse sick, so I'll need his help around the ranch."

"There." I nodded to Lachlan. "It's settled, I'll stay here."

"Lachlan," Abi growled his name, turning to our cousin. "I seriously hate you right now. He needs to go to Washington. It's called a grand gesture."

Rolling my eyes, I leaned against the gate, folding my arms to try to clear my head before I answered Abi. I had pictured a grand gesture several times. I would find Kyla at her new office, ask her to play her game and let me guess five facts about her—not that I needed to guess. I knew her. I *know* her. I'd get down on one knee and propose again—really propose this time. I had been carrying her ring in my pocket with me since she gave it back to me. Then I'd take her in my arms and kiss her, before I'd throw her over my shoulder and bring her home.

But that was only a dream. That couldn't happen.

"I can't. I'm giving her all the space she needs."

"I really hate how you're being a gentleman here." Abi stood up. "She doesn't belong in Washington."

"She belongs wherever she's happy, and if that is Washington—"

"It's not," she mumbled under her breath.

"You don't know that."

"You are frustrating," Abi snapped as she left the pen, leaving Lachlan and I with all the calves to be branded. Josie walked up to me and nudged my hand with her nose, forcing my arms apart. I scratched her nose as she left out a soft groan.

"I half agree with her you know," Lachlan said right before he placed the now cool iron in the fire. I could hear it begin to sizzle, and once he pulled it from the fire, the red hot iron smoked. I stood in front of Josie, protecting her from the iron. Lachlan looked at the calf, and then back at me. "I don't understand why you're not going after her."

"She told—"

"I know, I get it. You've said that so many times. You make that fact known. Obviously if she didn't want to be in your life anymore, she wouldn't be texting her friend about you, and you wouldn't be getting daily Kyla updates even though you don't answer her—"

"Okay, I'm out." I raised my arms and left the pen, with Josie turning to follow me. "I'll be back later. I need a break."

"You get fifteen minutes," Lachlan called after me.

I raised my middle finger, as I moved to get as far away from that pen as I could, with the small cow following me the entire time. I turned and watched her—her small trots and the way her head bobbed with each step, a small moo coming from her as we approached the horse pasture. It was a beautiful day, with the sun beating down on the green of the ranch, the September air making its way in. The heat of the summer was fading, and fall would take over soon, turning the greens to reds and oranges. I wished Kyla was here to see it. She would love the fall. The fact that she was missing it took away from the beauty.

Two days later I found myself mounted on Buckle—the rodeo arena abuzz all around me. Abi had followed me into my cabin and somehow convinced me to man up and—in her exact words—"go to the fucking rodeo." So here I was, at the fucking rodeo.

The rope was secure between my teeth as the lasso waved in the air next to me. Buckle took a few steps back, then one to the side, a routine she had picked up these last few rides. I was up next, and even though I knew the steps and I knew what to do, I could feel the tension sitting high in my shoulders. If I didn't loosen up, I'd get a foot stuck, or I'd drop the rope, something that would screw up all the hard work I did to get my standings.

Focus, Rhett. Get your head where it needs to be.

Lifting my chin, I closed my eyes and breathed in the cool Washington air. It wasn't Idaho air, but it was still crisp, and the chill of it hitting my lungs would help pull my focus.

"Not a bad run there, a 9.2... that calf was trying—" I heard the announcer bellow across the speaker.

I began to tune him out, focusing on Buckle under my thighs, my eyes taking a quick scan of the crowd. It wasn't a large arena by any means—just big enough that the crowd seemed to blur—but in the blur, a flash of yellow . . .

I paused and tried to focus in on the small spot of yellow in the sea of red and blue shirts and brown or dark hats—but it was only a glimpse—maybe it wasn't even there.

Only, it had to have been. The only yellow I'd seen like that was . . .

"Kyla," I whispered under my breath.

"And here's Rhett Hartwell, Idaho native and earning the money in the circuit, he's been keeping a high standing all year long, and tonight is going to be no different. Rhett. Hartwell . . ."

Blinking away the yellow, convincing myself it wasn't her—she didn't even know I was here—I swallowed and rolled my shoulders before giving the nod. The calf shot out of the chute and Buckle leapt over the gate. No broken barrier. The rope swung through the air, the whiz hitting my ear just in time to catch the calf. I jumped, my hand steady on the rope the entire time. The calf was right there, but all I saw was that damn yellow dress.

All I could see was her smile.

I could hear the cheers once I pinned the calf and tied its legs, waving my arms, and the crowd got louder.

But all I could really hear was her voice.

You did it, Cowboy. No 6.3, but look at you . . .

The announcer's voice boomed, rattling off my time and few facts, but every word was muffled as I mounted Buckle and scanned the crowd. My heart rate dropped. I didn't catch even a glimpse of yellow this time. But I did notice myself on that big screen, a look of confusion plastered on my face as I looked everywhere except on the ground where the calf stayed for the final six seconds. Licking my lips, I forced a smile and pulled back my rope as the calf was let free. Turning Buckle, I trotted off through the gate, my eyes up on the stands looking for that yellow dress.

Get out of your head. She didn't want you to chase her, remember.

And I wouldn't.

"Hartwell did not disappoint—" The announcer's voice grew clearer as I took deep breaths, finding myself thankful that I was only seven hours from home and that I could be back in my own bed tonight.

I dismounted Buckle and held on to her reins, leading her back to the trailer. Her hooves hit with a clunk as I tried to ignore everything around me. A fellow roper, whose name escaped me, congratulated me on my winning time as he guided his horse to his own trailer, stepping in sync with me.

"Where's that wife of yours, Hartwell?" he asked. "She's been with you ever since—"

"She stayed behind," I lied.

"Ah, well, tell her the guys missed her."

I gave him a curt nod before I stopped at my trailer, reaching up to scratch Buckle's neck. She needed to be brushed and rewarded for the run, then we could be on our way . . .

"Hey, Cowboy."

I stopped.

The voice came from behind me, the most perfect angelic voice rang through my ears as I forced my feet to stay where they were. I was imagining this, I had to have been. It was the adrenaline—the pure excitement from winning a rodeo I was going to back out of playing tricks on me.

"Cowboy . . . I'm not in the trailer."

I heard it again. I heard *her* again. With a quick inhale I turned and looked over my shoulder.

Kyla.

Kyla.

Kyla was here.

Wearing that damn yellow dress, white boots, and her white hat firm in her fingers at her side. Her hair fell along her shoulders, and when she smiled and tipped her head slightly, it fell and shined in the moonlight and my world stopped. Half of me wanted to run and gather her in my arms, allow myself to believe that she was really here. The other half kept me frozen in time and space, completely unable to form any kind of movement. All I could manage was a soft word.

"Kyla." I echoed my mind, the word breathless as it left my lips. "You're . . . here."

"Well." She took a single step forward. "I was going to go to the ranch, but when I called Abi—"

"You called Abi?" I asked, my entire body trying to remember how to move. I was still in disbelief that she was standing in front of me. That glimpse of yellow was her, and now she was here—meeting me like she would on the road. She was here. Really, truly here.

She nodded, the warmth of her radiating to me as she got closer and closer. *Vanilla.*

"A few days ago. I told her I was going to come home, but that I wanted to surprise you. You know, a grand gesture." She moved her hair off her shoulders. "But then she told me you would be here—"

Buckle moved, nodding her head as Kyla came closer. Kyla gave a small laugh, and reached out to her nose, touching her gently. After giving Buckle a few seconds of attention, she turned back to me. I swallowed, my Adam's apple bobbing with a gulp I'm sure she could hear.

"I just knew I couldn't—" she began, dropping her hand from Buckle. Taking a deep breath, she smiled lightly. "I figured out what I wanted, but it was up to me to make it happen. Nothing else mattered once that realization hit me. I had been denying it for so long, not accepting that I could be happy and loved the way I deserved—the way you loved me. You did something no one else has ever done. You gave me the time I needed, and you still loved me. It may have taken me way too long to figure it out, but I did." Kyla's free hand played with the tie on her dress. "Rhett, I have so much I want to tell you." She paused, a thin smile forming on her lips as she gave a small laugh. "We have so much to talk about, I'm not even sure where to start."

"Kyla, I—"

"David is done," she interrupted. "I wish you could have been there." A small laugh filled the space between us as she moved, her shoulders relaxing as she dropped the tie on her dress. "I almost hit him."

"You didn't?" My eyebrows shot up. "You should have."

"I didn't." She shook her head quickly, the motion barely visible as her lips tightened. "Restraining order is being filed. He's done. He's gone. He can't come near me or the ranch again."

"The ranch?"

"I added that to the restraining order since, well, I want to come home."

"Kyla," I gasp, feeling my heart beat faster. I turned to tie Buckle to the trailer before reaching out to touch her skin. I needed to feel her. My fingers feathered against her, the same spark shooting through my arm. It was her. It was always her. "Please tell me I can kiss you."

Her shoulders slouched as a shaky breath left her lips. "I left you, Rhett, and I—"

"Kyla." I brushed the pad of my thumb against her chin, slowly tilting her to look at me. "How about"—I sighed, my conviction bubbling back in me as I remembered my own grand gesture—"we make a bet."

The corners of her lips curled. "A bet?"

"I bet I can guess five things about you, and if I get them right, I get to kiss you. If I get them wrong . . . I'll still get to kiss you. Then we will talk about everything."

"Five things?" She raised an eyebrow.

I nodded, my eyes never once leaving hers.

"Okay," she whispered, rolling her lips softly as she placed her hand on her hip.

"One." I brushed the hair from her face, tucking it behind her ear. "When you're nervous, you'll roll your lips, almost as if you're trying to find the exact words to say, but I love it when those words finally come. Two, you hate sleeping with wet hair, even if it means you need to blow dry it before putting your head on the pillow, you will. Three." I smiled—all the small things I've noticed about her flooding back into my brain. Her eyes were glued on mine, as she hung on every word I said. "You love hotel beds. You say they are perfectly soft, even if the person sharing the bed with you keeps you from sleeping." She chuckled, a small blush appearing on her cheeks. "Four, you are insanely good at pool. Even without distracting your opponent, you would win every game. And five—"

"Oh, I can't wait for this."

"Your drink order."

"My drink order?" Kyla laughed, the sound filling my ears and hitting my heart. I never wanted to not hear that sound again.

"Rum and Dr. Pepper, because Coke doesn't give it enough of a kick—not that rum doesn't offer the kick already."

Kyla's lips moved, a tight line that was trying not to form a smile, but the corners pulled and tugged and finally the smile broke through.

"How did I do?"

"Rhett Hartwell, you better kiss me before—"

I closed the gap between us, my hand finding the nape of her neck with ease, pulling her towards me as our lips finally met. The scent of vanilla filled the air, and the soft skin of her fingertips brushed my chin. She left out a soft moan as she deepened the kiss, pulling me as close as she could.

When I finally came up for air, her forehead met mine. She inhaled, taking in that breath I knew she needed.

"I love you, Rhett Hartwell," she whispered, those five words filling my entire soul.

"I love you, Kyla." I stopped. "Kyla . . ." I dug my hand back into my pocket, her ring that was always there instantly finding my fingers. I pulled it out and held it up in between us, the small diamond glistening in the sunlight. "I love you more than anything. I don't want to be without you again, please . . . be my wife?"

Kyla let out a small laugh as the tears began to fall from her eyes as she took in the small diamond. "You just happened to have that with you?"

Holding back my own tears, I stammered, "I always keep it with me."

She kissed me, a sweet, fleeting kiss that felt like wind against my lips.

"Be my wife?" I repeated against her lips.

"Yes," she whispered. "And I will be changing my name."

"Mrs. Hartwell." I slipped the ring back on her finger.

"Rhett," she whispered as she brought our fingers up to her lips, "take me home."

FORTY-ONE

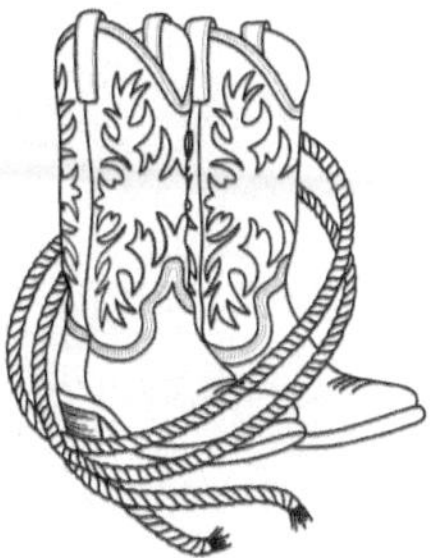

Kyla

THREE WEEKS LATER

Are you wearing the yellow sundress? Please tell me you're not wearing the yellow sundress.

I'm not wearing the yellow sundress. I'm wearing a white one.

Grace

White? I thought we said the vow renewal would come much, much later. I still need to get out there, you know.

Me

It's just a date, Grace. Not a wedding.

Grace

Hey, how was I supposed to know? You are married to the man. Mrs. Hartwell.

Me

Damn straight.

Grace

Where is he taking you?

Me

He's already there, I'm meeting him at The Steel.

A FaceTime call came through instead of a text. I propped my phone up against the counter and answered, working on my mascara.

"Hey—"

"What do you mean he's already there? He's supposed to pick you up and talk to your dad and take you to a movie and dinner. But instead he's meeting you at the bar?" Grace shouted, her voice echoing in the bathroom.

I laughed. "It's our first date, and my dad is dead so . . ."

"Your mom then."

"You already know how that conversation went."

It went very well actually. Everything since coming home had gone well.

Rhett swooped me up into his arms after he proposed, and promised to never let me go. He kissed me, over and over until I reminded him we had forever to explore each other. We headed back to my apartment after settling Buckle and talked. We talked about everything that had happened during the time we were apart. I told him about my mother, and how I was slowly mending my relationship with her. We called her—putting her on speaker phone—and Rhett smiled when he invited her out for Thanksgiving dinner. I was shocked, but grateful at the same time. I told him what happened with David, and how that was the final straw I needed to take what was mine. Even my therapist agreed with me.

And when I told him I still had a while in my dingy apartment, and that I wanted to finish the time with Ben before his school year started, he was supportive and instantly jumped at the chance to stay in Washington with me. He found a temporary stable for Buckle, and we lived together for a few weeks in my apartment, sleeping and making love in my small twin-sized bed. We went to rodeos, wandered bookstores and flea markets, enjoying every second with each other before we returned to Hartwell Hills.

We agreed to stay married because we wanted to—it just felt right. But we decided we would take it slower. We would date.

Tonight.

Our first real date since meeting him.

"I know, I know, your mom is on Team Rhett now—"

"Well, I wouldn't say she's one hundred percent on Team Rhett, but she's getting there. Thanksgiving is going to be interesting to say the least." I closed my mascara and grabbed my brush, running it through my hair. "But this date is going to be perfect. I can just feel it."

"Okay, I'll play along. What are you doing?"

"We're going to the bar where we first met."

"Oooo . . ." she cooed. "Recreating the first night, huh?"

I blushed. "Kind of, but different this time. We won't be getting drunk or having a one-night stand."

"But you will be coming home to have sex, right?"

The heat rose again, and I could tell the blush got deeper on my cheeks. "Oh yeah, but he's planned the night. All I know is I'm supposed to go up to the bar and order a rum and Dr. Pepper. He said he'd find me."

Grace sighed. "You and your cowboy. Hey, Kyla?"

I hummed in response, dropping the brush to look at her.

"I'm glad you stayed, I'm glad you found you."

I smiled, my heart practically bursting with her words. *I found me.* "Me too."

I walked into the bar, the country music crooning as I made my way to the bar top. Jason, the bartender who was here the night I first came here, smiled at me.

"Hey, Mrs. Hartwell, what can I get you?"

I smiled. I loved when people called me Mrs. Hartwell. I loved it even more when Rhett called me that. He had tried to slip more nicknames into the mix, but he always landed on Mrs. Hartwell.

"Rum and Dr. Pepper, please."

"You got it." Jason winked and turned, looking off to the corner and giving a slight nod.

I followed where his gaze went and saw my husband sitting at a table with his brother and cousin, wearing a white t-shirt underneath a blue button-down shirt that was open, revealing the gold belt buckle on his hips. A brown cowboy hat sat upon his head, his brown hair most definitely perfectly disheveled underneath. I couldn't wait to run my fingers through it tonight, it had gotten longer—perfect to pull on. Our eyes met for a millisecond right before Jason placed my drink in front of me.

I took a sip and waited, knowing he was going to approach me at any minute. The butterflies grew in my stomach, and I waited and watched. He seemed like he was deep in conversation with Lachlan, even though every few seconds his eyes would flick to me. He was stunning, and I desperately wanted him to come over and wrap me in his arms and kiss me until I couldn't breathe.

Instead, I sat here alone, drinking my Rum and Dr. Pepper, the tension and butterflies growing stronger every passing minute.

I sighed, taking another sip, realizing that my drink was almost gone. I had maybe one more gulp—one more pull—before I would get up and ask him if he wanted to dance. A glass hit the table with a thud and then I heard the most smooth, soothing voice hit my ear, and I melted.

"Hey, girl. What'cha drinkin?"

EPILOGUE

Rhett

3 Months later

Las Vegas. I made it. The final round.

The arena for the NFR was packed. It always was. I'm not sure why that single fact shocked me, but as I mounted Buckle, ready to take my shot, nerves began to settle in my stomach. I had been here before, but never expected to lead the boards. This was my year. So why the hell did I have these damn nerves circling my stomach?

I exhaled through my mouth, watching the lasso fly through the air next to Buckle. Darren had just gone and Jaxson was up next. Then it was Shane and Riley . . . then me. The best time to beat tonight was 8.3, and Jaxson had just blown that out of the water with a 7.0. I looked up at the big screen, watching Shane control the calf and rope it down, but that broken barrier kicked him to the bottom. My lips tipped. A broken barrier . . . I could work with Shane getting a broken barrier.

"Hey, Rhett—" Jeff came up to me, waving my phone in the air. "It's the wife."

I smiled, shaking my head. The nerves that had taken permanent residence in my stomach slightly vanished. Kyla was in the crowd, with Wyatt, Grace, and Abi, and yet she was distracting me by calling. A deep chuckle rumbled through me as I took the phone. It wasn't a distraction. She knew that. She knew it would be the perfect pick-me-up.

"Hey, Mrs. Hartwell," I said, looking in the general direction of where she was sitting. I always knew where to look for her. In the past months she has traveled with me to every rodeo, always sitting where I was able to kiss her after each run without her having to leave the stands. Then she would meet me behind the gate once her favorite event (which was Bull Riding even though she wouldn't admit that to me) was over. She would join me for after events and help with Buckle, then we would go to the hotel and repeat everything all over again. Kyla had become the constant—the grounding force I needed to get to where I was today. And honestly, knowing she was calling me told me she knew I was nervous.

Here at the NFR she was sitting further away. A kiss over the railing wasn't going to be possible here.

"Hey, Cowboy. You nervous?"

Called it.

"Not one bit," I lied.

"Liar."

"Okay, maybe a little bit."

"I'll make you a deal. You rope that calf and beat Jaxson's score and I'll come running down towards the chutes."

"And what if I don't beat his score?"

"Then I'll come running down towards the chutes."

"So, either way—"

"I'll meet you at the chutes."

"You'll miss the Bull Riding if you take off now."

"You know I don't care about the bull riders."

"Now who's the liar?" I raised an eyebrow.

"Cowboy, you're gonna have to get back on the podium to get that gold buckle." Her voice dropped lower, becoming hypnotizing. "I can see you on Buckle, she can sense when you're nervous you know, so you need to breathe."

I smiled, trying to pick her up from the crowd. I tried to convince her to wear her yellow dress, but she said it wasn't fitting for the NFR. Instead, she and Grace had T-Shirts made with a rope and the name HARTWELL written along their shoulder blades.

"I am breathing," I responded, looking up at the board. "Jason just finished—"

"8.7. You can beat that."

"Up next is the man we've been waiting for. Sitting at the top slot, it's been a wild road for Rhett getting here, but he's expected to take it all. Rhett Hartwell from Idaho who is currently . . . on the phone?" I heard the announcer's voice, missing Wyatt's voice. He'd make it to the NFR one day. Until then he was in the stands with my wife—wearing a matching T-shirt.

"Shit, Baby, I gotta go."

"I love you."

"I love you. Meet me at the chutes." I tossed the phone back to Jeff and looked at the camera, giving it a cheesy smile.

"You don't see many cowboys using the phone before their run, but Rhett is a newlywed, and I guarantee you that was his wife he was talking to."

"He seems a bit nervous, maybe she had to give him a pep talk?"

"Mrs. Hartwell has become known in the arena, almost as much as Rhett himself . . ."

I shook my head, ignoring their banter as I shifted my focus. That calf . . .

Ignoring the sounds and sights that surrounded me, I pulled my attention to the rope in my hand. I focused on Buckle's warmth under me, her muscles moving as she waited for me to give her the go ahead. I looked at the chute, the small brown calf already moving with force, ready to give me a good run. I closed my eyes and saw Kyla. Her smile. Her eyes. I focused on her, and the prize at the end of all of this: her lips on mine. It didn't matter if I beat Jaxson's score, it didn't matter if I broke a barrier, all that mattered was after I finished this ride, the NFR was done for the year and Kyla would be waiting for me.

Opening my eyes, I jammed the rope in between my teeth, and nodded.

"There he goes! That little calf already shooting past—"
Buckle moved, only flying a few feet until she halted to a stop. I grabbed the calf and jumped off, the dirt flying around my boots as I felt the rope along my palm as I approached, grabbing the calf,

lifting her up and down . . . to the ground. Three legs, one rope, twist and tie . . .

Done.

I waved my arms and ran back to Buckle.

1, 2, 3, 4, 5, 6 . . .

"And that's *exactly* what we were expecting from Rhett Hartwell! 6.9! The first six second run of the night and Rhett is officially on his way to that gold buckle. Maybe more men should take a call from their wife before their runs. Hot damn, Hartwell—"

I turned Buckle and ran off, stopping her right before the gate, jumping off and handing her reins to Jeff. I didn't even look at him, I didn't pay attention to anything.

"Hey, Rhett!" he called after me, but at this point his voice was a blur among everything else. I ran past the cowboys waiting and the rodeo workers . . . I had to find my wife.

My heart was racing, but my mind was clear. I just jumped to the top slot—I pretty much just won the NFR—and all I could see was that light blue t-shirt and white cowboy boots that were running towards me. She made it in record time, making me think she missed my run, but I didn't care. I didn't care one bit.

Her smile shined brightly as she jumped into my arms, her laugh filling the air as her legs wrapped around my waist. I grabbed her rear and held her close, the feel of her in my arms lifting any and all nerves that still lingered. Maybe those nerves were adrenaline at this point. But whatever they were, they were gone. And she replaced them.

"Cowboy!" she shouted in my ear. "6.9! SIX. POINT. NINE!" Her legs tightened around my waist, my arms holding her steady as she arched her back away from me, her hands sliding to the nape of my neck. Our eyes met and I melted. "You did it." Her voice had turned to a whisper.

I smiled at her, my gaze dropping to her lips. I kissed her, lifting a hand from her to hold on to her head, pulling her as close to me as possible. Each kiss sparked a new sensation in me, and this one was no different. Her vanilla scent enveloped us as I felt her fingers run through my hair, the tips finding their way under my hat. This was the best part of every rodeo. The kiss at the end of the run. Kyla in my arms, her lips on mine.

I broke the kiss, leaving my lips against hers. "I love you," I whispered, my voice shaky.

"I love you more, Cowboy. Who knew all I needed was somebody like you." Her lips tipped in a smile.

"Somebody like me?" I smiled, resisting the urge to kiss her again.

"Only you."

"What, no cowboys?" I emphasized the "s," knowing very well she had dubbed last summer her Summer of Cowboys.

"Nope, just one. And I love that cowboy more than anything." She smiled, giving me a small fleeting kiss. "You did it."

"Rhett, come on man, you need to get out there for the ceremony, you got the gold. Get your ass out here!" Jeff had caught up to us, completely out of breath.

I turned to look at him, only now seeing just how far I had run. We weren't far from Kyla's seat—I had definitely traveled further than she did. I turned back to her, getting lost in her once more as I gave her one more deep kiss, wishing it could turn into more.

I dropped her, my lips still on hers as her feet hit the ground.

"Get out there," she whispered.

"Rhett . . ." Jeff urged.

"I'm coming." I held onto Kyla as long as I could until her fingers slipped free of mine as I turned and ran back towards Jeff. "See you after, Mrs. Hartwell?!" I turned, jogging backwards to face her.

"See you after, Cowboy."

God that woman. She was all I wanted—everything and more. And from now until forever, I got to call her Mrs. Hartwell.

I got to call her mine.

ACKNOWLEDGEMENTS

Here we are, at the end of another novel. I honestly can't believe it. *Somebody Like Me* has my whole heart and soul and this novel is truly my favorite. It's not just because it focuses around rodeos, cowboys, and Rhett and Kyla's love story—but because while I was writing it, I had the best support. I had the most amazing people on my side which made it so different than any other book. So many people helped make this novel possible—without them I would have given up.

Michelle—Thank you, for everything. My solid, my sister, my support. Thank you for everything you did for this novel. I love you.

Katherine—the first person to read this messy, messy draft, all the way in India. You were Rhett and Kyla's first fan and you stuck with them to the very end. You even supported Abi's name change a million times. I am so grateful for you!

Tessa, the love you have for me and this novel is more than I could ever ask for. You pulled me out of so many spirals you and assured me this book was amazing, gushing over everything just as much as I did. This book is just as much yours as it is mine, it wouldn't be here without your love. I wouldn't be here without your friendship. I love you more than anything. And yes—Lach-lan will get his cat.

Jessee, I'm not sure where to start here. You've become my best friend, the one I can turn to for anything, and I'm not sure I would have gotten this far if we didn't connect over our shared loved of a certain fantasy book. You have the voice of reason, you have the control and the hype. You are my favorite person I have ever met on Bookstagram and you give the best hugs. Thank you for accepting me for me, and loving Rhett and Kyla, and for giving them the best scene in the entire book. You're the best critique partner, and best friend I could ever ask for. I love you!

Kate Cole—I constantly thank the powers that be that a book hangover brought us together. I feel like I've known you forever. Your constant words of affirmation push me to do better, to write to my full extent, and push myself to the next level. You offer the love that I need to go go go, and I know because of it, I'm growing. Rhett and Kyla wouldn't be here without your help and for that—I'll always hold you close. I can't wait to give you a hug!

My amazing editors. Cait and Allie, you two helped the magic happen. This book wouldn't be where it is today without Allie and her phone calls, without Cait and her brainstorming sessions. These two ladies are miracle workers. I apologize for all the drama dots . . . you guys know how much I love them . . . (hehe) . . .

My beta readers—Kate, Hannah, Shannon, Courtney, Grayson, Laura, Hannah, and Tessa, for providing the feedback I needed to make this book even better! You all are absolutely amazing. Thank you for being the first ones to start the Lachlan Hartwell Fan

Club. I know he loves you as much as you love him, even if he doesn't show it.

My amazing Street Team! You guys are the BEST and I owe you the WORLD. Thank you for sharing every post, for reading every word, and for helping me with all my content! It was the best decision in the world to get you guys together, and I know because of you, this book is going to shine.

My "Cowboy" Husband! Spencer—how many times did I say "it's done!" and then head right back into the editing cave. You know how much I put into this book, thank you for supporting me for the past year in order to get it right. You're love and encouragement means more than you know.

My writing group—MJ, Cindy, India and Grayson. I love our chats and they way we lift each other up, even though the tough times. I love that you pulled me in and accepted me! You ladies are the best!

My illustrators, Melody and Erika. You both brought Rhett and Kyla to life, and the ranch! The character art and cover are things I could have only imagined and I still look at them with awe. You two are absolutely amazing and I hope you're reading for three more books! I love you!

I know I'm forgetting so many people—so so many. It takes a village to write a book and this book had a HUGE village helping it come to life. I love each and every one of you and I am so grateful!

Here's to the next one.

With Love-

Stefanie K Steck

Also by Stefanie K Steck

Standalones

All Because of Elowin

Under the Marble Sky

The Moments of Us Series

That Right Moment

That Next Moment

That First Moment

About the Author

Stefanie K Steck is a romance writer, full-time dental assistant, Army wife, mom of three crazy kids, and curator of a small zoo. She currently lives in Utah and has recently found joy in camping. In the little spare time she has, you can find her writing, reading, cuddling with her favorite Guinea pig, Nugget, or rewatching the *Back to the Future Trilogy*...again...or obsessing over *Twisters*.

Follow her on Instagram @authorstefanieksteck
www.stefanieksteckbooks.com